THE BUCKET LIST

Also by CJ Murphy
frame by frame

THE BUCKET LIST

CJ Murphy

Desert Palm Press

The Bucket List

by CJ Murphy

© 2018 CJ Murphy

ISBN (trade) 978-1-948327-06-0
ISBN (epub): 978-1-948327-07-7
ISBN (pdf): 978-1-948327-08-4

Desert Palm Press
1961 Main Street, Suite 220
Watsonville, California 95076
www.desertpalmpress.com

Editor: CK King
Cover Design: TreeHouse Studio, Winston-Salem, NC

Printed in the United States of America
First Edition October 2018

DEDICATION

For Chris and Kelly Stadelman, who taught me that a bucket list should be about making memories and not just a list of items on a piece of paper—or in this case, a fictional work in progress. From our three-hour beer-and-burrito vacations, Pittsburgh pub crawls, kayak floats on the Allegheny, Pirates spring training and regular season outings, right down to watching fireworks in your backyard on the Fourth of July, we have been grateful for every adventure in your company.

Darla and I have been blessed from the first day we met you both and will always consider you more than friends. You are the closest of family in every sense of the word. For showing us that the check marks should come sooner than later, we raise a mason jar in your honor.

Sadly, we lost Chris before he could read this dedication. His life with Kelly certainly made me understand the importance of making the 'dash between' count.

"When we try to pick out anything by itself, we find it hitched to everything else in the Universe." John Muir- *My First Summer in the Sierra*, 1911

Chapter One

PROFESSOR JORDAN ARMSTRONG TRAILED her fingers along the spines of numerous books in the National Parks section of the library at Cornell University in Ithaca, New York. *How could it be so hard to find a specific book?* Two former staff professors had authored the groundbreaking publication about the role of the time-honored landmarks in relationship to the environment.

Although it had to be here, it wasn't in its designated space. *Shelved wrong?* She continued down the rows and rows of books, until her eyes caught a bold script across a cloudless sky. There it was, a thick text entitled *The National Parks Reaction to Climate Change*. "Found you," she whispered. Pulling the volume down, she looked at the cover shot that displayed a panoramic view of Grinnell Glacier in Glacier National Park. *God that's gorgeous.*

She opened the book and studied the photo credit, *Professor N.F. Scott*. Her pulse rate increased and a trickle of sweat formed on her upper lip. As she turned to the photo pages in the middle of the book, a piece of paper slipped from inside and drifted to the floor. Looking around, she bent to retrieve the folded yellow document. Jordan closed the book and tucked it under her arm, carefully opening the paper to reveal a seemingly nonsensical dictation full of letters, numbers and symbols, and random quotes. *What the hell*?

Jordan frowned, puzzled as to the meaning, until she was interrupted by a rustling sound. Someone was searching books a row over. Jordan nodded, having made up her mind. She shut the book and took it to the circulation desk, where she presented her university ID in order to check it out.

The librarian scanned her selection and ran her finger across the cover. She looked up at Jordan. "Ah, Professor Armstrong, nice to see you." A small smile crossed her lips while she ran her finger across the authors' names and tapped the book. "These two were favorites around here. When this first came out, we did book signings here. Such a tragedy."

Jordan formulated her next statement carefully. "I remember. Professor James passed unexpectedly from an undiagnosed heart condition, right?"

Sadness crossed the slight-of-stature woman's face. "Yes, Aggie and Noeul were out for their daily run. There were some complications and Aggie died two days later. I was sad when Noeul resigned her professorship shortly thereafter. Losing one of them was bad enough. Unfortunately, in the end, we lost both of them that day. A true tragedy for all who knew them and the students that would have benefited from many more years of their experience."

Feeling that exact sentiment, Jordan continued to gently pry, hoping to find an easy answer to the growing mystery. "I agree with you. Where did Professor Scott go?"

"After she sold the house here, no one knows. She took off on what she called her bucket list, and no one here ever heard from her again."

"She must have left a forwarding address?"

The librarian smoothed back her silver hair and adjusted the clip holding it off her shoulders. "If she did, I wasn't privy to it. I hope you enjoy the book. They worked on the research together with Aggie doing the majority of the writing, Noeul the photography. Such a shame and an incredible loss." She handed the book back to Jordan. "On a brighter note, how's your research going?"

Jordan was a Professor in Agricultural studies and a biogenetical engineer in the field of plant genetics. "When Professor Scott was the Biology chair, the research she was working on was closely related to what I'm trying to do now. It would go much faster if I could find her." She held up the book. "Thus, the book."

"Ah, I see. I wish I had more information for you. If I think of anyone to ask, I'll let you know."

Jordan thanked the librarian, tucked the book into her messenger bag, and left the formidable building. She threw her leg over her mountain bike and made her way back to her rental on Forest Home Drive. Her studio apartment was slightly off the beaten path, close to campus, and perfect for her needs. She was anxious to get a closer look at the paper. The unexpected find was burning a hole in her shirt pocket. The mile and a half ride was substantial enough to build up a light sweat as she peddled past the botanical gardens. It was still a bit cool for things to be in full springtime, the air crisp and clean.

Upon her arrival, Jordan locked her bike into the rack and sprinted up the outside staircase. Her mailbox held a stack of letters. Unfortunately, they displayed only her own handwriting on the envelopes. Three in all, each with a large red stamp across the mailing address. *Return to sender-Attempted not known.* "Dammit".

Frustrated, she sorted through the stack finding nothing more interesting than a five dollar off coupon at the local pizzeria. She clipped that notice to the refrigerator and tossed the rest of the day's mail in the trash. Walking over to the counter, she picked up the leather-bound notebook where she was keeping all her notes and information about Professor Scott. She peered down at a list of nine previous addresses, six already crossed out. "The last three down," she grumbled as she scratched through the final addresses still on her list in the notebook. "Another dead end. She certainly doesn't want to be found."

Finding Professor Scott was turning into more of a mystery than the Nevada Barr books she coveted. She pulled a bottle of water from the fridge and walked to her recliner, dropping into it ungracefully, only to hear a *scratch, scratch* at the door as she reached for the paper in her pocket. She rose and walked back to the entryway to let in an Australian shepherd. She bent and dutifully paid Bandit the attention he craved, his sky-blue eyes staring back at her as his head turned into her scratches.

"You know, if you had opposable thumbs, you'd be the perfect roommate. Maybe we should install a doggie door, so you can come and go as you please. On second thought, maybe that would be a bad idea. I'd come home to find a collar hanging on the door handle signaling me you had a girl dog in here. Or a boy dog, for that matter." She kissed his forehead and walked over to fill the water bowl she kept for him and called Max to let him know that Bandit was visiting.

"Your boy is hanging out with me, don't worry about him. I'll send him home at dinner."

"That dog. I swear he lives with you more than me."

"I'm better company. I speak doglandish."

"Ah, you'll have to teach me that, so he'll actually understand when I tell him no."

Jordan chuckled. "I'm not even sure doglandish has a word for no."

"Well that explains why he never listens. Send him home when you've had enough."

"If that's the case, don't expect to ever see your dog again. I promise that I'll send him home to eat."

"Fair enough."

By her nature, Jordan was a solitary individual, something her landlords Max and Sam Keller had worked tirelessly to change as they became like family to her. Her mind was always on her work, on her goal to eradicate hunger. Jordan's research project involved devising a way to graft a superfood onto a plant stalk capable of growing in little to no water. Max helped her develop complicated algorithms to manage the data she collected from growth rates as well as scheduling irrigation. These complex equations helped to keep his diagnosed dementia at bay for as long as possible.

Her mystery document still hadn't been examined closely. She opened her bottle of water and took a long drink as she made her way to the bar in her rarely used galley kitchen.

"Okay, Bandit, let's see what I found."

Gingerly, she pulled the paper that had fallen out of the book in the library from her shirt pocket. After she laid it on the bar, she gently smoothed out the creases and looked at the information written in a distinctive script. "I'll be damned." She'd seen Professor James' handwriting before, an elegant calligraphy with sweeping tails on the y's and a distinctive capital A and J. At first glance, the information seemed random and unorganized.

The dog sat at her feet chewing on a cow hoof. "I think it's time we call the expert, Bandit. I'm out of my league here." Bandit stopped chewing at the sound of his name and turned his head sideways as if contemplating what she'd said.

Jordan's sister, Dava Armstrong, was her go-to expert when it came to all things in puzzle form or code. Born with spina bifida, her sister had a powerful intellect that was in stark contrast with the physical impairment that confined her to a wheelchair. Outside of the US military, Dava was one of the east coast's premier cryptologists. Jordan pulled out her cellphone and speed dialed her number while tapping the speakerphone icon. Two rings later, a familiar greeting filled her kitchen.

"Atchawhay antway eengray umbthay?"

Jordan laughed. "Ovelay ouyay ittlelay istersay." Their use of pig Latin had irritated their parents who had never gotten the hang of it, leaving them to be able to speak in code much the way a parent would spell when they didn't want little ears to know what they are saying. Dava's greeting translated to 'whatcha want green thumb.' Hers in return varied slightly, telling Dava that she loved her little sister.

Jordan had a hard time not letting her adoration show in her voice as she took on a more serious tone. "Your mission, if you choose to accept, is to use that super computer brain of yours to help me decode a document."

Dava snorted. "Did you hack into the Department of Agriculture or something?"

"No. I found a document that may help me find Professor Scott. It appears to be in several different codes. It may be nothing. All I know is it's the first clue I've found in a long time. Unfortunately, my last three letters came back today marked 'attempted, not known.'"

"Are you even sure she's still alive, JJ?"

Jordan could feel the corners of her mouth pull into a smile at her sister's childhood nickname for her. At three, Dava couldn't pronounce her full name. Dava had long outgrown that inability. The term of endearment would always warm Jordan, even on her worst days.

"I have a web alert set up for anything on her. No obituary, no legal notification, and nothing even closely related to her has come back, even with the paid searches. If she died in the last ten years, I'd know."

"Well whatcha got for me?"

"There are a series of paragraphs. One is a short story about a brown fox, another set looks like binary, and the last one might be Morse code. I'm sure there are others, so I decided to come to the expert."

Dava's rich laugh emanated from the speakerphone. "I'm only an expert because I spent my entire childhood trying to find my things by deciphering your poor attempts at code."

Jordan laughed. "Hey, it worked didn't it? You loved it and you know it." The sisters were six years apart in age, gifted with extremely high IQ levels. They were blessed with parents who taught them that the only limitations in their lives were the ones they put up for themselves.

"I loved that you took the time to do it. You always made me feel special, JJ."

The stinging in Jordan's eyes was for a different reason. "Watson, that chair doesn't define you. It's a mode of transportation for your body not your brain."

"I know, Sherlock, and I love you for saying that. Now send that paper to me so I can get back to saving the world."

"Ovelay ouyay ittlelay istersay"

"Ittoday igbay istersay."

After she'd scanned the document to her computer, Jordan emailed it to her sister. There was no doubt in her mind that Dava would crack all those codes in record time. The Armstrong sisters' brains still shocked the scientists who often included them in studies. The two had hyperthymesia, which manifested as the ability to recall every day of their lives in perfect clarity and detail. Researchers had no explanation how their parents tested at normal intelligence levels with both daughters testing off the scales. Jordan's mind craved information as she pulled out a stool at her kitchen bar and began examining the book the two professors authored. The entire volume would be devoured in a few hours as she used her freaky ability to speed read. The photographic memory she possessed would make it possible to commit the information to the data bank in her head.

Jordan's eyes pulled in every word as she began to read the preface.

This book, The National Parks Reaction to Climate Change, is dedicated to the women and men who have struggled for decades to preserve these extraordinary places of grandeur. Without them, these lands would be opened to industry and the destruction would be catastrophic. President Roosevelt believed this to be true and established the United States Forest Service in 1905 to begin preserving these wonders. He said, "We have fallen heirs to the most glorious heritage a people ever received, and each one must do his part if we wish to show that the nation is worthy of its good fortune."

He argued that, "We have become great because of the lavish use of our resources," but recognized that these treasures would need protection for years to come. May these national treasures be protected as well as those items we house in museums for safekeeping. Their overall importance to our environment cannot be reclaimed once they are devastated by industrialization. - Dr. Tybee Agnes James and Dr. Noeul Finnegan Scott.

Jordan read the words once again, realizing how closely they resonated with her own thoughts. She loved the national parks and frequented them as often as she could in her travels. Dava had given her a directive when they were young. "Experience every adventure with double the excitement because you're doing it for two." Dava's ringtone filled the room.

"Whatcha got for me?"

"What I've got for you, is the decoded information you wanted."

Jordan laughed and looked at her watch. "Thirty minutes. You must be slippin' babe."

"Ha. I had them done twenty minutes ago. For your information, some real work came my way that took precedence. You, my big sister, are a small fry in comparison to Silicon Valley."

Jordan huffed a protest. "Hey now, I should always be at the top of your list."

"Let's say they pay better than you do. Now, do you want to know what these codes say or not?"

Jordan scrambled for a pen and paper. "Yes, yes. Please, oh wise one, enlighten me."

"The brown fox paragraph uses the first letter every third word. That one says *decipher the bucket list in this code, my love.* The next one is actually the Dewey Decimal System for a book called..."

Jordan finished for her. "*The National Parks Reaction to Climate Change?*"

"Hey, did you need my help or not? Don't be stealing my thunder here. I'm sharing my brilliance with you. Now, where was I? Oh yes, the code. So, that one leads you to that book you're apparently holding. Use those numbers to find the page number, line number, and word number. Since I don't have that book, you'll have to figure that out yourself."

"Ok, I'll do that later. What else have you got?"

"The Morse code says *Find the treasure at latitude 42.4524 longitude -76.485703.* That turns out to be Fall Creek Gorge in the Cornell Botanical Gardens."

Jordan stopped to ponder that, as she clicked her pen top rapidly. "Okay, so I'm looking for a spot that can be found here on campus, right?"

"Yes. Now, the next one is a polyalphabetic cipher, the Vigenère cipher that was used by the Confederates in the Civil War. Decoded, the message reads *follow the clues to each bucket-list destination. Love Aggie.*

"So, if I'm understanding this, it appears that Professor James planned out a bucket list for them to follow. Unfortunately, she dies before they can complete it, and Professor Scott retires to parts unknown." Jordan paused and scratched her head absently with her pen. "Well, I guess I start by finding the location here on campus and see where it leads."

"By George, I think she's got it. Now, if we're done with this treasure hunt for the day, Silicon Valley is in need of my skills to find a hole in their most recent software."

"I think I can take it from here. Thanks, Watson."

Jordan hung up and bit her lip in concentration while looking at the sheet. Bandit's persistent whine got her attention, and she put away her notes. "Okay, okay. Geez, impatient today, aren't we? Alright, let's go." Bandit barked enthusiastically, as Jordan walked across the room and grabbed three tennis balls.

Upon reaching the yard, Jordan started throwing the florescent-yellow balls. Bandit needed the exercise. He could wander back and forth indoors, between Max and Sam's level and Jordan's, if he chose to. If Max went outside, Bandit understood he was to always stay with him. Sam and Jordan had hoped that by forming that bond, Bandit would stay with Max if he ever wandered off and was unable to find his way home.

A familiar, deep voice filled the backyard. "You spoil him."

Bandit immediately wandered over to Max, who came outside and sat down. Jordan watched the dog put his soft nose under Max's hand and urged him to pet him. Jordan made her way over to the seat opposite Max.

"He's deserving."

Max smiled as he smoothed back the soft fur. "Glad to see he got you outside. Your nose is buried too deeply in those books when you're home. Any progress?"

"A little. I found their book in the library. It had a piece of loose paper inside, with some things in code."

Max's eyes twinkled. "Ah, and you called your source?"

"You know I did. Dava cracked the codes in ten minutes. She hasn't failed me yet."

"How is Dava by the way?"

Jordan smiled. Max and Sam had met her sister several times at different functions over the years. "Busy solving the ails of Silicon Valley and who knows whatever else the government throws her way."

"Remarkable young lady." He paused. "Both of you are, you know?"

"Although I'm barely qualified to carry her luggage in comparison. I hold my own."

Max tilted his head and squinted his eyes at her. "Always so self-deprecating my dear."

Jordan reached out a hand and Max placed his in hers. "Nice to know I've got a fan."

He squeezed her hand. "You are destined to solve one of the world's greatest problems, Jordan."

"Not if I can't find a way to graft a heartier and more drought-tolerant root base to my stalk. Everything I've tried so far fails. I need to find Professor Scott and, to date, she's a ghost."

"This new lead promising?"

She sighed and rolled her neck. "Possibly. It seems that Professor James made a bucket list for Professor Scott to decode."

Max leaned his head back, looking out over the yard. "Ah, Noeul always did like puzzles. Aggie searched the world over for jigsaw puzzles and other items to stump her."

"You knew them pretty well?"

"Aggie and Noeul were on staff while I was still teaching at Cornell. They were frequent guests at the restaurant where Sam used to work. A truly lovely couple, different in so many ways and yet perfect for each other. I met Noeul's parents, when Aggie and Noeul moved them into their guest cottage. Both parents passed within six months of each other. I think grief killed Noeul's father after her mother passed, not unlike how Noeul was lost after Aggie's untimely death." His voice trailed off wistfully. "Funny, I can remember all that. The sad reality is I can't remember what I had for breakfast this morning." He ran a hand across his face and stopped to look at his wedding ring. "I hope I never forget Sam."

Jordan squeezed his hand and noted that his Project Lifesaver bracelet was in place. The system was designed to provide protection and safety to individuals who wandered due to some cognitive condition like dementia, Alzheimer's, or even autism. "We'll make sure you don't. Now, have you been working on those irrigation calculations for me?"

"Yes, I've input all the data you provided and played with conversion tables, trying to calculate the rock bottom amount of water needed for your plant to survive. It's still more than what will ever fall in Mogadishu."

Jordan pulled her hand from Max's and ran her fingers into her short dark hair, tugging on it slightly in frustration. "That's why I'm so desperate to find Professor Scott. Her work was on the cusp of perfecting this grafting technique that will allow me to combine my superfood cereal strain with a drought-tolerant root ball. I've tried over and over to find the right one using different variances and treatments, still, they continue to fail. If I could find her and help her complete her work, we might find a way to plant a crop that could survive those drought conditions."

"I wish I could be more help. I don't have any idea where she went after Aggie died. Noeul stayed long enough to close out everything here. After that, she vanished."

Jordan blew out a long breath. "Well, I'm hoping that coded page I found will give me a clue as to where she vanished."

***

Later that evening, Jordan brought back a large number of containers that had at one time held the dinners Sam sent her. "Thought you might be missing these."

Sam hugged her in greeting. "Thank you, it will make next week's canine courier delivery much easier."

"You don't have to do that, Sam. You know that, right?"

"If Bandit didn't bring it to you, you'd live on ramen noodles. You geeks are all alike. You put your face in a book, get lost in your work, and forget about the world." He tenderly caressed her cheek and took the containers from her.

"Well, I do love the company Bandit provides, and the food is better than my cooking will ever be."

Bandit brushed by them in search of Max. "Best thing I ever did was get that dog, well, other than convincing Max I wasn't too young for him."

"You are the best thing that ever happened to Max and my stomach too. No doubt about that."

Sam carried the basket over to a cabinet and placed the containers back inside. "Nice to be appreciated. Now about Noeul, Max said you found something today. I remembered she told me one time, she and Aggie had a plan to see as many national parks as they could. That's where the idea for the book came from. I'd forgotten about that until Max mentioned it."

Jordan thought about what she'd read earlier that day. "I've counted ten parks so far in the book. Most of them are the biggies: Arches, Yellowstone, Grand Canyon, and the like. They wrote very vivid descriptions of the ecosystems involved in each. It's hard to believe there are still places untouched by industrialization."

"They both took the environment very seriously. Aggie taught geography and ArcGIS and had a degree in mechanical engineering as well. Noeul, as you know, was chair of the biology department and a very serious scientist...driven you might say."

"I've heard that from several people. I remember her intensity from my few classes with her. If I could find her, we could perfect her technique and possibly feed millions."

"You make me proud to know you, Jordan. I have no doubt you'll find a way to do that, whether you find Noeul or not."

Jordan smiled at the confidence Sam placed in her. "I wish I believed in me the way you do."

"Don't worry, Jordan, I have enough confidence in you for the both of us. Now, you look like you need a good night's sleep." He leaned in to kiss her cheek.

Jordan wasn't sure sleep would come, as her mind raced around the few tenuous threads of connection she was building to the elusive Professor Noeul Scott.

Chapter Two

SATURDAY MORNING, JORDAN WOKE without the aid of an alarm. She hadn't needed one since the day her sister Dava had been born. She woke at five thirty religiously, from that day on. She stretched and got out of bed, as she recalled the morning of her sister's birth with perfect clarity. The thought brought a smile to her face. She hadn't completely understood as a child. Within a few hours, after they'd made it to the hospital, everything would change. Being born 'differently abled,' as her mother called it, made no difference in the Armstrong family. Their parents never treated either of them differently and did everything they could to make life inclusive instead of exclusive. Dava would, however, live her entire life dealing with mobility issues and illness. She flourished, despite her physical limitations, her intellect propelling her far beyond where her wheelchair would take her.

Waking with Dava on her mind, she pulled up her sister's number, knowing she would be awake. Jordan stretched and scratched her head, as she listened for her sister's voice.

"What's on your mind?" Dava asked.

"I actually woke up thinking about the day you were born."

Dava laughed. "Really, what brought that on?"

"I'm not really sure. You know how my head is. I remember every minute of every day. That one was the best in my life."

"The day you were saddled with a sister who would never walk?"

"No, the day I got the best promotion ever."

"What the hell are you talking about? You were six."

"Yup, and the day you were born, I got promoted to big sister." Jordan knew her grin was wide enough to bring out her dimples.

Dava chuckled. "You're such a sap."

"True. I will easily admit to being a sap that loves you."

"There is that."

Jordan stretched again. "So, now for why I called. I guess I need a little reassurance. I've got to start somewhere, so I'm going to make my way over to the botanical gardens today, see where it leads me. I can't come up with the grafting combination on my own, and I've tested every theory I could find of Professor Scott's. She left incredibly detailed notes, but something is missing, something I can't put my finger on. Maybe it's just that she didn't finish her work here. I don't know. I've read everything she ever wrote that was either published or was in her lab reports. There's something missing."

"Maybe you're trying too hard or overthinking. Could be it was something she couldn't complete? It's possible you're the one who's meant to find the solution."

Jordan could hear her sister taking a drink of her morning creamer with a shot of coffee. Completely opposite, Jordan had come to love the taste of deep, rich, dark coffee. It didn't have to be expensive; good and strong was the only requirement. After she poured her own first cup, she settled into her morning routine of working through a problem with her sister.

"I guess so. I know this could make such a difference. I've got a viable superfood that I need to be able to grow in hostile conditions. By the time we grow a crop in an ideal location, process, package, and ship it over there, the cost is unmanageable. Those people deserve a chance. I could give it to them if I could get this damn plant to grow in sand with next to no water. I need to graft the superfood stalk on something like a cactus root ball."

"You're the agricultural version of young Frankenstein."

That brought a huge belly laugh from Jordan. The sisters shared a love of cheesy movies and had always been drawn like magnets to anything from *Blazing Saddles* to *The Princess Bride*, quoting from the movies frequently.

"That's Fronkensteen. Well, Abby Normal, I guess I'd better get my butt in gear and go find those coordinates."

"You'll call me, won't you? Don't keep me in suspense, Sherlock."

"Watson, you'll be the first to know. Now go save Silicon Valley while I try to save Death Valley's cousin."

***

Jordan scratched behind Bandit's ears as she left the yard. She unchained her bike and started toward the botanical gardens. Her GPS and other small hand tools were tucked into a backpack and secured to a rack on her bike. She bit the tube of the hydration pack slung across her shoulders and sucked in a drink of ice water. The general area the coordinates pointed to wouldn't be difficult to reach. The problem was, she didn't have any idea what she was looking for when she got there.

Is it buried or laying out in the open? She couldn't believe that there wouldn't be some challenge to this. After all, it was a coded message. *Probably meant to be an adventure.* She continued to picture the couple, whom she'd done a great deal of research on. Both were accomplished academics. After numerous interviews with former students of Aggie's, she was remorseful that she'd not had the opportunity to learn from her. Jordan had excelled in Professor Scott's class. She was saddened and disappointed that Aggie's death caused Noeul to leave the university before she could learn more from the esteemed professor. *Now if I can somehow find Professor Scott.*

Ten minutes later, she arrived at the gorge and strolled over to the visitor's center to pick up a trail map. She'd learned the hard way that it never hurt to have a backup that didn't require batteries. She smiled at Clarice, one of her students, as she approached.

The bright-eyed, young student perked up. "Hey, Professor A, out for a hike today? Or are you looking for the holy grail?"

Jordan smiled at the name. Her bosses insisted she be addressed as Professor. Since Professor Armstrong was too long and formal, she'd settled on her students calling her Professor A. Everyone knew of her quest to find the needed methodology to successfully graft her superfood to the perfect root ball. She pushed on toward her holy grail. "Morning, Clarice. A little of both I think. And yes, before you ask, I'll likely be going off trail. So, don't squeal on me. I promise not to swim in any of the restricted areas, and I promise to be cautious."

Winking at her, Clarice slid her a trail map. "Well, since you pretty much single-handedly keep our wildflower program going, I'm sure the powers that be will turn a blind eye as long as you don't attract followers."

Jordan patted her backpack. "I have about three pounds of native seed ready to go."

Clarice screwed up her mouth for a second. "Where are you going to be concentrating today? Just so I'll have a general idea if something, uh well, you know."

Jordan noted the concern in Clarice's face. Everyone knew Jordan's skills, and she'd never gotten into trouble on any of her ventures into the gorge. That didn't mean problems couldn't happen. "I'm going to be down around the bottom area. My plan is to be back by five this evening. I'll check in here with..." She stopped and thought about her other students' schedules. "Rick, I think. That will set everyone's mind at ease."

Clarice shook her head. "Your memory is uncanny."

"You don't know the half of it. Now, if I'm going to reach my destination, I've got to get going. Have a great day." Jordan waved as she settled her backpack over her shoulders and turned to go.

She immediately headed to what she'd determined was the closest point of access. The coordinates indicated an area deep into the gorge area and well off the beaten path. Her wildflower efforts would start along the more popular trails that would see visitors. More than once, she'd seen young lovers plucking a vibrant flower as a token gift. A year ago, she'd witnessed an engagement at the base of one of the waterfalls. A tall, athletic woman had dropped to her knee and presented a flabbergasted woman with a velvet box. Jordan had quietly watched the scene with admiration, as the redhead nodded an enthusiastic acceptance. The first woman rose and placed the ring on her companion's finger. She picked her up and twirled her around while they embraced. "She said yes," echoed off the rock walls and drowned out the water that rushed over the falls.

Jordan remembered her own proposal that hadn't gone as well. She and Tina Holden, a mathematics professor on loan to Cornell, had hiked down in the gorge and were enjoying a picnic. The memory rushed at her with the velocity of the water crashing down onto the base of the falls.

Jordan pulled out a travel brochure and handed it to Tina.

Tina furrowed her brow and looked at the colorful images of a Hawaiian adventure. "What's this?"

Taking another drink of her water, Jordan paused. "Someplace I'd like to take you." While Tina examined the pamphlet, Jordan removed a chain from around her neck and slid a ring into her palm. She put the necklace in her pocket, not bothering to put it back on.

"Hawaii? What brought this on?" Tina looked up from the brochure. Jordan was holding a large solitaire diamond ring between her index finger and thumb.

"For our honeymoon." Jordan shifted closer and placed a finger under Tina's chin, lifting her face so that their eyes would meet. "Tina, I love you, and I want to spend my life with you. Will you marry me?"

Tina looked stunned as her hand came to her mouth. Tears formed in her eyes.

"Hey, hey, this isn't supposed to make you cry. It's supposed to be one of the happiest moments of our lives." Jordan wiped an escaped tear off Tina's cheek with her thumb. "You haven't answered me." Jordan flipped the ring in her fingers.

"Oh, Jordan."

Jordan shook her head violently, as she gritted her teeth. Tina had been unable to say yes to the proposal. She had to admit she'd been legally married to a man for over fifteen years. The betrayal cut deep and resulted in Jordan being unable to open her heart to anyone since that day.

Dammit, Jordan, that was a long time ago. She crushed the memory beneath her hiking boots and followed the GPS points farther into the gorge. As she walked, she left the memory behind, while she looked all around the clearing she'd hiked into. A small creek above her cascaded down over several rock ledges and pooled into an ankle-deep pond about five feet in diameter. Jordan sat down in the almost hidden area and watched the water tumble over the rocks, the sound soothing and mesmerizing. She closed her eyes briefly and listened to the quiet. The bright light made Jordan squint when she opened her eyes to scan the area for anything out of place.

There was no record of when Professor James had created the bucket list, which made it difficult to know how much had changed since then. She sat on the soft grass near the water's edge and took off her boots to remove the small pebbles that had accumulated there. Without any more thought, she stood and accepted the clear water's invitation to walk in and cool off. Small minnows swam around her toes, as she allowed the water to ease the built-up heat and tension in her feet. She waded toward the small waterfall. A ray of sunlight broke through the trees and landed squarely on one point of the ledge, illuminating an area where the water shifted at an odd angle. Jordan squinted as her eye was drawn to something that reflected the sunlight back at her, something shiny. *What the hell?*

Under one of the rock ledges, a small niche existed, hidden behind the water. Her eyes focused on the space and on an object that looked like a small, reusable water bottle. With her phone in hand, Jordan confirmed that the geocoding was turned on to capture coordinates for the object in its exact position, before she snapped a picture to document the find. She reached through the frigid water and retrieved the cylinder. There were no markings other than normal scratches and dents on the polished metal. She walked back to the area where she'd been sitting and retrieved a towel out of her backpack.

Jordan carefully dried the cylinder and screwed off the top to pour out the contents. *What've we got here?* There were two folded pieces of paper and a small capsule about the size of a thirty-five-millimeter film canister. Engraved on the metal were the words, *A drop in the bucket...ashes to ashes.* A small heart separated the message from the initials *TAJ and NFS.* She whispered to herself, *"Tybee Agnes James and Noeul Finnegan Scott."* The gravity of what she was holding in her hands hit Jordan with the force of a sledgehammer, and she reverently placed the remains of Professor James back in the cylinder.

"Oh shit."

The letters still lay on the towel untouched. She felt like a tomb raider digging up ancient remains that were meant to be left in peace at their final resting place. Her stomach soured, and the guilt nearly overwhelmed her. Her search suddenly felt all wrong. Obviously, Professor Scott had visited this location again after the death of her wife and placed her remains in one of the spots Professor James had listed in the coded adventure. Why the location was important to the couple was unknown to Jordan. She was sure it held some significance in the two women's lives. *Did they get engaged here? Did they make love in this secluded area? Did they...?*

She paused, trying to determine the best way to proceed. *I should close this back up, put it back, and drop this whole thing. I feel like I'm violating their privacy.* She looked toward the sky. *I guess it is possible Professor James might be watching me from the afterlife.* She mulled all the possibilities around in her head before determining she'd already intruded on this private part of their lives. It wouldn't be any worse if she read the letters, in comparison to what she'd already done. She carefully unfolded the first piece of paper and began to read.

July 1, 2001
My love,

I know that you won't be pleased to know I hiked in here by myself to place this first clue. Now before you scold me, let me tell you why. In a few years, we'll leave Cornell in pursuit of a different dream, our dream. We've been creating a bucket list of what we want to see and do. Now it's time to start filling the bucket with memories instead of making a list. Your next clue is listed below. Hopefully, by July of next year, you'll have deciphered the code and we can plan our next trip.

My life changed in epic ways the day you walked onto the campus of Cornell. Your quiet, stabilizing grace saved me. Here in this place, we had one of our most incredible dates, and I knew I would never again be without you by my side.

So, on to our next adventure. Here is your mission—if you choose to accept it.

Love Aggie

Jordan read down the rest of the page to reveal the clue and pondered its meaning. She smiled at the use of the *Mission Impossible* line. She'd used it on Dava so many times it was automatic. Her sister's help would be needed again, if she planned to continue the quest to find Professor Scott.

Deep-seated guilt rose like bile in her throat, threatening to choke out her desire to continue. These were private thoughts and plans between a couple deeply in love and torn from each other by a premature death. Jordan placed the first letter on the towel and eventually picked up the second piece of paper from the cylinder.

November 2009

Aggie,

I've been thinking about plans, the plans we made for our happy ever after. These were plans we made together and never got the chance to fulfill. The day you died, you took my heart and soul with you, and every day, I feel I lose another piece of you. I wrap my arms around your pillow at night; your lingering scent grows fainter every day. I never wanted to do this without you. Now, in your honor, I work toward experiencing everything we had left to do.

I'll place a part of you in each place your codes lead me to and check off the boxes beside each item on our bucket list. The memories of you keep me going, driving me to the destinations, closer to you. I'm going to build our place, Aggie, exactly like we'd planned it. I know you'll be able to see it from where you are. I long for the day when I see your face again. Until then, I'll remember the list and the effort you put into this adventure.

Rest among the stars until I'm with you again my love,

Noeul

Jordan sat back, wiped out emotionally by what she had read. *How cruel to lose the love of your life that way. I could only hope to find a love like that, although I'm not sure I'd recognize it or trust it if I did.* She carefully documented the clue with photos and several notations into the research notebook she carried, before she tucked all the items back in the cylinder. Jordan was careful to reseal the canister and place it back in its final resting place. She ran her hands through her dark hair and gently tugged to relieve the tension headache she felt coming. She needed to ground herself and settle her spirit.

A glance at her watch made her rise quickly, surprised to see an hour had passed. She gathered her things, mentally calculating the time it would take her to get back to the visitor's desk to check out with Rick. Jordan had about a sixty-minute hike out, and it was fast approaching three in the afternoon. Turning for one final look at the area around her, she thanked the heavens for her time in this now sacred place.

A brisk pace would allow her to reach the center in time. *I need to get these seeds spread. The forecast called for rain, that should help set them.* Some of the seed would be eaten by birds. The majority should get washed down to the soil bed with the rain and have a chance to sprout.

Jordan hiked back up the trail with an empty seed bag and waved to Rick on her way out. She climbed into her Jeep, anxious to get home and call Dava to discuss what she'd found.

Chapter Three

NOEUL SCOTT WALKED THROUGH her walipini, an underground, greenhouse-like structure, and cut a handful of leafy greens for her evening salad. She checked the progress of her root crops and selected a ripe tomato. *The cabbage looks good. I promised Kelly and Miranda their own winter stash of kimchi. I think Miranda's as crazy about it as Aggie was.* Noeul thought back to a time when she'd tried to produce enough of the spicy, pickled cabbage to satisfy Aggie's addiction. Her wife had eaten kimchi with almost every meal since the day Noeul first took her home to meet her parents. Noeul stopped and closed her eyes.

"Twelve years since you left me, Aggie, and it feels like yesterday." Noeul still thought of Aggie as alive; she was gone on a long adventure and would be arriving home any minute. Noeul sat the basket she was holding and readjusted the long, black ponytail that was now streaked with silver. Strands of hair constantly escaped the cuff-and-pin style holder that Aggie had given her during their first trip to Ireland. She'd commissioned a local silversmith and presented it to Noeul. The Celtic knot incorporated the Korean symbols for wife and infinity. It was the most cherished item Noeul owned and a reminder of their commitment. Muscular and roguishly handsome, Aggie had completely swept Noeul off her feet, literally.

Noeul melted into the favorite memory.

Noeul rounded the corner on the Cornell campus, smacking into another body coming at her with speed. She squealed as strong arms wrapped around and lifted her up. Startled, Noeul grasped for anything to stop her fall. When they were under control, she realized she was being held eye to eye with one of the most gorgeous women she'd ever seen. The strong arms slowly lowered her back to the ground, and a shy grin crossed the taller woman's face.

"I'm so sorry." Aggie scowled at her companion. A tall, redheaded man, young enough to be a student, leaned over and held on to the bottom of his shorts. He was breathing rapidly. "Jackass over there,"

Aggie pointed with her thumb, "challenged me to a race and decided to shove me off trajectory when he started losing."

Noeul was still too stunned to speak. She stood looking up into blue eyes the shade of a perfect sky.

"Since we seem to have had our first embrace, how about we exchange names to make this less awkward. I'm Professor Aggie…"

Noeul found her voice and took in the Rollerblades and helmet. "Aggie James, I know."

Aggie scrunched her brow up in question. "Huh?"

Noeul blushed. "I'm Professor Noeul Scott from the agriculture department. You helped figure out the calculations for the timing on the new irrigation system with Professor Max Keller last year. I never got to meet you personally. Max was the go between. He told me all about you and pointed you out in the faculty directory."

The tall woman ran a hand through her sweat-soaked bangs, pushing them up under her helmet. "You know Max too? Well, I'll have to scold him for not introducing me. Can I rectify that by buying you dinner?"

Noeul craned her neck upward. "It might make for an easier conversation if I don't have to keep looking up to talk with you, high tower. Sure, what time and where?"

Aggie readjusted her helmet. "Six this evening, Fat Paddy's."

Noeul grimaced and shivered. "Only if you plan to take me to the cath lab after. The amount of saturated fat in a single burger there is more than I eat in a week. Do you like curry?"

Aggie laughed, "I could eat curry every day. The spicier the better. Rogan's?"

"Yes. I'll meet you at six. Now go finish your race. And you," Noeul pointed to the young man, "if she's your professor, I'd think trying to cheat would reflect poorly on the impression you're trying to make." The redhead laughed, shook his head and saluted her.

"See you later, Professor Scott. I think this race is over, and clearly, I'm the winner. Now, if you will excuse me, I'd like not to smell like this for dinner. Slán."

Speaking back to her in the same Gaelic, Noeul smiled, "Slán abhaile."

A look of shock crossed Aggie's face. "You speak Gaelic?"

"Well I do favor my Korean side. With a name like Noeul Finnegan Scott, you should have a pretty good clue where the other side of my DNA comes from."

Aggie laughed, the glint in her eyes full of mischief. "Marry me."

"Not until we've had our first date, Professor James. Now go, I'd like to be able to enjoy the curry without the smell of the gym locker."

Aggie began to skate backward, watching Noeul. "I'll hold you to that."

She had. From that first date, they were inseparable and married within six months. Shaking her head at the memory, Noeul walked back outside into the sharp, bright afternoon. The sun was still high in the sky, as she turned toward the house. The unique home built into the side of a mountain near Green Bank, West Virginia was designed to take advantage of the earth's natural thermal properties. The windows faced a breathtaking view of the expansive mountain range surrounding it. Forty feet out the front door, the property dropped three hundred feet down into a river gorge.

"Come, Kyo." She patted her leg to bring the border collie to heel at her side. Kyo sneezed and looked up at her, with a pink tongue lolling out of her mouth. Noeul opened the heavy sliding door into the kitchen. Large, floor-to-ceiling, thickly insulated windows faced the southern exposure and allowed the greatest amount of heat and light into the space. Kyo immediately went to her water bowl and lapped vigorously.

"If you would quit chasing those squirrels, you wouldn't be breathing so hard." She looked back at the dog, who stared at her with one brown eye and one light-blue one. "I've never even seen you catch one, although not for lack of effort." Kyo loped over beside her and nuzzled her hand with a wet nose, encouraging Noeul to stroke her ears. "Okay, I know. Maybe tomorrow you will. Way to be the optimist, girl."

She checked a stack of junk mail her friends had brought when they visited several days ago. "Oh look, Kyo. We might have won a million dollars. Too bad they spelled my name wrong on the check." The junk was easy to identify, because her Korean name, Noeul, was anglicized to Noel. "Used to tick me off as a kid." Noeul put a hand on her hip. "Never once did I have a key chain or a pencil without having to draw in an extra letter. Being born on Christmas didn't help either."

She smiled remembering the stories her parents told of her birth and their decision to name her. Kyo whined at her. "I know, I know. You don't have to tell me they had their reasons." The black-and-white dog blinked at her then went to lay down. Her journal lay on the bar. Writing down her thoughts had become a habit from her research. The habit now served to exorcise the pain and heaviness of her existence. She picked the notebook up to jot down a few thoughts.

I'm still grateful for the generous life insurance policy Aggie secured several years before she died. I'll never know if she was concerned or just thinking far into the future. Our plan was always to be completely self-sustained and isolated from the changing world. I've built the house and the life exactly as we'd planned it...almost. I added a barn into the rock face, where I keep a small cache of animals. Enough chickens for eggs and a continual supply of poultry, goats for milk, and a few lambs for wool. Rico, the tuxedo cat, is a one-eyed master who keeps the mice out of the feed and still manages to supervise me in the barn.

Kyo pawed at her, and Noeul put her finger in the journal as she carried it with her to let her companion out. She sat at the bar and continued her entry.

Kyo, my Korean mountain dragon, isn't much on conversation, but I couldn't ask for a more faithful companion. The vet bill was a small price to rescue that black-and-white ball of fluff. A true border collie, she herds the animals in at night with only a nod from me. I'm beyond grateful for her company, as my solitary days have stretched into months and the months to years.

As a way to escape nine years of sheer boredom, I've learned to speak French, Spanish, German, and Russian. My mother, Mi-ya, had taught me Korean, and thanks to one Finnegan Scott, I can also speak the Gaelic my great-grandfather taught him. A fat lot of good seven languages do me, since there's no one to speak them to.

At least I have the research I developed back at Cornell. At this point, I can graft almost anything onto any other compatible plant stalk. Back at the university, that missing link had eluded me like a lost treasure ship. After trying an entire list of variables including different types of cuts, stitching, clips, experiments with growth environments, soil types, lighting, and dozens of other factors, I've finally started to see some repeatable success.

Noeul closed the journal and went to the sink to rinse off the vegetables she'd collected earlier. *I need a distraction, to lose myself for a bit. Who will it be? Ah, Thoreau will do nicely.* She pulled the volume down from the shelf and headed to her small, comfortable living room.

There was no television in the living room. Even if she'd wanted one, living in the National Radio Quiet Zone made it impossible to have a live feed. The area was designated free of most electromagnetic signals to allow for scientific research and military defense. A TV in the guest bedroom allowed visitors to watch movies on DVD, if desired.

Without the distraction of the internet or television, she spent her free time reading, writing in her journal, or experimenting in the makeshift laboratory she'd set up in the greenhouse. It still wasn't perfect, though she'd come a long way since her days working with millions of dollars of equipment at Cornell.

Kyo jumped up against the window and startled her from her musings. "Silly dog. Get in here." Noeul returned to the couch, and Kyo settled over her feet as she'd done since she was a puppy with a broken pelvis and shoulder. Noeul stared out at the mountains, as she stroked the dog's soft ears. She closed her eyes and lost herself in the memory of dreaming with Aggie.

Aggie wrapped Noeul in her arms as they lay in bed. "Windows, lots of windows out the front view. We'll construct it for comfort, efficiency, and minimal maintenance. We'll have a green roof with solar panels, a small windmill, and a spring-fed water supply with a geothermic heating system."

Noeul snuggled into Aggie's side, drawing in the unique scent of her wife. The tropical lotion Aggie used religiously left a hint of coconut. When she was dressed up, she wore a dark, rich cologne that Noeul had created for her with the help of a friend in the fragrance industry. Hints of earth and freshly milled lumber hung around Aggie when she wore it. The scent Noeul loved most of all was the one they created together when they made love. She ran her index finger along the well-defined muscles of Aggie's bicep.

"I agree. Whatever we design as our retirement home, I want it as easy maintenance as it can be. I don't want you out crawling around on a roof when we're in our seventies."

"I'll second that, even though heights don't scare me. Our rock-climbing vacation was perfect. Climbing up behind you gave me the best view of your ass." Aggie laughed and pulled Noeul closer, catching the hand that was about to smack her.

Laughing softly, Noeul kissed the hand holding hers, reveling in the moment. "Happy to be able to provide you visual stimulation my love."

"Oh, it's stimulating alright." Aggie pulled Noeul on top of her.

Noeul enjoyed Aggie's direction and straddled her wife's hips with an audible groan, as Aggie began to move below her.

"I love you, Noeul, I have since the moment I saw you."

Noeul wove her fingers through Aggie's light hair. "And I fell in love with you the minute you wrapped me up in your arms after almost mowing me down."

"It was original."

Noeul leaned down and kissed her. "And effective."

"Obviously, because I walked away with a date." Aggie moved her hands to Noeul's breasts, lightly squeezing as she rose to take a nipple in her mouth.

"And I walked away with a marriage proposal and shortly thereafter, the girl." Noeul closed her eyes as the passion began to build and her hips began to rock without conscious thought.

Noeul felt Aggie slip a hand between their bodies, finding Noeul's wet center.

"I did get that a bit bassackward. Although, if I had to do it all again, I wouldn't change a thing."

Noeul felt Aggie's fingers slide into her, as she allowed her head to lean back, eyes closed, her body shuddering with the sensation. "And neither would I. Now make love to me like you did our first time together."

Noeul lost herself in the passion, riding her lover's hand to a bone-melting climax that left her weak and satisfied. Aggie climaxed soon after, with no other stimulation than the sight of Noeul and the sound of her guttural release. When they lay together in the waning light with shadows from the trees dancing across the walls, Noeul relaxed into the security of the strong arms that held her and the promise of a long life together.

Noeul woke from the memory, her cheeks wet with tears. She threw the book in her hand and startled Kyo. "I'm sorry girl. Don't mind me." Loneliness overwhelmed her, as she missed those intimate moments with Aggie. There were times when she could still smell her, hear her, and even see her when she touched herself before going to sleep. The problem was that after the brief moment of release, there were no strong arms to hold her through the night. When she woke, she would still be alone. Whispering to herself, she spoke the truth of it. "My God, Aggie, I still miss you so much."

She rose, wrapping her arms around herself, as she walked over to the kitchen to begin the preparations for her meal along with Kyo's. "How about some dinner, girl?" Constantly hauling big bags of dog food up the mountain was no issue as there was no processed dog food she'd ever give Kyo. Noeul had always prepared for Kyo a steady diet of poultry mixed with vegetables that could easily be put on her own plate, though she wouldn't because it lacked the spices she loved. There were only a few food items she required from outside her mountaintop world: coffee, tea, and the spices she got from Mr. and Mrs. Anderson at the farmers' market.

"I really need to get to town. I'm running low on a few things, Kyo." The dog cocked her head at Noeul and panted softly. Her mismatched eyes twinkled, and that made Noeul smile. Twice a month, Noeul would ride one of her horses two miles down the mountain and take the truck she parked at Miranda and Kelly's to town for supplies. They also accepted deliveries for things Noeul ordered, as well as the mail the attorney would forward to her. Most of her online orders were things she couldn't pick up at the general store in the small town of Green Bank. "I probably need to schedule dentist and eye doctor appointments while I'm down there. I think I need new glasses, or longer arms." She chuckled at her own joke. At fifty-five, she enjoyed excellent health and was still in very good shape. Living on the mountain left her no option to be anything else.

Kneeling, she put her arms around Kyo's neck and kissed between her eyes. "I think we need a trip to see Aunt Miranda and Aunt Kelly. Bet they have a cow horn or two for you." The couple were her closest friends since she'd moved there. They were her source of comfort when the sound of her own voice began to grate on her nerves or was too raspy from lack of use. "We'll get an early start in the morning." She looked out the windows as the shadows grew long. Her life had its joys, without a doubt, but she knew the solitude was never meant to be her day-to-day reality.

"Our Life was supposed to be so very different, Aggie. We were supposed to be watching the sunset here together."

***

Jordan climbed the stairs to her apartment, with Bandit carrying her dinner basket from Sam. Once inside, she pulled out a portion of lasagna, a small salad, and some bread. "Bandit, it's a good thing your dads are married." Bandit tilted his head sideways and whined at her.

"Don't worry buddy, I've sworn off love forever."

She finished her meal and fed Bandit his reward. While she booted up her computer, she copied the information from her pictures into her leather-bound notebook. Her eyes were drawn to one set of numbers that seemed extremely familiar. She traced the numbers over and over, making the marks darker as she thought about the range. The light in the room changed, and her attention was drawn to a piece of stained-glass window art in the shape of a rainbow. Jordan snapped her fingers. "That's why it seemed familiar. The numbers could be related to the wavelength range of blue and green light." Excited, she called her sister. The phone didn't have time to ring more than once before the rapid-fire questions started.

"How did the search go? I've been waiting for hours. What did you find? Come on, start spilling your guts, JJ!"

Jordan shook her head at the impatience and laughed. "Can't I call because I want to talk to my amazing little sister?"

Dava growled. "Good God, Jordan, I'm going to have to get my chair's wheels cleaned with all the bullshit you're making me travel through. Now give."

"Okay, okay, Miss Impatient. I hiked down into the gorge and looked around. I didn't see anything until sunlight glinted off something in the waterfall area. It was a cylinder about the size of one of those reusable aluminum water bottles. The contents were two letters and a small sealed canister with engraved initials. If I'm not mistaken it likely contains ashes of Professor James.

"Oh, that's creepy, JJ."

"Don't I know it. I felt like a grave robber."

They were both quiet for a moment before Dava finally spoke. "Okay, creepiness aside, what else did you find?"

"The letters were dated at different times. Aggie's letter was written back in July of 2001 and the other is dated November 2009, over a year after Aggie passed away. I'm going to send you pictures of both, and before you ask...yes, it feels weird to read what wasn't meant for me." Jordan drew in a deep breath and let it out slowly. Dava didn't speak as she waited on the pictures.

"Ok, I've got them. Let's see."

Jordan read over the letters again, and she knew Dava was doing the same. "I think I figured out at least one part of Aggie's clue, see what you think. I'm looking at that set of numbers, 4 0 - 4 9 0 to 5 0 0 - 5 6 5. I'm going to take a guess that those are the wavelengths of blue and green light. It's possible I'm wrong."

After a few seconds, Dava finally spoke. "Nice, JJ, that's a really good possibility. At this point, I tend to think you're right. Noeul and, for that matter, you would have dealt with this in agricultural research. Let's see about the others and if they fit together. The first clue contains two sets of Roman numerals and comes out to forty-eight and nineteen twelve. We'll figure out what they mean after we've deciphered the rest of the clues."

Jordan looked at the numbers. She didn't have any idea what they meant. This was Dava's area of expertise; it would only be a matter of time for her to crack it.

Dava laughed in triumph. "Ah, simple letter number substitution for the one clue that starts with twenty-three. Those numbers correlate with the word water."

"Humm, so we have blue, green, and water. Where can you find blue-green water?"

"Several places around Florida at first thought, the Florida Keys come to mind. Maybe we can narrow it down with some of the other clues. Let's look at the next set. An up arrow and a series of numbers separated by slashes, with the last set of numbers including dashes. Hang on for a minute and let me try something."

Jordan sat looking at the numerical clues. "Twelve, twenty-four, and six fifty." She could remember creating puzzles like this for Dava when she was a child. Their endeavors had never materialized to this extent.

"Gotcha, you little bugger." Dava's enthusiasm filled the phone.

"What is it, Watson?"

Dava made a drumroll sound. "It's the element magnesium, Sherlock."

"What?"

"Twelve is magnesium's position in the periodic table, twenty-four is its molecular weight and the six fifty..."

Jordan finished for her. "That's magnesium's melting point in degrees Celsius. I'm almost positive that last number is the chemical abstract service number, now that I really look at it. It's the unique numerical identifier assigned to each chemical substance by the registry. As researchers, we must use the reference in all our scientific publications. Damn, I wonder if the arrow means elevated or high magnesium concentrations? That can cause water to have a blue-green tint." Jordan giggled. "I'd forgotten how much fun creating these for you were."

Dava's deep laugh came through the speaker. "Glad you enjoyed my misery. Okay, what haven't we decoded yet?"

"The last clue is the word *metimur* with the set of numbers five, zero, six, eight, eight, zero. *Metimur* means measure in Latin." Jordan mused.

"Well, if you put those numbers into a distance conversion calculator, it gives you a list of measurements from nanometers to nautical miles. This one could be tricky, Jordan, because we don't have any idea if this measurement is on land or water. The clue has to do with water, so it could be nautical miles."

"True. Let me try something. The book they wrote together was about national parks. I wonder if there are any that might have blue-green water. Something with a high magnesium concentration." Jordan scratched her head. "I'll work on that while you work on that first clue in Roman numerals. Maybe that will help pinpoint the location."

"Okay, and by the way, I'm having fun doing this with you. Thanks for making me a part of your project."

Jordan could hear Dava's smile through the line. "I love you, little sister, don't you ever forget that."

"Okay, enough mushy, back to work. I did a simple internet search for forty-eight and nineteen twelve. Arizona became the forty-eighth state in 1912. Does that fit with anything?" Dava asked her sister.

"Let's recap for a second and bring it all together."

"Okay, Sherlock. Putting it together in simple terms, we're looking for blue-green water in Arizona with a high magnesium concentration. Got any ideas?"

"Well Google hasn't failed us yet, putting that in..." Jordan stopped. Simultaneously they yelled, "Havasu Falls!"

Dava filled in a few points. "Havasupai means..."

"People of the blue-green waters. Wow, I think I found the measurement too. It's eight miles from Hualapai Hilltop to the village of Supai, according to the official page of the Havasupai tribe. Then another two over to the falls. That's got to be it. The Grand Canyon is in their book. Not Havasu specifically, but the canyon itself. Maybe it was a place they visited or wanted to go back to. I've got to do some planning, if I'm going there to look for a clue." Jordan thought about her schedule. "I have some annual leave coming to me."

"Now hold your horses, my dear sister. You can't just jump on a plane and take a hike. Mom will worry, not to say anything about me."

Jordan stopped to consider the wisdom of a trip like this. Over her summer breaks, she'd worked in various national parks throughout college. She had the money and the time to do this, not to mention she was stuck in her research and truly believed her next breakthrough would be in finding Professor Noeul Scott. Jordan knew she might not even be able to find the next clue once she got there, but she had to try.

"Watson, I know you worry about me. I have a gut feeling this is something I have to do. I promise to take every precaution and keep in touch as much as I'm able to. We're in this together, if not in body, in spirit."

There was a long pause before Dava answered. "So, when do you leave?"

* * *

Noeul finished her list and tucked it into her backpack. Kyo was jumping around like a jack in the box. "Be patient, silly. I need to go set the timer to drop the food for everyone." Along with training Kyo to bring the flock in at a whistle, the animals had been trained to come to a buzzer on a digital timer. That same timer-controlled feeders that allowed her to be gone for the evening and morning feedings. Rico had a big bowl of food and water. Before the animals had joined her existence, it wasn't a problem to leave the property for a few days, or even a week if she'd needed to. After she made the decision to include them in her life, she developed a system to feed them while she was away. The solar-powered, electric fence added an extra layer of protection around their grazing area.

All systems were double-checked before she and Kyo headed down the trail to Miranda and Kelly's. With the horses being re-shod, the trip on foot would take them almost two hours at a steady clip, longer if Kyo found she needed a dip in the stream. Noeul couldn't begrudge her that simple pleasure. Dealing with the wet dog smell was the only downside. Hopefully, when she and Kelly took their evening run, Kyo would dry out.

"Kyo come," she called to the border collie who dutifully took her place at Noeul's side as they set out. Noeul adjusted her backpack to sit more comfortably on her shoulders and pushed down the holster holding the Glock she carried when walking the trail. Kyo's presence normally kept the large black bears and occasional coyotes at bay, but Noeul took no chances when Momma bear might be out for a stroll with her cubs.

About halfway down, they reached the stream that ran off the mountain and right through Miranda and Kelly's property. Noeul scanned the clear creek bottom for any fish. "This time of year, the fishing should be good, Kyo." Native trout were plentiful in the area, and Noeul had joined her friends in catching their limit of rainbow trout many times. Her mind drifted to where it always did when she thought about fishing. *Aggie loved to fly fish and put a line in the water. She was so beautiful in that element.*

Aggie was a patient teacher as she taught Noeul both the art of tying the flies and the movement needed to cast the line in fluid arcs without hooking herself. Their bucket-list trip to Havasu Falls had included a side trip to fly fish near the Grand Canyon in the Colorado River. They'd spent their summer vacation each year visiting several of the national parks in the Grand Circle. Parks like Arches, Bryce, Mesa Verde, and Zion had given them ample research for the book they'd coauthored.

Cold water splashed up on her as Kyo bounded into a deeper section of the stream and took a drink. Noeul wiped water from her face. "Thanks for the bath, goofball." Noeul had to laugh at what looked like a smile on her dog's face as water streamed out of her mouth. "Okay, break time. You swim." Noeul sat on a log she frequently used to watch Kyo play in the water and pulled out a small bag of dehydrated peaches to nibble on.

Kyo showered her again when she bounded after a squirrel. "I'd really like to know what you're going to do if you ever catch one of those." Noeul absently chewed and thought about the trip to Havasu Falls. It was still a favorite memory. They'd spent many hours each day around the falls, swimming and enjoying the area free of electronic distractions and modern life. Unfortunately, they'd only managed a few more trips from Aggie's list. Two months after they'd returned from one of them, she'd sat by Aggie's side, willing her to live. The memory of Aggie collapsing on their run still haunted Noeul's dreams.

Noeul noticed for the second time as Aggie rubbed her chest. "Honey, are you okay? You look a little pale. Let's drop the pace down a little bit."

Aggie grinned at her, sweat rolling off her jawline. "I'm fine, babe. I think it's a little muscle pull."

Noeul protested. "Let's find a place to cool off and let me look at you.

"Honey, I'm fi—"

Noeul watched in horror, as Aggie stared blankly and reached out for her. "Aggie!"

"Noeul...love you."

"Aggie! Aggie! Somebody, help." Aggie was slumped against her, as Noeul tried to ease the much-taller woman to the ground. They fell into a heap, and Noeul positioned Aggie on her back. She was conscious, but not responding. Her color was pale, and she was sweating profusely; her hands felt cool and clammy. Noeul placed her fingers on Aggie's wrist to find the pulse thready and irregular. Reaching into her small pack, she found her phone and dialed 911.

"911, where is your emergency?" The dispatcher asked.

"I've got a woman collapsed on the Bebee Lake trail at the Cornell Botanical Gardens. We're at...shit! I can't see any markers. We're about three miles around the loop, starting from the visitors' center."

"Is she conscious?"

Noeul screamed as the felt Aggie's forehead. "Barely, she's not responding to me. Please, I need an ambulance!"

Anything the dispatcher said to her after that was lost, as Aggie clasped her hand and went completely limp, her eyes closing. Noeul felt for a pulse in her wrist. Finding none, she moved her hands to the carotid artery in Aggie's neck. Again, she found no pulse. She screamed at the phone something unintelligible and put her face near Aggie's. "Aggie, please don't leave me, please."

She tried to feel for breath against her cheek and failed to detect any. She moved down Aggie's body and said a silent prayer for the first aid and CPR classes they attended every year. Placing her hands in the middle of Aggie's chest, she began to count. She continued by herself to the point of exhaustion, before a side-by-side ATV came barreling up the trail. A police officer jumped out, carrying a small box. He asked Noeul a few questions, while his partner took over CPR. Noeul tried to make sense of what was happening, as the officer cut Aggie's T-shirt and jog bra open. He attached two pads with wires that ran to the small box. She heard the box say, "analyzing," while the officers held their hands up. After a few seconds, the unit's mechanical voice announced, "shock advised." The officer quickly yelled, "clear" to Noeul, and his partner depressed the button on the unit. Noeul blanched as Aggie's body jumped from the current.

Noeul moved to Aggie's head, placing her face very close to Aggie's ear. "Tybee Agnus James, don't you dare leave me. We still have so much to do." Tears streamed down her face, and the breath froze in her chest. The unit again called out, "analyzing," and advised a shock was necessary. Noeul moved away from Aggie and closed her eyes briefly, as the shock jolted her wife's body. "No shock, pulse detected." Noeul thought those were the sweetest words she'd ever heard and looked up expectantly at the officers.

"I'm feeling an extremely week pulse. I'll radio the ambulance."

Everything was a blur from the time they arrived at the hospital until hours later when Noeul sat at her bedside. Max and Sam had brought her a change of clothes and something to eat. She hadn't been able to bring herself to do more than sit holding Aggie's hand.

A young man, who looked like he'd only recently graduated high school, stepped into the room. "Ms. Scott, I'm Dr. Riker. I understand you have medical power of attorney for Ms. James?"

Noeul wiped her eyes with a Kleenex. "Yes, she's my wife."

"Well, gay marriage isn't legal here in New York, so technically you aren't her wife. Your status as her medical power of attorney allows me to consult you about Ms. James condition and treatment."

Noeul's focus narrowed on the man standing in the white coat. "Stop right there." She rose continuing to hold Aggie's hand in hers. "I don't give a shit how you feel about gay marriage. She's my wife and if you have one second of doubt about that, I will request another doctor so fast you'll be looking at your own ass as I go past you. We married in Massachusetts in 2004, when it first became legal there. In your small mind, it may not be valid in this state; however, I put that band there in 2004 and my vows mean as much to me as any straight marriage. Now, either you can deal with the fact that we are lesbians, or I'll find her another doctor. Do I make myself clear?"

Red faced and properly dressed down, the young man apologized. "I meant no disrespect. I apologize. I need to discuss the patient's condition with you." He took a deep breath. "She—"

Noeul's stare cut him into a million small pieces. "Aggie, her name is Aggie."

"Aggie. Okay. Aggie suffered a cardiac arrest, as you know. What you may not know is she apparently has a congenital heart condition. She...Aggie suffered an arrhythmia called ventricular fibrillation or V-fib. She experienced a run of erratic, electrical impulses that basically caused the heart to flutter instead of pumping blood the way the cardiovascular system is intended. There are three electrical nodes in the heart that fire in a particular sequence, causing the chambers of the heart to pump blood through the body. Aggie's sinus node malfunctioned."

Noeul took a deep breath. "So how do we fix it?"

The doctor looked at the tablet in front of him and touched the screen. He turned it to Noeul. "She needs a pacemaker to make sure the heart fires in sync."

"Her parents are on their way from Tybee Island in Georgia. They are flying into Ithaca. When do we need to do this?"

"As soon as possible."

"Can we wait for them to get here? From what they told me, they'll be here in the next two hours." Noeul kissed and caressed Aggie's hand, turning the wedding band that matched her own.

The doctor sighed with impatience. "We are monitoring her. If she goes back into V-fib, we would have to shock her again. We'd like to avoid that if we can."

Noeul fixed him with a hard stare. "Fine, then we wait. In the meantime, I want another surgeon."

The doctor tilted his head and looked at her over the top of his designer glasses. He spoke in a clipped tone. "Ms. Scott, I assure you I am more than qualified to perform this surgery. I've done hundreds."

"Well, this is one you won't be doing. Thank you for your time, Dr. Riker." She turned abruptly from him and back to Aggie's side. "Max, can you call Kendra and see how much longer she'll be?"

The doctor visibly paled. "Kendra?"

"That's right, Dr. Riker." She turned back to him, narrowing her own eyes. "Kendra Powers, the head of this hospital, is a personal friend. I'm sure she will be able to give me excellent medical advice on which physician would be best suited to care for my wife. I called her as soon as I got to the hospital and made sure Aggie was stabilized. She's on her way here from her summer home in Lake George. Good day, sir."

His hand holding the clipboard visibly trembled. "Ms. Scott, please. I'm sorry if you've felt like I have insulted you. I..."

Noeul dismissed him with a pointed finger. "Please leave, Dr. Riker, you've said enough. Nothing you say now can change the past. You can't unring a bell. Thank you for your time."

Noeul shivered as Kyo's wet nose touched her arm and roused her from that terrible memory. "Hey girl. Guess you struck out again?" The dog, still smiling and dripping wet, stood at her side as Noeul stroked her head. She always seemed to know when to bring Noeul back from a memory. "Guess we'd better get going."

Despite all the best doctor's efforts, Aggie hadn't come out of the coma, even after the surgery to put in the pacemaker. Sometime during the procedure, she'd suffered a bleed in her brain. She passed away two days later. Noeul had collapsed when Dr. Rita Hamilton, Aggie's surgeon, told her there was no brain activity. Only the machines were keeping Aggie alive. Tom and Bell James were with Noeul at Aggie's bedside when they turned off the machines, the grief ripping each of them into tiny pieces. Five years later, Noeul lost both of them to a sailing accident near Tybee Island, the place they'd named Aggie for. She was truly alone.

Noeul rose, closed her eyes and whispered to the sky, "I love you, Aggie." She started back down the trail, Kyo at her side. She planned to stay the night with Miranda and Kelly for some restorative conversation after making a run to town. The next morning, she'd saddle Thor and Athena, her two horses she'd left with them for a farrier appointment and make the return trip up the mountain with her supplies. The couple ran a small retreat for those who were on internships at the Green Bank Observatory or were desperate to get away from the trappings of modern life. The area relied on landlines for phone service and was regulated by a long list of restrictions as to what could and could not be used to avoid any interference with the ongoing research. Forty minutes later, Noeul arrived at the wide, front porch of the rustic cabin only to be wrapped in a bone-crushing hug by a tall, muscular woman with a long, salt-and-pepper braid hanging down her back.

"Miranda, I've missed you."

"Missed you too. About time you came down off that mountain." Miranda kissed her forehead.

Her wife, Kelly, was a slight woman with a mop of red curls. She came out the door with a fresh blackberry cobbler and placed it on a rack. Kelly removed her oven mitts to wrap Noeul in gentle embrace and kiss both cheeks.

"God, it's good to see you, stranger. Good lord, we've got to put some meat on those bones. A good wind will blow you off that mountain. Noeul, you've got to eat." Kelly was a caregiver, always putting something delicious in her hands and urging her to eat.

Noeul smiled at her friends and enjoyed the interaction with another being. "I eat just fine, Kelly. Remember, I'm Korean and five foot nothing. I can't put much weight on, or I'll be as big around as I am tall."

Kelly smiled and wrapped her in another hug. "Well, you could do with another five pounds. I'm sending a few things back with you tomorrow, so don't argue."

Noeul shook her head and laughed. "I might as well go argue with that porch post over there, because it would listen about as much. Thank you, Kelly. I know I'll enjoy whatever you fix. However, now I've got to head to town. If you two will entertain Kyo, I'll go take care of business and get back here for some good food and better company."

Miranda knelt and briskly scratched Kyo's sides. "I'll take her with me to check the cabins. She'll be good and tired by the time she runs that five-mile loop. That way, when you go with us for a run later, you might be able to keep up."

"Very funny. See you for lunch." Noeul waved at the couple, as she trotted to her truck. Within minutes, she was making her way down the dirt driveway and toward the closest thing to a big city in the area.

Chapter Four

TWO WEEKS HAD PASSED since Jordan and Dava deciphered the clues. Jordan loaded up the Jeep and turned to Max and Sam. "Guess that's it." The two looked at her, their expressions sad. *I'm going to miss them more than I imagined.*

Sam walked forward first and put his arms around Jordan. "Please be careful. You're family to us. Please don't forget to eat."

He pulled away as Max stepped toward her and placed his hands on her face. He ran his fingers over her cheeks. "I want to remember you. Don't stay away too long."

Jordan pulled him into a hug and held him tightly. "I won't, I promise. We still have to finish our chess game." Jordan's heart was breaking in two. The fear that he might not remember the chess game or her, wracked her with pain and guilt.

"I think you should email me with your next move every few days. I'll send you mine, and we'll keep a running game between us. Stay safe." Max kissed her temple.

Jordan pulled Sam into a group hug and felt Bandit jump up so she could scratch his head. When she pulled out of the hug, she dropped to her knee and buried her hands and face in his thick coat. "Keep Dad safe now, Bandit. I'll be back before you know it. Please don't eat the couch." Bandit licked at the salty tears running unimpeded down her face. She stood and wiped at them furiously, as she climbed into her Jeep and leaned out the window. "I'll call you when I get near Fort Wayne. That's my target for tonight. I have no idea whether I'll make it there or not. I love you both. Make sure you give Bandit a scratch every night from me." She waved at them and watched them grow smaller in her rearview mirror.

She'd promised to connect with Dava at the halfway point, somewhere around Cleveland, Ohio. Her sister was far less worried about her venturing than Sam, who'd made an impassioned protest. Max had calmed him down, knowing how important her search was. Jordan looked at the seat beside her and smiled at the snacks and sweets Sam had packed for her journey. Without a doubt, she was going to miss his culinary skills. As long as she had her staples, she would be fine.

James Taylor's "Fire and Rain" came pouring out of speakers, and she sang along while the Jeep chewed up mile after mile of hot pavement on I-86. This route would take her over near Erie. The farther she drove, the more the scenery changed. Fields of hay and grain, forests of trees, and the familiar, whitewashed farmhouses dotting the landscape gave way to the industrial gray of concrete lots, glass high rises, and cookie-cutter shopping malls. *I could never live in a place like this. I need green.*

The soothing voice of Carol King filled her ears, and she realized her playlist was circling back. This list had about six hours of pure, 1970s gold. Jordan ran her fingers through her hair and rubbed her eyes vigorously, trying to wake herself up. Exhaustion was setting in, and the need to find a place to camp or stay was becoming urgent. Up ahead, a small gas station came into view, giving her the opportunity to fill up and check with the clerk about camping arrangements.

He gave her the change from a five-dollar bill, for a pack of salted peanuts. "About three more miles down on the left, take Parnell Ave. Nice municipal park with camping."

Jordan thanked him and got back in her vehicle. It was nearing five in the evening, and she wanted to cook her noodles and make some hot tea. A few minutes after purchasing her permit to stay the night in the park, she set about getting a fire started and erected her nylon and flex-pole tent with a practiced ease. Her food was stored in bear-proof containers, a lesson she'd learned the hard way on a trip into the Vermont mountains. Yogi tore through her Jeep and snacked on her food stocks while she was out hiking. She could forgive all the destruction, but not the ransacking of her must-have comfort foods. *Who knew bears could be so cannibalistic to eat the Teddy Grahams?*

In a small pull off surrounded by pines, Jordan pulled out her cook pot and kettle. The dried noodles were easy to pack, quick to fix, and filling. She would consume the entire pot leaving no leftovers, facilitating an easy cleanup. Add a sleeve of Ritz crackers, and she would be set. She poured boiling water over the Jordanian tea mix her mother had given her and filled her campsite with a pleasant aroma. Her cellphone sat beside her, and to her surprise, she had service. As she blew across the mouth of her mug to cool the tea, she punched in Dava's number.

"Hey, Watson."

"Sherlock, I didn't expect to hear from you after our call earlier. Where did you end up?"

"I'm in Fort Wayne, Indiana, at a little place called Johnny Appleseed Campground. This place has a headstone for Johnny Appleseed with an inscription, 'He lived for others.' The stone is dated 1774 to 1845."

Dava's laugh was rich. "God, you're such a geek."

"Hey pot, meet kettle. We just geek on different things." Jordan pulled up her first forkful of noodles with the phone cradled to her ear. "Ow!" She'd burned her tongue and set down the pot to look for her water bottle.

"What'd you do?"

"Ah bwerned ma ung."

Dava snickered. "Let me see if I can translate. I'm going to guess it was ouchy ow wow. You burned your tongue, didn't you? You barely have the patience of a three-year-old."

Jordan shook her head. "You're a riot. Now, did you find anything about the area I'm headed to?"

"Only that it's gorgeous and you'll have to hike in. You can camp there. It appears to have some basic amenities. In reference to exactly where you're going to find your next clue, I'm not sure."

Jordan admired the setting sun's lines of color in broad swaths of pinks and yellows feathered through the sky. The blazing campfire was chasing the shadows to the base of the trees, orange tongues of flame licking the air. *I guess that's where the saying like a moth to a flame comes from. Mesmerizing.* "I'll send pictures, though I'm sure it won't be until the adventure is over. I'm guessing the only service I'll have in some of those parts, will be the satellite phone." She heard a sigh followed by a sharp chomping sound. Dava was chewing on her fingernails.

Dava's voice sounded small and timid. "You'll call me before you drop off the radar, right?"

"I will, please don't worry about me so much and stop chewing on your fingernails."

"I wasn't."

"Liar."

"Okay, okay. I can't help it. I hate when you go off grid. I'm going to slap a GPS tracker in your ass the next time I hug you." Dava quipped.

Jordan laughed and took a sip of her tea. "I'll keep in touch as much as I can."

"Be safe and call me tomorrow."

"I will. Love you, kiddo."

Jordan sat watching the last embers of the fire die down. The sky was a million tiny dots of lights against an ebony background. "Beautiful. *'If the stars should appear one night in a thousand years, how would men believe and adore.'"* The writings of Ralph Waldo Emerson and John Muir were some of her favorites. She'd always been a voracious reader. Childhood summer days meant lying in the backyard hammock with Dava, silently disappearing into the world of an author's mind. They'd spend hours indulging their imagination. Reading was one activity where both girls were on completely equal footing and needed no assistance.

Jordan's other love had been growing things. Their backyard had a vegetable and flower garden where Jordan began to sow seeds on her first birthday, according to her parents. Her mother told about giving Jordan several packets of wildflowers and watching as her small hands released the seeds on their lawn. As a child, Jordan had frequently presented her mother with a handful of freshly cut flowers from their garden. Now, she made sure, on every holiday and anniversary, that her mother received a bouquet of in-season, fresh-cut flowers.

Jordan grew weary and crawled into her sleeping bag. She lay there for a long time, listening to a lone whippoorwill calling out its sharp, repetitive song into the night. Her thoughts quieted as she closed her eyes and fell asleep, confident in her mission.

***

Noeul stood with a pail in her hand and patted the goat she'd finished milking. "Thank you, Pip. This will make some excellent cheese." She walked through the barn and stopped to run her hand over one of the lambs, feeling its soft, black wool. With her free hand, she grabbed the basket that contained the eggs, radishes, and carrots she'd gathered and carried everything into the kitchen. After pouring the milk into glass jars, she placed them and the eggs in the refrigerator. The vegetables went in the sink.

Her next task was to make another batch of medicinal salve. The previous week, when Kyo cut a pad on her paw, the salve had helped it heal rapidly. Noeul grabbed a double boiler to heat up a small amount of olive oil and set a portion of bee's wax beside it to add during the last step. She adjusted the heat on the electric burner and began to measure out dried yarrow and petals from the arnica flower into a mortar. She used the pestle to grind the ingredients and release more of their essence. "That should do it." When complete, she added the mixture to a cloth teabag and lowered it into the oil. She would let it steep for about twenty minutes to let the herbs infuse the oil. She would create the salve by adding the beeswax. The all-natural remedy was less likely to make her animals sick when they invariably licked it off.

Her hand grazed the bar and landed on her journal, which she picked up as she headed outside. Fingers of despair crept up her spine, as she stepped over to the black-and-white fur ball that leaned into her shoulder from atop the fence post. She kissed the cat between his ears and scratched his face. A V8-engine purr rumbled deep in his chest, albeit with a slight miss. "Such a sweet boy."

A large boulder sat at the edge of the yard with a view looking out over the mountains. Warmth spread throughout her, as she closed her eyes and lifted her face to the sun. She sat down on the large, flat surface and relaxed as she absorbed the heat from the stone into her legs. The journal's ribbon marking her last entry.

As I sit here, off in the distance I can hear a woodpecker's repetitive tap-tap-tap as it works for its dinner, chipping away at a tree where its meal of insects hides. In the meadow, my sheep bleat softly, and the hum of my bees working their hives drifts in on the breeze. I can smell the honeysuckle and the laurel blooms, fragrant and sweet. I love my life here, it's peaceful, satisfying...and lonely.

She raised her face again to the sky. Dazzling oranges, reds, and blues flashed on the inside of her lids as she moved her eyes, closed tightly against the brightness. Kyo made her way up on the rock and laid her head across Noeul's thighs. One hand buried itself into the soft fur, as she quieted her heart and opened the journal again.

Every day that passes without human contact and conversation makes this life grow harder and harder to withstand. The term social butterfly never applied to me in any way, but I did enjoy personal interaction. When I first moved to the mountain, I only went down to Miranda and Kelly's every few months. Now it's hard to go more than a week without seeing them.

One of the chickens let out a terrifying squawk and the sound of flapping feathers and urgent clucks drew her away from her journal. She sprawled off the rock and ran over to the enclosure area.

"Dammit! That coyote is back!"

Kyo heard her and ran past at a blistering pace to reach the intruder, barking her head off at the brush rustling beyond the pen. "Kyo! Heel!" The dog obediently ran back to Noeul, panting as she looked up for approval. "Good girl, Kyo, good girl." Noeul stroked her head and led her over to the pail of water, where Kyo drank with great gulps. The excess water streamed from her jowls.

"Kyo, I think it's time to find you a friend." Noeul had been thinking about acquiring a Great Pyrenees because they were known for being incredibly protective of their flock and territory. It was something she would investigate when she went back down to the girls' house, maybe find a rescue. Kyo came to her side and her fingers ran across her head. "At least it will give *you* someone to talk to."

After passing through the gate, she looked over each of her chickens, ensuring herself that the only damage done was some ruffled feathers. With a sigh, she checked over the entire run, confirming that there had been no breach. She walked out of the enclosure and locked the gate behind her. "Well Kyo, let's go see about some supper and maybe an evening with John Muir...or maybe a good dystopian novel. A. J. Adaire's latest came in the mail the other day. I need a moment of escape, and a good book is always a wonderful way to accomplish that."

***

It was still dark when Jordan left the camping area in Peach Springs, Arizona and dawn still hadn't broken when she turned onto Indian Road 18 and into the Hualapai Hilltop parking area. She'd leave her Jeep there and hike down to get the permit that would allow her to camp at Havasu Falls. She got out and rummaged through her hiking pack to ensure that all her essentials were there. Her pack held a few clothes, a tent and bedroll, a small cook stove with utensils, dried noodles and tea bags, a shortwave weather radio, a supply of water, and purification tablets. She was also carrying her journal and a paperback version of Professor Scott's book, in case she needed to show someone else what she had stored in her head.

Jordan was physically fit and able to carry a larger load than the average backpacker. She'd hiked the Appalachian Trail and several other through-hikes in her lifetime. "It's all in knowing the difference between what you need and what you'd like to have," she whispered. The one thing she didn't skimp on was water. In this area, it was a precious commodity. She wouldn't run into a stream at every turn like she might back east. Her hydration pack was full, and she had more than one container of water with her. If she did happen to run into a source on the descent, she had purification tablets to make it potable. *Chances of that are slim to none.* This wasn't a trek that you could begin in the dark. She would start out at first light to avoid hiking in the heat of the day. Temperatures would be well into the triple digits shortly after the sun began its climb into the sky.

Jordan had spoken with Dava the night before, trying to pin down where the next clue would be. She hoped she would be able to find it on her own when she got to the bottom. She thought through the book's last chapter about the Grand Canyon. Whatever might lead her to where she needed to look still eluded Jordan. Her colleagues at Cornell were enthusiastic about her work, though there were few that knew the true nature of her quest. Ellie had personally known both Aggie and Noeul. In talking with Elle, she'd hoped to glean any clue, any tidbit of information she could from Elle's memories. Jordan was looking for the place she was sure would hold another of Aggie's memorials and a cipher to the next spot on the bucket list. She had to find Noeul. Something deep inside was driving her forward with the hope that, together, they could bring about monumental change. "She's the key. I know it."

The light had barely broken the horizon when Jordan put her head torch on and set out on the narrow pathway. Several others joined her in silent communion at the top of the grade before their descent. The first rays of light began to bounce off the laminar clouds that lay in lines across the sky, while bright reds and oranges began to tint the thin layers. She was reminded of John Muir's words, *"Everybody needs beauty...places to play in and pray in where nature may heal and give strength to body and soul alike."* His words resonated with her every day of her life, and she wanted nothing more than to spend time in the grand cathedral of this place that was holy to the Havasu.

The heat was sweltering, as she continued down the trail. Dust rose with every pounding step Jordan took. She'd been passed by pack mules and riders who had chosen to commune in the cathedral without setting foot on its dirt pathways lined with rock. Jordan couldn't imagine not treading the path under her own power. She had considered renting a mule to carry her equipment. This wasn't a trail for the faint of heart. What she had found was that it didn't have to be lonely.

For the last hour, she'd struck up a conversation with one of the area natives who had been away on a short vacation. Jordan adjusted her pack, as she looked around at the changing landscape. As the sun rose, the colors of the layered rock changed, giving everything a completely different look. "So, Kelea, did you grow up at the village?"

The beautiful woman with long, shiny, black hair pulled into a leather binding, hooked her thumbs in the straps of her daypack. "Yes. There are less than two hundred houses at the falls. My parents and grandmother still live there, too. I went away to college to earn degrees in economic development and accounting, and now I take care of some village financials and work in the economic development office. It's a delicate balance maintaining the sanctity of the area and being able to support the families that still work and live there."

"I can imagine. I've never been here. I find the lore of it fascinating." Jordan sucked on her bite tube, drawing tepid water into her mouth. It didn't cool her in any way, merely staved off the constant thirst caused by the amount of sweat pouring off her body.

"Stories from the ancients tell of how our people came to settle here. Two Hopi brothers traveled through, one returning and one continuing on to Hopi land to plant abundant corn. We are people of the blue-green waters because we have made our home near the one thing you can't do without here...water." Kelea raised her tanned face to the sun and closed her eyes briefly. "What's your story, Jordan?"

"I'm trying to find a way to grow something without water."

"You've set yourself up for an impossible task." Kelea brushed her hand down Jordan's arm. "Water *is* life and without it there is *no* growth."

Jordan shivered at the light touch, despite the heat. It had been a very long time since she'd enjoyed the company of another woman or even noticed one with something that resembled desire. Kelea stirred something in her on a primal level, something she couldn't understand. The dark eyes shimmered in the sun, and the easy companionship they experienced on their shared path unsettled Jordan.

As they continued down into the canyon, Kelea continued her gentle information probe. "Jordan. I like that name."

Jordan smiled. "My given name is Jordan Moriah Armstrong. My mother's family is from the country of the same name. When my parents decided to have kids, they talked about using Jordan as a first name, boy or girl." Jordan smiled at the memory of her parents. Unfortunately, her father had passed away a few years ago. Losing him felt like her legs had been taken out from beneath her. Her mother had yet to recover and still grieved his loss. Dalia Armstrong had thrown herself into her work with the disabled children's organization they'd started together. Her parents had worked tirelessly to raise funds to increase accessibility for those with disabilities, and her mother still immersed herself in that work.

"Where'd you go?" Kelea asked.

Jordan shook her head and smiled shyly into the dark, twinkling eyes. "I was thinking about my mom. Strongest woman I've ever met, next to my sister."

"Sounds like you come from a long line of strong women."

"That I do. How about you?"

"My dad is on the council circle and my mom and grandmother are medicine women." Kelea brushed at a few strands of escaped hair.

"Really? I'd love to talk to your mom. I'm fascinated by Native American medicine."

"I'm sure she'd love that. Will you stay with us one night? I'll fix you dinner, and you can talk with my mother."

Jordan felt Kelea's smile was genuine. "I couldn't impose on your family."

"It's no imposition. Please, stay with us."

"Thank you, Kelea, I'd love to."

They continued down the trail until they caught sight of the falls. The view took Jordan's breath as they stopped.

"It's still the most beautiful scene I've ever taken in, no matter where I go." Kelea said, stepping close to Jordan.

"I've never seen it in person before, and I have to agree."

They walked down to Kelea's house. The small, wood-frame dwelling sat at the base of the canyon walls and was within a stone's throw of what Kelea said was her parent's house. They entered through a small opening in a stone hedge that surrounded the structure. The yard was so unlike the mowed lawns of the east coast. The desert landscape dotted the space with small scrub trees and sparse vegetation. Kelea showed her to a guest room and offered her the shower, while she went next door to tell her mother they would have a guest for dinner.

Jordan relished the hot shower, but wanted to be considerate of the resources in the area. She didn't linger. It felt good to shed the red dust and grit of the trail. Once she'd dressed in a clean pair of swimming shorts and tank top, she exited to see Kelea coming out of her room in a short, silk robe. Jordan eyed a long expanse of thigh, along with an enticing triangle of burnished skin that showed between her breasts where the robe fell open. Jordan briefly took in the beautiful woman, before she returned her eyes to the dark ones that smiled at her with amusement.

"I hope those are swimming trunks you put on. As soon as I clean up, I'm headed to the falls for a swim. When I get home, I always have a need to immerse myself in the waters to wash away any bad spirits I may have carried in with me, or so I tell myself. We have horses we can ride over with."

Jordan shook her head, trying to focus on Kelea's eyes. "Well, you'd be correct, they are swim trunks. I like that idea. I hope it opens me up to find answers to the questions I have."

"Give me a few minutes and we'll go. There's bottled water in the fridge, or beer if you'd like one." Kelea pointed to the kitchen, as she made her way to the bathroom.

"Water sounds great. Even with all the water I drank, I feel a little dehydrated."

"Help yourself. I'll be right out."

Kelea disappeared, and Jordan retrieved a bottle of water while she looked around the small house. Native American pottery peppered the tiny space, along with pictures of the area. A beautiful painting depicted a woman with long black hair floating on the breeze. She stood on a cliff top, wrapped in a colorful blanket. She bore a striking resemblance to Kelea. The Grand Canyon stretched before her, and to her side, a vision of the falls tumbling into a turquoise pool. Jordan took another drink of the cold water and ran the bottle along her forehead. She felt a soft hand on the small of her back. She used her bottle to point to the painting.

"You?"

Kelea stepped to her side and kept her hand in place. "Yes, my grandmother painted it when I was seventeen."

Jordan looked at the woman beside her. She was truly beautiful. Her hair hung in damp strands around her shoulders. "She's very talented."

"Yes. She's very accomplished." Kelea held two towels in her free arm. "Ready to go for a swim? Dinner will be ready in a few hours, and

Mom is expecting us. She actually said something strange."

Jordan furrowed her brow and tilted her head. "What?"

Kelea squinted at her. "She said grandmother has been expecting you. Did you contact her before you came?"

"Does she work for the permit office? That's the only person I talked to before I started out from home."

"No, my mother has the clinic here at the falls and my grandmother retired when my mother took over. Currently, she's an artist. Humm, we'll have to ask her later. For now, let's go enjoy a swim." Kelea reached out her hand for Jordan's and folded it into her own.

They walked down to a holding area to reach the horses. It was a short ride to a small side path that opened up to one of the most beautiful spectacles Jordan had ever seen. There were groups of people enjoying the pool, and someone dove off a rock ledge into the deepest part.

"Don't even think about it. Raj has been diving for years."

Jordan smiled and shrugged at Kelea. "I'll take your word for it. Can't say it didn't cross my mind. I promise, I'll settle for a swim."

They tied the horses, and Kelea laughed as she led Jordan to the edge of the pool. She pulled off her pale-green T-shirt, exposing a white bikini.

Jordan was doing everything she could not to stare at the beautiful woman before her. She busied herself by taking off her own tank top. Before she'd pulled it completely over her head, soft fingers on her ribs caused her to shiver. She continued to undress and held the shirt in one hand while keeping her left arm up. She watched Kelea trace the lines of her tattoo, sliding along one of the wings.

Kelea looked into her eyes. "It's beautiful. In our culture, the phoenix is the symbol of renewal."

Jordan shuddered against the gentle touch. "I got it a few years ago, a rebirth of sorts."

"Painful rebirth, if the waves of energy coming off of you are any indication." Kelea dropped her hand and walked into the pool of water. She spread her arms and dove under. She broke the surface and turned back to Jordan, wiping water from her face.

In more ways than I can even begin to explain. "You could say that." Jordan followed Kelea in, and the two swam over to an area near the falls. They spent the next hour enjoying the spray and cooling off from the heat of the day. They went back to Kelea's to clean up for dinner and walked the short distance to her mother's. A short woman with long, gray hair and deep lines in her face met them at the door.

"Jordan, this is my grandmother, Maiah. The woman peeking out of the kitchen is my mother, Solanya. Addressing the others, she said, "This is Jordan Armstrong."

Solanya walked out of the kitchen, drying her hands on a red and white dish towel. "Welcome, Jordan. Did you enjoy the falls?"

"Yes ma'am, I did. It's one of the most beautiful places I've ever been. I've never seen anything like it. Your daughter has been kind enough to play tour guide. She also generously offered a place for me to sleep instead of my tent. It'll feel good to sleep in a real bed tonight." Jordan watched Solanya look at her daughter with obvious affection.

"We've taught her to be a good host. I'm happy to meet you. Please come in, dinner is almost ready." Solanya waved her hand and led them into a dining area where a formidable man sat at the head of the table.

"Jordan, this is my dad, Pasqual."

Jordan observed the man dressed in a dark, long-sleeved shirt buttoned to the neck, and extended her hand. Pasqual took her hand and motioned for her to sit. She looked to Kelea who nodded. Kelea sat to one side of Jordan, with her grandmother occupying the other side. Maiah had yet to say anything to her, and Jordan was a little unsettled by her gaze. It felt more like she was looking inside of her instead of at her.

They enjoyed dinner and retreated to wooden rockers in a small, outdoor area. Kelea and Solanya conversed easily with Jordan. Dusk was falling, and an earthen chimera held flickering embers of mesquite wood that filled the air with a fragrant smoke. Jordan watched the sunset paint the canyon walls and streak the sky.

Finally, without prompt or warning, Maiah spoke. "You must seek the rooted dragon. Your phoenix will find its answer there."

Jordan turned to her. "I'm sorry?"

Maiah spoke no more. She sat back in her rocker, eyes closed.

Jordan looked to both Kelea and Solanya for some explanation. Kelea shook her head, while Solanya steepled her fingers, her elbows resting on the arms of her rocking chair.

"My mother is a vision holder. She sees what others cannot."

Kelea looked to her mother. "How does she know about Jordan's phoenix tattoo? Grandmother, were you over at the falls?"

Maiah spoke again. "It is not the marking on the skin that I've seen, only the one on her spirit." She looked at Jordan with soft, narrowed eyes. "You must seek the dragon to find balance." With that, she rose, touched Jordan's face, and went inside.

Jordan sat there for a long time, gently keeping her rocker in motion by flexing her feet.

Solanya broke the silence. "Why did you come to the falls, Jordan?"

Jordan blew out a breath. She told Solanya and Kelea about her quest and why she was seeking Professor Scott. She explained that somewhere, here at the falls, was a clue to her next destination on the bucket list Aggie had created for Noeul. Solanya slowly covered her mouth with her hand, as if she was holding something back. She put her head back and closed her eyes for a moment.

"I know what you are seeking. A few years ago, a woman came into my clinic. She'd slipped on the trail on her way down here. When she went to catch herself, she jammed her hand, dislocating her index finger. I put it back in place, and she told me why she was visiting. She was unsure how to accomplish what she wanted to do." Solanya opened her eyes and sat forward, turning to Jordan. "She was trying to find a place to put a memorial with a small capsule of her wife's ashes."

Jordan's eyebrows shot up, her mouth gaping open. "Solanya, I know this is asking a great deal, given the personal nature of her request. It's important I find her. She may hold the only key to what I'm trying to do, and I need her help to complete this research." She stopped for a moment. "I've read many of your legends, about how your people came to be here. Even in the harshest of habitats, they were able to thrive. I'm trying to help those in this world who are barely surviving under circumstances even more dire. With global warming, we can only predict that these conditions will continue to get worse for them. I need to find a way to help them grow food to support themselves and their communities."

She stopped and took a deep breath, trying to calm herself. Jordan had been racking her brain trying to figure out how to find the next clue. Here it was, right in front of her, and yet out of reach if she couldn't convince Solanya to help her. She watched the woman's face as she seemed to wrestle with the decision. "Please."

Solanya turned to Jordan. "I will help you. First, my mother must cleanse you from all negativity. The place I must take you is sacred to my family and must not be defiled in any way."

Jordan grabbed her hand and held it tightly in hers. "I'll do anything you ask. I will try to disturb the memorial as little as possible. Most likely, it leads me to the next location that Aggie chose for them. I can't tell you how important this is to me. I've taken a year sabbatical to accomplish this task, that's how committed I am."

"I will speak to my mother and make preparations." With that Solanya rose from her chair and turned to Kelea. "If your grandmother is agreeable, we will do this at dawn. You know where to bring her."

Kelea rose and kissed her mother. "Yes."

Solanya walked into the house, leaving the two young women sitting quietly in the waning light. Jordan was watching the fragments of light disappear above the canyon walls. The rock faces were in a state of constant change, going from deep reds to dark grays and eventually into black obsidian. She could hear Kelea's quiet rocking beside her.

"Do you think your grandmother will agree?"

"Yes."

Kelea's quiet reply left many questions in Jordan's mind. Did she hear hesitance or resistance? Did Jordan have something she needed to be worried about, or was Kelea centering herself for what needed to be done? She had no answers and resigned herself to whatever was to happen.

Hours later, Jordan lay awake in the wee hours of the morning. Her mind hadn't let her rest, no matter what she did. She'd tried her usual technique to relax herself, tightening every muscle from her head to her feet, one area at a time. Usually, after three tries, she could drift off. She'd only been able to achieve a twilight slumber, constantly feeling as if she was running. From what or to what she had no idea. She'd awakened several times in a drenching sweat. Lines of code, complicated formulas, graphs, and data scrolled through her head. She'd sat up only a few minutes ago, her heart racing, searching the unfamiliar room for a voice beyond her consciousness. A light tap at her door startled her, and she ran both hands across her face to clear the vestiges of her restless night. It was still dark, even with the shades completely open. She rose and walked to the door to find Kelea standing there, fully clothed.

"It's time." Kelea touched her hand and walked away.

Jordan quickly dressed in a pale, cotton T-shirt and khaki hiking shorts. She slipped into her short socks and pulled on her hikers. At the door, she met Kelea who handed her a bottle of water.

"Drink this now and save the other one. We need to hike about twenty minutes from here. Leave everything behind except what you're wearing."

Jordan began to follow Kelea, slowly drinking the cool water. Their route led them to the canyon wall.

Kelea turned and spoke quietly to Jordan. "Watch your step, take my hand."

Jordan gratefully accepted and instinctively followed Kelea's lead, even though she couldn't see where she was going. Her steps were not as tentative as she would have expected. Something inside her told her to follow and not worry. Ten minutes later, they'd climbed to a small plateau. Kelea led her to a small, dome shaped structure made from hides.

"Drink your other water."

Jordan drank and was led to the inside of the dome, where a small fire illuminated the faces of Solanya and Maiah. They sat beside each other, legs crossed beneath them as their eyes rose to meet Jordan's. Maiah motioned for her to sit in front of her, and Kelea took a position behind her mother and grandmother. Maiah spoke softly.

Jordan reconsidered. *Not really speaking exactly, singing or chanting.* Jordan didn't recognize the language or the song, yet something stirred deep inside her. She sat in what she would consider the lotus pose. In this setting, that terminology didn't seem appropriate. She began to sweat profusely as the song continued, and she grew increasingly sleepy. The song grew fainter, and the light from the fire appeared to grow brighter until it seemed she was sitting directly beside Maiah. She noticed they were no longer inside the dome. They were sitting at the edge of the canyon wall. Before her, a wide stretch of blue sky opened up and the clouds shifted, casting shadows on the ground.

Jordan turned to Maiah "Where am I?" She watched, as a breeze blew back the silver strands of hair that surrounded the older woman's face.

"You are in between earth and sky."

A vision dream played out before her, vivid and striking, foreign and yet familiar in nature. Jordan heard a gentle voice calling to her and found herself curled on her side, as Solanya wiped her face with a damp cloth. Maiah was chanting and walking around the dome. She held a sprig of smoking sage in her hand and used a large brown and white feather to spread the smoke over her. The chant was so soft now, it nearly made Jordan cry with its whispering caress. Kelea helped her sit up, and she stared straight into Maiah's eyes that still echoed the flames between them.

Maiah ended the song, she rose looking at Jordan. "What did you see, my child?"

Jordan could barely speak. Her words came out on a strangled breath. "Uh...a...phoenix and a dragon. The dragon's tail became roots that deeply pierced the earth. A branch sprouted...A giant tree grew with the phoenix...The dragon became its heart. Sunlight so bright, it was blinding."

"Ah, then what I told you last night was true. You must seek the rooted dragon. Do you understand the rest of the vision?" Maiah was covering the remnants of the fire with sand from around the pit.

"I'm not sure, the vision was tripping something in my mind. I need to figure that out. Maybe something in the memorial will point me in the right direction. I know I have to find Noeul, no matter how long it takes."

"If that is so, you must continue your quest. Solanya and Kelea will lead you from here. I must talk to the ancients to help you in your journey."

Jordan stood on shaky legs, Kelea supporting her under one arm and Solanya's hand at the small of her back. "Thank you, Maiah."

With that, the three of them left the dome.

Chapter Five

A FEW DAYS AFTER returning from Miranda and Kelly's, Noeul found she was one chicken short. Feathers she'd discovered at the fence line gave away the culprit's entry point. Sweat ran into her eyes, as she finished reinforcing the fencing by setting another post. It saddened her that even with all her efforts, she'd been unable to keep them all safe. *Damn coyote.* She carried her tools to the barn and put them away before returning to the house to clean up. She decided a light lunch was in order and loaded a pita pocket with some fresh greens, shredded carrots, and steamed edamame she'd glazed in some ginger and sesame seed oil.

After lunch, she grew sleepy and sought out the solace of her favorite napping spot. Noeul had no idea how much time had passed when she woke from a light doze. Her back felt relaxed, as she lay against the warmth of the big rock in the sun. At her side, Kyo's fur was hot to the touch. When she dug her fingers beneath the thick coat, it was surprisingly cool. She shook her head, trying to remember a dream through the fuzziness that lingered beyond the edge of her conscious mind. *Something about a phoenix.* She could remember that but nothing more. *Strange.* A wave of dizziness hit her as she sat up. It felt like she was dehydrated. Noeul couldn't understand how that was possible, as she was always careful to drink water frequently through her day. Standing, she brushed off the seat of her pants and took a few tentative steps toward the pens.

There was work to be done and some experiments she wanted to do today. Her lab sat idle, as she walked through the doors and checked the progress on a few of her trials planted there. The in-ground bedding row, as well as several raised table beds, lay basking in the heat of the greenhouse. Tomatoes, legumes, and quinoa grew in their individual spaces and were all doing very well. *Remarkable.* She bent down and placed her hands in the soil around the plants and dug her fingers into the warm earth. She reached for her journal on the work bench and made a few notations of the progress and her thoughts on the process.

Ever since I turned my attention to the stalk and root ball of specific weeds, my results have been much easier to replicate. The weeds I'm using now are the bane of most farmers' existence. The remarkable thing about them is they seem to flourish under any conditions. In normal field crops, these weeds are a nuisance and can render a crop unharvestable. Bioengineering specific weeds to accept a graft of a useful plant has shown great promise in my research. The procedure has taken me years, as I consider the plant structure, its defenses, and nutrient pathways.

Noeul read back over what she'd written and placed the journal back on the bench. Head down, she was checking two of her test rows, when she heard the approaching clip-clop of hooves on the stone path leading up to the house. Delight crossed her face, as she looked out the tilted glass panels of the greenhouse to see Miranda and Kelly riding into the yard. She rose and wiped the dirt from her hands on a rag, as she watched Kyo dance around the front of the horses. The dog obediently sat as Miranda directed before she climbed down from Comet and tied his reins to the fence. Kelly followed suit and dropped to her knees to show her pleasure at Kyo's enthusiastic greeting.

After making her way outside, Noeul wrapped her arms around Miranda. "God, it's good to see you two."

Miranda hugged her back and held her at arm's length. "It hasn't been that long, but that doesn't matter. It's always good to see you too. We got some mail for you that we had to sign for and decided to leave Leo in charge for a few days. It was beautiful weather for a ride and a good excuse to come for a visit. You spend too much time up here on this mountain by yourself."

Noeul couldn't disagree. Sadly, she saw no solution to the issue. She hadn't planned on living this dream alone. Every night, it grew harder to go to bed, reaching out for someone that wasn't there and waking alone the next morning.

Kelly walked up and drew Noeul into a motherly hug. "I'm going to grill us up some prime—A steaks tonight and fill your stomach until you pop. I'll fatten you up yet."

Noeul shook her head and laughed. She missed the comfortable comradery she had with her friends and relished this unplanned visit. "I'll go grab some fresh vegetables for sides. Will potatoes and carrots be alright?" Kelly nodded her head in agreement, and Miranda rubbed her stomach in delight.

Miranda pulled two bottles of Noeul's favorite red wine out of the saddlebags, holding them up in triumph. "Here's my contribution."

"Now, that I look forward to. You guys go in and get cleaned up. I'll unsaddle Comet and Vixen and put them in with Thor and Athena and give them all some feed."

Miranda kissed her on the cheek and grabbed their saddlebags. Noeul walked the two horses into the barn and scratched each on the muzzle. "Your mommies might be a little confused about you two being reindeer. I'll admit, they certainly *seem* like the Clauses to me." She rubbed the horses down and filled their buckets with feed and water. Kyo ran around her feet, dancing like a puppy. "Yes, we'll go for a run before supper. Now go find Miranda and tell her you're ready." Kyo barked her approval and ran out of the barn toward the house.

Noeul walked over to the garden and found the items she was looking for. She already had an onion and enough lettuce and tomatoes for a salad in the fridge. She found Miranda attempting to tie her running shoes while Kyo was licking her face. Noeul shook her head in amusement. "I'll change, and we'll go before she busts something."

Once in her bedroom, Noeul stripped down and was about to put on her jog bra when she glimpsed a redness to her side. In the mirror, she examined the area, noticing that the roots on her dragon tattoo were irritated. Noeul probed with her fingers all around the area. Nothing felt tender. She decided she must have brushed up against something while she was fixing the fence. Once dressed, she carried her shoes to the couch and felt Miranda touch the red area on her side as she sat down.

"Honey, what's wrong with your tattoo? It's all red."

"I don't know. I just noticed it." Noeul stretched to look at the area. "I'll put some salve on it after our run."

"Almost looks like a burn. You didn't get up against any of your lab equipment, did you?"

"No. Honestly, it's fine. Not even sore. I'm guessing Kyo told you what she wanted?"

"No mystery there. You ready?" Miranda stood and bent over to stretch her back.

"We'll see if you can keep up on my trails. That pasture you run in doesn't hold a candle." Noeul smiled and twisted sideways, loosening her obliques. "I'll help you when we get back, Kelly."

"Young whippersnapper, I'll have you eating so much of my dust you won't need any supper." Miranda grumbled good-heartedly.

Kelly planted her hands firmly on her hips. "Miranda Leigh, if you pull something trying to outrun her, I'll kick your ass. Now behave yourself." She walked over and kissed her wife. "I'm good on fixing dinner. You two get that pup on the trail before she pees all over herself. I'm fine."

Miranda pushed Kelly back and sprinted out the front door, Kyo on her heels.

Kelly kissed Noeul on the head and sighed. "Try to keep her from killing herself to show you how good she is. Remember, she's got ten years on you."

"Don't worry, Mom, I'm letting her think she's got a head start. I promise, she'll come back a little tired and still in one piece." Noeul hugged her, then took off after her dog and one of the best friends she'd ever had.

After the first mile, Miranda quit trying to outrun Noeul and they settled into a comfortable rhythm on the trail, allowing them to talk without much difficulty. Despite the years Miranda had on Noeul, she was extremely fit and always gave her a run for her money if they went all out.

"So, how are you?" Miranda held her hand up to avoid a small branch in front of her face on the trail.

"Honestly, I'm fine." Noeul jumped over an exposed tree root and noticed one of Miranda's laces was coming untied. "Hey old woman, tie your shoe before you fall and break a hip. Kelly would kill me if I let you get hurt out here."

"Look here, funny girl, who you calling old woman?" Miranda laughed, as she slowed and bent to finish untying and retying her lace.

Noeul paced to keep from developing cramps and to keep her body limber. She absently rubbed her side.

Miranda finished her lace and stood, pointing to Noeul's side. "Is that bothering you?"

Noeul looked where she was pointing and dropped her hand. "Not really. Did you ever feel like there's something you've forgotten and can't figure out what it is? Or that feeling that..." Noeul didn't finish the thought. "Shit, forget I said anything. It's nothing."

"No, I won't forget it. Come on, let's cut our pace a bit so I can actually talk while we run." Miranda squinted and put her hands on her hips. "And if you tell Kelly I asked to slow down I will personally kick your ass."

Noeul threw her head back in raucous laughter. With her hand on Miranda's shoulder, she winked at her friend. "Don't worry, your stud credentials will still be intact when we roll in. Want me to let you pull ahead so she thinks you ran me into the ground too?"

Miranda shoved her. "My wife's anything but stupid. She'll see through that ruse in a microsecond." They turned and started back to the house. "Tell me what's going on."

Noeul was silent for a few moments, as they jogged past a grove of trees. The pine fragrance surrounded them and she breathed it in, as the fallen needles crackled under her running shoes and forced her back to Miranda's question. "I'm not sure what's going on. Some days I feel like I'm crawling out of my skin. I'm so lonely, and I miss Aggie more and more. This was *our* dream. We were supposed to be running these trails together."

She had to slow down, as she could no longer see where she was going. Her emotional haze was turning everything into a blurry kaleidoscope. Noeul stopped to wipe at her eyes. Her sobs could no longer be contained. A sharp pain stabbed through her, and she grabbed her side, turning from Miranda's gaze.

"Noeul," Miranda wrapped her arms around Noeul from behind, "I know this isn't how you planned it. You've been so strong to even continue this dream at all. You've built a life here, a sustainable life. Don't hate me for what I'm about to ask you. What would you have wanted for Aggie if the situation was reversed?"

Noeul cried harder and the tears fell in hot torrents across her cheeks. Her insides screamed as if they were being shredded, and her heart felt like it was being torn from her chest. She cried out in great sobs of anguish that she couldn't hold inside. "I would want her to love again."

Miranda tucked an escaped strand of the long black hair behind Noeul's ear. "Don't you think she'd want you to take your own advice?"

Noeul squeezed Miranda's arms and broke the embrace to walk over to a large cherry tree that stood in the middle of all the pines. Her fingers traveled over the rough bark, and she leaned into its strength. She heard a disembodied whisper from above her.

"Why aren't you listening, my love?"

The voice was so familiar, Noeul startled as she gazed up and backed away from the tree. She turned to look around then back at Miranda. "Please tell me you heard that."

Miranda moved closer and touched her forearm. "Noeul, heard

what? Are you okay?"

"Miranda, tell me you said that." Her hands trembled, and her head pounded.

"Noeul, you're scaring me. Said what?"

"Tell me you asked me why I'm not listening." Noeul couldn't focus her eyes. Everything around her started spinning. Her vision closed in, as all light dimmed then faded into blackness.

"Noeul!" Miranda lurched and reached out to catch Noeul as she fell to the ground.

Noeul heard nothing more, as she collapsed onto the soft, pine bed beneath her.

* * *

Jordan sat with her head resting on her arms. After another bottle of water and the placement of a cool rag on her neck, she was starting to feel like herself. Solanya was busy checking her vitals. "Will I live?"

Solanya pulled the blood pressure cuff from her arm. "I think so. You're still a little dehydrated. That's to be expected. I'm prepared to give you an intravenous dose of fluids if you need them."

"I think I'll be fine."

Solanya looked into her eyes. "Do you feel like walking?"

"Depends." Jordan gave a nervous laugh. "Are we going on a short hike or a day trip? If I have to go more than a few miles, I might need to wait a bit more." Jordan rubbed the cool rag across her face and shook herself, clearing the last bit of fuzziness from her head.

"It's not far, just over that knoll," Kelea said. "Think you can make it?"

Jordan stood, her legs feeling a bit like wet noodles. She shook her head in the affirmative, sure she could travel.

Kelea and Solanya stepped to her side, as they began to walk the short distance. Jordan still felt like she was in an altered state, somewhere between the physical world and one she really didn't understand. They hadn't gone more than sixty or seventy yards, when they came upon a large boulder that looked like it had fallen from the top of the canyon wall and come to land at the base of the fissure. Solanya walked to the side and disappeared behind the rock. Kelea stood beside Jordan, supporting her with a warm hand to the small of her back.

When Solanya reappeared, she waved for them to approach. They followed her into a torch-lit opening, barely wide enough for them to enter. Solanya continued to light torches protruding from the cavern walls every fifteen or twenty feet.

"What is this place?" Jordan asked quietly, her voice barely above a whisper.

"My people used this as a refuge in times of bad weather or danger from our enemies. It is a well-guarded secret passed from generation to generation. We keep dried food stocks and essentials here, and our history is written on these passage walls. She swept her arms wide.

Jordan slowed to examine the pictograms on both sides of her. She was fascinated and wished she had more time to examine the carvings and paintings depicting Native American life. A driving need to follow her own quest pushed her forward.

The end of the long passageway opened up into a large cavern full of stalagmites and stalactites. A small stream of turquoise water dropped into a pool. Jordan's mouth gaped open, and she spoke in soft reverence, "It's incredible."

"Yes, and a very guarded secret. If my mother hadn't been sure of your integrity, you wouldn't be here now. I trust you will tell no one about this. If you find the woman you seek, she will know your intentions were true because we brought you here. Remember, she too had a quest." Solanya led her to a small crack in the rock face. "May you find your next step here."

Jordan looked at the rocks surrounding her. Layered gradient marks recorded the passage of time. She ran her hand over the stone, feeling the earth's recorded history under her fingers. She reached into a break in the rock and felt the smooth canister she expected to find. She opened the bottle and gently removed the letter. She'd made a conscious decision to leave Aggie's remains in their protective shell, not wanting to disturb anything she didn't have to. Her eyes had finally adjusted to the low light conditions, unfortunately she still couldn't easily read the letter. She knew she would have no trouble recalling every word and symbol with her photographic mind if she could clearly see them. She walked a few paces to a flickering torch and began to read, murmuring the words that were written for her eyes. They belonged to someone she wanted to find more than anything. She closed her eyes for a moment and started again.

May 2010
My Dearest Aggie,

61

I know that you must be watching over this journey, because you led me to Solanya and Maiah. I saw you in a vision, diving from the top of the falls into the turquoise waters of Havasu Falls. You were so strong and beautiful. I asked Solanya to help me find a place worthy of your love, a place to leave a small piece of you behind. I think you would be thrilled to know that a part of you will rest in the secret dwelling of an ancient people, among an incredible record of the earth's formation. I carry you with me on to our next destination, as I live out our dream. I miss you my love, now and forever.
Noeul

Jordan closed her eyes and murmured, "How do you survive a loss like that?" She returned her focus to the task at hand. Inside the canister, Jordan noticed that there was a second paper with the next clues. She read down through a list that included a John Muir quote she'd never heard, something called the BAFTA award in 1983, along with the name Kit West, and "Blue Harvest." Further down the clue was the word hexaploid, followed by a series of numbers. After that was what Jordan recognized as a list of musician's names, the words *Alces alces* along with the name Rocky, Natasha, and Boris. Finally, something in a language she was able to translate.

Without access to any of her computer equipment or the ability to call to her sister, she would have to wait to do any research until she made it back to Peach Springs. There was a good bit of information to be deciphered from this clue. With her eyes closed, she committed the items to her internal hard drive, replaced them to their resting place, and stood for a moment of silence.

"Seek the highest point."

A voice Jordan didn't recognize echoed in her skull, and she turned to look at Solanya and Kelea. "Did you say something?"

The two women looked at each other and turned back to Jordan. Solanya stepped forward and rested her hand on her shoulder. "No, I didn't. In this sacred space it would not be unusual hear the voice of those who have passed on to be with the Great Spirit. Many come here to seek the guidance of those who can see beyond this world, beyond this time. Whatever the spirit said to you, it will be important in your journey. You must listen to it."

Jordan felt moved and yet disturbed somehow. The voice had penetrated her skin, like it had settled deep in the very marrow of her being. "I'll try."

"You must do more than try. To ignore the spirit is a great disrespect to the gift you've been given. Heed the message and follow its guidance. Do not be surprised to hear the voice again, as visiting this place means that you are now connected on a different level, inside your own spirit." Solanya placed her warm hand on Jordan's cheek. "You are now a daughter to a Havasu mother, Jordan, and you are welcome back with us at any time."

Jordan leaned into the touch and said a silent prayer to the spirit that was guiding her. She hoped that it could lead her to her final destination, the place where Noeul Scott had disappeared.

***

Noeul felt cool water running down the back of her neck and shivered. "What?"

Kyo licked her face and hopped around her, whining. Noeul reached out and buried her fingers in the dog's ruff, pulling Kyo to her.

"For God's sake, Noeul, you scared the shit out of me." Miranda continued to pour the water down the back of her neck.

Noeul shook herself and ran a hand around the back of her neck and over her face. "What the hell happened?" She stared deep into Miranda's eyes that were full of concern and something more—fear. Shaking herself, she tried to pull herself together for the sake of her friend. "I guess I pushed too hard. It's okay, Kyo. Mommy's okay."

"Bullshit, Noeul, we'd already slowed down, and you're in peak shape compared to me. Honey, before you went down, you asked me if I'd said something, something about not listening."

The voice came again.

"It wasn't Miranda. You know who it was."

Kyo jerked, tilted her head and looked at her. Noeul shut her eyes tightly. "I'm okay, Miranda, I've been pushing too hard. Let's walk back to the house. Kelly will start to get worried, and dinner will be ready by now. I could use a glass of wine or seven." She smiled and wrapped her arm around Miranda's shoulders. "Hell, I'll even tell her you ran me into the ground, and I had to walk most of the way back."

"You can try peddling that and fool yourself. I want you to consider this, my wife's bullshit meter is better than mine. You'll peg it with the way you look." Miranda grinned at her and smoothed back a few strands of Noeul's hair that had stuck to her cheek.

Noeul shut her eyes, knowing Miranda was right. "Ok, how about we tell her the truth and hope for the best."

"Winner, winner, chicken dinner." Miranda winked at her and helped her up.

They walked back to the house, where Kelly was waiting at the door for them. "I was about to come looking for you two. I was…" She stopped and quickly walked to Noeul's side. "What happened? What's wrong?" She placed her arm around Noeul's waist and helped her into the house. "Sit your ass down right there and tell me what's going on."

Noeul looked up into Kelly's eyes, not exactly sure what to say. She was grateful for her friends and their concern. She took a deep breath, as Kelly knelt before her and Miranda went to get her a glass of water. Kyo lay beside her, head resting on her thigh. She took the glass from Miranda and used the few seconds it took to consume the water as a chance to organize her thoughts. "I honestly don't know how to even begin to tell you what's going on. Miranda's shoe came untied, and we were talking. She asked me why I wasn't trying to find someone to share my life with and what I would have wanted for Aggie if the roles had been reversed." She shuddered, hearing the voice in her head again. "I think Aggie spoke to me while we were out there."

Miranda touched her on the shoulder. "Is that why you asked me if I'd said something? Something about not listening?"

Noeul started to cry again, the sobs racking her body as Miranda slipped an arm around her and held her.

Kelly got up and found some tissues for her. "Noeul, are you sure it was Aggie's voice?"

Noeul angrily stood up and moved to the windows, hugging her sides and wiping briskly at the hot tears. "I was with her for eight years. I think I would remember her voice." Her own grew thin and quiet. "Thirty years from now, I'll still remember that voice."

Kelly walked up beside her. "I'm sorry. It's hard to wrap my head around it. I'm not saying it's impossible, but I've never spoken to anyone who's passed to the other side."

"Trust me, I haven't either. I have no doubt it was her. I think she's trying to tell me to move on." Noeul shook her head quickly trying to dispel the lingering tendrils of sorrow. "I don't know how to do that."

Kelly drew her into her arms and let her cry until the pain became a dull ache.

***

The next morning, Noeul stared out the glass windows as the sky began to lighten. Everyone was still in bed. Kyo was next to her, drifting in and out, paws twitching in small fits of movement. Noeul ran her fingers through the soft fur and stroked the velvet ears without thought, drawing comfort from the repetitive motion. On her lap lay the journal she was filling with her current thoughts and some of her fondest memories.

This morning, when I woke, the knowledge there were other human beings in the house felt strange. Yet I thirst for the interaction and conversation Miranda and Kelly provide. The one thing I truly need is something they can't give me. I miss the feeling of a solid body beside me at night, cleaving tightly to my back, encircling me in strong arms. I miss sleeping with my cheek against warm flesh, the sound of a muffled heartbeat in my ear, and soft breath in my hair. I long for the sight of naked skin, lightly misted with perspiration and hovering above me. I ache for the passionate feeling of being desirable and the smell of arousal filling the room as I'm touched.

My Aggie was always such an attentive lover, only rushing when we'd been teasing each other in ways only longtime lovers would understand. I can remember how Aggie would close her eyes and shudder, when I'd slide my hand discretely into her lap as we dined with friends. I would play my fingers along the seam of her jeans, lightly brushing her center, bringing her so close to release before I'd pull away. When we'd get home, Aggie would barely be able to make it inside before she'd back me against the door and strip me out of my jeans. She'd lift me to her waist and kiss me like she was possessed. On nights like that, we could never make it farther than the steps to our second floor, before Aggie would slide between my legs and bring me to climax over and over before cradling me in her arms and carrying me to our bed.

Writing the words down made Noeul miss those moments with her wife more and more. She could feel herself get wet merely thinking about Aggie making love to her. She ruthlessly brought her body to heel, slamming her journal shut and shoving the memories back into the box she held deep within herself.

The grandfather clock struck seven bells, and she went to the kitchen, knowing her friends would soon be awake. She looked around the gourmet kitchen and pulled the cast iron skillets from the hanger above the stove. She lifted the eggs from the refrigerator and grabbed a green pepper, an onion, and a block of sharp cheddar cheese. Sipping her coffee while she prepared the omelet, she was transferring the bacon out of the other skillet when she heard a bedroom door open. As Noeul placed the bacon onto a paper-towel-covered plate, she forced a smile at a bedheaded Kelly shuffling toward her.

With a sleepy yawn, Kelly came around the bar with a quick hug for Noeul. She poured her own cup of the dark, hazelnut roast before adding a small amount of goat's milk. Noeul watched, as she parked herself on a high barstool and took a deep inhalation over the steaming cup.

"God, you make good coffee." Kelly stole a piece of bacon before Noeul could smack her hand.

"Yes, I do. Coffee is one of those things I spare no expense on. It's one of the few things I can't grow or raise myself. I'm damn sure not going to get it out of a red plastic container if I don't have to."

Kelly laughed. "Yeah well, when you come to my place, don't look in the cabinet."

They both turned to see Miranda squinting at them from one eye, before she stole Kelly's coffee cup and drank deeply. "Shit that's almost orgasmic. Don't suppose you still have my favorite mug in those cupboards, do you?"

"Yes, dear, your sippy cup is still here." Noeul walked over to the cabinet and pulled out the large black travel mug with the *X Files* logo and the words, *"The truth is out there,"* printed on the surface.

"Nice to know you still love me." Miranda kissed her on the forehead and accepted the cup from her.

Noeul watched Kelly eye her diagnostically. "I'm fine, Kelly."

Kelly shook her head. "Did you sleep at all? I heard you up prowling around before dawn."

"Off and on. Sorry if I kept you up." Noeul slid two plates in front of her friends and laughed as Miranda suspiciously poked at her omelet with her fork. "There's no mushrooms, you big baby."

Miranda smiled sheepishly, chewed a bite, and childishly poked her tongue at Noeul.

Noeul screwed up her face in disgust, as she laughed at her friend's antics.

"You up for a ride today?" Kelly popped another piece of bacon in her mouth, looking at Noeul.

Having her friends here was exactly what she needed. "Of course, I am. We could take the south trail down to the falls and have a picnic if you guys are up for a longer ride."

Miranda bounced on her stool with enthusiasm.

Kelly rolled her eyes and shoved her. "You are such a three-year-old sometimes."

Miranda pouted, pushing her lower lip out. "Pweeeese, Mom? Can we, can we, pweese?"

Noeul laughed and covered her face, as she almost snorted coffee out her nose.

"Finish your breakfast and go get cleaned up, goofball. If you're good, I'll take you for a pony ride." Kelly pulled her coffee cup to her lips and shook her head.

Miranda sat on the stool grinning from ear to ear. Noeul loved her friends and knew they were doing everything they could to fill the voids in her life left by Aggie's death. She looked around her living room at the comfortable furniture, the tasteful decorations accented by simple lighting, and the floor-to-ceiling bookshelves that lined two walls. These were the things that filled this space. What made it a home, was the laughter and companionship her friends brought with them when they visited. She vowed to enjoy the here and now in their visit.

***

Jordan woke to the sounds of birdsong outside her tent. It was still extremely early in the morning. She unzipped the flap and stared up into the sky, where pastel colors were beginning to streak across the horizon. A thin stratus cloud floated across the sky. She pulled her cellphone from beside her head and answered the incessant ringing. The ringtone told her it could only be Dava.

"Let me guess, you couldn't care less that it's before five in the morning?"

"Correctamundo. Get out of that tent, it's almost eight here. Half the day is gone. You want this information or what?"

Jordan yawned and crawled out of her sleeping bag. She climbed from her tent into the chilly morning air. "I'm awake, I'm awake. I don't even have coffee on yet, so be gentle." She stretched and lit her small camp stove, while Dava decoded the clues for her.

"So, you've used your decoder ring to discover that I'm headed to...." Jordan left the sentence open, as she hung the coffee pot full of water over the fire to heat.

Dava huffed. "One puzzle piece at a time, Sherlock. Let's put all the outside pieces together first, or did you forget the system?"

Jordan couldn't help the laugh that bubbled up. Their father was methodical in the way he went about putting together a jigsaw puzzle. They would separate all the pieces with a straight edge first, find and assemble the corners. When the outside frame had been completed, they would sort pieces by color or pattern. It was a family activity, one they could all do together. "No, I haven't forgotten. Proceed."

"That's more like it. I started with the John Muir quote. "God has cared for these trees, saved them from drought, disease, avalanches, and a thousand straining, leveling tempests and floods; but he cannot save them from fools[,]—only Uncle Sam can do that." It came from his writing *Our National Parks*, in 1901. From a good bit of debate on the internet about the exact meaning of the quote, I settled on a protected forest because part of it had to do with only 'Uncle Sam' being able to protect them. Now, if I combine that with your vision at Havasu, I tend to believe that you're headed to either the California or Oregon coast, where the giant sequoia and redwoods are. The BAFTA award was for special effects in a film that was originally titled *Blue Harvest* for secrecy. That movie ended up being titled *Return of the Jedi*. Remember those air motorcycle scenes through giant redwoods?"

Jordan added the coffee grounds into the percolator parts of the percolator and hung it on the tripod above the flame of the stove. "Oh yeah."

"I'll let you fill in the meaning of the word hexaploid here…"

Jordan smiled, as Dava let her pull from her education specialty. "That there are six copies of each homologous chromosome in the genome."

"Exactly. From there we get the numbers 2,100/2.7/274.9/100. 2100/274.9/102.6/36.5. These are numbers given by the National Park Service for the largest tree on earth. Which is?"

"General Sherman Tree in Sequoia National Park." Jordan shook her head, enjoying the game with her sister.

Dava clapped loudly. "Give that girl a gold star."

Jordan delighted at the infectious laughter coming over the phone line. "Ok, so I know I'm going to Sequoia or Kings Canyon. That's a really big area. Any clue how to narrow it down?"

"I considered the list of names you gave me. Most are recognizable singers like, Bob Dylan, Van Morrison, and Ani DeFranco. There were a few obscure names like Bill Fay and Midge Ure, which I'd never heard of. I did a commonality search and came up with the word watchtower. The other names had songs that mentioned the word watchtower, and Bob Dylan wrote 'All Along the Watchtower' made famous by?"

"Jimmy Hendrix." Jordan laughed at her sister and listened to the telltale sounds of the water working its way up the metal tube and bubbling over the coffee grounds.

"From all those clues, I believe you are supposed to make your way to the Wolverton trail which will eventually lead you to..."

"Let me guess, The Watchtower?" Jordan inhaled deeply as she began to smell the aromatic grounds producing the liquid gold brewing over the hum of the propane burner.

"That's where I'd put my money. Next, Alces alces is the scientific name for moose, which also ties into that weird string of Rocky, Natasha, and Boris. The missing link in that is Bullwinkle the moose from an early 1960s cartoon *Rocky and His Friends*. My extraordinary codebreaker skills say you are headed for...drum roll please."

Jordan obliged and made a drumroll sound by vibrating her tongue across the roof of her mouth.

"Moose Lake in Sequoia National Park."

Jordan poured her first cup of strong, dark coffee. Raising it to her lips, she blew across the top of her stainless-steel mug. She sipped slowly, allowing the steaming liquid to slide over her tongue and down her throat. Chuckling at her sister, she paid appropriate homage. "Thank you, Watson, you're brilliant. You've done it again, in spectacular form."

"Lastly the foreign language clue doesn't really give any particular location. *Ardú do shúile go dtí an pointe is airde,* translated from Irish Gaelic to English, reads *raise your eyes to the highest point*. It will be up to you to determine what that means when you get there. I have no idea. I guess when you get to Moose Lake you'll need to see if your spidey senses start going off and it clears up. Well Sherlock, I've got a busy day ahead of me working at the five side."

Jordan knew this was Dava code for working at the Pentagon. "That last clue ties in with what I heard in the cavern. Go do your thing, geek. I love you. I've got a pretty good drive to Sequoia National Park. When I get there, I'll plot my course. Have a great day and try not to run over any five-star toes this time."

"Occupational hazard, easier for them to move out of my way than it is for me to move out of theirs. Love you, be careful and call me later."

They signed off in their unique way and Jordan set about making herself breakfast. She pulled out her laptop and connected to her phone's hotspot to begin plotting her course from Peach Springs to the next bucket-list item in Sequoia National Park. She'd allowed herself a much-needed day to rest and recover, giving Dava time to decode everything.

While she drank her coffee, she journaled about her previous day's call to Dava and her reaction to the recount of her experience and her visions. Dava was a big believer in the afterlife and didn't doubt a second of Jordan's account. Jordan did find part of her sister's observations interesting.

Dava said she looked up the relationship between the phoenix and the dragon. She found that in Korean lore, the two symbols compliment and complete each other in sort of a yin and yang style. That made me think about my own tattoo and what it means to me. The design came to me in a dream after my break up with Tina. The symbolism of rebirth fed a need deeply hidden within the most inner parts of my soul. That feeling chewed at me until I laid down on the table at Skin Deep. At that point, I was a blank canvas. Deidra transformed that surface into a work of art.

Over twelve long sessions, Deidra and I became close friends. It was like she understood this was a way to document my pain and celebrate my survival and rebirth. She used her unique abilities to create the intricate crimson wings with yellow-and-black-tipped flames that edge up my back and along my shoulders. The long feathers from the tail travel around my side and seem to caress my left breast. My talisman is a record of where I've been and what I've become because of each and every painful step, my journey permanently integrated into my being.

Jordan closed the journal and prepared a simple breakfast for herself, while she enjoyed the still-breaking dawn. She turned her attention to finding the quickest route to Moose Lake and the next phase of her journey.

***

Noeul led the group down the trail toward the falls. Beneath her legs, she could feel Athena's muscles ripple. The horse was amazingly graceful on the trails. Surefooted and spirited, she was a perfect companion to the larger and calmer Thor, whom they'd left munching contentedly back in his stall. Each woman carried a portion of their planned picnic. The closer they got, the louder the water tumbling over the outcropping of rock became. Kyo took off like a shot to the pool of water as soon as it was in sight.

"No matter how many times I see this, it still takes my breath. The way the sunlight makes a rainbow in the spray, it's incredible." Kelly pulled up on her reins, bringing her horse to a halt beside Noeul.

Noeul reached up and patted Athena's strong neck. "I know exactly what you mean. I ride down here quite a bit. You guys have never seen it in the winter. It's both eerie and spectacular."

"I, for one, am thankful you own this little piece of heaven." Miranda took a drink from her water bottle and placed it back in its holder. "And that you're willing to share with your besties."

Noeul smiled at her friends. She cherished their company and was more than grateful that they seemed to know exactly what she needed when she needed it. There was no doubt that the longer she was isolated, the more restless and unsettled she felt. Near the base of the falls, they stopped in a shady spot and tethered the horses to allow them to graze for their own picnic. Kyo came out of the water, shaking out her thick coat. She trailed around the water's edge and smelled everything her nose encountered.

Miranda spread a blanket out on the ground, as Noeul and Kelly gathered their lunch. Plastic containers of sandwiches, chips, and pasta salad were spread out on the red and white checkered blanket beneath them. Kyo found a patch of sunlight to lay down in, her tongue lagging out to the side, her breath in quick pants.

"Take a nap, sweet girl." Miranda smoothed the fur on her head.

Kelly held up one more container, as she handed Miranda the bottle of white wine and the small plastic cups. "For dessert."

Noeul's eyes grew big. "Tell me that's what I think it is."

"If you are asking if this small box contains your favorite peppermint-patty brownies, then I would say your psychic abilities are tuned into the right wave length." Kelly laughed, as Noeul launched herself and wrapped her up tightly in an appreciative hug.

"Have I told you that you are beyond amazing and my favorite person in the whole world?" Noeul placed a sloppy kiss on Kelly's cheek, as she slyly grabbed for the container, missing by a fraction of an inch.

Miranda placed her hands on her hips and attempted to pull off a glare. "Hey what am I, chopped liver? I thought I was your favorite person in the whole world?"

Kelly laughed, as she continued to hold the brownies out of Noeul's reach. "Honey, you don't stand a chance in hell while I'm holding these in my hands." She squeezed Noeul tightly and narrowed her eyes. "Lunch first, then dessert."

Noeul sat back down and crossed her arms in a fake pout. "Yes, Mom. And Miranda, you are my favorite Amazon friend. She," Noeul said pointing to Kelly with her thumb "is my favorite person in the world, who also happens to make my favorite brownies."

Miranda grumbled under her breath. "I could make brownies." She paused, "As long as my wife measured it all out, wrote all my instructions down, turned on the oven, and set the timer. So there." They all fell into a fit of laughter until they could barely breathe.

Kelly reached over and caressed Miranda's face. "It's okay, my love. You keep the tractor fixed and the truck running. I'll make the brownies."

Kelly leaned over and placed a soft kiss on Miranda's lips, causing Noeul to blush. She envied the connection they shared, that same kind of connection she'd shared with Aggie. She pushed the melancholy back into the shadows, determined to enjoy this much-needed companionship with her best friends.

"You okay, honey?" Miranda placed a hand on Noeul's back.

Noeul shook herself. "Fine, just hungry. Pass those plates around so I can eat lunch, or Mom there won't let me have dessert. You have that wine open yet, or am I going to have to resort to buying screw tops for these adventures?"

Miranda screwed up her face. "I'm working on it. I'll admit, it's quite taxing." She bugged her eyes out and placed a hand on her forehead in a show of theatrical despair.

Noeul raised an eyebrow. "Yeah, before you met me, I imagine it was a bit easier to screw off the plastic cap and pull the ring."

"Hey, I've learned my lesson and vowed to never buy wine in a box again. You've thoroughly schooled me." Miranda flipped her hand in a posh move that had both Noeul and Kelly choking on their sandwiches.

Kelly rolled her eyes and shook her head. "Honey, pass the wine before we need boots over here to wade through the bullshit you're peddling."

Miranda leaned across and kissed Kelly, handing her a cup of wine. She poured one for Noeul and passed it to her.

Noeul raised it to her lips and took a sip of the very sweet moscato. She held it in the air in approval. "Well done, my worthy student."

The three of them ate and laughed in the afternoon sun. Kelly sat with her back against a rock, Miranda's head in her lap, and ran her fingers through the salt-and-pepper strands she'd freed from her wife's braid. Miranda breathed evenly as she napped.

Noeul caught Kelly's eye and whispered. "I'm going to take a little walk. Take a nap with her, I'll be right back."

Kelly nodded her head and closed her eyes. Noeul smiled at her friends and slowly rose to her feet. Kyo stood, obviously unwilling to be left out of any adventure. Noeul walked down to the water's edge and slid her hands through the cool liquid. She scrubbed them together, rose, and shook the water free. Wiping her palms over her face, she raised her chin to the warm afternoon sun and started walking toward a clearing beyond the edge of the pool. Kyo padded softly beside her. Noeul reached out to pet her, the soft coat warm and dry from the sun.

Kyo traveled at Noeul's heel. Reaching a small outcrop of rocks, Noeul climbed up to enjoy the view and take in a few minutes of solace in the bright sunlight. Kyo sat beside her, turning her head curiously from side to side, as if she was listening to something. Noeul listened. Faint at first, yet still audible, the words were familiar. She'd learned the Bible verse from Ecclesiastes in Sunday school.

"There is a time for everything, and a season for every activity under the heavens: a time to be born and a time to die, a time to weep and a time to laugh, a time to mourn and a time to dance." Noeul knew the voice, and her eyes searched frantically for the face she longed to see more than anything. She squinted and held her hand to her eyes in an attempt to shield them from the bright light of the sun.

"The time to mourn and weep is past and gone. A new season is blowing in, and with it, a chance to laugh and dance. Don't hold your heart back. There is a time to plant and a time to uproot, a time to tear down and a time to build. Our time was short, I know. I'm gone, my love, and it's time for you to live. Listen to your heart, my love, not your head."

Noeul rose and thrust her hand toward a very bright light. "Don't go, Aggie, please don't go. I need you."

"A time to search, a time to throw away and a time to keep. A time to tear and a time to mend. When the seeker finds you, know that it's time to mend and time to love again. Do this for me, my most precious one, and I'll rest happy."

Noeul ran forward, crashing through the brush and the laurel. She could feel the briars tearing at her legs and heard Kyo yip in pain behind her. She stopped and turned back to see her faithful companion limping behind her. Kyo stopped and held one of her paws up. Noeul's face drew back toward the light and the fading voice. She knew it was Aggie and desperately wanted to run after her, to hear her voice one more time.

Tears streamed from her face and she cried out. "Please don't go!" Kyo limped up beside her, whining softly. She dropped to her knees and buried her face in the black fur. She wiped the tears away as best she could and tried to focus on Kyo's injury. A large crabapple thorn had pierced one of the pads on her front paw. "Oh God, baby, I'm so sorry. Hold still." She grasped the injured paw in one hand and the thorn between the thumb and index finger of her other. Noeul quickly removed the thorn and pulled Kyo into her lap. She looked up to see Miranda and Kelly pushing their way through the brush to them. Sadness threatened to overwhelm her. She pulled Kyo closer. *Am I losing my mind?*

"Noeul, are you alright?" Kelly dropped down beside her and brushed back the long black strands that had escaped the cuff at Noeul's nape.

"No. No, I'm not." Noeul collapsed into Kelly's embrace and felt Miranda's strong arms envelop her from the back. "I think I'm going crazy. Check Kyo's paw for me, please. I pulled a big thorn out of it, and I can't tell if I got it all or not." Noeul wiped at the tears and pushed through the soul-searing panic currently piercing her heart. Two messages from Aggie in two days. Something was happening or was about to. Something she had no clue how to face or handle. She knew, deep inside, she wasn't going insane. It *had* been Aggie's voice. Both encounters carried a single basic message. *It's time to move on.*

Miranda cupped Noeul's jaw. "You think you can get up? You've got some pretty serious scratches. Your face is bleeding, and so is your arm."

Noeul took a deep breath and shivered. "I think so. I've got some medicinal salve in my saddlebag. Can you get it and put some on her paw? I'll put her in the saddle with me for the trip home. I don't want her walking that far."

Kelly stood and reached a hand down to help Noeul up. "We can do that. First, let's get you back to the water and clean you up. Once we get back to the house, I want to know exactly what happened. And don't tell me nothing, because something made you tear off into a briar patch. I'll give you time to find a way to put it into words."

Kelly placed an arm around Noeul's waist, as they made their way back to the pool with Miranda carrying Kyo in her arms. After cleaning and treating the cuts and scratches, they packed everything up. Miranda passed Kyo up into the saddle with Noeul for the trip back. Noeul had taken her for numerous trail rides when she was a puppy, when Kyo would eventually wear out and make the trip home riding across Noeul's lap.

Today she found it beyond comforting to feel her constant companion so close to her. The return trip was silent, a striking contrast to their comfortable banter on the way to the falls. Thankful that Miranda was in the lead, Noeul let Athena follow at a gentle lope. Noeul blanked her mind to all the things around her, while she tried to process what had happened.

A few hours later, they sat on the butter-soft leather furniture, facing the fireplace. Noeul was wrapped in a soft afghan and held a steaming cup of coffee. Her friends sat on either side of her. The silence in the room was louder than the impending storm outside when Kelly finally broke the silence.

Pushing a strand of hair behind Noeul's ear, she started. "Are you going to tell us what sent you on a dead run into the brambles, or am I going to have to pry it out of you?"

Noeul took a deep breath, blowing it out through puffed cheeks. "Aggie spoke to me again."

Kelly stroked her back. "Okay, and what she said made you run away or what?"

Miranda bent down to catch Noeul's eyes. "Honey, we believe you, so stop worrying about that. What did Aggie say?"

Noeul let her head fall back onto the couch and stared into the flames that danced in the fireplace. "She was quoting a Bible verse from Ecclesiastes." She watched as both women squinted in confusion. "The one that says there is a time for everything. Think about the song "Turn, Turn, Turn" by the Byrds. The scripture says, 'a time to be born and a time to die, a time to weep and a time to laugh.' I think she is trying to tell me to start living, and I don't know that I can do that. Aggie also said something about a seeker. I don't know. I'm so confused." The tears started again, great sobs that caused her shoulders to rise and fall. The pain lanced through her chest, white hot and searing. It felt like she was losing Aggie all over again.

Two sets of arms enveloped her, as her friends wrapped her in a protective cocoon while she cried. Mourning this recent connection with Aggie was almost as painful as when she'd died. Trying to figure out what everything meant was draining both her strength and her emotional well-being.

Miranda kissed her temple and continued to hold her close as she spoke. "Noeul, you don't have to figure it all out this minute. There must be a reason all this is happening. I won't lie. I want you to find happiness and love. We never got the chance to know Aggie, but your stories about her humor and tenderness have made us come to love her through you. I have no doubt how much love the two of you shared. I'm having a hard time believing she would have wanted you to live alone for the rest of your life. You have a great deal of knowledge to pass on. The things you can do with a plant could change the world. Don't waste that gift."

Noeul pondered Miranda's words. Her heart longed for someone to share her world with, the intimate touch of a lover, and the security of leaning on someone who would share all the hopes and dreams that only a partner could. Her heart craved that soul-deep connection. It was her head that kept telling her no one would, or could, measure up to Aggie. She feared another relationship would only lead to heartache. "I'm not sure I know how to love again. I've had the very best. It's hard to imagine settling for anything less than what I felt for Aggie."

Kelly tilted Noeul's chin up and turned her face toward her. "Noeul, it will never be what it was with Aggie, because that could only happen with Aggie. It doesn't have to be less either. Not better, not less, just different. Isn't it worth a try? You'll never know what could be if you don't take the first step to try. Honestly, it may be enough right now to admit to yourself that you'll be open to the opportunity."

Noeul closed her eyes and tried to let Kelly's words sink in. There was so much to think about and a great deal of soul searching ahead of her. Aggie said that when the seeker found her, she needed to let them in. Could she even recognize the opportunity if it knocked on her door? Only time would tell. She needed to find the courage to answer if the knock ever came.

***

Noeul lay in her bed, trying to let her mind settle. Kyo sprawled out on her back beside her, paws in the air. She'd applied another layer of medicinal salve to Kyo's wound and wrapped it to keep her from licking it. That hadn't lasted too long; she quickly chewed through it and promptly sneezed indignantly. After she realized the futility, Noeul had given up and waited until the dog fell asleep to apply a final dose that she hoped would keep it from getting infected. Kelly and Miranda had brought the latest Cornell newsletter with them, and it was open on her lap as she read. The subscription was in their name to avoid any link to her old life. It had taken some convincing and cajoling from Noeul to get them to go home after their ride back from the falls. They'd tried to argue with her that they could stay another day.

"Go home, you guys. I'm ok." Noeul hugged her friends as they cleaned up the kitchen.

"Noeul, there's no reason we have to be back. Leo can handle it. I really don't like the thought of you being alone after what happened today. I worry." Kelly drew Noeul into a hug, and she allowed herself to melt into it.

Miranda kissed the top of her head. "You're family to us, and family sticks together. We're here for you, day or night. That doesn't stop because we aren't physically in the same room."

Noeul turned in Kelly's embrace and reached out a hand to cup Miranda's cheek. "I love you both and, I promise, I'm fine. I have work to do in the greenhouse, and you two have a business to run."

"Our business is nowhere near as important to us as you are. It's what family does." Miranda sandwiched Noeul between her and Kelly.

Noeul welcomed the love and concern from choice. How she would have survived all these years without them was something she wasn't even willing to think about. She only wished Aggie could have been here to be a part of it. "Now, let's get you guys on your way before it gets dark. I've got some work to do. After that, I'm going to park myself on the couch in front of the fire and read."

Noeul lay in bed trying to concentrate on the newsletter and not on Aggie's words. Her eyes caught a story about a Professor Armstrong's sabbatical. She remembered Jordan as a student, years ago. She'd shown incredible promise in the field of plant genetics. In Noeul's mind, Jordan was a prodigy. The article revealed that Jordan was headed out on a cross-country trek seeking missing elements into her research involving a promising superfood. Noeul was intrigued. Maybe the next time she was at Miranda and Kelly's, she'd look into publications from her former student and do some internet research. It gave her great satisfaction to know that her beloved Cornell was still one of the leading institutions of higher learning with a focus on agriculture.

Brenda Schoepp came to mind, an advocate for both women and agriculture credited with saying, "Once in your life you need a doctor, a lawyer, a policeman, and a preacher, but...three times a day you need a farmer." Noeul believed that there was a coming storm in relation to growing the goods needed for a healthy society. Climate change, urban sprawl, and big agriculture's failure to properly care for the soil and the environment in general, were constantly pushing the boundaries of food production. *I can only hope something I taught her is helping in her quest.* Noeul laid the newsletter on the nightstand and switched off the light. She heard a soft snore from her canine companion and turned to rub a soft belly, as she closed her eyes and prayed for a night of sleep, without dreams full of hidden messages.

***

Jordan opened one eye to judge the time. The tent was beginning to filter in the morning light. She could see faint wisps of her breath in the muted illumination and feel the stinging cold on her face. "Why couldn't you have chosen Hawaii, Professor James?" Her body was warm inside her sleeping bag and urged her to stay right where she was. Her brain, on the other hand, demanded coffee, and her stomach growled with an angry request to be fed.

A great deal of energy had been burned yesterday to reach this point, and she needed to refuel. *A few packages of instant oatmeal, dried fruit, and a squeeze of honey should do the trick.* She wriggled into the jeans she'd kept in the sleeping bag with her and donned her thick wool socks. No matter what the temperature, she couldn't sleep in socks or pants. She preferred sleeping completely naked. That wasn't really practical in the great outdoors, where anything could happen.

Her polar fleece skull cap had kept her head warm all night. Currently, it was making her itch. She pulled it off and scratched at her scalp until the frigid temperatures forced her to pull it back on and rummage for her gloves inside the bag. Once she'd sufficiently braced herself for the cold, Jordan unzipped the subzero sleeping bag and shivered against the frosty morning. Her boots were like ice blocks. After she laced them up, she unzipped the tent to watch a brilliant sunrise inch its way above the horizon. Jordan prepped her breakfast and poured a healthy measure of freeze-dried coffee into a mug. She munched on a power bar as the light began to dance off the rocks and the lake.

The solitude was incredible, though part of her wished for someone to share this moment with. The last person Jordan let that close had ripped her heart out and crushed it into the ground like a discarded cigarette butt. *Not going to happen. Your time will be better spent figuring these clues out and finding Professor Scott.* She poured water into the metal cup and stirred. With the coffee held close to her nose, the strong aroma stirred her senses as she pulled it deeply into her sinuses.

She tore two oatmeal packets open and dumped them into the pan of hot water. She sat back, holding the pan in her gloved, but still chilled fingers. She gingerly brought the coffee mug to her lips and took a careful sip in an attempt to avoid burning her tongue. Waiting for the coffee to cool before the first drink was proving too difficult. The scalding, bitter brew slid down her throat, instantly spreading warmth throughout her chest.

A thought worked its way into her brain, as she pulled a flask from her backpack to add a small portion of Irish whiskey to the mug. As she took another drink, she closed her eyes and let the caffeinated liquid take the edge off her growing anxiety. Finding the resting place of the next clue weighed heavily on her, as she consumed her breakfast.

Jordan was aware that she might not locate the memorial, and her quest could come to an end right there. Something made her believe she had to keep searching, that the answers were there. She also had to believe, given her experience at Havasu, that she was being guided by something beyond the physical world. She finished her meal, cleaned up, and made a few preparations in case she made a discovery.

With her own allotment of two days at this location, she wasn't looking forward to another night in the cold, sleeping on the unforgiving ground. The thin foam pad only did a fair job at keeping her from feeling every rock and twig under her tent. She rubbed at a sore spot on her hip and grabbed her day pack, determined to get an early start at climbing to the highest point in search of the memorial.

Gravel crunched beneath Jordan's boots, as she climbed up the frost-slicked path. She watched the steam trail of her exhalation float up, before her lungs inhaled the next breath of sharp, clean air. After ten minutes of exertion, her muscles were warmed up and she considered removing a layer to prevent overheating. *Hard to believe I could be burning up in these temperatures.* Within fifteen minutes, she'd reached the summit she'd been directed to and removed her beanie to allow steam to rise off her head.

Having no idea where Aggie's memorial rested, she closed her eyes and waited for a moment of inspiration to direct her next steps. She lifted her eyes to watch the sun flit in and out of long, thin clouds, as its reflected light shone off the mirror-like surface of the lake. She tried to look for things that would be out of sight from below. Anything was suspect, and she only hoped whatever had guided her up to this spot would point out the anomaly. She didn't expect the soft voice floating on the wind.

"Listen."

She looked around and saw no one. *What the hell?* Jordan closed her eyes and sharpened her auditory senses, blocking everything else out. A thin whistle pierced the quiet. The sound was only audible when the wind blew. That fact led her to believe it wasn't a person creating the sound. In her mind, Jordan pictured a clock face and rotated her body clockwise to the various numerical positions. Each time she heard the high-pitched whistle, she adjusted until she could hear it better. At the five o'clock position, the whistle was the strongest and clearest yet. She looked for anything that could create the noise. A bare scrub tree sat alone off in the distance, visible only when the cloud cover was just right. She watched it and waited.

A gust came up and the sound pealed out, while she zeroed in to find something capable of producing a whistle. Visually, there was nothing there except the scrub. *That has to be it–there isn't another damn thing anywhere near there.* After she shifted her pack to a more comfortable position, she mapped out a path to reach the tree and again looked for a source of the voice that had told her to listen.

"I know what I heard. I'm not losing my mind". She was also sure it was the same voice that had led her to the high point. Jordan had to believe she was being guided by something well beyond her understanding. Something was revealing each step along the treacherous path, as she worked her way to the tree. She scaled small rock faces and navigated deep crevasses that meant certain injury if she took a wrong step. "This is crazy. If Mom or Dava knew what I was doing, they'd have a fit." Painfully, she moved forward on instinct, stopping occasionally to listen for the distinct whistle. After a grueling, hour-long trek, she approached the tree with an eye to identifying anything like she'd seen in the previous clue sites.

"Follow your heart."

Jordan turned around quickly. This time the voice was much louder and resonated with greater force. A hand held to shield her eyes, she searched for anything that could explain what she'd heard. There was nothing within sight in any direction. The pull toward the scrub was growing ever stronger and attempts to resist seemed futile. Nothing seemed out of place; nothing looked like a potential source of the whistling. She hadn't heard it since arriving at the tree.

Jordan repeated the disembodied message, "Follow your heart." Where was her heart? Work...her family...her roots. *Wait a minute. Roots, could that be it?* The roots at the base of the tree were partially exposed. She bent over to examine them more closely, circling the tree counterclockwise. Her eye caught something peculiar. Two rocks, lying side by side, formed an oddly shaped heart. There was no way this was a natural occurrence, because the two rocks were of different composition. She inspected the formation closely and took a picture of the orientation. She moved them to reveal what she had driven across the country to find, a silver cylinder. Jordan stopped for a moment and raised her face to the sky. "Thank you, whoever you are. I know that I wouldn't be this far without your help. I can only ask that you keep helping me. I need to find her." She took a few minutes to hold the cylinder in hands. She closed her eyes and swore she heard the whistle again.

Chapter Six

NOEUL WOKE UP THE next morning to a heavy rain. She'd cared for her animals and spent time in the greenhouse recording some data that she'd fallen behind in categorizing. Her outside tasks completed, she'd curled up in front of the fire and read from an Ann Rice novel. Her last trip to New Orleans had been when she'd traveled there to leave Aggie's memorial. That was not the memory that pulled her mind.

Aggie patted her stomach, as they entered the room. "I'm so stuffed, I could pop."

"Oh my God, I've never seen a steak that big. I can't believe you ate all of it. I'd be crawling out of there on my hands and knees if I'd eaten that much." Noeul flipped on the lamp and collapsed back onto the beautiful, ornate wooden bed in the historic Havana Hotel. It'd been a long day of travel, and she wanted to climb under the sheets and curl up in Aggie's strong arms. She closed her eyes and felt the bed dip, a knee pressed up into her center. "There is no way you can even think about making love. You have to be exhausted." Noeul rolled her head from side to side. "The mind's willing, but the body..."

"Well I can dream, can't I? I still think you're the sexiest thing I've ever seen." Aggie placed her hands on each side of Noeul's face, leaned down, and kissed her. "You still have a clue to figure out. We're close, but we aren't there yet. I brought you to San Antonio because I've always wanted to see The Alamo."

Noeul wrapped her arms around the strong shoulders of her gorgeous wife. Aggie's wavy hair fell into her eyes, and Noeul ran her fingers through it. "You're such a tease."

Aggie rose up and pulled her red-checkered flannel shirt out of her jeans, exposing the washboard abs that lay hidden beneath the soft material. Noeul reached up and unbuttoned the shirt until she could run a single finger over the defined muscles. Aggie lowered her body until she lay pressed against Noeul. "About that mind willing quip." Noeul nipped at the chin near her lips.

Aggie rocked her knee, "Yes?"

Noeul slid her hand between them and cupped Aggie through her jeans. She smiled as her lover's head fell to her shoulder and her breath hitched in. Her tongue found Aggie's ear and traced the edge, dipping inside. She smiled at the delicious groan Aggie emitted and shared the shiver from the body she held close.

Aggie rose above her, pulled her shirt the rest of the way off, and helped Noeul to sit up and remove hers. Clothes became unnecessary barriers that were soon discarded, as two hungry mouths met, and hands explored sensitive skin. This was a dance they'd performed hundreds, maybe thousands of times. Their bodies rose and fell, arched and bent, into the ultimate submission.

Noeul lay beneath her lover, legs wrapped around the strong thighs as their bodies became one. Fingers teased and claimed possession of the deepest parts of her. Aggie's touch never failed to bring her right to the edge. Noeul searched the blue eyes that held her captive, as she used blunt nails to scratch down Aggie's back and urge her to take what Noeul was desperate to give. She felt her heart pound in her chest, as she spiraled closer and closer to the moment of ecstasy. She focused on those penetrating eyes, so dilated she could stare directly into Aggie's soul. A silken voice called to her.

"Come for me, love."

Aggie's words were all she needed to slip over the edge and crash into oblivion. Her back arched off the bed, and her screams were smothered with a searing kiss, as Aggie tumbled with her against her thigh and drove Noeul straight through another soul-searing orgasm.

They lay spent and breathing hard, their bodies slick with sweat. Aggie had yet to withdraw from her heat. Noeul knew if that touch was ever missing, the fire within her would surely go out. They lay for a long while, kissing softly and recovering from giving everything of themselves to the other.

"I love you, Aggie, with all I am." Noeul nuzzled closer to the woman she loved, who slipped gently from inside her, rolled them over, and drew Noeul into her arms.

"I love you, Noeul. Rest tonight. Tomorrow, we'll put your detective hat back on. You have clues to decipher." Aggie kissed the top of her head as they drifted off.

The next morning, they'd showered together which led to another round of making love. Side by side, the two explored the city and eventually found a small café to have dinner. A brilliant red sunset captured their attention as they enjoyed drinks with a succulent meal. Their table was on the restaurant patio, surrounded by nets of tiny white lights and small glowing candles that flickered lazily in the evening air. Noeul held a few pieces of parchment paper in her hands.

She knew the paper wasn't as ancient as it appeared. She smiled. Aggie's gone all out to set the scene for me. The paper crinkled as she unfolded it and read through the next series of clues. "Okay, so this first cipher stands for the Coup of 18 Brumaire in November 1799 in France. After a bit of research into the subject, I found the answer to part two of the same cipher about who came to power when the directory was defeated. The answer, my love, is Napoleon." She watched as Aggie sipped her whiskey and smiled.

"Okay, you've got that part. How about the next?" Aggie rolled her hand indicating for her to continue.

"I called Max and had him translate the binary code."

"Hey, that's cheating!"

"I don't remember any rules to this game that strictly forbid me from phoning a friend. It translated to the numbers 15000000 and 828000. All on my own, I figured out that these two numbers represent largest land deal in American history, the Louisiana Purchase. A total of 828,000 acres were sold for $15 million dollars."

Aggie lightly clapped and tilted her head in acknowledgement. "How about the next one? Did you have to cheat on that too?"

"No, smart ass. I used an alphanumeric code related to a page, line, and word number of our book to reveal your question. Where was the surviving son of the Black Prince born? I had to uncover who the Black Prince was, first, in order to figure out who his son was. The Black Prince was Edward IV and his son, Richard II, was born in Bordeaux, France, nicknamed *La Belle Endormie* or sleeping beauty."

"You know, you're pretty twisted my love. My brain is on overload with all this sleuthing." Noeul reached out and clasped her lover's hand.

Aggie smiled back at her with that devilish grin and quirked her eyebrow. "That was the easy part. I am a bit devious. I have a pretty good idea you're loving this adventure. You know it and I know it. Think of it as a way to keep your brain young and your spirit alive and well."

Noeul picked up her wine and swirled the dark red liquid around before raising it to her lips. "You like to watch smoke pour out my ears."

"Well, if that's what it takes to make you hot, then I'll keep your brain..." She wagged her eyebrows up and down. "busy for years to come."

Noeul smacked Aggie's arm and followed it up by pulling her hand to her lips. "I love you, you fool."

"So what clue are you working on now?" Aggie took a pull on her Jameson's.

"Well, I've worked out another code, giving me the name Alexandre Frédéric." Noeul looked at a series of pictograms and a word. "The anchor tells me it's something nautical. The cannon ball makes me believe it was a battleship. The French word *barateur*, roughly translated, means cheat. None of that makes a lot of sense until you read about Alexandre and two of his brothers, Jean and Pierre Lafitte. Jean is rather famous it seems. With the help of his..." She stopped, and her lips moved silently over each line. "oh my God—band of privateers. They were pirates who helped Andrew Jackson defeat the British in the War of 1812!" Her voice had risen a few octaves and was almost a squeal. Noeul looked up to see Aggie laughing at her. "What?"

Aggie smiled. "I love watching you turn into a little kid."

"Well, you've turned this into a treasure hunt. What kid doesn't dream of finding treasure?"

"Well, I found mine when I ran you down all those years ago."

"Yeah, one of us is a bigger kid than the other." Noeul leaned over and lightly kissed her cheek. "That honor belongs to you, *a chuisle mo chroí.*"

"You are the pulse of my heart too." Aggie softly kissed her lips. "Why don't we take this back to the room, so you can try your key in the treasure chest?"

"I'm all for that."

They left the restaurant and walked back to their hotel, where Noeul worked out the remaining clues about the escapades of Jean Lafitte. Aggie finally handed her a pictogram of a fleur-de-lis and a crescent moon. Noeul had no doubt where they were going.

"Are we headed to New Orleans?" Noeul bounded over to straddle Aggie's hips and look into eyes whose mischief swirled like smoke rising off a magical, smoldering fire

"You're pretty good at this, babe. I hope you're having fun, because I'm truly enjoying watching you." Aggie ran her hands up Noeul's sides and arched her hips, pushing their centers together.

Noeul closed her eyes and rolled her head back at the sensation. "God, I love when you do that." Noeul felt hands drawing her down and soft lips meeting her own.

"*Laissez les bon temps rouler*, my love".

"Let the good times roll, indeed." Noeul rolled over to feel the secure weight of her wife above her, wrapping her in a haze of desire. They made love under a crescent moon before drifting off to sleep, arms and legs entangled.

***

Jordan held the phone to her ear, as she walked through the French Quarter talking to Dava. The smells of gumbo, beignets, and good coffee filled along the historic streets. She'd camped where she could on the way from California and was looking forward to sleeping in a comfortable bed.

"Have you checked into your hotel yet?" Dava asked.

"Not yet, it's next on my list." Together, they'd worked through the clues and discovered that she was headed for New Orleans. It was someplace she'd never been to. The lore of the crescent city was legendary. The French Quarter, Bourbon Street, and the madness of Madri Gras, all played into the magic of the city.

"Talk to me, Sherlock, do you have a plan for your next move?"

"I do. It involves a huge meal, a few beers, and something sinful."

"Sinful, I like that plan. Not sure it's going to bring you any closer to Professor Scott, but it's a damn good plan."

Jordan smiled at her sister's statement of the obvious. "Me neither. I know I think better on a full stomach. I'll call you later. Love you."

A few hours later, she pushed back from her seat at Mother's Restaurant on Poydras Street. Jordan looked over the remnants of her meal. A small piece of a Debris Po'boy sat beside an empty cup of gumbo. A different plate bore the ghost of some decadent bread pudding. She licked some whiskey sauce off her thumb and caught the waitress watching her.

"Can I get you anything? Refill your coffee maybe or…" She paused and arched an eyebrow. "something else you might need?"

"Thank you." Jordan grinned at the attractive young woman. "Just my check please."

"Let me know if you change your mind."

"I will."

The server turned and swayed back to the bar before bringing her check and accepting the cash Jordan placed in the narrow, leather folder.

Finishing her chicory coffee, Jordan grinned and looked over the clues she'd written down. New Orleans was a huge city. All the things she'd deciphered on the Sequoia clue had led her here. Once again, she didn't have a snowball's chance in hell without some divine intervention. She thought about the whistle and the voice that had led her to the tree at the lake.

She'd had visions at Havasu, of great sequoias and the mystical phoenix. Her own phoenix burned, and Jordan could only hope for the guidance to continue in some form or another. She left the restaurant and walked to her Jeep. A few minutes later, she pulled into her hotel on Bourbon Street. She was fortunate that a vehicle was pulling away from the private lot, giving her the opportunity to snag one of the limited parking spaces. The clerk met her with a smile and an appraising glance that traveled down Jordan's body from her eyes, to her waist, and back up.

"Welcome to Lafitte's Guest House, may I help you?"

"Uh yes, reservation for Armstrong?" Jordan glanced around the small, ornate lobby. A steep staircase lined one wall and led to the upper floors.

A melodious voice coming from behind the reception desk caught Jordan's attention. "You were lucky we had an opening. Most of the time, our rooms are booked. We'd had a last-minute cancellation when you called. I have you in room twenty-one. Unusual for that room to have a cancellation. Do you know anything about our history?" The receptionist raised her eyes above her tortoiseshell reading glasses and again, appreciatively eyed Jordan.

"I've read a bit about the paranormal activity here. I think it adds to the mystique." Jordan smiled at her and watched, as she continued to type into the computer with long, delicate fingers tipped with dark, maroon polish.

"Well, Ms. Armstrong, I..."

"Jordan, if you please."

The receptionist smiled seductively. "Jordan. That's beautiful. My name is Angèle. Again, your room is number twenty-one and has a private balcony overlooking Bourbon Street. It's our most infamous room, where more than one guest has reported, shall we say, unusual things."

Jordan returned the smile and felt something like warm honey run through her chest. "Well, that would be nothing unusual in my life, of late."

"Here's your key. We serve a complimentary continental breakfast and coffee that's worth waking up for. If you need anything else, don't hesitate to ask for me."

Jordan accepted the key and didn't fail to notice that Angèle's hand lingered in hers a bit longer than necessary. She felt her heart speed up at the contact, and heat radiated off her. "Thank you, I'll keep that in mind."

Jordan carried her duffle up the steep staircase to the second floor and located her room. The off -white, four-paneled, door was adorned with a brass twenty-one. To the left of the door, hung a large mirror surrounded by an ornate, dark, wooden frame. Jordan briefly gazed into the reflection, as she slid the key into the lock. She squinted at what she saw and quickly turned to look back down the empty hall. She turned back to the mirror looking for the young girl she'd caught a glimpse of. Nothing but her own reflection stared back at her. Jordan shook her head, as she pushed open the door and stepped into the room. *As if this whole quest isn't strange enough, now I'm seeing things that aren't there.*

A tall, four-poster bed greeted her, along with a few beautiful pieces of Queen Anne style furniture scattered around the room. Two walls revealed exposed brick. One, built with a double set of French doors, led out onto a wrought iron balcony. After depositing her duffle on the small settee, Jordan opened the glass paneled doors and walked out onto the terrace overlooking Bourbon Street, taking in the sounds of New Orleans. Jazz drifted up from below, along with the strong smell of whiskey. She briefly closed her eyes and wondered how in the world she was ever going to find her next clue.

A realization hit her that it had been over six months since she'd seen Dava in person, or her mother for that matter. *Regardless of this quest, that must be rectified.* Seeing family only at holidays was not how Jordan had grown up, and she wouldn't allow it to continue. Regardless of where this quest went next, she was going to D.C. to visit her mother and sister.

Dava had her own apartment, and her mother had moved into the same neighborhood after the girls' father passed. Dalia had said she wanted to be closer to political resources. In reality, Dalia had confided in Jordan that she wanted to be near Dava in case she ever needed her. Jordan was proud of her sister's independence. Still, any of spina bifida's health complications could occasionally rear their head. It was not unusual for Dava to suffer from infections and serious gastrointestinal issues that warranted hospitalization.

Jordan worried less about Dava since their mother's relocation. *She's my greatest confidant, smart ass or not.* Jordan's favorite role ever was being Dava's big sister. Keyed up and anxious, she pulled her cellphone from her back pocket. A few moments later, Jordan found herself lost in her sister's voice

"I'll assume by the jazz I'm hearing in the background, you've made your way near some entertainment?"

"Yeah, you'd love it here. Live music in a ton of places and more delicious food than you can even imagine." Jordan's smile broadened. "You need to come down here with me sometime, maybe at Mardi Gras."

Dava's laughter rang through the phone. "JJ, I love you. A bunch of drunken people pissing in the street isn't my cup of tea."

"True. Watson, I can tell you there's a lot more to the city. Right across the street from me is Lafitte's Blacksmith Shop Bar. The bar is fabled to have been where Lafitte and his band of pirates had planned their operations. You remember from the clues that he helped General Andrew Jackson defeat the British in the War of 1812, saving the city. The blacksmith shop is alleged to be the oldest structure in the United States used as a bar. How cool is that?" Jordan loved sharing parts of her adventure with her sister. Their thirst for knowledge was unquenchable.

"That is pretty cool. Have you been there yet? You can't leave there without tipping one back in a famous setting like that."

"I'll probably wander over there after I relax a bit. I was on the road all day. I did have a fabulous supper, and you'll be happy to know, the bread pudding is all it's cracked up to be. The whiskey cream sauce is absolutely sinful."

"Well, you are in a city known for it, enjoy. Now, are you any closer to knowing where the memorial is?"

Jordan puffed out her cheeks and let out a slow breath. "Not a clue. I'm hoping I can go back through everything we have and see if I missed anything. Other than that, I'm here on a wing and a prayer. The professors knew where they were going. I'm trying to follow the footsteps of someone who didn't leave a very detailed map. It's like finding a needle in a haystack. Say, I was thinking..."

"I thought I smelled smoke."

"Very funny, Watson. I was thinking I'd make a run to D.C. after I get finished here." Jordan rubbed her eyebrow with her thumb and forefinger.

"Sherlock, are you okay?"

"Just missing you. That a reason for alarm?"

Jordan heard Dava sigh.

"Big sister, you never need a reason to come and visit. You're on an important mission, halfway across the country."

Jordan began to pace across the balcony, phone to her ear. "I know. I can't help it. I miss you, and nothing is more important than family. It's been almost six months since I've seen you and Mom, and that's too long."

"I won't argue. Let's see where this clue leads. You never know, the next stop might be right next door."

"You're right. That is possible. It doesn't matter. I'm coming anyway. I'll treat you and Mom to dinner."

"As long as you aren't cooking it. I'm not into ramen noodles or your beloved Nutella and Teddy Gramhams."

Jordan laughed from deep inside. "You always did know how to bring me out of a funk, Sis."

"The only funk you're in probably has to do with not being able to shower while you're camping. Now, go have a drink among the ghosts of pirates. Love you, JJ."

They signed off and Jordan put her phone back in her pocket. Walking back into her room, she shut and locked the French doors. She opened her duffle, pulled out her sleep shorts and tank top for later, and threw them on her bed. She patted her back pocket for her wallet and slipped in her room key. At the last second, she grabbed the professors' book before stepping into the hallway.

"Thirsty?"

Jordan turned quickly in the direction of the voice, finding no one behind her. She shook her head and reached for the banister. Near her room, she saw what she could only describe as a fleeting apparition. *I must be more tired than I thought. One drink, then I'm going to bed.* An attempt to shake away the cobwebs and the gnawing feeling failed, as she descended the stairs and headed out the door and across the street.

Jordan entered the establishment and made her way to the bar. It wasn't a very big place with a large brick chimney in the center taking up a good portion of it. Illuminated with candles, she couldn't detect any electric lighting at all. The massive ceiling beams were exposed, as were the wide, wooden planks above them. The L-shaped, wooden bar top was well used and had only simple wooden barstools in front of the brick face. She took one of the stools and looked around the room, as she waited for the beautiful bartender to finish with another customer. Jordan laid the book on the bar beside a well-used coaster. There was absolutely nothing fancy about the room or the furnishings, and she was surprised to find herself completely at ease. The bluesy sound of a piano came from across the room.

"What can I get you, *ma chère*?"

The lithe bartender spoke with a distinctive, low-country accent that settled a pleasant warmth around Jordan. She smiled into the striking gold eyes surrounded by mahogany skin. "Makers Mark. Neat, please."

The woman tipped her head sideways and reached up to the third tier of the liquors behind the bar and grabbed for a short cocktail glass. She poured the honey-colored liquor to the two-finger mark Jordan indicated and winked at her. Jordan smiled back and spun the glass in a slow circle while she watched the musician play to the small crowd in the room. She looked at the book she'd brought with her and realized, in the extreme low light of the room, she would never be able to read anything. She turned the book over and looked at its cover as she picked up her drink.

The whiskey slid down her throat, and she closed her eyes to savor the bite as it hit her tongue. She waited for the smooth warmth to spread over her. Jordan rarely drank to excess, that didn't mean she didn't enjoy a good glass of whiskey or a good wine. She turned on her stool so that she was able to see both the L-shaped section of the bar and the musician. After about fifteen minutes, he took a break and the bartender made her way back to check on Jordan.

"First time visitor?" The woman asked.

"Yes. I certainly hope not my last."

"Business or pleasure?"

"A little of both," she extended her hand, "Jordan Armstrong. I'm pleased to make your acquaintance. I heard the music from my hotel across the street and had to come."

The bartender took her hand. "Draws them in every time. I'm Joëlle, pleased to meet you too. Can I get you another or are you okay?"

"I'm fine for now." Jordan pointed to the musician, "He's good."

"That's Mike Hood, he's a regular. He keeps the patrons happy and my tip jar full." Joëlle looked down at Jordan's book. "You won't get any reading done in here. Not too many people bring a book with them. What brings you to New Orleans?"

Jordan turned squarely back to the bar and placed both arms on the surface while she cupped her drink. "I'm not sure how to even describe it other than to say I'm on a quest."

"A quest? That's a new one. Most people say vacation, or of course, Mardi Gras. Somehow, you don't look the type." Joëlle wiped at a condensation ring on the bar and threw away a discarded beer bottle from the seat beside Jordan.

"It's kind of a weird story, and I'm not sure you'd believe me." Jordan sipped from her glass, allowing the aged whiskey to mellow her thoughts.

"I'm a bartender, try me."

"Well, I'm a professor from Cornell University in New York. I'm trying to develop a superfood to eradicate hunger in drought-stricken areas. I'm on a quest to find the missing piece of my research," Jordan picked up the book she'd brought, "that one of the people who wrote this book might have. Only, I can't find her."

Joëlle picked up the book and looked over the names on the cover. "Which one are you looking for?"

Jordan studied her for a moment. The woman's eyebrows were drawn together, as she looked at the cover. "Professor Noeul Scott."

"Good thing, because reaching Aggie would be a much harder quest." Joëlle continued to study the book, opening to the middle where the pictures were.

Jordan was momentarily stunned. The cover didn't say Aggie James. The cover only had A. James. Joëlle had it in her hands less than ten seconds and not long enough to really see anything written inside. "Do you..." Jordan shook her head. "You know Aggie James?"

"Knew her. I met her and her wife, Noeul, years ago."

Jordan placed her hand on the book, lowering it to the bar top and bent forward to peer into Joëlle's golden eyes. In an excited voice, she probed. "You've met Professor Scott?"

Joëlle looked at Jordan, walked over to the bar, and removed a photograph she had tacked up near the register. She brought it back and handed it to Jordan. "I guess six degrees of separation actually applies here. I met them as a couple several years ago, when they stayed across the street at the guest house and became regulars for about two weeks. They were fun. It's not often visitors become regulars. Noeul visited a few years later, by herself."

Stunned, Jordan stared at a photo of Joëlle, Aggie, and Noeul at the bar. "After Aggie died?" she said with a hint of hope in her voice. How in the world, in a city the size of New Orleans, had she come across someone who had met the woman she was traveling the country to find? She had no explanation for the strange forces that were propelling her through this quest and had long ago given up trying to find any logic to it.

"Yes. It nearly tore me up to see Noeul come in by herself. She stayed about a week the last time, visited with me every evening here at the bar." She pointed to Jordan. "Sat on the exact stool you're sitting on. We became pretty good friends. I haven't seen Noeul in years," she tapped the photo, "after Aggie died, so did a piece of Noeul."

Jordan looked down and quickly to her left and right. "This is going to sound extremely strange. Did she happen to mention a memorial to Aggie here?"

"Not to me, at least that I can remember. I can tell you she did go visit *Grand-mère* Montieu." Joëlle said the second part with an almost reverent tone.

"Grand-mère Montieu? That means grandmother, right? Is it your grandmother?"

Joëlle laughed quietly. "She's everyone's grand-mère. She's one of our local Santeria priestesses and yes, she is my biological grandmother."

"Santeria?" Jordan was reaching for her phone to make note of the term.

"It's a blending of different spiritualities from West Africa to Cuba and others. It's worship of the Orishas or more understandably, head guardians." She paused, squinted as if looking for the right word. "Supreme beings."

"Ah, are we talking voodoo?" Jordan asked.

Joëlle scowled. "Voodoo is something made up by those who want to cash in on something inexplicable to them. Don't use that term with Grand-mère Montieu or you're likely to find yourself on your ass. Santeria is as much a religion as Catholicism or any Protestant spirituality. The interpretation and practice are different. Don't make the mistake of dismissing it."

Jordan held her hands up in earnest. "No disrespect meant, I promise you. The concept is all new to me. Rest assured, I do respect all forms of belief. The terminology is foreign to me and I apologize." Jordan pleaded with her, afraid to lose this fragile thread connecting her to Noeul. "Where can I find Grand-mère Montieu?"

"Call this number." Joëlle handed her a slip of paper. "If Grand-mère Montieu is available, I'll take you to her." Joëlle pointed to her glass. "You want another? You look like you could use it."

Jordan stared at her empty tumbler, having no recollection of finishing it. She simply nodded to Joëlle and stared at the picture. Once again, she felt as if forces beyond what could be seen were at work, and she had to believe they would eventually lead her to Noeul. When Joëlle set the glass down, Jordan toyed with it absentmindedly. The picture showed three women with their arms around each other, smiling for the camera. *What are the chances?* Absolutely certain something had led her to Joëlle, Jordan handed the picture back to the beautiful woman on the other side of the bar. She was both confused and excited by this chance meeting.

Joëlle lifted her chin in the direction of a new patron and walked to the end of the bar to take his order. Eclectic music floated around Jordan, and she took a healthy swig of her drink. After an hour, mellow and relaxed, she paid her check and tucked Grand-mère Montieu's contact number in her pocket. She'd also traded numbers with Joëlle. "If she can see me, are you available tomorrow?"

"Yes, I'm actually on staycation. That's why I can help Tim out. I'll be around, just call." Joëlle reached out a hand and clasped Jordan's forearm. "You okay to make it across the street?"

"I'm good. Thanks for all your help. I'll call you." Jordan gave a small wave and made her way across the street and up the steep staircase to her room. As she unlocked the room, she again looked into the mirror to her right. A young girl, almost translucent, stood in a white flowing gown, staring back at her.

"Ashes to ashes, what is hidden will be revealed."

Jordan spun on her heel so quickly she nearly fell, managing to stay upright only by grabbing the door frame. There was no one in the hall with her, and yet she knew she'd seen the girl and heard her speak. *Ashes to ashes, what is hidden will be revealed. What the hell does that even mean?* She shook herself and pushed open the door to her room. The alcohol on top of her large meal was beginning to make her very sleepy, and she longed to stretch out on the soft bed. She readied herself by brushing her teeth and changing into her sleep clothes.

The sheets were startling white and cool against her skin. The comforter was light but still heavy enough to feel it. After wrestling the pillows into submission, she drifted off with disembodied voices and apparitions floating through her thoughts. "What a long strange trip it's been."

Chapter Seven

NOEUL SQUINTED INTO THE sunbeam that streamed in through her window. For the first time in several nights, she actually felt rested. Kyo stretched, yawned her doggie good morning, and then twisted quickly and leapt up, wagging her tail furiously.

"Okay, okay, I'm up. Let's get you outside and find me some coffee." Noeul rose and slid her feet into her slippers. She looked around the bedroom absent mindedly, yawning and scratching her side lightly across the area of her tattoo. Lately her whole side had been itchy. No matter how many times she applied creams or lotions, it still felt itchy. *No, not itchy. Tingly.*

She let Kyo out to survey her domain before sliding her favorite mug under the coffee dispenser and filling it with the dark brew. Dawn was slowly breaking through into her eastern facing kitchen, leaving the large expanse of glass that formed the southern side of the house still shadowed in darkness. Kyo scratched at the door. Noeul let her in and laughed as the dog immediately ran to her food bowl.

"Find anything out there interesting? Any ninja squirrels waiting in the shadows?" She filled Kyo's bowl with the baked chicken, brown rice, and vegetable mix. A few embers of the fire remained. She spread them out till they glowed brightly and laid some split cherry wood on top. In a few minutes, the room's morning chill disappeared, and the flickering light gave off a cheerful glow.

She sat on the couch and sipped at her coffee as she watched the shadows recede and the shapeless objects turn into familiar forms. The newsletter again caught her eye, and she read over the part that intrigued her the most. There was little she could learn about her former student until she made a trip down the mountain. Although there really wasn't anything she needed, the temptation to discover more about Jordan's research was quite compelling. She and Kyo could go down and spend the night. "I can do this. I'll make the preparations for the animals, and we'll get started, Kyo."

Three hours later, Noeul and Kyo traveled down the mountain. She rode Thor and used Athena as a packhorse. Kyo bounded in and out of the stream when Noeul stopped midway to water the horses. When she finally reached Kelly and Miranda's, Kyo ran to Miranda and turned over to receive her customary belly rub. Kelly came off the porch and held Thor as Noeul dismounted. The two women embraced.

"Well this is a pleasant surprise. What brings you off the mountain off schedule, love?" Kelly grabbed the reins and started walking Thor toward the corral, as Noeul took the saddlebags off Athena and led her to the paddock as well.

"Kyo and I were a bit restless, so we decided to seek out some good company and found ourselves here." Noeul walked into the grassy area and removed Thor's saddle. After it slid from his back, she hung it across the split rail fence and kissed his nose. "Go eat."

Miranda walked up to them and hugged Noeul. "It's always good to see you. You're welcome any time."

"I need to do some research if your internet is up and running. In the newsletter you brought me, I read a story about one of my former students. I got curious. I also need to order some supplies for the greenhouse." Noeul threw the saddlebag over her shoulder and walked with the two women back to the small house.

"It's working okay, and you never need to ask. I put fresh sheets on your bed the other morning, so it's ready to go. I was planning on chicken parmigiana for supper tonight...that work for you?" Kelly picked up a stick and threw it for Kyo, who happily ran full out to retrieve it.

Noeul clasped Kelly's hand and squeezed. "That sounds wonderful. You know what they say, feed a stray and it keeps showing up."

"Well, I'll make sure we open a good bottle of merlot for dinner, and we'll be good to go."

Noeul made her way to the computer and sat down in the large, leather office chair. The room was furnished with pictures of the couple as they'd built the cabins and from their time working at the Green Bank Observatory. Noeul appreciated the evidence of the couple's deep devotion to each other. She opened a browser on the computer and pulled up her former employer. Locating Professor Jordan Armstrong in Cornell's faculty and staff directory was not difficult. *Her looks haven't changed much from all those years ago.* The accolades shown under her bio attested to Jordan's accomplishments. There were numerous links to her work, and Noeul was thoroughly impressed. Jordan's research was fascinating. *So thorough.* Noeul could see the basic threads of her own research that Jordan was building on. There were missing pieces, things she herself had discovered only within the last few years. Transfixed, she sat in front of the computer completely absorbed in the data and research. She had no clue of the time passing until Kelly brought in a sandwich and a glass of iced tea and set them beside her hand.

"Honey, it's been three hours, why don't you take a break and eat something? It's well past lunch. We still have a good while before dinner, and you're too skinny as it is. Eat." Kelly kissed her head and leaned on one arm to look at the screen. "What has you so captivated?"

"Do you remember that former student I told you about?" Noeul looked to Kelly for confirmation. "Well, it seems she was a better student than I thought. Jordan Armstrong took my basic research and ran with it. She's so far advanced in her technique and research, I feel like an amateur. I've been able to accomplish some of what she's been trying to do on a very small scale. This," Noeul pointed to her screen, "is a game changer."

Kelly furrowed her brow while squinting at the screen. "How so?"

"What she's trying to do is graft this superfood onto a root system that will grow with little to no water. If she can combine what she's doing with what I've been able to accomplish up in my crude lab, famine in Africa could be eradicated. Hunger could be a thing for the history books. It's fascinating."

Kelly laughed out loud. "I haven't seen you this excited since you figured out how to get more light into that underground greenhouse of yours. It's nice to see. Any chance you'll contact her and see if you can collaborate?"

Noeul rolled her shoulders to release some of the tension. She couldn't remember the last time she'd sat in front of a computer for so long. Her stomach rumbled, and she gratefully chewed a bite of the sandwich while she considered the question. "I'm an out-of-the-loop, retired professor. What she's doing is so far beyond my simple grafting techniques. Jordan has made incredible advances in her research. I'd only be more of a stumbling block than a stepping stone."

Kelly rubbed her shoulders, and Noeul moaned in pleasure. She continued to chew the sandwich, as Kelly's strong hands worked the knots out. As good as it felt, a wave of sadness hit Noeul. Aggie used to rub her shoulders when she'd been hunched over the computer for too long. It was always Aggie who pulled her from the screen and urged her to take a mental and physical break. If it hadn't been for the insistence of her wife, Noeul would have worked around the clock when she was elbow deep in a project.

Aggie had been her balance and voice of reason. Noeul missed those gentle admonishments that enough was enough. No extra hour granted, Aggie would give her enough time to save everything and then bodily remove Noeul from her chair. At work, their labs were not close in proximity by any stretch, yet Noeul would look up to find a jar of Nutella and graham crackers, along with a mug of warm coffee. Aggie made it a priority, and Noeul had enjoyed the rewards of her nurturing. She felt Kelly pat her shoulders and kiss her head again.

"Are you at a place you can go for a run with Miranda and Kyo? She sent me in to ask." Kelly picked up the empty plate and left the half-full tea glass.

Noeul stretched and rubbed her face. "I really want to read a bit more and get those things ordered. I may even make some inquiries from some old colleagues. It's been a while since I've checked in up at Ithaca. I'll bet it's been close to eight years now. I'm not even sure anyone up there would know who the hell I am anymore."

"Ok, I'll leave you alone for now. You'll be a mess if you sit there in front of that computer too much longer. That's one part of my old job I don't miss. I'd rather be in the kitchen or out in the garden. I'll call you when dinner's ready. If you're still on that thing, I'm pulling the power cord." Kelly was in the doorway of the office and only turned her head as she emphasized the last statement.

"Okay, Mom, I hear you." Noeul opened her email program and looked through her contact list for her former associate professor, Alice Timmons. She began a how-are-you email and asked if she remembered Jordan and her research. After placing an order on her favorite agriculture-supply website, she emerged from the office to find Kelly kneading bread at her butcher block island.

"Why don't you go take a walk, clear out all that data and computer work from your system? I've decided on *japchae* in your honor instead of the parmigiana. I got an order in of those sweet potato noodles you love so much. I've already marinated the beef and cut the vegetables by the time you get back, dinner should be ready."

Noeul's disposition brightened in anticipation. "Oh, that sounds wonderful!"

"Go already, get out of my kitchen."

Noeul grabbed a matchstick carrot and was met with a swipe of Kelly's dishtowel. "I'm going, I'm going." She pushed through the kitchen door and out to the yard. She chose a path that led down to the creek and slowly let her mind clear. Sitting down beside the brook, she listened to the water roll across the rocks and drop down into the deeper pools. She rolled a small pebble in her fingers, before she dropped it into the water, watching the ripples reach out in ever widening circles.

"You never know how far those ripples reach or when one will return."

Noeul glanced around, knowing she wouldn't see the face. The voice was unmistakable. "Why are you reaching out now? All these years alone, I've begged to hear your voice one more time." Noeul kept her breathing as even as possible, as she fought the despair. "I've missed you so much."

"The sorrow is not yours alone. I watch over you constantly. I can only speak to you now because your life is about to change chuisle mo chroí.*"*

Noeul grew angry. "I remember the first time I called you that. We were in New Orleans. How can I be the pulse of your heart when you're not here? When I can't feel you near me? I want you here!"

"In the annals of time, our lives are merely a blink of the eye, my love, some even shorter. If I could have stayed, I would have. All I can say is your life is not over. There is one who seeks much from you. Be willing to use all your gifts, my love. You have much to offer, and the one coming deserves all you can give."

Noeul rose to her feet and spread her arms. "I don't know that I can, Aggie. Love like ours comes once in a lifetime. How do I go beyond the perfect love we had?"

"Please be open to the possibility and let yourself take a chance when the opportunity arises."

"Will I lose you again?"

The voice grew fainter and sounded as if it was high above her. *"I will always be with you, inside. You need to know a seeker's heart is destined to find you."*

Noeul hugged her sides and let the tears fall for a love alive only in memory and the possibility of one yet to materialize. She started back toward the house, mentally and emotionally exhausted, unable to analyze all that Aggie had said. Her heart felt the loss, while her head argued adamantly about her sanity.

Each step closer to the house seemed harder and harder to take. Her need to be reassured that she wasn't losing her mind kept her lifting one cement shoe after the other until she'd reached the porch.

Miranda and Kyo were returning from their run, and the dog sprinted to her side, vying for her attention with excited wiggles. Reaching down, she ran her fingers into the soft coat and bent to scratch behind her ears. Noeul accepted Kyo's warm tongue bath to wash away the tears, until she was laughing more than she was crying. "You always know how to chase away the shadows, Kyo." She kissed her head and faced Miranda.

"You okay, Noeul?" Miranda wiped sweat off the side of her face.

Noeul freed her long, black hair. She gathered the escaped strands and placed the silver cuff back in its traditional spot at the base of her neck. "I will be. After a plate of japchae and a glass of your good bourbon, I'll be right as rain. Good run?"

Miranda bent at the waist and stretched. "Kyo and I should both sleep good tonight. She's good for me, doesn't let me slack at all. Takes after her momma and Aunt Kelly."

"Somebody has to keep you in line. How about we go in and see if I can at least help by setting the table while you shower?"

"Sounds good. The taskmaster in there will have a fit if I come to the dinner table with all this mud on me. I'll take Kyo and wipe down her fur too. We'll join you two in about fifteen minutes." Miranda patted her side and called for Kyo as they went through the side door of the house and headed up the stairs.

Noeul detoured to the office to see if there was any reply from her Cornell contact. She was pleased to find an email from Alice waiting on her.

Noeul,

It's wonderful to hear from you. What's it been, close to eight years now? Well, even one year is too long. I've missed you. How are you and what have you been up to?

Yes, I'm familiar with Professor Armstrong's research. She's a rising star around here. I checked with a few of our former colleagues, who tell me she's on the cusp of a major breakthrough along the same research lines you were working on during your tenure. She's well published, and I've included some contact information in this email, if you are interested in reaching out to her.

You inspired many during your years here, my friend, and you still do. Your name continues to carry weight here, and you are dearly missed. I do hope you come back and visit some time. We could call together a group of the old guard and meet up for dinner and drinks.

Let me know if you are interested, and I'll be more than happy to set it all up.
Love, Alice

Noeul closed the email program and wondered if she could emotionally handle the trip. She hadn't been back to Ithaca since she'd packed everything up, sold the house, and moved to West Virginia. Going back would surely stir painful memories along with the pleasurable ones. *It's worth considering. For tonight, I'll let it simmer and enjoy a night with my family.*

***

Jordan sat at a small café in the French Quarter, enjoying a very good local microbrew with her lunch. The humidity made her shirt stick to her skin. She'd never been much for air conditioning. If it was tolerable, she'd choose to sit outside every time. The sights and sounds of New Orleans were unlike any she'd ever seen. In almost every direction, she could hear some kind of blues or jazz. Unique improvs and highly addictive riffs resonated from the buskers' brass instruments. Jordan caught herself bobbing her head to the sound of a slide trombone and tapping her foot with a snare drum pulsing out the heartbeat of the city. *The carnival atmosphere continues, even though Mardi Gras has long since come and gone.*

Anxious to share what she'd learned with Dava, she had waited for the time her sister had texted, when she'd be out of her morning meeting. The phone didn't ring more than once before she heard her sister's customary greeting and answered in kind.

"So spill, Sherlock," Dava implored, "I'm not getting any younger and neither are you".

Jordan put her head back and turned her face to the sun. "Okay, okay. First let me tell you that the place where I'm staying is infamous for paranormal activity. Last night, while I was leaving to go across the street to have a nightcap, I distinctly heard someone say I looked thirsty. I swear Dava, there wasn't a soul in the hallway with me. More than once, I've caught a glimpse of an apparition."

"You're kidding me. How cool."

"Lately, that's turning out to be more of a norm than you can imagine. Anyway, turns out the Blacksmith Bar is pretty awesome, as was the woman tending bar last night."

"Oh, do tell."

A chuckle rose from Jordan's belly. "Not that way, goof. Well on second thought, she was pretty hot. However, that's not the interesting part." Jordan could hear Dava laughing on the phone.

"Okay, okay. What was so interesting?"

Jordan proceeded to relay all the strange coincidences and experiences of the night before. She shook her own head to clear the cold chill she felt at the totality of it all.

"JJ, this gets weirder by the minute. You know I believe in the paranormal. Even for me, this is pretty wacko."

"I know, Sis. That's why I'm sure I'm going to find Noeul. Something is leading me, putting me where I'm supposed to be. I would never have found that memorial at Moose Lake, never. Now, you want to hear the kicker to this whole story?"

"There's more? You've got to be kidding me?"

The waiter came by, and Jordan ordered another beer. She shifted restlessly in her chair; the prickle of her phoenix tattoo grew, the more she told Dava. She'd noticed that she felt the tingling anytime she started talking about the quest.

"Oh yeah. According to Joëlle, she hasn't worked in the bar for over a year. In her real life, she's a civil engineer working on the levees for the Army Corps of Engineers. She was there because the bar owner desperately needed help and begged her to cover for a few days. Now tell me that's a coincidence, and I'll run a marathon pushing you in a wheelbarrow."

Dava's deep laugh rang through loud and clear. "Well, I'm not much of a believer in coincidence, so I'd say she was put into your path on purpose. The probabilities of you running into someone, in a city that size, who would have met the woman you are looking for, are astronomical. You've got a better chance of being struck by lightning—twice."

Jordan sipped the microbrew that held hints of chocolate and coffee. She looked around her and down at her watch. *Close to two.* She needed to call Grand-mère Montieu. "Don't I know it, which is another reason I'm sure I'm being guided or led. I've got to call that Santeria priestess and see if she'll meet with me. Joëlle said she'd take me if the priestess agreed."

"Well, get off the phone, chug that beer, and make the call. I'll expect a full report tonight."

"Copy that, Watson. We've got work to do. I love you. Don't forget to look at your schedule, because I wasn't kidding about making a run to see you and Mom."

"Will do, Sherlock. Be careful. From what I've read, the Santeria religion is nothing to take lightly. Make sure you give it due respect."

Jordan thought about what Joëlle had said when she'd inadvertently referred to it as voodoo. "I promise. Now go decrypt some deep, dark secret until I have the next clue. I'll call you."

They signed off, and Jordan called for the check. She pulled up the number she'd stored in her phone and tapped the contact to make the call. After a few rings, a thick Creole accent announced she'd reached Grand-mère Montieu's phone, but Jordan was unsure if she was speaking directly to the priestess herself. After explaining who she was and how she'd come to have the number, she inquired about an appointment.

"You think I can lead you to what you seek?"

Jordan felt the tingle again and ran her hand across her side. "I presume I'm speaking with Grand-mère Montieu?"

"'Das correct."

The street noise faded into the background, and Jordan leaned over, her elbows on her knees. "I can assure you that my purpose for looking for Agnus James' memorial is honorable. I wish to take nothing from it except for the knowledge of where I am to look next for Noeul. My quest to locate her is in the hope that I can join our knowledge into a solution for an age-old problem. If we can, it may be possible to eliminate something that has plagued mankind for centuries. Hunger."

"Your purpose may be honorable, like you say. I more concerned about you heart. If you have dis number, you must have been in contact with my Joëlle. Come to me, seeker, and we see what will be. Joëlle will bring you."

"Do you think you can help me?"

"So many questions, tis good you are a professor. To be a good teacher, you must be a better student. Joëlle is my *pitit fi*. You come, we talk."

***

Noeul sat back, a steaming cup of tea in her hands, as she listened to Kelly strum her guitar and Miranda played the harmonica. Listening to her talented friends play music in complete harmony was pure joy. Once or twice a year, they would all go camping at a makeshift site they'd cut out between their two houses. They would cook over an open fire and enjoy friendship in the great outdoors. The evening air would be filled with the sounds of their wonderful music.

Noeul loved being with her friends. The house they owned was as comfortable to her as her own. The walls were lined with overflowing bookshelves in place of a TV. They'd carved out a simpler life for themselves in this isolated community and hadn't looked back. Noeul sunk into the soft, leather couch and closed her eyes. Even with her two closest friends right in the room with her, she felt alone. Kyo sat curled up on her feet, her paws twitching at some dream.

"You okay, Noeul?" Kelly reached out and stroked the top of Noeul's head over the arm of the couch.

"I am...relaxed and very full. You know how I love it when you make Korean food. Given my mother's isn't an option, yours is always exceptional." Noeul reached up and clasped her friend's hand, holding it to her cheek and kissing the backside of it. The fire crackled in the corner, throwing off flickering amber light that warmed the room even more.

Miranda spoke up. "That's why I love having you come down the mountain. Kelly makes special dinners. I'm worried she might be ready to boot me out the door and have you move in, so she'll have someone to impress." Miranda laughed and playfully scooted away from Kelly's flailing arm.

"Keep that up and you can make yourself comfortable on this couch when Noeul vacates it, smart ass." Kelly leaned over and kissed Miranda.

"You'd miss me. Who would you put your cold feet up against at night?" Miranda traced the side of Kelly's face with a finger.

"You two kill me. So, in love after all these years. It's sickeningly sweet. I love both of you." Noeul opened her eyes to watch the antics of the people closest to her heart. She sipped her tea again and rubbed her eyes. "I got an email back from one of my colleagues, about my former student. Seems she's a rising star in my old field and on the cusp of a major breakthrough. Alice asked if I was planning on a visit and offered me some contact information on Jordan. "

Miranda's eyes brightened. "Are you thinking about going? We could send Leo up to watch your place for you. He loves going up there."

"Slow down there a bit. I haven't even really thought about going back there. Honestly, I don't know if I can. The memories of Aggie might be overwhelming. I don't know that I could take all the trips down memory lane my old friends would want to travel. I think I'll stick to doing some information searches on Professor Jordan Armstrong and her research. I may even try to make contact with her. We'll see. I'm a long way from going back to New York."

Kelly softly strummed her guitar and the sound floated through the air. "Only you know what you can and cannot endure. We'll help you no matter what you decide."

"In other news, I've been thinking about something I'd like to try with you guys. The reality is, with no phone or internet service up at the house, I need to think about a communication system, so we could at least send messages when needed. One of my magazines had an article on homing pigeons. I was thinking we could raise a set trained to roost at your place and another for mine. We could occasionally use the pigeons instead of the travel time to actually ride up or down. It's something to think about anyway. Something new to develop." Noeul sipped at her tea, thinking about the logistics of pigeon post.

Miranda walked over and stood with her back to the fire, arms crossed behind her. "I'd be game. They wouldn't be very reliable until we got them accepting our places as home. Doesn't mean it's not something to consider, given you're never going to have a telephone up there."

Noeul's eyes were growing heavy, and she rubbed at them while yawning out her next thought. "It would take a good bit of research first. I'll start working on some information and we'll see where it goes. For now, I think I need to make my way to bed." She pulled herself off the couch, rousing Kyo, who leapt down to be let out one more time before retiring. Noeul walked over to kiss Kelly and turned to meet Miranda's open arms. She melted into the embrace and absorbed some warmth from her friend. "I'll see you two for breakfast. If I get up first, I'll start the coffee and biscuits."

"I may stay in bed to see what it would be like to be Miranda." Kelly laughed and set her guitar down. "Think I'm turning in too. See you in the morning."

Kyo turned circles before she lay down behind Noeul's knees with a huff. Noeul pulled up the soft quilt and reached back to stroke furry ears, as she drifted through a fitful slideshow of her past. Her dream landed her in the parlor of Grand-mère Montieu.

The smell of fragrant cigar smoke floated around her, as Noeul watched the cowrie shells being poured from the bowl onto the table. The room was alight with the soft glow of candles that cast shadows on the ceremonial articles all around the room.

Grand-mère's thick Creole broke the silence. "*Aleyo*, what bring you to me? I can tell...your energy is wounded."

Noeul drew her brows together in confusion. "*Aleyo*? I'm sorry I don't understand?

"Ah, dat mean stranger to our ways."

"My apologies, Grand-mère, Joëlle thought you might be able to help me with a request."

"We get to dat. First, I do a *diloggun consulta*, and petition da orishas to read your energy."

Noeul sat with rapt attention, as Grand-mère walked over to a small shrine adorned with several water glasses. She rubbed something on her hands and flicked them in the direction of the glasses. Soft words were spoken, as the woman dressed in brightly colored robes lit a white candle among the glasses and small items that sat on a white covering. Grand-mère puffed deeply on her cigar and blew a steady stream of smoke across the altar. Noeul's only cultural references made her think about a Catholic priest using incense and the lighting of candles for offered prayers.

Grand-mère came back to the table, rattled a wooden bowl, and rolled the shells out onto the surface. Some of the shells landed with the openings up and some were down. She positioned the shells so that they were in four columns, each containing four shells. Noeul could hear the woman mumbling, as she stared at the shells and said something about their mouths. Her fingers pointed back and forth.

"Elegguá say your energy is *osogbo*, unbalanced, my child."

"Grand-mère, what does that mean?"

"It means, we need to find you some peace, child."

Over the next hour, Grand-mère performed a spiritual cleansing in an attempt to balance things in Noeul's wounded spirit and to dispel the darkness she said surrounded Noeul. Nothing could bring Aggie back. By opening herself up to the possibility of spirits who were capable of aligning things outside of her control, Noeul hoped she could find some of the peace Grand-mère spoke of. When they were done, Grand-mère offered to create a *bóveda* for Aggie in a back room of her own home.

"We make a small shrine adorned with des offerings, my child. You are welcome here anytime to pay your respects to da one who has passed over." In among the water glasses and candles, she'd left a picture of Aggie, along with the memorial cylinder.

Grand-mère had explained everything and led Noeul through each step. "Now, my child, know dis, no life can thrive in a place wit'out hope. To stay in balance, you can't lean too far on one side of da path. I have seen da future. A seeker come, and you must be open to da path yet to be revealed. I know you do not understand. Be patient. All will be revealed."

Grand-mère walked Noeul to the door. "Grand-mère, thank you more than I can say. I feel more at peace than I have since Aggie left me."

"Only her body leave you, child. Now her spirit watch over you. You listen close, and I know you hear her." The larger woman embraced Noeul in a bone-crushing hug. She'd left New Orleans feeling like a completely different person, or at least feeling more like the person she was before Aggie's death. Noeul had been given a gift and she intended to use it to the best of her abilities.

***

Jordan sat at the Blacksmith Bar, once again listening to the house musician and sipping on another brand of bourbon that Joëlle recommended. Her mind was full of information. Everything she'd experienced was like a giant jigsaw puzzle that she needed to systematically separate and categorize. She thought back to her afternoon with Joëlle at Grand-mère Montieu's and tried to decipher and make sense of the day.

"Elegguá say your energy is *iré*. Dat mean you are in balance. Dis good. He show me a vision of you on a path, a path dat take you to a child of Orishaokó. He say, you a child of da same."

Joëlle looked at Jordan. "What Grand-mère is saying is that these are both good things. You are doing exactly what you are supposed to be doing, and your path will take you to another child of Orishaokó. That particular orisha, or god, is called the tiller of the land." She raised an eyebrow and grinned at Jordan. Jordan studied her and reflected on the concept that her path was somehow preordained.

Grand-mère Montieu's spoke again. "You are a child of da light and a daughter of Orishaokó. You must live in da light for life to grow, my child."

Grand-mère Montieu had led her to the *bóveda* Noeul had created for her wife. She cleansed Jordan's spirit and had her pay homage to the dead, before she was allowed to open the capsule where she carefully removed Noeul's letter and the other paper that contained the clues, which she committed to memory. She'd placed everything back exactly where it had been found. With Grand-mère's permission, she'd added a piece of turquoise from Havasu Falls and a small stone she'd found near the tree at Moose Lake, in tribute.

Now, Jordan sat at the bar watching the beautiful bartender take care of customers. Joëlle returned with a smile and motioned to Jordan's glass for a refill. She retrieved the bottle she'd poured the earlier dram from and poured one for Jordan and one for herself.

"So where do you go from here, Jordan?"

Jordan took a deep breath and gathered her thoughts, as she took a sip. The excellent whiskey had a dark smoky flavor with a touch of sweetness. "Well, the first thing I'm going to do is go see my sister and mother in Washington, D.C. It's been too long since I've shared the same space with them, and I have to fix that. I've been so caught up in my work and now this quest. I don't know, I...I need to touch base with them. While I'm there, my superbrain of a sister and I will work out the next set of clues."

"What will you do if you can't find Noeul?"

"I don't know. Probably return to Cornell and try to discover the missing research myself. This is my life's work, and it's too important to give up. That's why I'm traipsing all over the country, sleeping in my Jeep, on the ground, and in haunted guest houses for even the slimmest chance I can find Noeul. I have to believe I'm doing exactly what I'm supposed to." Jordan stopped and squinted at Joëlle for a second "What did Elegguá say? My path is true and that I'm following my purpose. I have to believe that's why all these extraordinary things keep making themselves known."

"I believe you're destined to find Noeul. Your path may be true. I wish Elegguá had given you a better idea about how long that path will be. Only you will know when you have found the end."

Jordan watched Joëlle's golden eyes drop from her own as she spoke. "If you don't, will you ever travel back this way?"

Jordan entwined their fingers and rubbed the outside of Joëlle's index finger with her thumb. "It's possible, though I can't make any promises. I will promise that if I do, I'll check in with you." She patted her pocket with her other hand, where her phone was. "I have your number, remember?"

Joëlle smiled. "When will you leave?"

"In the morning. I'm going to try and get as far north as I can before I camp for the night. I hope to make it to D.C. in the next few days, if I can. My sister, Dava, is off on Saturday and Sunday. If I can get in by Friday night, we'll have the entire weekend to visit."

Joëlle met her eyes and lingered. "I wish we had more time to explore this. As stupid as this is going to sound, I'm not a one-night-stand kind of girl. Somehow, I don't get the feeling you are either."

Jordan's gaze softened. "No, and you deserve more than one night. That I'm very sure of."

"I think you deserve that same thing, Jordan. How about we enjoy the music and the company?" Joëlle released her hand and moved up the bar to take care of a couple who'd entered.

Jordan waited until Joëlle had been relieved by the owner, who'd finally made it back from his unplanned trip out of the city. They walked hand and hand to Joëlle's convertible. Jordan leaned against its trunk and pulled Joëlle between her splayed legs, holding her around the waist while Joëlle leaned into her. Jordan felt toned arms snake around her neck, as she let her head fall against Joëlle's shoulder. Fingers stroked through her hair and held her close.

"You know, I wish I wasn't so honorable right about now."

Joëlle chuckled. "I was thinking the same thing. Damn shame that we are."

Jordan tilted her head and found Joëlle's lips. They were silky soft and tasted of bourbon. Jordan held her by the hips, as Joëlle's tongue darted in and out of her mouth. The night was warm, and Joëlle felt good in her arms. There was a stirring she hadn't felt in a very long time, not since—

"Hey, where's your head?" Joëlle gently bit her lower lip, bringing Jordan's focus back.

"Believe it or not, lost in you. It's been a very long time since anyone has churned me up like you have."

"I can believe it, because I feel the same way." She put her forehead against Jordan's and took a shuddering breath. "Just don't lose that number, *chercheur*."

Jordan kissed her once more then moved Joëlle back a fraction, until their bodies were no longer touching, their foreheads still together. "Idiot is more like it. *Au revoir*, Joëlle."

"*Au revoir, chère.* Joëlle pulled her keys out of her pocket and slid into her Corvette.

Jordan stood as the beautiful woman pulled out onto the street. She watched until she could no longer see the red glow of her taillights. She let her head fall back for a moment. When she had composed herself, she walked across the street to the guesthouse and dialed her sister.

"So, how did your appointment go? Did you find the memorial?"

"I did. Believe it or not, it was actually at the priestess's house. Grand-mère Montieu helped Noeul create a type of altar memorial, and still maintains it."

"Unreal. So, what's the next clue?"

Jordan laughed at Dava's enthusiasm. "We'll work on that when I see you. I'm headed out in the morning. I'll drive as far as I can tomorrow before I camp for the night. I should reach you guys by Friday evening, so we'll have the weekend."

Dava protested. "You might be driving right by one and not know if we don't decipher the clues as soon as possible."

"True, and it might take me even farther from you. Right now, I need to see you guys. Don't ask me to explain it, I just do."

"JJ, you never need to explain a thing. You get your ass here, and I'll have Mom make *mansaf*. With that amount of time, Mom will be able to marinate the lamb to perfection."

Jordan's mouth watered with thoughts of the layers of vegetables and lamb over rice. "And that's why I love you, little sister, you always know how to bring me home."

Chapter Eight

NOEUL WOKE IN A sweat around five in the morning. She tried to lay in bed and hoped for sleep to return. It never came. Frustrated, she got up and let Kyo out. Once she'd started the coffee and preheated the oven, she let Kyo back in and fed her some of the sweet potato noodles and cooked beef. Kyo buried her head noisily in her bowl, while Noeul began gathering ingredients for the biscuits.

The small kitchen was comfortable to work in, and Noeul felt at home pulling bowls and baking pans from Kelly's cabinets. Kyo lay near the door watching her. The ingredients for breakfast were lying out on the counter, and Noeul had placed the last drop biscuit on the baking pan, when Kelly entered the kitchen, yawning and scrubbing her eyes.

Noeul looked up at the pillow-crease marks that lined Kelly's cheeks. "I'm sorry Kel, was I making too much noise? I tried hard to be quiet. "

"No, hon, I'm always awake early. Twenty-five years of waking up at the same time will do that to you. When I was still working, I was actually up earlier than this." She took a seat at the counter and leaned on an elbow.

Noeul slid a cup of coffee in front of her and began cleaning up the mess from the biscuits. "What time do you think Miranda will stir? I don't want to start the eggs too soon."

Kelly sipped the rich coffee and let out a groan of appreciation. "Can I pretend I never met Miranda and ask you to marry me?"

Noeul stifled a laugh. "Kel, I love you. You know that."

Kelly held a hand up and stopped her next words. "I know, honey, I'm not near 'rugged' enough for you." She made air quotes. "I'll ask that you make it up to me by making another pot of coffee after I drink this one."

"That I can do for you and make you breakfast. Now, what time will Miranda be up?"

"Who the hell can sleep with all this lovey dovey racket in here?" Miranda walked up and put her arms around Noeul. "Can I score a cup of that coffee, beautiful?"

Noeul turned and kissed her cheek, as she pulled away to fill a cup. She put it on the counter near Miranda and checked on her biscuits, while pulling out a large, cast iron skillet.

Miranda leaned in and leered at her wife. "Don't think I didn't hear your plot to replace me either. You'd miss me in about, say, twenty years."

Noeul laughed at them both, while she arranged thick strips of bacon in the hot skillet and cracked eggs into a bowl. She added heavy cream and pulled out another skillet for scrambled eggs.

"Can I have cheese in mine, please?" Miranda sipped her coffee and, like Kelly, moaned in pleasure. "Ok, I'm on the bandwagon. If I divorce Kelly, will you marry me? I think I might even fit your type."

Kelly lifted one eyebrow and rolled her head on her hand to look at Miranda. "She'd divorce you in five, no three minutes. Probably after the first time you left your muddy boots in the hallway. Best stick with me, babe. I've learned to overlook your faults."

Miranda looked to the ceiling. "Probably so. Sorry, Noeul. I'll dance with the one that brung me." She leaned over and kissed Kelly.

"You two." Noeul used a fork to flip the bacon. Slowly, she filled the second skillet full with the egg mix and adjusted the heat.

After breakfast, Miranda headed outside to tend to the cabins that would have guests later in the day. Noeul went back to the computer for some more research and to place a few more orders. She was continually drawn back to the published works of her former student. The documents she accessed were comprehensive, detailed, and well written. It was obvious that Jordan cared deeply about solving the world's hunger problem. Noeul downloaded two of Jordan's books onto an external hard drive to read later, on her tablet. Noeul preferred to hold a real book in her hands and decided to order the hardbacks as well. It was about ten in the morning when Miranda stuck her head in the office, with Kyo at her side.

"Want to take Kyo for a run?"

"That sounds like a great idea. I've been sitting here for a few hours, and I could use the fresh air. I'll go change."

Noeul and Miranda took to the trails around the property, getting in an hour's run. They hit the trail that led them down by the lake, where Noeul gave Kyo a stern look to keep her from jumping in to chase the ducks. She and Miranda were good partners when it came to physical fitness, and they enjoyed this time together. As they came through the gate, the smell of warm bread hung in the air and both women picked up their pace. Kelly met them at the back door with towels and ordered both to remove their muddy shoes. Miranda wiped down Kyo after she finished cleaning off the back of her own legs. Both women came inside, as Kelly began to dish out the potato soup she'd started after breakfast. Miranda snagged a piece of hot bread. Kelly was fast with the dish towel draped over her shoulder, and slapped Miranda away from the plate.

"Go wash your hands. Land sakes, that woman."

Noeul entered the kitchen after she'd washed her own hands and caught the exchange. *I used to have that with Aggie.* She pushed the feeling aside and sat down at the table, breathing in the aromas of Kelly's extraordinary talents.

Noeul had learned to make cheese and butter from her extra goat milk, and the excess she produced supplied her friends with all they could handle. She pulled a roll apart and used a knife to slather it with real butter that melted immediately. "Mmmm."

Miranda joined them at the table. "Smells great, Kel, and from the sounds that one made, it must taste as good. I'm starving." Miranda downed a large glass of water quickly, and Kelly replaced it with a second almost immediately. They seemed to read each other's minds and functioned like a finely tuned machine, always being able to anticipate the other's movements and needs. Noeul laughed as Miranda dribbled soup down the front of her shirt.

"What can I say, you can dress her up, but you can't take her anywhere. You going to stay another night with us, hon? We'd love to have you." Kelly slathered her own bread and rolled her eyes at the first bite.

Noeul smiled. "No, I'm packing up right after lunch. Can't leave Pip and the girls too long without milking. They'd be miserable. I've got some work in the green house I need to do. I love staying with you two. Unfortunately, there's no one at home to pick up the slack when I'm gone."

Out of the corner of her eye, she caught the girls looking at each other, the look sad and pensive. Noeul knew her friends wanted her to be happy and worried about her being alone. *I don't see anything changing that anytime soon.*

***

Jordan inched along I-66, her hand fisted in her hair. She glanced at the dashboard clock with regret that she hadn't left earlier. *I should have left before six, dammit.* Rush hour traffic trying to get in and around Washington D. C., was a nightmare. Dava lived downtown so that she didn't have to commute long distances to the places she did business with. Their mother lived a few streets over and would be waiting at Dava's for Jordan's arrival, while cooking one of Jordan's favorite meals.

Jordan had called Dava twice in the last few hours to update her. She'd pulled out of the campground, outside of Knoxville TN, around eight that morning. She'd tried to wait out the rain that had fallen steadily all night. The farther north she drove, the harder the rain came down. Progress had been slow on the day's seven-hour drive. Twice, she'd been detoured around chain reaction pileups due to that same rain. The end was in sight. Unfortunately, the traffic was bumper to bumper, and she was at the point of no return. Diverting off I-66 would delay her arrival even further. Her phone rang again, and the radio automatically decreased in volume, as she used her hands-free device to answer it.

"Hey, Momma."

"How far out are you, honey? I don't want to start the rice until I know you'll be here in fifteen minutes or so. Your sister and I are so excited to see you."

"I'm on I-66 headed your way. Traffic is horribly snarled. If you guys are hungry, go ahead and start without me. I'll be there when I can."

"We'll do no such thing. I've been working on your *jida's mansaf* all day just for you. We'll wait. I need a good Jordan's hug. It's been too long."

"I agree, Mom. We started moving again, so I'm hoping it won't be much longer. I'm so tired of being behind the wheel. I need some family time and your home cooking. Think we can accomplish those things?"

"Piece of cake. Now pay attention and drive. See you soon."

"I love you, Mom. I'll be there in a bit."

Jordan disconnected the call and ran her hand through her hair again. She jammed on her brakes when a sporty BMW coupe cut her off, and she pounded the steering wheel in frustration. She let out a sigh of relief when she could finally see her exit. Fifteen minutes later, she found a parking lot about two blocks from Dava's. She hefted a duffle over her shoulder and pulled her collar up against the still-pounding rain. The lights of D.C. reflected off the blacktop, as water puddled in small ponds everywhere. A passing bus hit a particularly deep pothole, soaking Jordan from head to toe in muddy water and grit. She'd managed to block her face from the worst of it. Unfortunately, the rest of her resembled a drowned rat, as she entered the glass-fronted apartment building. One look at the doorman's face, as she dripped on the carpet, told her she looked like a vagabond seeking shelter. She sheepishly approached his desk.

"Sorry, Jordan Armstrong. Dava Armstrong's sister. I got drenched by a bus two steps before the door. Sorry about the floor." He smiled with a slight grimace and called down the elevator with the press of a button.

"So sorry about your bad luck. Ms. Armstrong asked me to call when you arrived. You can go on up. Don't worry about the floor, par for the course today. Have a good evening."

Jordan made her way to the elevator, her shoes squeaking with every step. She stepped inside and pushed the button to the fifteenth floor. The water dripped out of her hair and into her eyes. She closed them and let her head fall back against the elevator wall as she ran a cold hand over her face. The 'ding' of each floor echoed off the metal walls, letting her rest for a few minutes while she counted off fifteen bells. With great effort, she heaved herself off the railing and exited the elevator. She turned left and walked to her sister's apartment and rang the bell. Footsteps sounded from inside, and Jordan heard the locking mechanism open. The look on her mother's face was pure astonishment. Dalia Armstrong's hand covered her mouth, but the laughter escaped, nearly doubling her over.

Jordan placed her hand on her hip in protest, unable to hold back the grin from forming on her face. Dava had moved her motorized wheelchair within view and nearly ran Dalia down to get to Jordan.

"Get your ass in here, Sherlock." Dava stopped abruptly and took a good look at her sister. "And apparently straight into the shower. I know you've been living on the road, but this is ridiculous. What the hell happened to you?" The laughter infected Dava too, and all three were having trouble breathing.

Dalia stepped forward and used her hands to wipe off Jordan's face until she could kiss her cheeks without doing it through a layer of road grit.

Jordan fist bumped her sister. "A bus and a very large pot hole is what happened to me. I'll be back out in a bit." She headed to the bathroom, grateful for her waterproof duffle. After a long shower, she made her way to the modified kitchen, and stopped to properly hug and kiss Dava on her way. Jordan hauled herself up on the granite counter top and stole a carrot from her mother's cutting board. "I'm starving and that smells like heaven."

Dalia ruffled her daughter's still wet hair and kissed her on the shoulder as she stirred the last few ingredients. The *mansaf*, a traditional Jordanian dish, was Jordan's favorite food. Dalia had learned to make the creamy *jameed* sauce of fermented and dried, goat's milk yogurt from a master, her own mother.

The smells in the kitchen took Jordan right back to her childhood. She could see her mom and *jida* in the kitchen, simmering the lamb and making lime-mint juice. Her grandmother had been a beautiful woman like her mother was. Jordan was grateful to have inherited her dark hair and eyes from both of them. Dava's hair was a longer version of the same color, but she favored her father's features.

Jordan surfaced from her memories when a cold glass was pressed into her hand. The beverage had a soft, green tint, and she smiled as she brought it to her lips. The mint fragrance mixed with the lime, tugged at her heart. She leaned over to kiss her mother's temple.

"Momma, how is it you always know exactly what I need?"

Dalia placed a hand on her daughter's cheek and stroked her thumb lightly. "Because a momma always knows. Now, go set the table."

Jordan slid down from the counter and picked up the cream-colored plates with the thin, blue-lined pattern. The sisters had shopped together to furnish Dava's first apartment. It was a milestone in Dava's life, her first apartment away from her parent's home. Dava was starting her freshman year at MIT, and Jordan was overjoyed with pride.

"It's good to have you here, JJ. I've missed seeing that face." Dava distributed the silverware Jordan had deposited on the table.

Jordan stealthily watched her movements, attempting to judge if she'd lost any further motor skills. Nothing seemed different, and Jordan drew in a relieved breath.

Dava continued to move around the table in her wheelchair. "Okay, spill the beans. Tell me about this sexy bartender you met in New Orleans. Any spark there?"

"More like a slow burn. Yes, little sister, a definite attraction. Joëlle was exotically beautiful. Skin like mahogany, hair like black velvet, and eyes like golden sunlight." Jordan caught herself lost in the memory of their one and only kiss. "Definitely a spark."

Dava furrowed her eyebrows and waved the fork she held. "And?"

"And I had too much respect for her to have a one-night stand."

"You're kidding me?" Dava's tone was incredulous.

Dalia strode in with all the grace of a model, holding a serving platter in her hands. "I taught my children better than to disrespect anyone. I'm glad to see that lesson stuck."

Dalia kissed Jordan's hot cheek and motioned for her to move the trivet onto the table. "Obviously, Jordan cared for this woman, or she wouldn't have resisted the temptation. Now, tell me her name."

Jordan moved the trivet and placed her cool glass against her neck to pull the fire from her face. "Momma."

"Don't Momma me."

"Her name is Joëlle, and she's a civil engineer working on the levees in New Orleans. She was tending bar across the street from where I stayed. She took me to her grandmother's to find the clue I was looking for."

"Sounds like she was more than just a means to the end, my love." Dalia motioned for them all to move to their seats and began portioning out the mansaf.

"She was, Mom. It wasn't something I felt I could pursue, knowing I wouldn't be staying. Joëlle deserves to have someone who will treat her like the wonderful woman she is, all the time, not just once."

Jordan felt her mother's hand on her forearm and closed her eyes, knowing there was an unspoken request to look at her. Slowly, Jordan raised her eyes. Dalia cupped Jordan's chin in her soft fingers. "You deserve more than that, too. I'm glad to see the interest. There is more to life than just your research, my child. Life without love is empty, no matter what you accomplish."

Jordan knew better than to argue with her mother. Dalia had been a witness to Jordan's devastation after Tina's disclosure and had expressed her desire to unleash the wrath of a protective mother more than once. Jordan bent her head down and kissed her mother's palm. "Can we eat? I'm starved."

"We can. Know that this conversation isn't over."

Jordan caught Dava's laughing eyes and slowly raised the middle finger of her right hand. Dava nearly choked on her drink. This earned Jordan a smack on the arm and a disapproving look from her mother, who missed absolutely nothing when it came to her girls.

The comfortable apartment was filled with the sounds of conversation, as they ate and caught up. The three ate to nearly bursting. Full or not, they saved room for Jordan's favorite dessert, *hareesa*. With the texture of a dense brownie, the confection was made with a blend of almonds, *jameed*, and coconut. It had been a staple around the house when she was young, especially when her jida had come to live with them. The whole meal gave Jordan a warm feeling of being surrounded by love. She looked around the table at the most vital parts of her life, her mom and her sister. They grounded her and reminded her of all the good things she had.

The leftovers were packed away, and the dinner dishes done before the three sat around the dining room table playing *bastra* and enjoying dessert. "So, Momma, how's the foundation going?" Jordan fished a card from the board before the next play moved to Dalia.

Dalia smiled broadly. "It's been a good year so far. We're opening another playground in a few months, in Fairfax County."

Jordan and Dava's parents had established Unlimited Fun to serve a population of children with limited mobility issues. The specialized equipment made it possible for everyone to enjoy simple childhood pleasures. Hundreds of playgrounds around the United States had been designed and built using funds from the charity Dalia still ran. Jordan made sure that Cornell contributed every year, as did many of the companies Dava worked with. The swings were made so that wheelchairs could be rolled up into them, sandboxes had digging equipment that could be used from wheelchairs, and ramps were built so that children unable to climb stairs could use railings to help balance themselves or roll to the upper levels. All the equipment was painted in red, yellow, blue, and green. The bright primary colors added to the lively atmosphere each playground displayed.

"Jordan, where'd you go?" Dalia touched Jordan's arm.

Jordan smiled. "I was remembering your first park, Momma. I remember seven-year-old Dava cutting the ribbon."

Dava cleared her throat. "I remember it too, JJ. We spent the whole day swinging and climbing all over that thing. It was one of the first times I didn't feel different."

"Now you two stop, or I'll start. We all know what a leaky faucet I am." Dalia dabbed at eyes and started clearing the table.

Jordan rose and took the dessert plates from her mother. "I love you, Momma. The best things in my life always started with you." She set the plates on the counter and leaned her head against her mother's.

"You two are the best things I've ever done. You've both made me so proud." Dalia placed her hand on Jordan's face and held her close.

"Now, you two go visit. I'll clean these up. It's rare I get to do this for both my girls. Go work out your clue with Dava."

Jordan carried two cups of her mother's famous hot chocolate into the living room. Jordan sat on the plush couch and sipped at her mug. "So, still seeing that software engineer?"

Dava turned her head and rolled her eyes at her sister.

"What? You can ask me about my love life, but I can't ask about yours? That's a double standard, Watson. Nope, won't have it. Dish."

"Okay, fair's fair. Yes, Sarah and I are still seeing each other. She's incredible, although I'm not really sure what she sees in me." Dava sipped from her hot chocolate.

Jordan choked on her drink and sputtered, as she sat up trying to catch her breath. "What the hell's that about?"

"What?"

"You don't know what she sees in you?"

Dava rolled her eyes again and grinned. "Look, let's be honest. I got the brains, you got the body."

Jordan flipped her younger sister her middle finger. "I'm two points behind you, you ass."

"Two points is two points."

"Okay, okay. Knock that shit off. You're a beautiful woman, Dava, and your heart is three times bigger than that brain of yours. Sarah's a lucky woman."

Jordan watched the emotion swirl in her sister's eyes. There was much more to the relationship with her fellow technology geek than Dava was ready to analyze with her big sister. The determination to force Dava out of her comfort zone was a strong motivator for Jordan. She knew when to push and when to wait out the younger Armstrong.

"What's she been up to lately? Designing something to make the world more technology friendly?"

A twinkle gleamed in Dava's eyes. "Believe it or not, she's designing apps to help those with accessibility issues see what their options are for entertainment in relationship to their particular difficulty. She's also helping the National Park Service become more ADA compliant. Her algorithm helps identify potential areas where they can make improvements to existing access or creating new ones." Dava's grin slowly grew wider.

Jordan reached out and clasped her sister's hand. "Oh, Sis, you've got it bad. You better hold on for the ride."

Dava's voice was small and soft. "I've never met anyone like her.

She's so strong in every way. Nothing seems to matter to her about my disability. She's like you, Jordan, she sees beyond the chair."

Jordan leaned forward and kissed her sister's forehead. "What did Mom and Dad always teach us? The only limitations are the ones we put on ourselves. So, don't add love to your list of things you can't do. If she's important to you and she loves you, let her speak for herself as to what she sees. I'm betting it has nothing to do with that chair. If she's like me, she sees a dark-haired beauty with soulful eyes, an incredibly intelligent woman with quick wit, and a heart of a lioness."

Jordan held her sister tightly. Looking around the room, Jordan spotted the gift she'd bought her sister at Christmas time last year. The replica of the brass cryptex used in *The Da Vinci Code* was a tribute to her sister's skills, even though Dava had scoffed at the movie in general. Jordan smiled at its pride of place in the room. She also saw all the diplomas, accolades, and awards and knew her mother must have placed them. Dalia was devious enough to know that Dava could not take them down because they were out of reach. Their mother had spent her life telling her children to be proud of their accomplishments and not to hide their light under a basket.

A new photo caught her eye. She stood and took two steps toward the mantle and picked up a framed photo of Sarah kneeling beside Dava. Sarah was in a black tux with a rainbow-colored bow tie, a shock of turquoise right in front of her spiked blonde hair. Dava was in a black cocktail dress with a small set of pearls around her neck. Jordan brought the picture back to Dava. "Where were you guys when this was taken?"

Dava quirked a grin. "We were at an awards dinner held by *Smithsonian Magazine*, their American Ingenuity Award. We were joint winners for our work in digitizing literary works in over a hundred languages. We make it more affordable, allowing for greater accessibility for those with functional issues all around the world."

Jordan carried the picture over and knelt beside her sister. "A modern-day Martin Luther translating the Bible from Latin to German. Why didn't I know about this?"

"I might have forgotten to mention it."

"Dava! This is a big deal."

Dava sighed. "You know how I hate people making a fuss."

Jordan pointed to the picture. "This is fussworthy, Watson. I'm so proud of you." They were still in tears when their mother entered the room. "What happened? Why are you two crying, and if they're happy tears how come nobody invited me in?"

Jordan pointed her thumb toward Dava. "My little sister here has been keeping secrets, Mom."

Dalia wiped tears from both her daughter's faces with her thumbs. "Well honey, she is one of the country's foremost cryptologists. Secrets are part of her job."

"True, I'm guessing this was a secret she didn't have to keep. Did you know she and Sarah won an award together?"

Dalia's eyebrows shot up. "Dava Grace!"

Jordan watched with amusement, as her mother chastised her younger sister. "You stepped in it this time, kiddo." Dava became the five-year-old who'd been caught with her hand in the cookie jar.

"Save me, JJ."

Their mother leaned down and drew them into a hug. They'd perfected the ability to hold themselves at the right height to accept a hug from Dava long ago, and for the first time in as long as she could remember, Jordan felt like she was exactly where she was supposed to be.

"Now, about that clue, Sherlock." Dava pulled from the hug and rubbed her hands together.

Jordan tried to hide a yawn unsuccessfully. "Tomorrow, Watson, I'm beat. Tomorrow, first thing, I promise."

CJ Murphy

Chapter Nine

NOEUL BEGAN HER DAY with her chores and a quick run with Kyo. She was determined to get some work done in the greenhouse. There were a few new experiments she wanted to try with a different soil. Sandy soil was always a difficult medium to grow in, as it lacked enough organic material to supply the plant with necessary nutrients. Weeds fascinated her; they could grow anywhere, under any conditions. She'd always marveled at the way a dandelion could grow up through a crack in a concrete sidewalk. *Persistence pays off.*

Rounding out of the trees, she reached the edge of the property and slowed to a fast walk to cool down. Kyo was busy sniffing at the base of a pine tree and came away with needles stuck to her nose. "Come here, girl." She removed the sticky items from Kyo's face and fur and led her over to get a drink. As she pumped the handle up and down, Kyo happily lapped up the clean, cold water from her bowl. Noeul put her hand in and let the stream pool in her palm. She caught a drink and splashed some on her face.

Noeul dried off with the bottom of her T-shirt and walked to the pen to let everyone out for the day. Thor and Athena lazily loped out into the pasture, while her goats and lambs followed happily behind them. This was the part of life she enjoyed most, being truly present in the world she'd built. There were so many things that fulfilled her life here and that included the research that sustained her scientist's mind. She lacked almost nothing, and the one thing she did, seemed impossible to attain. *Amazing how one missing element changes everything.*

The greenhouse door creaked as it swung open and allowed the humid air to immediately wash over her in a wave of damp heat. Most of the plants she grew thrived in these conditions. Over in her test crop area, the grafted plants were doing well. It was time to take measurements on their size and condition. She also needed to evaluate the differences in the types of clamps she was using, based on stem size. Noeul wondered what she would do with all the information she gathered. *Should I publish another paper? A book? Or should I pass the research on to Cornell to allow the agriculture program to run blind tests? Let them prove or refute my methods?*

She thought of Professor Jordan Armstrong. Learning about her research was becoming more than a niggling feeling. It was more like a thirst, quenchable only by taking in more than a brief glance. A few hours later, Noeul placed her hands on the small of her back and stretched. Lost in the research, her eyes felt gritty from looking through the microscope and at the many spreadsheets that held her data. The growth she'd recorded was small yet significant. A rumble from her stomach told her it had to be near lunchtime.

"Kyo, where are you?" Noeul looked around and spotted Kyo lying in the sun on their resting rock. Rico, the one-eyed cat, was lying on the dog's tail. They both looked her way as she called out. The cat rose and arched his back. Kyo sprang off the rock and fell in beside her, as they went into the house. The clock on the wall read two in the afternoon. It was later than she'd thought. Time had little meaning; Noeul followed her own senses. *I eat when I'm hungry and sleep when I'm tired.*

Noeul put some chicken and rice in Kyo's bowl and fixed herself a small salad. Her laptop sat running a screensaver of a growing vine until she woke it and settled in on the couch to input her data. The growth tables and formulas played out from her fingers to the keys in a staccato rhythm while she chewed. The next time she looked up, it was dark and Kyo was scratching at the door.

"Damn. Sorry, Kyo." She grabbed her light jacket and walked out to put the animals in their safe enclosure for the night, while the dog made her nightly reconnaissance near the property edges. Noeul mucked out the stalls and fed everyone. She added the straw and manure to the compost and checked that the gates were closed and the electric fence was on, before she gathered a few pieces of firewood and went inside to shower.

Dressed in a faded, black, New Orleans T-shirt and plaid pajama pants, Noeul grabbed one of the latest lesfic novels she'd ordered and sat on the couch with Kyo across her feet. She fell asleep right where she was, lost in a story of passion, while her own body longed to be held and her center longed to be touched in ways she hadn't felt in many years.

***

Jordan woke to the delicious smells of bacon frying and coffee brewing. Knowing full well her mother would be puttering around in the kitchen, she sat up and swung her legs off the bed. She pulled on a Cornell hoodie and made her way to the bar. Her mother set a cup of coffee down in front of her and kissed her cheek.

"Good morning, Momma. Thanks."

Dalia was mixing blueberries into the pancake batter. "Morning, honey. How'd you sleep?"

Jordan yawned, as she brought the cup to her lips. "It took me a while to let the tension from the drive make its way out of my system. That full belly you sent me to bed with helped tremendously."

"About time you got up, sleepy head, it's after five." Dava rounded the corner, her laptop open on a table attached to her motorized chair.

"I know precisely what time it is, Watson. I wake up at the same time every day and have since the day you were born. Makes me think of you first thing, you know."

Dava's cheeks flushed. "I love you, JJ." After they'd finished breakfast, their thoughts immediately went to the task at hand.

"Okay, Sherlock, what's first?" Dava put on her eye-tracking glasses that would allow her to use her laptop with her eyes instead of her hands.

Jordan smiled, knowing the glasses allowed Dava to overcome some of the manual dexterity issues that accompanied her spina bifida. "You're such a high-tech geek, Watson. I'm guessing this first one is binary."

Dava pulled up her converter and used her eyes to type in the binary code. "Nine circles of hell."

"What?"

"Nine circles of hell. That's what the binary translates to."

Jordan shook her head. "Dante's *Divine Comedy*?" After a few seconds, Jordan had her answer. "Ah well, I was right. The nine circles of hell are part of 'The Inferno,' the first section of the poem as he goes through hell."

"What in the world would Dante's poem have to do with a bucket list? Other than the heaven part, that doesn't sound very fun. What's next?"

Jordan screwed her mouth up and repeated a set of letters to Dava. "There are three words. I-l-u-v-w D-p h-u-l-f-d-q W-u-d-q-v-o-d-w-r-u. I hope you can work your magic on that."

Less than twenty seconds later, Dava replied, "First American translator. Mean anything to you? "

Jordan shook her head in amazement. "How do you do that?"

Dava brushed her hands together. "Caesar cipher with a three shift."

"You are such a smartass, Watson."

Dava laughed and pushed at her sister. "A smartass whose services cost the government thousands of dollars per hour. Tick tock, Sherlock."

Jordan typed both the phrases they'd identified into a simple Google search. It brought up a large amount of research that would need time to weed through and narrow down the possibilities. "Let's see if the next clue gets us anything. It's something like an algebraic formula $f(x)=3+1$".

"That one seems to be an affine cipher. There's a simple mathematical equation that's used to do the conversion. The problem is in figuring out what the shift is that defines b in the equation $ax+b$. The answer to the cipher is fireside."

Jordan looked at her sister's raised eyebrow and burst out into laughter. "You talk about codes the way Mom talks about recipes. You never cease to amaze me."

Dava let her head fall back on the head rest of her wheelchair. "I'll bet when you were hiding all my stuff as a kid, you never thought it would turn into this."

Jordan reached out and clasped Dava's hand. "Baby sister, I knew the world was in for quite a ride with you. There's not a day that goes by that I don't think back on our childhood with incredible fondness. Mom and Dad gave me the best present ever the day you were born. You've challenged me and inspired me beyond my wildest imagination. Being your sister is my favorite thing ever."

Jordan admired the woman her sister had grown into. Jordan was sure Sarah felt that way too and could only hope that Dava would let the relationship grow into whatever its potential was.

"Ok, enough mush. We have a clue to decipher. What's next?" Dava turned her eyes back to the keyboard, releasing Jordan's hand.

"There is a series of dots in a grid-like pattern." Pulling from her photographic memory, Jordan drew out the series of eleven small grids and put them in front of Dava.

Dava looked the dots over and turned to her computer. "Looks like braille to me, let's check and see." Jordan's heart sang when the triumphant look spread across Dava's face. "Ok as I call out the letter, you write it down. E, I, N, H, E, I, M, I, S, C, H."

Jordan did as instructed and looked at the word in front of her. I think that's German for native. Can you confirm?" She repeated the spelling back to Dava and waited for a confirmation.

"Brilliant, Sherlock. Ok, we have the word native in German, what's next?

"The next was a series of little lines and dots." Jordan drew them out for Dava.

"Wow, this woman really did some research. Unless I miss my guess, this is the Freemason's cipher, known to Civil War confederates as a pigpen cipher. The first sets of letters are laid out in tic-tac-toe grids. S through V and W through Z are placed in X grids. You decipher by noting the sides of the grid that touch a letter. The first symbol you drew is an S, because it's in the form of wide V. Our next letter is a box missing the right side with a dot close to the left upright. That's an O. The last box is complete with a dot on the bottom line. That's an N. Put them all together and you have the word son. Tada."

Jordan's mouth fell open before forming a wide smile accompanied with a laugh. "Now I know why you scored that point higher than me. You didn't even look at your computer."

"Two points, thank you, and I don't really need the computer for most of the code. I use it to save time. The really simple code forms are stored in one of our shared gifts, our photographic memory. If I have enough of the code to determine what it is, I can almost see the letters below the code in my head." Dava looked at Jordan, her eyes glassy.

"Hey, hey. Why are you about to cry?" Jordan reached up and cupped her sister's cheek.

Dava covered Jordan's with her own. "You gave this to me, Jordan. You set me on the course to be what I am today. My love of code and puzzles comes from you. You found something that I could do almost completely with my mind. You gave me something incredibly precious, your belief in me."

Jordan pointed to Dava's head. "I didn't give you anything that didn't already exist inside you. The only thing I did was find the code to unlock it."

A sharp knock at the door drew them out of the emotional moment. Dalia answered the door, and they heard muffled voices. "It's Sarah, Dava."

Dava's face turned several shades of red, with the entrance of a blonde in worn jeans, black boots, and a white T-shirt.

"Hi, honey. Jordan, good to see you again."

Jordan stood and squeezed Sarah's shoulder. "Good to see you too, Sarah. Although, you both are in deep shit with me and Momma that you two didn't tell us about that Smithsonian award."

Sarah Reynolds looked at Dava, and together they said, "Busted."

Jordan took her seat back, as Dalia brought in a tray of glasses she placed on the small coffee table. She handed one to each of them and took a seat on the couch.

"My girls have been at it for a while. I thought they might enjoy a glass of their jida's lime-mint juice. I seem to remember you falling in love with it too, Sarah." Dalia pulled her feet up beside her.

Jordan marveled at her mother's timeless beauty. She could easily pass for the girls' older sister. Her hair was still long and as jet black as Jordan's.

"That I do, Dalia. I wish I could have met her. From everything I've heard from Dava about her grandmother, she was an incredible woman." Sarah reached out and placed a hand behind Dava's neck, stroking with her thumb.

Jordan watched the love and affection pass between the two women. Seeing someone she cared so deeply for being shown true adoration made Jordan happy on an elemental level. Still, she couldn't help herself from turning into the bratty older sister. "Want me and Mom to find something we need to do outside the apartment so you two can, uh, visit?"

Dava squinted at her and gave her the best one-fingered salute she could manage.

"Dava Grace!" Dalia scolded her youngest child and directed a withering glare at her oldest. Both girls apologized while Sarah laughed.

Dava rolled her eyes at her sister. "Can we get back to business? I thought we were deciphering some clues, if I remember correctly. Maybe you can help, Sarah."

"I'm always up for a challenge. What are we doing?"

"Jordan's trying to decipher that bucket list I was telling you about."

Sarah's eyebrows rose. "Oh, your search for Professor Scott."

"Correctamundo. We've been deciphering the latest clue Jordan found in New Orleans." Dava reset some of the programs on her computer.

"Dava told me some about your trip to the Big Easy. Very cool, Jordan. I'd love to help any way I can. What are you working on now?"

Jordan recited the clues they had to Sarah.

Sarah leaned in to look at the parts Dava had assembled in an Excel document. "Wow, they sure didn't make it easy, did they?"

Jordan shook her head at the understatement. "No fun if it isn't challenging, I know. In my case, the easier it is, the faster I find Professor Scott. That's why I came to the expert. If you want to know how to make it grow, I'm your girl. If it's in code, there's nobody better than your girlfriend, who also happens to be my favorite sister."

"I'm your only sister, genius. Now what's the next clue?" Dava was laughing at the two women sitting to the right and left of her.

"There's a series of circles and lines, some look like the Venus symbol for female." Jordan drew them out and handed them to Dava.

Dava went to work, her eyes shifting quickly right and left, up and down, moving through different tabs. "I give you the Giovani Fontana cipher. Giovani created this to encode Latin in the fifteenth century. Your clue reads *official flower is not a flower*."

Sarah's brows drew together. "Official flower of what?"

"That's part of the fifty-thousand-dollar question. Each little piece leads to the whole puzzle. The puzzle being, where I have to go to find the memorial Noeul left for Aggie." Jordan pulled her hair in frustration.

The smell of her mother's homemade pizza wafted through the room, causing Jordan's stomach to grumble. She looked into the small dining room in time to see her mother placing the large pan in the center of the table. Jordan loved her mother's need to nurture. Dalia had slipped out to cook, while they had been deciphering clues.

"Girls! Lunch. Come to the table." Dalia set down a bowl of salad and waved everyone over to the table. Sarah reached across the table and grabbed a plate for Dava, loaded it up with pizza and served her. Dalia made no comment, and Jordan tried to act as if she didn't notice. What amazed Jordan was the love in Dava's eyes as she looked at Sarah. Jordan was sure her sister had fallen harder for Sarah than she wanted to admit. She had a sneaking suspicion Sarah had no intention of letting Dava keep it a secret for long.

For the next hour, Jordan filled them all in on her adventures from Havasu Falls to New Orleans, while they devoured a second pizza and some of the salad.

Dava rolled away from the table. "Momma, I'm about to bust. I'm so full."

"I'm right with her." Sarah got up and started clearing the table. Jordan started to help when they were all shooed into the living room by Dalia.

"You all go on, figure those clues out. I'm happy to stay in my wheelhouse and do the things I'm best at, taking care of everyone. Go, go." Dalia used her hands to usher everyone out of the way.

Jordan kissed her mother. "You're a pushy broad, you know?"

"One more comment like that and I'll put you over my knee, smartass."

"Yes, Momma."

The three women went back to the living room and settled in. Sarah again sank into a seat on the black, leather couch next to Dava, and Jordan sat in the chair across from them.

"Now, where were we? Oh yeah, we decoded official flower that isn't a flower." Jordan pulled up the next code from her memory. "It's a series of dots similar to braille. It did look a little different." Jordan recreated the code and passed it over. She smiled as she watched Sarah lean in and put her arm around Dava. The blush she watched pass over her sister's face made Jordan warm inside. Sarah pointed to something on Dava's screen, and Dava shook her head up and down. They bumped knuckles, as Dava decoded the dots for Jordan. "One syllable. Bordered by one. Its number is twenty-three."

Jordan typed the variables into her laptop. "Maine!"

Sarah leaned over to see her screen. "What brought that combination together?"

"Maine is the only one syllable state. It borders only one other state, New Hampshire and—"

"It was the twenty-third state in the union." Sarah was almost bubbling over with excitement. "This is fun."

"Well done, Sherlock. You know we're going to need a name for her."

Sarah rubbed her hands together and looked like a little kid. "Oh, oh! Can I be Scully? I've had a crush on her for years!"

Jordan nearly doubled over laughing. "Scully it is, although you don't have the red hair."

"True, that. I'm sexy like Dana, right honey?" Sarah nuzzled in close to Dava's neck.

Dava kissed her and shook her head. "Sit down so we can finish this, Scully."

Sarah's arms shot up in triumph. "Ok, what's next?"

"While you two have been sucking face, I did a search with the clues we have. The common denominator is, Henry Wadsworth Longfellow. Born in Maine, he was the first American to translate

Dante's *Divine Comedy*."

Sarah was almost bouncing in her seat. "Okay, now what?"

Jordan rose and stretched. "Now, I could use a drink. Anyone want some of Jida's juice?"

"Great minds." Dalia walked into the room with glasses for everyone.

Jordan watched her mother walk past her. "Thanks, Mom."

"How about I give you guys a hand with these clues? I've got a pretty good head on my shoulders. Maybe I can show you where you two got your brains. Not that your dad didn't add a few points to the scale."

For the next twenty minutes, the four women worked through the final clues with Dalia adding the answer Cadillac Mountain, to a trivia-style question about who sees the sunrise first.

Dalia ran her hand across Jordan's back. "Honey, unless I miss my guess, you're headed to Acadia National Park. It's a huge place. Any idea of a more pinpoint location?"

Jordan closed her eyes. Each stop had been exactly like this. The clues got her to the overall location, while failing to divulge the specific site of the memorial. That was never revealed to her without help from another realm. Relaxing into her mother's touch, she let her mind settle into the feeling of strong hands running through her hair. When Dava and Jordan were young, Dalia would sing them to sleep while repeating this same gentle motion. Those wonderfully protective hands had soothed them through childhood difficulties revolving around the girls' intelligence and the stigma of gifted programs in elementary school.

Sarah sat forward and leaned her elbows on her knees. "I spent some time in Acadia, a few years ago. I was with a dive club hitting a few of the cold-water spots in October. Temperatures were in the fifties most of the time. I dove in a pretty thick wetsuit, so it wasn't too bad."

Jordan started pulling up accommodations for Acadia National Park, when an idea hit her. She couldn't control her giddiness as she typed in a search for handicapped accessibility and came up with the Bar Harbor Inn. The rumble of conversation penetrated her searches. Hearing her name, she looked up at everyone around her. "What?"

"You're mumbling to yourself, JJ. What are you smiling about?"

"I need everyone to check their schedules for the next week. I think it's time we took a family vacation." She looked directly at Sarah. "and I mean the whole family."

***

Noeul found herself drawn to the research material in Jordan's book. Miranda had sent Leo up with some mail and an apple chop cake from Kelly. Noeul had barely been able to put the book down since the minute she put it in her hands. As she lay on the couch, one hand behind her head, her eyes flowed over page after page of Professor Jordan Armstrong's research. It'd been a very long time since she'd been so engrossed, almost to an obsession, about anything. Jordan's research was extremely advanced and fell right along the track Noeul had been on when she retired. She smiled at the detailed work.

"She's brilliant, Kyo. Jordan's found a way to orchestrate growth in relationship to the available moisture or in this case, lack of it. It's like we've been working in parallel, only each in a different universe. Slightly different approaches, I'll admit. Water is her issue. Everything I'm reading says she's right on the cusp. Some of the things I've been doing here could put her over the edge toward a major breakthrough."

Noeul pulled herself up off the couch. Pots and pans came out of the cabinets, as she set about creating a lamb stew. Butchering was not one of her favorite things. With Miranda's help, she'd learned to do it when it was time. She could only keep a small flock, given her resources. Kelly had spent almost a week teaching her the finer points of cold-packing meat in a pressure canner. Her shelves were stocked with preserved foods that required no refrigeration. A jar of the lamb combined with carrots, potatoes and onions from her garden would make a satisfying meal. Once it was on slow simmer, she took Kyo out and checked on all the animals.

Noeul put them to bed, as she took the time to provide them with their evening meal and attention. Rico rubbed up against her, as she milked Pip. She squeezed and streamed milk right into his mouth. He meowed incessantly between licks of his face. "Nothing like fresh from the source, right Rico?" The cat circled her legs, until she rewarded him with a final shot before patting Pip's side. "Thank you, girl." Noeul carried the goat's milk inside and poured it into a large glass jar with a lid. "Tomorrow we'll make cheese, Kyo." She enjoyed the great purpose she found in being self-sufficient through simple tasks. Thoughts of Jordan's research began to creep their way back into her mind.

What Jordan had been able to accomplish in such a short life was truly remarkable. Everything she read about Jordan told her she was a talented professor. Her students had nothing less than high praise for her teaching ability. Noeul was fascinated that, in half the time, Jordan had taken her own most basic research and pushed the boundaries far beyond what she'd been able to do. What Jordan was on the verge of would change the world and fueled Noeul's desire to continue her own research. *What would we have been able to accomplish together, Professor?*

After filling a bowl with the thick stew, she grabbed a bottle of Miranda's home brew and settled on the couch in front of the fireplace. She found the page where she'd left off and began to read as she ate. Entranced at a particularly fascinating passage, her spoon sat poised an inch from her lips. Only when she stopped to ponder some point did she realize and place the cold bite into her mouth.

Kyo was scratching at the door, and the half-eaten bowl of stew sat on the table in front of Noeul. She shook herself from her reading trance and realized it was well past ten. Hastily, she let Kyo out for her nightly rounds. Kyo was back in a few moments time and nudging her empty bowl with her nose and a soft whine.

"Good Lord, I think Momma has lost her mind, Kyo."

Bowl in hand, she headed to the kitchen where she put the remainder of her own dinner as well as a generous helping of the stew into the bowl. Soft scratches behind Kyo's ears as she ate helped ease Noeul's guilt. The stove blazed with the wood she'd added, as she picked up Jordan's book and yawned.

"Bedtime, Kyo." The border collie jumped up on the bed and made her three circles before she settled with a huff in Noeul's direction.

"I'm sorry, girl. I've been a bit distracted. I guess I'm still a geek at heart." Noeul settled under the covers and held the book in front of her. Sleep claimed her in the middle of a page, and the book unceremoniously fell on her face, making her jump. She rubbed her eyes and placed it on the nightstand, as she reached for the switch on the lamp.

Her body was tired, and her mind was swimming in thoughts of research and a dark-haired student, turned professor. It was rare for Noeul to dream. Tonight however, was the exception. If she were honest with herself, she couldn't even swear this was a dream.

All around her, plants grew in raised beds. Vegetables of every color hung ripe on the vine, ready for picking. The fields rippled in waves of what she thought was grain. She couldn't be sure. Deep within her, something was intrinsically familiar about the plants. A noise to her right drew her attention. A rider, backlit by the sun, rode very near the planted field. Every so often, the rider would dismount and pull at the base of the plants. The person walked along, reins clutched in the right hand, leading a beautiful, black-and-white paint behind. The rider never looked in Noeul's direction. She made her way around the edge of the red-gold field, her left hand brushing through the thigh-high growth. The rider never came close to her. Eventually, she swung back into the saddle before skirting into the trees. Noeul did notice the long, lean form, as the individual rode away.

Was it possible she was watching herself as the rider? It didn't seem like it. Her ponytail was missing. To her, the person seemed much too tall to be a representation of herself. Not having seen the rider's face, she had no way to confirm or deny her suspicion, until Noeul heard a voice.

"It wasn't you."

Noeul spun in a wide circle, seeking the source of the voice. "Aggie? Where are you? I can't see you. Tell me where you are."

The voice was all around her. *"In your heart...and in your past."*

"No, no. In my dreams it's possible for you to be right here in my present. In my dreams I can touch you. You can hold me! Please, Aggie!"

Noeul's pleas were met with silence.

"Aggie, don't go!"

"Noeul, our time was too short. I know. We accomplished and experienced amazing things together, my love. I died, you didn't."

"Yes, I did! I died the second your heart stopped beating. Nothing has been the same for me. I'm empty and yes, angry at you for leaving me."

Noeul heard a sigh.

"It wasn't by choice. I would have stayed if I could have. Nothing can bring me back, my sweet Noeul. You have a choice to make in the not too distant future. Life isn't always what we planned. I never wanted you to be alone. I thought I would die of old age by your side."

Noeul dropped to her knees, grabbing handfuls of rich earth between her fingers. "You were supposed to be here."

"I was, and in a way, I still am...in your heart. Life is short, too short in my case. You, on the other hand, have years left and much to do. That rider is your future, and she walks the same path you do. Her journey brings her closer to what she's seeking, and you are part of her quest."

"Who the hell are you talking about? How am I supposed to even know who she is? I'm up here on this mountain, and the only people I ever see are Miranda and Kelly. No one knows I'm here."

"None of that will matter, your paths are moving closer together. The crossroad isn't in sight yet. Be open, that's all I ask."

"Aggie why would you ask this of me? How can you ask me to move on from you and the greatest love I've ever known?"

"Because it's time."

Noeul sat upright in bed, drenched in sweat. Her face was wet from the tears that poured liberally down her face. Kyo's warm tongue swiped at the moisture, as Noeul wrapped her arms around the dog's soft neck and cried. She cried for all the things in her life that had put her in this place and time, alone.

Hours later, Noeul got out of bed and walked to the bathroom. Eyes, with dark circles underneath them, met her in the mirror. *Well, Noeul, you look like shit.* At some point, she'd fallen asleep with her arms around Kyo. The cold water she splashed on her face braced her, while she tried to compose herself. She held onto the sides of the sink, as water ran down her jaw and dripped onto the collar of her sleep shirt. Noeul smoothed back her hair and tried to shake off the shadows from the night. Every nerve was on high alert.

Sunlight streamed through the windows, as her feet made connection with the hallway. The wood was smooth and warm from the radiant heating that ran beneath it. She let her hand brush along the tongue and grooves of the pine walls, taking in every tactile sensation. Something felt different today. It was as if an ember had sparked into a small flame within her. Noeul felt things. Things that seemed impossible yesterday. A growing feeling of hope swirled through her.

Last night's dream felt so real. I can still hear Aggie's voice, asking me to be open to possibilities not yet revealed. Noeul let Kyo outside and stood on the threshold. She pulled her eyes to the rising sun. Each day, the sun rose in the east and set in the west. These two things happened without fail. Although she was grateful for the constants in her life, she was growing restless. Noeul shook herself and concentrated on the here and now. She grabbed her journal from the end table by the couch and took it to the kitchen.

First Aggie talks to me in my waking hours, now in my dreams. She keeps talking about a change in my life. None of that seems possible, even if I wanted it. My heart is still so broken from her leaving me. How can I think about moving on when I can't get her out of my thoughts?

I'm lonely. I need to go visit Miranda and Kelly more, possibly take an overnight trip out of the area.

There's always so much work to do here, though. Pretty soon I'll need to build cold frames for kale and a few other leafy greens. The cabbage should be ready to mix the kimchi I'll can and put in the root cellar. The cabbage, ginger, and scallions are easy. I'm not sure the daikon is ready yet. That long, white winter radish is key to getting the recipe right. The smell alone takes me back to days in the kitchen with my mother. At least the lingering smell will give me happy memories for weeks.

For centuries, my ancestors buried the mixture in clay pots. I use modern safety precautions. I always make a big batch of it for the girls as an anniversary present. I swear there must be some Korean in Miranda somewhere, with as much as she loves the stuff. I also need to check on my turnips and carrots. I need to put out a second crop for the winter months, when the snow is too deep to walk down the mountain. Thor and Athena will get spoiled over the winter, down at Miranda and Kelly's. I wish I had a way to make or have hay delivered up here. The terrain makes that impossible. I need to get some things ready to take to the farmers' market, too. Haven't been there in a while. It will be good to see Mr. Anderson.

Noeul closed the journal and decided that breakfast was the first order of the day. She attacked it with gusto before slipping into a pair of worn jeans, a West Virginia T-shirt, and work boots. With Kyo at her side, she made her way through the barn to feed everyone and turn them out. Noeul's chickens left the roost with appreciative clucks and pecked around the ground. "That should keep them busy while I look for the eggs."

Once the morning chores were done, she curled up in the hammock with Professor Armstrong's book. Noeul was allowing herself an hour break before she set about planting the winter vegetables. Page after page, Professor Jordan Armstrong drew her deeper into the material with her words and thoughts. Each chapter engaged the reader in the research and Professor Armstrong's passion for solving world hunger. Noeul let the book fall to her chest, as a familiar voice called out to her.

"Ollie, Ollie oxen free!"

Noeul turned and rolled out of the hammock, a huge smile plastered on her face. "Kelly! What a great surprise!"

Kelly dismounted and stretched. "I come bearing gifts." She pulled a stack of mail and packages out of her saddlebags. "What in the hell did you order?"

Noeul looked over the stack of mail, quickly dismissing the junk and moving it to the bottom of the pile. "More books that my former student wrote and some correspondence from former colleagues. You up for some lunch? I made lamb stew last night."

Kelly rolled her eyes back in her head. "I'd kill for your lamb stew. Count me in."

The two made their way to the kitchen so that Noeul could prepare lunch. She pulled the lid off the goat butter and set it in front of Kelly with a few slices of her homemade bread. Once the stew came up to temperature, she dished out a generous helping into each bowl and slid onto a stool beside Kelly at the granite-top bar. Kelly clinked spoons with her and they both dug in.

"You know this is one of my absolute favorites?"

"That I do. I'm glad I decided to make it. After all these years, I don't know how to make just enough for myself." Noeul caught herself and bit into the bread to keep from expanding on that thought.

Kelly put her spoon down and turned to Noeul. "We aren't made to be alone, honey. I'm sorry I didn't get a chance to meet Aggie. I'm guessing this was not what she had envisioned for you." Kelly took a few breaths. "Look, Noeul, what would you have wanted her to do if you would have been the one to pass?"

Noeul's heart was aching, and so much of her world seemed to be crashing in around her. The signs were getting more apparent, all the time, that change was coming. She didn't have any idea if she was ready for that change, or if she would even recognize the signs. Her eyes were stinging, and she closed them tightly.

"Please don't cry, Noeul. I didn't come up here to badger you or to make you sad. I thought you could use a little company."

Noeul rubbed the back of her neck to relieve the tension. "You're always welcome here. It's an open invitation."

"Good, because that wife of mine is on my reserve nerve. I figured, before I said something I'd regret, a long ride up the mountain and a friendly face were a much better choice."

"I love you, Kelly. You never need a reason to visit and will always be welcome to vent about the *Looney Tunes* character you married. I'm sure by now, she's cleaned the house for you and probably has made a dozen no-bake cookies in apology."

Kelly laughed. "Probably." She shivered, "If they turn out like her last bunch, we'll have to eat them with a spoon. I have no idea how you can screw up a recipe that has so few ingredients and doesn't require you to even turn on the oven, but my wife can."

"Well, this is Miranda we're talking about, so nothing should surprise you after this long." Noeul paused for a long time. "I'm so envious of you two sometimes. I'd give anything to have Aggie screw up no-bake cookies for me." She felt Kelly's hand slide over hers, as she did her best to push the melancholy thoughts away. "How about you help me harvest some bok choy, and I'll send some back with you tonight?"

Kelly squeezed her hand. "Throw in some kohlrabi and you've got a deal."

"You drive a hard bargain. Come on, I want you back off this mountain before it gets dark. Thanks, Kelly, more than you know."

Chapter Ten

JORDAN HELPED HER MOTHER gather the luggage, while Sarah eased Dava into a companion style wheelchair they were using. The group had collectively agreed to make the trip less stressful by taking a flight to Boston and then a commuter to Bar Harbor, in comparison to a long drive from D.C. The family had flown together before and had worked out a system that was effective.

Jordan was inordinately pleased when Sarah had claimed full responsibility for helping Dava, and that her fiercely independent sister hadn't protested. One call to a medical equipment company in Bangor, and Sarah had been successful in renting some specialized equipment, including a motorized wheelchair, to help make Dava's stay more pleasant.

They had reservations at the Bar Harbor Inn for three rooms, one that was handicapped accessible for Dava. The rest of the arrangements were fluid, and Jordan left that up to the others for those decisions. Jordan was almost positive where Sarah wanted to stay, and she knew it would not be an issue with their mother. Dalia adored Sarah. *Little sister, you are going to have to let go of some of those insecurities around me and Mom. I hope you can admit that your feelings for Sarah are moving to another level.*

"You all set, Watson?" Jordan found a cart and loaded the luggage. Their rental van had a lift and was waiting for them in the lot. Sarah had called ahead to ensure that special arrangements were made for it to be on hand.

"You thought of everything, Sarah." Dava reached out for Sarah's hand.

"When was the last time we took a family vacation, and I don't mean a day trip?" Jordan asked. "It has to be five years, I'll bet."

Dava smiled up at her sister. "At least. We all went to that beach house belonging to your fellow professor...down at the Outer Banks."

"Professor Taylor thought it would be a good fit. He built that house with his son's needs in mind. Marcus is starting college next year.

What an incredible kid." Jordan squeezed Dava's shoulder, as their mother joined them.

Dalia adjusted her shoulder bag. "Need help with the luggage?"

"I think I've got it. Sarah, you two good to go?" Jordan started pushing the cart toward the automatic doors.

At Sarah's nod, they made their way out to the van and got everyone loaded. The van's ramp made it easy to get Dava in and secured for the twenty-five-minute ride to the Bar Harbor Inn on Mt. Desert Island.

Dalia was reading from her tablet about the things they could do that were accessible to all of them. Jordan drove, enjoying memories of the road trips they'd taken when her father was still alive. "Mom, do you remember playing road games whenever we traveled with Dad?"

Dalia reached over and ran her fingers through Jordan's fringe. "I do. It helped pass the time. I hear so many of my colleagues talk about their kids being buried in their electronics during their family vacations."

The Loop Road took them along the cliffs that led down to the water's edge lined with boulders and farther along, through tree-lined areas. The smell of the salt air relaxed Jordan, as she let the anxiety of her quest fade. She would be present with the people she adored and enjoy this time. Jordan was brought back out of her musings, as her mother asked her a question she didn't quite hear.

"What did you say, Mom?"

"I wonder if we can schedule one of these Dive-In theater tours. It says people with mobility issues can schedule a cruise at high tide. Apparently, there is a ramp that is more accessible during those times. I don't think we can take the chair on the boat. I think we could manage to get Dava on board. What do you think?"

Jordan caught Dava's eyes in the rearview mirror. "How about it, Watson? Want to go for a boat ride?" She watched as Sarah pulled their joined hands to her mouth and kissed Dava's knuckles.

Sarah's smile lit up her face. "Come on, honey. Live dangerously. I promise not to let you drown. I'll swim you back to shore if I have to." Sarah's enthusiasm was infectious and hard to fight.

"I'm game as long as you two don't mind doing the heavy lifting." Dava let out a contemplative sigh.

Jordan nodded her head. "Then it's settled. We'll call when we get checked in."

A few minutes later, the large, stately inn came into view. Perched high above the water, it's white and gray exterior starkly contrasted against the backdrop of azure-blue sky. Jordan wasn't sure she'd ever stayed any place as majestic. Many of the rooms faced Frenchman Bay and Porcupine Island. Frankly, it was stunning. She pulled under the tall awning to check in. Sarah walked in with her, while Dava and Dalia waited in the van.

Jordan thought Sarah might be trying to have a moment alone with her. Inside the large front doors, the entrance lobby was decorated in shades of maroon and cream and accented with small touches of white trim. Several areas were set up to relax around a large, white-faced mantel piece framing a beautiful fireplace.

"Jordan..."

Jordan watched Sarah rub her palms against her khaki shorts. "Spit it out, Sarah. What's bugging you?" Jordan checked her phone for their reservation confirmation and met Sarah eye to eye.

Sarah took a deep breath. "Jordan, would I be overstepping to ask if Dava and I can stay in the same room?"

"I'm not sure I'm the one you should be asking."

Sarah looked a bit shocked and stammered. "Do you think your mom will mind? Or Dava? Crap, maybe she won't want to. I mean..." Sarah rubbed her hand over her face. "I'm sorry, Jordan. I don't want to make you uncomfortable. I should go wait in the van."

Jordan reached up and placed her hand on Sarah's shoulder. "I'm rooting for you, Sarah, trust me. What I think you should do is trust Dava. I'm only saying you should ask my sister, not me. Mom and I want only the best for her, and as far as we're concerned, that's you. The thing is, Dava doesn't much care for us making decisions for her. Let's get the keys, and let me see if I can help you figure out where to put your luggage."

Jordan walked to the desk, where a young man with a perfect haircut and a bow tie waited for her to approach.

"Hi, reservation for Jordan Armstrong and company."

The young man typed on a keyboard while he looked at a screen in front of him. "Welcome, Ms. Armstrong, I have your reservation right here. Two kings and one wheelchair accessible room, correct?"

"Yes, that's correct."

After a few moments, he gave her some directions and told her where she could park. He handed her three keys.

"We hope your stay is enjoyable. If there is anything we can do to help, don't hesitate to call on us."

Jordan nodded, and they went back out to the van. Sarah got in and helped Dava out, as Jordan heaved the luggage onto the cart.

Jordan parked the van, while the rest went inside. She joined them a few minutes later and knelt beside her sister.

"I checked, and your motorized chair will be delivered tomorrow."

Dava's quirky grin was infectious. "I'll be fine if one of you is up to pushing me around, literally."

Jordan met Dava's eyes. "Watson, you know I love you."

Dava shook her head and laughed. "I didn't know that was in question. Thanks for the confirmation."

Jordan flipped her sister's ear. "Sarah loves you too."

Dava's eyes dropped, as her cheeks turned crimson. "I know that."

"I think you love her too, so I'm giving you the room keys to distribute. No matter what you decide, Mom and I will support you, okay?"

Dava brought her eyes back to Jordan's.

"Take a chance, Dava. I don't think you'll regret it."

Dava took a deep breath. "JJ, I will if you'll watch for your own opportunities and not be afraid to take that same chance."

Jordan pulled her sister's hands into her own. "We'll see. I have something else I'm destined to do right now. I'm not sure I'd know the right one if she walked up and introduced herself to me."

"I have faith in you, Jordan. At least keep your eyes open to the possibility."

"Come on. Mom and Sarah will think we've gotten lost." In front of their block of rooms, Jordan stopped beside Sarah and waited. *This must be Dava's decision.*

"Here's your key, Jordan." Dava paused and looked at her mother. "And here's yours, Mom." She looked up to Sarah, who stood at her shoulder. "How about we take our stuff into our room and lay down for a bit? Between the early departure time this morning and this all-day adventure, I think I'd like to rest before dinner."

Jordan looked at her mother and winked. She squeezed Sarah's shoulder as she unlocked the room and helped Dava inside. "I'm going to work some on trying to figure out where Aggie's memorial site is. How about we meet downstairs at six for dinner? Mom, will you be ok on your own for a bit?"

Jordan's mother kissed her on the cheek while she held the other with her palm. "I'll be fine. You are more like your father than you know. I love you, Dear Abby."

Dalia's wide grin told Jordan, her mother knew exactly what she'd done.

After retiring to her room, Jordan pulled out her laptop and opened the files she'd been transferring clues from her notebook into. Everything led her to Acadia. Nothing so far had pointed her to where Noeul had placed Aggie's memorial. She kept waiting for a sign, something that would give her an idea of which direction to go. *At all the other locations, something has spoken to me, caught my attention, and put me in the right place at the right time. I'll have to be patient and wait until that happens again.*

Jordan looked around her hotel room at the luxurious, king-sized bed. She was too restless to lie down. Jordan had made a reservation for the four of them to have dinner in the Reading Room there at the inn. Until it was time to go, she would see what she could dig up with research.

The hours passed quickly. The group was shown to their table looking out into Frenchman Bay. Stately yachts, with their towering masts, dotted the waterway. Off in the distance, large tourist boats ferried patrons out into the waters around Bar Harbor. Jordan allowed the buttery soft flavor of pear to flow across her tongue with hints of apple. *This chardonnay is good.* She didn't get to enjoy a good wine very often. The menu had a variety of seafood items along with lamb, beef, and chicken options. Jordan waited while her family ordered and settled on the fresh Maine lobster for herself.

Jordan ordered and handed the server her menu. She cocked her head toward her mother. "Did you know that Maine provides nearly ninety percent of the nation's lobster catch? When in Rome."

"That's why I ordered the lobster pie. Have you been able to do any more research on what you're looking for?" Dalia picked up her own glass and sipped.

"I haven't found anything else yet," Jordan unfolded her napkin across her lap. "I keep hoping I'll get inspired. All along this path, I've felt like I've been led to where I'm supposed to be. This time, nothing has pulled me to anything particular."

Sarah idly fiddled with her silverware. "Maybe you're supposed to enjoy yourself while you're here. Sometimes we can focus so hard on the end game that we miss the journey. I'll bet, if you relax, it will make itself known before you know it."

"The whole quest has a pretty strong hold on me, and I can't help think that I'm this close." Jordan held her index finger a fraction from her thumb for emphasis.

"You've always been a driven child. Both of you feed off the need to explore, to decipher and explain. I'm a proud mother of two exceptional children." Dalia reached out and took both of her children's hands in hers. "And the company you keep is as exceptional." Her gaze landed on Sarah.

Sarah pulled Dava's hand up and kissed it. Her eyes drew back to Jordan. "While we wait for our meals, what's our plan for tomorrow?"

"Well, I thought maybe we'd take in a few sites around town. Did you know that John D. Rockefeller Jr. built forty-five miles of carriage roads here? Wildwood Stables has two donated carriages that are wheelchair accessible. I thought I'd call about scheduling one for us. The Wild Gardens of Acadia have some hardpacked trails, and there's Hulls Cove Visitor Center. I definitely want us to see the sunrise at Cadillac Mountain. I checked on that boat tour Mom talked about and..." Jordan looked up to see Dava's lip quivering as she bit it. "Hey, what's wrong? You don't want to do any of those things?"

Dava leaned forward and reached for Jordan. "No, I want to do them all. This reminds me of all the vacations we used to take when we were little. Our family always did things that we could all do. I never had to sit out of anything." She looked at Sarah. "You do that for me, too. Sometimes I forget what that's like when I'm in a mixed group. Most of the time, people tend to forget I can't do everything they can, and it becomes awkward. With you two and Sarah, I never have to worry about a suggestion that wouldn't include me."

Jordan rubbed a thumb across her sister's cheek. "That's one of the reasons I was so excited the clues led to Acadia. It's one of the most accessible national parks in the system. It's not what it should be, by any means. What I will say is it's better than many. I noticed on our drive in here that the sidewalks are pretty congested. I think we can still make it if people will be reasonably accommodating. They say the population spikes in the fall when everyone comes to look at the leaves. We seem to be here at a good time."

Dalia spoke with determination. "More should be done to make all the parks accessible. I know it's not cheap, and in some places not even possible. Every effort should be made to make sure our national treasures are accessible for all. It's what your father and I fought for with the parks we helped build. Every child should know what it's like to swing."

Dava grabbed her mother's hand. "That's why you're my hero, Mom."

Dalia cupped Dava's cheek. "Trust me, it's the other way around."

"I know what you mean about the accessibility issues, Dalia. It's why I'm working with the National Park Service to make them more inclusive. There are ways that can be implemented that aren't cost prohibitive. I'm developing a rollout pathway to be able to get wheelchairs over the sand and down to the water's edge."

Jordan watched the love between her sister and the woman who was speaking about accessibility with such passion. *Sarah's so good for her.* Jordan decided she wanted to have some time to talk to Sarah alone, to make sure she knew she was always welcome wherever they were.

Their waiter approached and began serving their meals. Jordan took in a deep breath, inhaling the smell of lobster and melted butter. *Heaven on earth.*

After dinner, they retired to their rooms. Jordan wanted to make a few phone inquiries for reservations. She intended this to be a vacation they all would remember for some time. She could only hope the memorial clue would find her. Until some inspiration hit her, she planned to be mentally and physically present for every moment with her family.

***

Noeul made her way through downtown Marlington, West Virginia. She truly did live in an out-of-the-way place. Her proximity to Green Bank and the Quiet Zone kept her distant from many of the modern conveniences she'd known in New York. The trade-off was getting lost in a good book, a glass of wine in her hand, and a crackling fire nearby. Noeul did miss the ability to pick up the phone and make a call. Kelly's words kept coming back to her. If the tables had been turned, what would she have wanted for Aggie?

The little brass bell jingled when she pushed open the door to the local mercantile. Her senses were overwhelmed with the scents of vanilla, coffee, apple, and cinnamon. Just inside the door sat a display of homemade soy candles. Noeul browsed the labels, picking up one occasionally to remove the lid and inhale. She chose one that smelled of vanilla and toffee, and carried it with her through the store as she browsed. It was Kelly and Miranda's anniversary and she was on a mission to find them something useful that they didn't already have or something that needed replacing. They weren't much for having a lot of material things. What they did have was of the highest craftsmanship and purpose. In the corner of the store stood a selection of fireplace tools made by a local blacksmith. A set of black, wrought iron tongs, with poker and shovel, caught her eye. They would be perfect.

Charlotte, the store owner, was minding the register. "Well hello, stranger, nice to see you. What brings you out of the clouds?"

Noeul's face heated at Charlotte's teasing. "An anniversary gift actually. I was looking at that handcrafted set of fireplace irons. Can you wrap them for me?"

"Sure, I can. They are a heavy-duty set, should last a lifetime." Charlotte wrapped the candle up in paper to protect it and went to retrieve the tools.

"How's life up there?"

"Really good now that summer's here. Cold and windy in the winter, near perfect in spring, summer, and fall." Noeul handed Charlotte the cash.

"Problem is that, around here, those three seasons are each about a week long. Not sure how you stand being cooped up in that house all alone for those long days and nights." Charlotte shook her head. "To each their own." She went about boxing the irons and wrapping them for Noeul.

"It's not as hard as you'd think. I keep busy with the animals and some research projects. Sometimes, it's nice to sit and watch the sunset in complete silence."

"I can understand. I remember several of the guys that built your home said it was unlike any place they'd ever seen. Anything else I can get for you while you're down here among the lowlanders?"

"Not that I can think of. Thanks, Charlotte."

"Are you free for dinner? They opened a new Mexican restaurant down the street."

The words of rejection sat on the end of Noeul's tongue, as they had all the times before. Charlotte was nice enough, and her offer was sincere. "Thanks, I appreciate it. I need to get back."

Charlotte handed over her change. "I think I'd fall over if you ever said yes. Can't blame a gal for trying."

Noeul's cheeks heated. "I'm sorry, Charlotte."

"No need to be sorry, honey, I'm teasing. Stop in the next time you're in town. "

Noeul gave her a genuine smile and picked up her packages. "I always do."

She loaded everything in her truck and headed toward Green Bank. She wanted to be back to the girls for dinner. She had a bit more research to do. Jordan's theories were right on track with Noeul's own research. Noeul had even used some of what she'd recently gleaned in her own experiments, with very promising results. Several more publications were on order, and Noeul felt a sense of excitement and discovery. For a very long time, her research had only been about how to become self-sustaining in her own little microclimate. Lately, with the addition of Jordan's research, she was feeling accomplished and at the cusp of something. Noeul found it easy to imagine working alongside Jordan, and she'd caught herself, more than once, having a one-sided conversation with her. The miles of dusty blacktop rolled beneath the truck tires, and soon she was back at Kelly and Miranda's.

Kelly was stirring a large pot on the stove. "Good, you're back in time for dinner. I made Miranda's favorite cake. She and Kyo are checking on the horses. They should be back soon. How was your trip?"

"Fruitful. I picked up a few things I needed and stopped in at Charlotte's store in Marlington." Noeul popped a strip of yellow pepper in her mouth and chewed through the crisp skin.

"And did Charlotte hit on you like normal?"

Noeul sighed. "Like always. She asked me to dinner. Luckily my dance card was already punched for dinner with you two."

Kelly laughed and pulled the bread from the oven with a potholder and set it on a cooling rack. "Saved by us again, huh?"

Noeul closed her eyes and snickered. "Seems so."

They heard Miranda's rhythmic footsteps crunching on the gravel and Kyo's lighthearted yips. A few scratches at the door, and Kyo pushed her nose inside, tongue lolling out the side of her mouth.

"Go get a drink, girl." Noeul pointed to the water bowl her friends kept by the door. Kyo's nails tic-tacked across the hardwood floor. About every third gulp, she would look up and pant. For all the world, she appeared to be smiling, as water dripped from her jowls.

Miranda pushed through the door and kissed Kelly. On her way by, she grabbed a piece of carrot and pulled her sweaty T-shirt over her head, leaving her standing in her sports bra. Kelly threw her a towel and pointed to the bathroom.

"Welcome home, stranger. Someday I'm going to beat that dog back here. For now, I'm going to go get less covered in ick so we can eat. That meatloaf smells wonderful. Is that French onion soup I detect too?"

"Well, it is our anniversary, dear. If you don't get showered, Noeul and I are going to eat it all by ourselves. I love you, but go." Kelly pushed Miranda away and again pointed her toward the bathroom.

"See that, Noeul, for better or worse, just not smelly and gross. I'll be right back. Don't eat my soup!"

"I love being around you two."

"We love having you. Can you set the table?" Kelly ladled the soup into bowls, added hunks of the homemade bread, and laid large pieces of mozzarella cheese over top before slipping the bowls into the oven.

Noeul put out the plates and silverware. She pulled the bag of lamb and vegetables out of the fridge to fill Kyo's bowl, before washing her hands and opening the wine.

Within minutes, a freshly showered Miranda swept back into the kitchen and kissed the top of Noeul's head as she passed on her way to her seat. "I'm starving."

"Good thing, because we have enough food for an army. I made three more of these ahead of our incoming guests. We can quickly pop one back in the oven for our first meal together." Kelly set the meatloaf down in the middle of the table and pulled out the soup bowls from the oven.

The small, quaint kitchen, the comfortable conversation, the clinking of silverware against the stoneware plates and bowls allowed Noeul to relax into the warmth of her family of choice. She felt warm and content.

"Charlotte hit on Noeul again."

Miranda raised an eyebrow and ran her hand over the long, gray braid that lay across her shoulder. "Do tell."

Noeul rolled her eyes. "There's nothing to tell. It was an invitation for dinner. I declined, because I was committed to dinner with you guys."

"Yeah, that's your only reason, huh?" Miranda raised an eyebrow and displayed her crooked grin.

"Don't quit your day job, detective. You know I don't want anything with Charlotte. No matter how many times she asks, I'm not having dinner with her. Not a week from now or a year from now. I'm not interested."

Kelly pointed her finger, wagging it between the two. "Okay, okay you two. Don't go spatting on my anniversary. Leave room for cake."

They ate and talked about the incoming guests and Noeul's plans for the next few days. She was going to be trying a few new things in her greenhouse.

"I have a gift for you two. I'll be right back." Noeul went out to the truck to retrieve the present. Miranda held the door open, as Noeul carried in the gift-wrapped tools and a jar of the kimchi she'd canned. She placed them on the counter. "Happy anniversary. I have more kimchi for you. This is just a sample."

Kelly tore through the paper and opened the box. Miranda pulled out the tongs. "These are beautiful. Heavy duty, too." Miranda opened and closed the jaws of the tongs. "And you know how much I love that kimchi."

"Thank you, honey. You didn't have to get us anything. Your company is enough." Kelly wrapped Noeul up in her arms.

Noeul melted into the hug. "I don't know many people who have been as happily married as you two, for so long. I saw these and thought they'd be perfect."

"They certainly are. These puppies will come in handy this winter. Thanks, Noeul." Miranda gave her a sloppy kiss on the side of her cheek.

"Okay, okay. Let's get this kitchen cleaned up. I need to do some research before I head back up the mountain tomorrow."

Hours later, Noeul finally fell into bed, her head full of as many questions as the searches she'd run about Jordan Armstrong. She knew there were ways to contact her, but she wasn't sure she was ready to make that kind of leap. In the morning, she'd go home and try some of the techniques she'd uncovered. *Maybe, if I can work through some of the variables...*Sleep claimed her, but it wasn't restful, even with Kyo curled up at her feet.

The following morning, She'd started the coffee and was mixing up pancake batter, when Noeul beat Kelly into the kitchen.the sound of loose slippers flapping against the hardwood floor drew her attention to the doorway. Kelly yawned and wrapped her robe around herself tighter. Noeul put a hot cup of coffee in her friend's hand, kissing her on the cheek. "Morning, Kel."

A big yawn escaped Kelly. She grunted a good morning and cupped the coffee between her hands as she sat at the bar.

"Rough night?"

Kelly rubbed her eyes and sipped at the coffee. "Weird ass dream."

Noeul loosened the cap on the pure maple syrup bottle. She licked a small drip off her thumb and furrowed her brow. "What kind of dream?"

Kelly shivered and took another sip. "Miranda and I were scuba diving, only it wasn't near some tropical island. It was like we were swimming in the arctic. All I could see were these damn icebergs floating by, in the shape of giant fish. No more pickled cauliflower before bed."

Noeul put her hand up to her mouth, trying desperately not to spit coffee out her nose. "Oh my God, Kelly, don't say things like that as I take a drink." Shaking her head, she took another sip, contemplating a memory. "Aggie and I went scuba diving quite a bit. When we were doing a few of her bucket-list stops, we took advantage of some pretty spectacular dives. Our last dive was when she led me on a hunt with a crazy set of clues that ranged from Dante's *Divine Comedy* to the fireside poet, Longfellow. In the end, we were headed to Acadia National Park." Noeul turned on the stove and slid the griddle into place.

"Seems like Aggie had the soul of an adventurer."

Noeul smiled at that thought. "She did. It was hard finishing out our bucket list without her." Noeul dribbled a small amount of batter on the cast iron griddle to test the temperature. She watched it sizzle and turn golden brown. Scraping it off, she poured out three silver-dollar-size pancakes.

"Bucket list?"

"Have I never told you this story?" Noeul furrowed her brow, as she ran her spatula around the edges of the pancakes.

The sound of shuffling feet behind them drew their attention. Kelly rose and poured a cup of coffee for a sleep-disheveled Miranda and placed it in her hands as she entered the kitchen mid yawn. Noeul smiled, as Kelly kissed Miranda and smoothed down the bedhead her partner sported. "You mentioned you and Aggie traveled. I'm trying to remember if I've ever heard you mention a bucket list."

Yawning through her words, Miranda entered the conversation, "Whaaa bucket list?"

Noeul stacked the pancakes on a warm plate in the oven until she had enough for everyone. Kelly started the bacon on the burner beside her. Kelly's bacon was legendary, because she took the time to turn it and focused on nothing else during the process. Noeul poured more batter onto the griddle and answered the question at hand.

"We'd been together for a year or so, when Aggie started making this list of places she wanted us to visit. Sort of a bucket list. For each place, she made up these coded clues that she assembled into a sort of treasure hunt. I used to laugh at the amount of research she did for those things, which in turn, meant I had to do a bunch of research to figure them out. That woman had everything from pictograms to Morse code. Sometimes she would find these obscure hieroglyphics, and other times it would be a series of trivia clues. Thank God for Google. It was how we'd spend our quiet time. I'd have a whole year to solve a clue and figure out where we were going. A few times, she had to help when we would get too close to the time we were supposed to leave."

Three more pancakes were placed in the oven, while Kelly meticulously turned the bacon. Miranda sat with her hands cupped around her coffee, eyes glued to Noeul.

"And?"

"The destinations were mostly in national parks. Some of them were well known, others were different places she wanted us to visit near the park. We hiked down to Havasu Falls and swam in the most gorgeous turquoise water. I've never seen anything like it. It was spiritual in a completely different way. Sadly, we didn't make it to very many before she died."

Kelly finished the bacon and Miranda set the table, while Noeul pulled the warm plate out of the oven and set it on a trivet in the middle of the table. She took her customary seat and watched as Kelly put the bacon down and refilled everyone's coffee.

Miranda filled her plate and poured maple syrup over the stack. "Where else did you guys go?"

Noeul bit into a piece of the crisp bacon, allowing a few moments to collect herself. It wasn't that she couldn't talk about the journey. She was actually finding it cathartic. The hesitancy came from thinking about the incredible places she'd visited alone, wishing she was visiting them with more than Aggie's ashes. "One time, there was this whole set of clues that led us down to New Orleans. Aggie loved the music. And the food, I swear I gained ten pounds while we were there." Noeul realized she hadn't taken a bite in some time and her friends were quiet.

Kelly reached across the table and placed her hand on Noeul's forearm. "It sounds like you and Aggie attacked life with gusto."

Noeul looked at her friends with affection. "I know. It feels strange. I have so many amazing memories I made with Aggie and having her talk to me lately has put me in a bit of a spin. It's like I'm being flooded with her presence. She's been telling me something's coming, and I can feel it too. I just don't know what it is."

Miranda poured more syrup on her pancakes and shrugged off the stern look from Kelly. "Whatever it is, it's time for you to do more than just sit on that mountain and talk with your flock. Time for you to live in the here and now. I can't pinpoint when your life will take a different path, I only want you to not discount it."

"Honey, we're always here for you. I want you to know that if you ever need to get away for a bit, Leo could take care of the animals. For that matter, Miranda and I will go up, and Leo can take care of this place like he does when we come stay with you. I want you to know you have options. Whatever you need, we're here for you." Kelly rose and began clearing the breakfast dishes.

"I can't say what I'm going to do." Noeul picked up her napkin and wiped a dribble of syrup off Miranda's chin. "but I'm eternally grateful to have both of you as part of whatever comes next."

Chapter Eleven

THE SUN WAS SHINING brightly overhead, as a soft breeze blew strands of Jordan's hair into her eyes, reminding her she really needed a haircut. The day was positively gorgeous. Her arm rested on the side of the carriage, and the clip-clop cadence of horseshoes against the packed gravel path soothed Jordan into a peaceful lull. Her mother sat beside her. Dalia's hair lay intricately braided across her shoulder.

Jordan loved the way her mother's eyes glinted with mischief and small lines formed at the corners as she smiled. It pleased Jordan to no end that a donation of two special carriages allowed her sister and others like her to enjoy a ride under the trees that lined the sides of the carriage roads. They'd been able to maneuver the companion chair into the carriage easily.

Dava sat beside Sarah, their hands folded together. Their guide, Ross, was originally from Ohio and regaled them with many facts and stories about the creation of the carriage roads, the park, and the surrounding area. *Such a simple thing. I haven't had this much fun in forever. No worries about clues, quests, or anything beyond this perfect moment.*

Jordan tilted her head and smiled over at her sister. "You having fun, Dava?"

Dava's smile could light up a stormy day. "It's wonderful! More people with accessibility issues need to know about this."

Joy spread through Jordan's chest like warm honey. "I'm pretty sure we know someone," she raised her eyebrows and tilted her head toward their mother, "who's pretty good at getting the word out."

Dava rubbed her hands together. "Mom, do you think we could find a way to do something like this over at the Fairfax Park? It wouldn't have to be as long as this one, by any means. It would be wonderful for kids to have a chance to ride in a carriage made to accommodate their chairs. That would be something we've never done."

Dalia's eyes glinted with delight. "I was thinking the same thing. I even think we could contact someone like Anheuser Busch to see if it would be something they could help with. I'll make some calls."

Jordan hugged her mother. "And that's why you are such a rock star, Mom."

For the rest of the day, the group went to some of the visitor centers, including the Abbe Museum. Dalia and James had made it a point for their young girls to learn about other cultures, and both had been fascinated with Native American history. This museum was all about the Wabanaki. The People of the First Light referred to their area as Dawnland.

Jordan watched as Dava touched a soapstone carving in the shape of a turtle hanging from a leather necklace. "Turtles have always been your favorite. It's gorgeous."

Dava let a slight grin escape her lips. "That's because I've always felt like a turtle on its back when I'm out of my chair. Not able to do a damn thing until someone takes pity on me and helps me out."

Sarah knelt before Dava and looked at her with a serious expression. "You are the most resourceful person I know, in or out of that chair."

Jordan nearly cried when Dava reached out and placed a hand on Sarah's cheek.

"That's because you love me."

Sarah let her most brilliant smile shine through, as she turned and kissed Dava's palm. "That is true, with all my heart."

Jordan and Dalia watched Dava move on to another exhibit, while Sarah picked up the soapstone turtle and took it to the counter. Moments later, Dalia drew a hand to her mouth as Sarah walked up from behind and placed the gift around Dava's neck.

"Sarah's so good for her. I don't want Dava to push her away for fear of tying her down. Sarah is deeply in love with her."

Jordan drew her mother in tight with an arm around her shoulder. "I don't think my sister could run her off with a cattle prod. Don't worry so much. Dava is the smartest person I know. She doesn't make stupid mistakes."

Later that night, they were enjoying the sounds of the harbor. The water splashing against the boats and the crisp snapping of sails in the breeze were a perfect accompaniment to the end of the day. Dava had to take a call and moved off to the side. When she came back, Jordan could tell there was an issue.

"Hey, I've got a mess brewing out at one of my small companies on the west coast. We're working through some server trouble, and I have a bad feeling they've been hacked. I may have to spend tomorrow on the computer helping them. I know we're on vacation, and I'm sorry. This is a start-up company of a friend. I can't let this happen to them."

"And it pisses you off, admit it." Jordan had a smirk on her face.

"Hell yes, it pisses me off. Especially since everything I'm hearing is that the situation was totally preventable. Introduced by a foreign thumb drive that hadn't been scanned. Follow the policy and it doesn't happen. One of the new employees went to a trade show and got it as a freebie." Dava sighed. "I know we were excited about going to Cadillac Mountain. If I can get this straightened out, maybe we can go later in the day. Until that happens, how about you three do something I wouldn't be able to."

Jordan drew her brows together in protest and crossed her arms.

Dava reached up and tugged Jordan's hand. "I'm not kidding, Sherlock. I'm ok with you guys doing something without me. I need to take care of this. I won't be slighted because you did. It'll be like all those years you worked in the national parks and sent me pictures. I can live a little through you guys."

Jordan turned and looked to Dalia. "Mom, what would you like to do?"

Dalia held up her phone. "Sadly, I got a notice that I have an emergency board meeting. I can do it by teleconference. There is an issue with the site over in Prince Georges County. I want to get that cleared up before the equipment installation gets derailed. It's on schedule for two weeks from now, and the grand opening is in a month."

Jordan's hands went to her hips. She was used to things going off the rails. Learning to roll with the punches had become second nature. "Well Sarah, do you have some urgent, unexpected meeting that will keep you holed up in your room, or are you willing to ride shotgun on a yet unknown adventure?"

The wide grin that came across Sarah's face said she was more than up for the challenge. "I'm amazed these two are willing to leave us to our own devices. Who knows what mayhem we can manage to get into without our handlers?"

"Mom, I'm not so sure it's a good idea to let these two out of our sight. How much cash do you have ready for bail money?" Dava's laugh was infectious, as they headed for the van.

Dalia crossed her arms over her chest. "I do not expect to have to visit either one of you in a police station or an emergency room. Do I make myself clear?"

Jordan and Sarah looked at each other and shrugged. Jordan raised a finger.

"I'm not kidding, Jordan Moriah Armstrong. Do I need to make myself any clearer? I've bandaged up enough of your mishaps."

Sarah tried to smother a laugh by coughing when Dalia turned her steel gray eyes on her. Jordan burst out in a deep belly laugh, and Dalia cracked a smile. They pulled into the hotel, and within minutes were standing in the hallway outside their rooms.

Dalia pulled Jordan into a hug and kissed her cheek. "I'll see you for breakfast before we spread out to the wind. Sleep well."

Jordan decided to look back over the clues that had led her to Acadia. *Maybe I'm missing something.* Carefully, she went back over each clue and the coding of it. She hadn't missed anything. The clues had brought her to Acadia, however the memorial was still concealed. She'd received no message from the world beyond, as yet. *This can't be the end of it.* If it was, why would all the other memorials have been revealed to her? She closed the leather-bound notebook full of clues and observations and rubbed her eyes. Sleep might be hard to come by. If it came, she hoped that it would offer guidance if not rest.

***

The next morning, Jordan met her family for breakfast. She and Sarah decided they might take a bike ride around Eagle Lake. Riding was one of the things she'd missed during her quest. Back in Ithaca, it was her main form of transportation and a prime source of her mental wellbeing. After agreeing to check back with Dava and Dalia around three in the afternoon, Jordan and Sarah took the van and headed to the Bar Harbor Bicycle Shop.

Jordan watched something she couldn't identify cross Sarah's face. It seemed she was deep in thought, chewing absently on her cheek. It was something Jordan had seen her do when she was contemplating something she needed to come to terms with.

"Penny for them." Jordan watched Sarah startle a bit. She smiled sheepishly at Jordan, while she ran her hand across her short spiky hair.

"Do you..." Sarah stopped.

"Sarah, there is nothing you could say to me that would make me upset unless you were thinking about breaking my sister's heart. Take a chance."

Sarah took a deep breath and blew it out between pursed lips. "I want to ask Dava to marry me."

Jordan's grin eclipsed her face. She pulled the van to the side of the road at a beautiful overlook and reached across the console to place a steadying hand on Sarah's shoulder. "Let's step outside and I'll play devil's advocate. Or in this case, let me play my sister and the myriad of things she is going to say to you."

Sarah laughed and unbuckled her seatbelt. They stepped out and found a place to sit overlooking the harbor as water rolled into the rocks.

Jordan started the dialogue. "I don't want to become a burden to you."

Sarah sat up a little straighter and squared her shoulders. "We've been dating over a year, and not for one second have I felt burdened. If I've learned anything dating you, it's that you know full well how to take care of yourself."

"I'll get sick and end up being a big burden."

"And we'll go to the doctor and you'll get well."

"I'll hold you back from doing things you want to do."

Sarah narrowed her eyes at Jordan. "Like what? I've never felt like I've been cheated out of anything, unless it's more time with you."

Jordan chuckled. "Nice one. That will earn you a slap on the shoulder, just saying. Okay, back to it. We've never lived together on a day-to-day basis. My life requires a lot of adaptation."

"Everyone's life requires some adaptation. I'm allergic to bees, so I carry an EpiPen. You aren't an invalid, and I have no intention of treating you like one. You will be my wife, not my obligation."

"I might become an invalid, Sarah. My condition won't get better. Over time, I'll have more issues. How will you cope with that?" Jordan knew these questions were hitting Sarah hard. She also knew that Dava would throw every one of these at her and probably some she wouldn't think of. Sarah had to have responses that would show Dava she understood exactly what she was getting into.

"And tomorrow I might get sick too. We're human with all the fallibilities that entails. Becoming sick or dying is a when not an if, Dava. If the roles were reversed would you walk away from me? Would this be a consideration in your mind, or would you stand here resolute in the love you have for me? Isn't that what it means when you vow to love, honor, and cherish, in sickness and in health?"

Jordan watched as Sarah's eyes flashed. *Oh, little sister, you are so wrong if you think you can scare her away.* Jordan drew Sarah in and held her, allowing her to let the tears flow and wash away the fear of rejection. She held her there for a long time until Jordan could tell the butch in Sarah needed to pull herself together. "You alright?"

Sarah's fierce determination quickly returned. She shook her hands and pulled at her shirt front as if to dispel heat. "I am. Hit me with the next one. I know my girl, and this isn't all she's worried about. You know it and I know it."

"No, you're right. Okay. Ready?" Jordan waited for Sarah to shake off the release and gird herself with her truth. "What if, over time, you get tired of making love with someone who's handicapped?" Jordan looked at Sarah and screwed up her face. "I know this is personal so you don't have to answer that for me. Actually, thinking about my little sister having sex weirds me out. I'm sure she's going to hit you with it, so you'd better have an answer."

The crimson blush reached well into Sarah's blond scalp. She coughed and tried not to laugh. "Jordan, all I'm going to say is that we have that part worked out. Your sister..."

Jordan put one finger in her ear and the other over Sarah's mouth. "La, la, la...Just keep that answer ready. Dava needs to know that one, I don't. I have no doubt you two can figure something out, or already have." Jordan shook herself and laughed with Sarah. "Next question. What about kids? You're great with them, and I know you want them. That's not possible for me after my surgery." Dava had developed severe endometriosis in her early twenties, requiring a complete hysterectomy. Jordan had sat with her through hours of painful flare-ups and doctor's visits before the last resort had been necessary.

"Dava, do you know how many amazing kids with special needs are out there waiting for good homes? With all that we know and your incredible mother and sister, you think we couldn't open our home to one or more of them? You and I would give our child every advantage when it came to living up to their potential. I think Dalia wants grandchildren, and both of her daughters are fully capable of making that happen. I happen to think we are ready for the challenge sooner than Jordan is."

Jordan couldn't hold back her smile. Sarah was exactly what her sister needed, and if she didn't say yes, Jordan would lock her wheels until she saw reason. "Let me be the first to say, I'd be honored to have you as my sister-in-law."

Sarah walked back to the van and pulled out her backpack. She motioned Jordan to come over and opened a navy-blue velvet box. Inside sat a gorgeous diamond ring.

"Wow, that's beautiful." Jordan gently touched a finger to the stone.

"It was my grandmother's. My mom loves Dava and has been giving me the stink eye for three months over asking her. I kept waiting for the right time. I think...I think I was waiting for this time. To be here when I did it."

Jordan's grin grew even wider. "When are you going to ask?"

Sarah looked at the ground and tilted her head to the side. "I've been looking online. I really like what I see about Jordan Pond House. I thought maybe we'd stop by there today and scope it out. If it feels right, make reservations for all of us tomorrow evening for dinner. I'd like you guys to be there. What do you think?"

Jordan drew her friend, and hopefully soon-to-be sister-in-law, into a hug. "I think my mom will be ecstatic to see one of her daughters tie the knot. I'll be there to pelt you with bird seed after you say I do. Now, how about we go for that bike ride? You call the Pond House. I'll get us to the rental shop."

***

Noeul brushed Athena down and filled the water buckets for both horses. It was lunchtime before she got back home, and she hadn't taken the time to eat yet. She hauled another pail of milk to the house. She'd probably gone off the mountain more in the last month than she had in years. Several things were driving her—her need to be with Kelly and Miranda, her conversations with Aggie, and her near obsession with Jordan Armstrong's research.

Noeul looked at the black-and-white dog lying at the edge of the kitchen. "I've got way too much milk, Kyo, which means you and Rico get a little extra dairy for the next few days. Time to make some soap and cheese. Maybe even some yogurt." She'd learned a variety of uses for the milk she didn't use and kept Miranda and Kelly in handcrafted goat's milk soap and lotion they were able to use in their rental cabins and as gift merchandise. The girls collected a variety of jars and small bottles to put the lotion in, and for the cakes of soap, Noeul ordered small, canvas, drawstring bags. It gave her something to do.

"Now, let's see about something to eat." She opened the

refrigerator and pulled out the hardboiled eggs she'd made before she went down the mountain. "How about an egg salad sandwich and a green salad? For me, I mean. Sorry girl, you and eggs make for a noxious cloud." Kyo wagged her tail. *This is what my life has become, talking to my two friends. One's a dog...and the other's a ghost.*

Once she'd finished lunch, she poured two quarts of the bounty from her goats into a sauce pan to heat and gathered her lemon juice. Because her milk was unpasteurized, the cheese she made would have to sit for at least two months to make sure it was safe. Being up on the mountain alone meant you didn't cut corners. Help, if you were sick, was too far away. For the lotion and soap, she'd melt emulsifying wax and add a variety of essential oils for fragrance or other beneficial properties.

A few hours later, she'd cleaned everything up and parked herself in her Adirondack chair in the sun with a glass of wine. She pulled the leather-bound journal into her lap and began to write.

There are days when I can't find enough things to keep me busy. Yes, I have my research and my hobbies. Unfortunately, you can only eat so much goat cheese and I've got an ocean of lotion. Kyo is my constant companion.

Rico jumped up in her lap in need of a soft place to rest. Noeul stretched out her legs, propped them up on a stool, and let him lay, paws up, on her shins. After a few chin scratches she went back to the journaling.

Rico felt a bit slighted at that comment. He's here with me too.

It's been years since I've climbed into bed beside another human being. My animals are great cuddlers. I'm still human, and I'm lonely. I haven't felt this lonely since the first few years after Aggie's death, even while I completed our bucket list.

Kelly and Miranda do all they can to keep my spirits up. I know that even they can see the restlessness.

And then there's Aggie. All those years ago we committed to each other and spoke those famous words...til death do us part. Well, that came way too soon for what we had planned. I built this house as a tribute to her and the great love we'd shared. I want for nothing materially, Aggie made damn sure of that.

Noeul took a satisfying drink from her wine, then placed it back on the ground. She held her face to the sun, absorbing the warmth, and began to write again.

The strange thing is that everything I've worked for doesn't seem like it's enough anymore. My research fulfills me to an extent. What am I doing with it? Experimentation for the sake of activity is one thing. If I don't share the knowledge, is my effort wasted? I keep reading Jordan Armstrong's goal to eradicate hunger. A worthy goal. I've read her published materials. It's stunning work and she's going to make history. I keep thinking, what if I'd stayed? It's obvious she's built on what research I left behind. She even mentions it was her inspiration. What if I'd still been teaching as she made her breakthroughs? Would we have the answers? Maybe. And maybe it's an old woman's musings. What if Aggie hadn't died, would we still be here, or would we be traveling the world on some crazy bucket-list item?

I'm back to Aggie, the woman I've loved for longer than I can remember. Physically, she's gone, and I'd come to accept that. Suddenly, she starts showing up, telling me change is coming. What change? Is it anything I have a choice about?

I have more questions than I have answers. Aggie tells me there is an opportunity coming, a seeker. Who and what do they want? Questions. More questions. Didn't I just say I was restless? Well, I certainly am. That I can fix with work. Loneliness is a totally different animal, and I have no idea what to do about that.

* * *

Jordan and Sarah biked around the Eagle Lake trail and found themselves having popovers with blueberry jam at the Pond House. It was a spectacular spot for what Sarah had planned. They could have dinner overlooking Jordan Pond and relax around the beautiful scenery. Jordan licked jam off her thumb and watched Sarah try to stifle a laugh. "Hey, they're good. If you aren't wearing it, you didn't put enough on." Jordan stopped and wiped her hands and mouth with her napkin. "So, what's your plan? Talk it out with me."

"God, Jordan. I'm as nervous as a technology virgin with a fried hard drive. I'm trying to find the right words. I know we practiced all those things, and I'm appreciative. What do I do if she still says no?" Sarah buried her face in her hands and rested her elbows on her knees.

Jordan took a deep breath and a long drink of iced tea. She looked out at the beauty of the calm water surrounded by lush vegetation rippling in the light breeze. Jordan wanted astute words of wisdom to miraculously form in her head. She couldn't imagine Dava saying no. It was more than evident to her how much Dava loved Sarah, and she had no doubts about Sarah's feelings. What she couldn't shake was what had happened in her own life. Jordan had been so sure about Tina's answer when she'd held that diamond ring up to her. It had never crossed Jordan's mind that Tina wouldn't say yes. She thought about why Tina hadn't been able to. None of that was present here. There was no baggage from the past holding them apart, only Dava's self-doubt about her ability as a lifetime partner. Jordan knew her sister better than anyone on this earth, even more than their mother. Jordan and Dava were more than sisters, they were best friends.

"Sarah, you love Dava. You love her like a partner should. You see beyond the steel, rubber, and wires that surround her. Some see her wheelchair as an anchor. The truth is, it's no different than my Jeep that transports me from point A to point B. The difference with Dava is that she must have it to move from point A.1 to A.2. Once people can see the real Dava, the chair fades. Her wheelchair has helped her travel in a world that, a hundred years ago, would have written off one of the most outstanding minds I've ever known. She's smarter than both of us put together, and that far outweighs the limitations of the body she was born with. She needs you, Sarah, and you need her. It's that simple. You'll never know the answer until you ask the question, my friend. I don't see a coward sitting here beside me." Jordan picked up her tea and finished it.

Sarah looked at Jordan for a long time and let a wide grin form below mischievous eyes. "Let's get these bikes loaded and go check out a few more things before we go back. Dava sent me a text saying she's still deep into the servers at TechFuture1. She thinks she'll be done by our reservation time."

"Sounds good. Mom is elbow deep in the new tell-all book about our former train wreck of a president's impeachment and subsequent federal indictment. It was written by a member of the prosecution team, the retired Lt. Col. Bishop, who's also one of her board members for the foundation."

"Thank God for Robert Mueller and his investigation. I've met Colonel Bishop. I watched her play in the wheelchair basketball tournament your mom organized to raise funds. She's an American hero."

"She is to me. Margo's been a family friend for years. Personally, I think she has a huge crush on my mom. I don't know if anything will ever happen. I've learned to believe what they say—never say never."

Sarah placed a hand on Jordan's shoulder. "You need to listen to your own words my friend, never say never."

"Yeah, well. Come on, let's get these bikes back and go visit Thunder Hole." The two women loaded the bikes into the van and a short time later stood in line at the bike shop. Flyers and pamphlets of local attractions stood in a display rack near the door. Sarah looked over the numerous options and squinted when she picked a brightly colored leaflet. She opened the pamphlet and held it closer.

"This was the shop that helped arrange that dive tour I went on. It's the same guy from that boat tour we have scheduled for later this week."

Jordan scanned the full-color pictures of the diving and boating adventure. Half way down the page, she came to an abrupt stop. Jordan stumbled and Sarah caught her arm.

"Jordan, are you okay?" Sarah asked. Jordan stepped out of line and found a counter she could lean against. She stared, wide eyed, at the brochure. She couldn't say anything.

There, staring back at her in neck-deep water, were Professors Aggie James and Noeul Scott, holding up a beautiful purple starfish and what looked like a toy figurine. From beneath the goggles pulled up on their foreheads, they looked into the camera with broad grins and sparkling eyes.

Sarah stood directly in front of her, stretched out her arms and placed a hand on each of Jordan's shoulders. "Jordan, you're scaring me. What the hell?"

Physically shaking herself, Jordan reached up to cover one of Sarah's hands. Drawing a shaky finger to the picture of the couple on the brochure, she swallowed hard. "That's Professor Scott." Jordan tapped the photo. "That's the woman I'm looking for."

Sarah quickly moved to her side and pushed her sunglasses up. She pulled the brochure closer. "How in the hell?"

"That's what I've been trying to tell you guys all along. Something, or someone, is guiding me through this. You explain to me how in the thousands, maybe millions of pictures this company has probably taken...how does this picture," she flipped her finger against the brochure, "end up in a brochure that you pick up in a bicycle shop that has nothing to do with scuba diving?"

Jordan stood transfixed. She had a direction, someone in this town that had been in direct contact with Noeul Scott at some point. There was nothing to date the picture other than the fact that Aggie James was in it. The photo had to be more than twelve years old. Would anyone at the dive shop remember Noeul?

"Sarah, I don't care about returning the bikes right now. Jordan pointed at the brochure. "We need to go here, now. Do you remember how to get there?"

Sarah grabbed the keys hanging from Jordan's pocket. "I'll drive."

Jordan pulled up the business's website. She kept scanning for anything that would lead her to the picture of Noeul and Aggie. She clicked on a link to a social media site. There were hundreds of pictures of the boat tours and a few diving expeditions. Professor Scott's picture didn't seem to be there. What she did find were toy figurines. Some were duplicates of the previous version and some were very distinct. The one thing they all had in common was a three-digit number written on them. The captions detailed the antics of the figurine being held in the claws of various lobsters or pictures of the figurine missing limbs that some sea creature had relieved him of. The numbering on the toys started to niggle at her. She started opening the pictures and paying attention to the numbers.

Jordan turned to Sarah. "I think I figured out a way to determine the year on the photo in the brochure." Her pulse raced. She used her phone to take a picture of the brochure and zoomed in until she could make out the number *128* written across the top of the figurine's dive mask.

Sarah negotiated a left turn. "How?"

"This guy, Jon, takes this little toy diver with him."

Sarah shook her head. "Yeah, I remember that, calls him Mini-Jon, I think. I might even have some pictures from my trip."

"Well, they're all numbered, and I'll bet those numbers have particular years associated with them. The one in Noeul's picture looks a lot like this one he has designated as *128*. I can't make it out. When we get there, we can try to leverage that information to jog some memories."

The *Wave Bobber* was a large, blue and white boat moored at the dock when they pulled in to the lot. Adults and children were clamoring off the boat and chatting excitedly. A man, probably in his fifties, and a woman with a long, white braid were waving goodbye and high-fiving the departing kids. Jordan and Sarah stood back until everyone disappeared and the pair turned back to the boat.

Jordan held up her hand. "Excuse me."

The woman stopped and caught her companion's arm, turning the pair back to Jordan and Sarah. "Can I help you?"

"Hi, my name is Jordan Armstrong and this is Sarah Reynolds. We have a tour scheduled with you tomorrow at high tide. My sister's in a wheelchair."

The man's eyes brightened and he extended his hand to her. "Oh yeah. Hi, I'm Jon Everett and this is my wife, Lynn. We have another group of people that will be going with us. The couple has a young son who's in a wheelchair too. Don't worry, we'll get everyone safely on the boat."

Jordan blushed as she took his hand. "Pleasure to meet you both. I'm not worried. I'm grateful. It's rare to find an adventure activity that's willing to make accommodations."

Lynn smiled softly. "Our son, Jon Jr., was confined to a wheelchair. We wanted to make sure he had the opportunity to do all the things his sister, Yvette, could whenever possible. He loved going on the boat."

Jordan noticed a sadness cover Lynn's eyes. Jon was shuffling his feet and not making eye contact at all. "I'm sorry if I've brought up something painful."

"It's not your fault." Jon raised his head and managed a smile. "We lost Jon Jr. about two years ago, complication of his muscular dystrophy. We miss him and keep his memory alive in our hearts and business. How can we help you?"

Jordan took a deep breath. "Is there someplace we can sit down for a minute?"

Lynn waved them up onto the boat. "Come aboard. We don't have another tour today, so we were about to reset everything for tomorrow. There's a table on the deck where we can sit."

Jordan and Sarah followed Jon and Lynn onto the deck. Scuba gear, crates, and mesh bags lay near the stern of the canvas-covered deck of the vessel. Jordan pulled out the brochure.

"Okay, before I get started, I ask that you keep an open mind for a minute, while I tell you sort of a winding tale. You need to know this part, so you will understand what I'm asking. Okay?"

Jon raised his eyebrows and shrugged. Lynn smiled at her and waved for her to continue.

"I'm an agricultural studies professor at Cornell University. I'm also a bioengineer, working on a project to grow a superfood without water." Jordan looked up at each of them to gauge if they were following.

Jon scratched his face. "As someone who makes his living by the sea, I certainly hope there isn't a time when it won't be around."

Jordan explained the reason for her journey and what brought her to Maine. She brought her hands together and steepled her fingers, bringing them to her lips. "Now, here's where it gets pretty strange. Noeul," she pointed to the woman on the left of the picture, "never got to complete this list with Aggie before her untimely death. After the funeral, Noeul quit her job at the university, and from my understanding, set off to complete the bucket list Aggie created. At each of the locations, Noeul left a memorial to Aggie with a small portion of her ashes, a list of clues for the next location, and usually, a personal letter. The last clue I decoded brought me to Acadia. However, it didn't give me a location for the memorial."

Jordan closed her eyes and took a deep breath trying to find the words to explain the unbelievable things guiding her. "All along this journey, I've had someone, or something, guiding me to these memorials. I've been directed, you could say, to areas or people who have helped me find the final resting place of these memorials. In Havasu Falls, I found an Indian medicine woman who'd helped Noeul. In Sequoia National Park, I heard a voice and a whistle that led me to the site. In New Orleans, I ended up at a bar across the street from where I was staying. Out of the millions of people that live there, I ran into a bartender who'd met them and even had a picture of the three of them together. Her grandmother had helped Noeul create the memorial there. Oh, and this grandmother, happens to be a Santeria priestess who can talk to the dead. I know this all sounds crazy, and I appreciate that you are still listening to me at this point."

Jordan put her head into her own hands at the ridiculousness of the story. She pinched the bridge of her nose. "Which leads me to you. After arriving at Acadia, I kept hoping something would lead me to the memorial. Sarah and I rented bikes at the Bar Harbor Bike Shop and went for a ride today. When we went to return the bikes," Jordan tapped the brochure. "Sarah pulled this brochure off the shelf, and I recognized Aggie and Noeul in this picture. Now, sometimes I think I'm losing my mind, but to me," she slid the brochure closer to them, "is like a giant, flashing billboard telling me this is my clue. I'm hoping you remember them." Jordan felt Sarah's hand on her back.

"I can vouch for the fact this woman is sane." Sarah laughed. "Well, let's just say she isn't crazy. Jordan's a bit driven, because she's on a mission to end world hunger. If you know anything that could help us find Aggie's memorial. Is there any chance you remember one or both of these women?" Sarah slid her finger back and forth between Aggie and Noeul on the glossy brochure. "The little Mini-Jon's number seems to indicate they would have been here around 2007, if we understand your numbering system."

Jordan watched, as Lynn looked at Jon and took his hand. She pointed out something on the back to him, and he shook his head in wide-eyed wonder.

"Jordan, I'm about to add to your story with a few more pieces of divine intervention. This particular brochure," she held it up and waved it a bit, "never went to print. There shouldn't be a single copy of it anywhere, because the printer messed up several things on the proof." She pushed it back over to Jordan. "If you look at the cover, our company name is spelled wrong. You might not catch the other things, but we can tell. The phone number, hours of operation, and even the website is wrong." She tapped the brochure. "This never left the shop. The gentleman who'd always designed our brochures got sick during the process. His less than enthusiastic son took over. Mr. Daniels passed away, and Roy didn't know how to make any of the changes or finish the project. This layout never made it off the computer. We've used a completely different service for our marketing for the last, what..." Lynn looked to Jon.

Jon shrugged. "At least twelve years." He scrubbed his jaw, making a sound akin to sandpaper from the stubble of his beard. He sighed and closed his eyes. "I remember them, Noeul in particular. They came on this trip," he pointed to the picture, "as an anniversary present. Aggie told me all about the clues she had Noeul decipher." He chuckled. "I thought it was the coolest thing I'd ever heard." He looked at his wife. "Jon Jr. was still with us when they were here, and Aggie was amazing with him." Jon looked out into the bay. "About four years after this picture was taken, Noeul came back and told us what had happened. Our son was still alive and it almost broke his heart. Noeul asked me to help her with the memorial she wanted to place." He stopped and looked at Lynn again.

Jordan could see some hesitancy. "Jon, I know you might not want to tell me where that is. I completely understand that. I promise we will respect the remains and do no harm. All I'm asking is for you to consider it, because I'm not sure how else I'm supposed to find the next clue. It's a step by step process, and I have to believe I would never have known any of this if Aggie wasn't directing me in some way. How else do you explain this brochure, or Sarah being with me to find it? I wouldn't have picked this up. I was standing in a line trying to return our bike rentals. It was Sarah, who was here before. She picked up the brochure to show me your company that she'd been on a group dive with. The same company that we have a boat trip scheduled with, yours. No one, until now, has been with me on any part of this journey. We made this trip to Acadia into a family vacation, because there are activities accessible to my sister, Dava. She has spina bifida and is the one in a wheelchair. We booked an adventure with you because of your efforts to be inclusive." Jordan knew her voice was bordering on desperate. "You created a way to do it for your son, who met both Aggie and Noeul. I must believe I was meant to find you and put two and two together. Please?"

Jon and Lynn shook their heads. Jon massaged his temple as he spoke. "The picture you see here was taken at Anemone Cave. Aggie loved it when we all dove there together. It's a really beautiful place. I'm trusting you, because what I'm about to tell you could get me in big trouble." He stopped and folded his hands. "I helped Noeul put Aggie's memorial in an underwater cave and found a place to hide it out of the public eye. By now, it will probably be grown over with colorful sea life. It's illegal to put anything like that there. I justified it because environmentally, there was no harm. Can you dive? High tide tomorrow morning will be around five thirty. Meet me here at the boat at four thirty. I've got wet suits you can use."

Jordan looked at Sarah and both nodded affirmatively. She stretched her hands out to Jon and Lynn. "I thank you both, more than you will ever know."

After leaving the boat, they returned the bikes before heading back to the hotel. They checked the rack for more of the brochures but weren't surprised that there were none. It was close to four in the afternoon when they returned to the hotel to clean up for dinner and share what they had learned.

Chapter Twelve

NOEUL RAISED THE COFFEE cup to her mouth and took in a deep breath. There were certain scents in this world that made her smile, fresh brewed coffee, the smell of hay drying in the sun, a ripe tomato, lilac, and honeysuckle. *Puppy breath, that's another favorite.* She smiled and let Kyo out as she walked to the chair, cup and journal in hand. Raising her face to the sun, she sat quietly listening to sounds of the world waking up around her.

Chickens clucked behind her, the bells around the goat's necks rang off the surrounding rocks, and the horses nickered low in their throats. The breeze moved through the branches, causing them to creak and the leaves to rustle. Birdsong sounded in the distance and all seemed right in her world. Well, mostly. The growing feeling of loneliness was as stifling as heat in the desert. Sometimes, it literally stole her breath. She opened the journal and noted the date.

I've been able to replicate several pieces of my former student, Professor Jordan Armstrong's research. I find it completely fascinating how far she's been able to take the bioengineering aspect of the grafting process. She does seem to be missing a few elements that I've documented in my research logs. The processes that I've been working on in my own greenhouses mesh beautifully, resulting in a stronger grafting process.

I am intrigued by her ability to articulate the processes. Her data isn't just factual, it correlates to its usage to end world hunger. I wonder what we would have been able to accomplish together. There are times I miss teaching and seeing the light bulb moment when the student gets it. The real satisfaction is when an exceptional student, like Jordan, takes what they learn from the classroom and puts it to practical use. That's what a true teacher strives for.

The more I read about her, the more I want to know. At this point, I don't know what I want to do about that. I do know the desire grows stronger every day.

Aggie's been quiet of late. No dreams or long conversations. I don't know, maybe I've been imagining it all. Maybe I'm losing my mind talking to a dog, a cat, and a goat. All I know is I'm less and less satisfied with the life I've made. It's certainly not the life I'd imagined.

Noeul closed the book and decided she needed a run. She had too much pent-up energy with no outlet. The trails would offer her a place to clear her mind and tire her body. Kyo would love it. She'd put her journal, a sandwich, and a bottle of water in a lightweight pack and head out to the waterfall, maybe take a swim. After changing, she tied on her trail shoes and walked out to do a few stretches before choosing her route.

Kyo perched at her feet, body in a full downward dog. Her tail wagged slowly, her eyes darting around the yard. Noeul couldn't help but laugh as Kyo's ears twitched. "Come on you nut, let's go."

A brisk pace pushed Noeul's body and thankfully cleared away all thoughts of ghosts from her past. Her research, former students, and loved ones long gone silently faded into the forest. A pleasant heat hummed through her legs, her arms pumping in synch to each step. There had been a time, right after Aggie's collapse, when she wasn't sure she would enjoy this ever again. Pine and damp earth filled her nostrils with each deep inhalation.

Time ceased to have any real meaning once her mind and body entered that zone of perfect harmony. Up ahead lay the waterfall. As they approached, Kyo's excitement was almost palpable, and Noeul laughed as the dog ran in front of her and hurled herself into the water. Noeul stopped and paced back and forth, inhaling deeply and letting her pulse rate drop. Once she was no longer panting, she began to strip down, untying her shoes and pulling off her clothes. She climbed up the side of the falls and dove into the cool water. Noeul let her body absorb the temperature change. It was a shock at first, brisk and breathtaking. It reminded her of the scuba diving adventures with Aggie in Acadia. That bucket-list location had been the site of a huge argument and in the end, their final adventure.

Noeul heard her phone ping with an incoming message, the third of the morning.

Aggie frowned and stabbed a forkful of pancakes and sausage. "Really?"

"I can't help it, Aggie, it's my lab. There's a problem, and vacation or not, I'm responsible." Noeul opened her email app and read the message from her lab assistant.

Professor, I'm sorry to have to tell you this. Research plot 672 has developed lesions. We've identified it as stagonospora nodorum blotch. *What do you want us to do?"*
Amy

"Shit, I've got to call the lab after breakfast. We've got a major failure, a fungal leaf disease." Noeul threw her napkin on the table, grabbed at the sides of her head, and rested her elbows on the table.

Aggie let her fork clatter onto her plate. "We're on vacation, Noeul, nothing you do right now is going to change what happened. What it will do, is ruin our time together, because you'll obsess about this, looking for solutions, and you won't be able to try again until next freaking year."

"Aggie, I'm responsible for millions of dollars' worth of research. If I can't fix the issue, that money won't be around for as you say 'next freaking year.'"

"We've got a dive scheduled that I went through a lot of trouble to arrange. Doesn't that count for a damn thing, or as usual, does that research mean more than our down time? One time a damn year, I pull you away from that lab...one time a year, for a week! Seven days isn't too much to ask to put as much into us as you put into that precious research. It's seven damn days, Noeul!" Aggie got up from the table and stormed away.

Noeul covered her face. Her whole life had been about research until she'd met Aggie. Her wife had introduced love and laughter to her life. Research was her career, a job. Aggie was her life. She'd grown up striving for excellence. Driven to succeed at everything. None of it meant a thing without Aggie. She signed the check, charging it to their room, and quickly typed out a message to Amy.

Handle it, I'm on vacation until next Monday. Figure it out. —Noeul

She pushed a button on her phone, flashing to the power-off screen. She watched the screen go black, then slipped the phone in her back pocket and took a deep breath. She headed out of the restaurant and in the direction of their room. "Now to fix what I can, something much more valuable than any research I'll ever do."

Noeul stroked though the water, coming to rest on some rocks under the waterfalls. She sat with the water beating a massage on her shoulders. The rocks around her were teeming with small layers of algae, moss and lichens, and other simple plant life as abundant as the sea anemone of the cave they dove in. The whole cave had brimmed with vibrant red and purple life. It was one of the most beautiful places she'd ever been. That day, she'd watched complete joy in Aggie's eyes. The inquisitive, childlike enthusiasm of her wife was full of wonder. Her eyes had sparkled through the scuba mask.

Kyo paddled up beside her and climbed onto the rocks. Noeul stroked her dog's head before she picked up a stick and tossed it out into the water for her. Kyo dove off the rock, swam over to the stick, clasped it in her teeth, and returned to her. "Good girl, Kyo." Noeul tossed it to her again, slid down into the water, and swam back to where she'd left her clothes. She dried off with a chamois towel and put her clothes back on. The journal called to her and she pulled it out while she ate half her cucumber and tomato sandwich. Kyo found a spot in the sun and lay down in the soft grass beside her. Noeul shook her head and picked up her pen.

I'd forgotten how much fun we had on that dive in Acadia. Jon, Lynn, and the kids were wonderful. Aggie took such a shine to Jon Jr. I used to call her the biggest kid I knew. Jon Jr. was big into maps, particularly ocean charts. I can remember packaging up some of Aggie's flea market finds and mailing them off to him. His mom would send us back pictures with them up in his room. I was devastated when I read online that Jon Jr. passed away from a health complication. That would have killed Aggie. Maybe they're diving together somewhere. I'd like to believe that.

"You know Kyo, sometimes I wish we'd have had kids. Maybe I'd still have a part of her. She wanted them. We'd even talked about it. Just like everything else, somehow we always thought we had time." Noeul shook her head. "Little did I know, time was one luxury we didn't have."

***

It was still dark when Jordan and Sarah stepped onto the dock where Jon's boat bobbed in the water.

Jordan took the big man's outstretched hand. "Thanks again for doing this, Jon. I don't know how to thank you."

"Let's get you two outfitted. I've got my underwater camera with lights, so we shouldn't have a problem finding it."

The trio boarded the boat and took some time to get the right fit for the gear before loading it all up in Jon's truck for the ten-minute drive. As they reached Schooner Head Overlook, Jon pulled the truck to the side of the road.

"Jordan, I need you to know something. This cave is accessible by foot at low tide. The entrance where the memorial is hidden isn't accessible until high tide. The height of the cave is pretty substantial, so we use the water to take us to the level where we placed the memorial. It's a dive you don't want to miss. I need you to understand, this is considered risky. The tide can push you into the rocky ceiling, so both of you watch yourself and follow my lead. Once we get it, we need to swim back out so you can do whatever it is you need to do."

Jordan placed her hand on Jon's shoulder. "Jon, all I need to do is look at the letter and the next set of clues. I promise, everything will stay intact and I won't take a thing other than what I commit to memory up here." She pointed to her temple.

"I have to trust you, Jordan. This story is too close to an episode from the *Twilight Zone* for it not to be true." He put the truck in drive and took them to the area closest to the cave. The trio dragged the equipment down to the entry point Jon picked out.

Suited up, they entered the water at the top of the cave. Jon switched on his camera with the brightest light Jordan had ever seen. As they entered, the camera's light beams bounced around the cave. Jon had made them promise one thing before they entered. He wanted them to enjoy fifteen minutes of the dive before they retrieved the memorial. He told them it was a once in a lifetime experience. Jordan felt privileged to experience it with someone who loved it the way their guide did.

Jon pointed out bright, neon-green sea sponges resembling a tie-dyed carpet, while all around them small anemone waved with the current. Hundreds lined the rocks everywhere, in color swatches of magenta, white, red, and green. There was one very small one that reminded her of the children's tea set her mother had given Dava. The color of the sea life closely matched the milky, light-green of that jadeite.

Watching Sarah's eyes light up inside her dive mask, Jordan was glad they were experiencing this together and wished Dava was able to do the same. For several more minutes, they floated above the undersea world, letting Jon and the current gently guide their field of vision.

It was all too brief, when Jordan noticed Jon tapping his watch. She reached out and touched Sarah's arm to get her attention, pointing to their guide. They followed the light deeper into the cave until they reached the back side. High tide completely filled the cave, allowing them to swim to the top where Jon pointed to a small crack in the ceiling. Jordan propelled herself upward, and with a substantial amount of trepidation, reached in until her gloved hand found a smooth cylinder. She closed her eyes and said a small prayer of thanks, showing it to Jon and Sarah. They had a finite amount of time to get out of the cave, open the memorial, and retrieve the clues to the next location.

Using Jon's light, they swam out and quickly made their way to the dry area they'd prepped. Jordan made quick work of pulling off her mask and the torso section of her suit. She meticulously dried herself and zipped up a fleece jacket and pulled on a skull cap to avoid getting a chill. Sarah had done the same, and Jon sat off to the side reviewing some footage on his video recorder.

Jordan dried the cylinder and began the process of carefully opening it to avoid any damage from residual salt water. Sarah grabbed her arm. "Wait, the light still isn't good enough to see. Let me get my cellphone out of my dry bag, so we can video what's inside."

Jordan felt her heart pounding as she held the cylinder in her hands, waiting for Sarah's return. With her cellphone aloft, Sarah came close by Jordan's side and indicated she was ready. Jordan slowly rotated the cylinder until a seam became visible. Each turn revealed more threads, until the two halves could be separated. Ensuring her hands were free of moisture, she pulled the first piece of parchment free and allowed Sarah to slowly film the entire piece as she read. After Sarah indicated she had it, Jordan pulled the next piece of paper out. It was the clue list. Several lines of text, numbers, and a few small diagrams filled the page.

Sarah lowered her phone. "I've got it, if you do."

Jordan shook her head up and down, while rubbing a coating of bee's wax to the threads. She wanted to provide an all-natural coating to ensure the watertight seal would stay intact. This was something she'd done with each of the memorials as an added layer of protection.

The last thing she wanted to do was destroy something that Noeul had gone to such great lengths to protect.

"We've got it, Jon. Thank you." She handed the cylinder to him. "Noeul trusted you with her secret, and I'm forever grateful you shared it. I think you should be the one to take it back."

Jon was visibly moved, and turned slightly away from them as he put his mask back into place and walked back to the cave edge. They watched as his light illuminated the water around him then trailed off. Jordan and Sarah tied the arms of their suits around their waists and gathered their equipment, while waiting for Jon's return. He surfaced about ten minutes later, and the three made their way back to the truck. They pulled the doors shut as the sun pushed away the shadows of the dawn's waning moments.

"I never grow tired of the sight," Jon paused and looked out at the sea. His voice was soft, the cadence perfectly timed. "The sea, full of power and might, releases its lover, the eternal shining light. The rolling waves, a good morning kiss, holding a promise of love's tender bliss." The truck grew silent as they watched the light's ascension.

"I've never heard that, Jon. It's beautiful," Jordan said softly.

"Lynn wrote it after we moved here. She's quite the poet. Just one of the thousand things I find amazing about her." Jon sighed and started the truck. "You guys ready to head back? We only have about two hours before your planned excursion on the boat. We have ten other people joining us, including two children in wheelchairs."

Jordan nodded, and he turned the truck back onto the main road. Sarah aimlessly rubbed her thumb hard into her right palm. "I wish Dava could have experienced that this morning. It was truly extraordinary, Jon. Thank you, for everything."

Jon waved off the comment. "Don't worry about Dava. She'll get to see everything you guys did today, in high definition. I filmed it all so you could share."

Sarah's grin grew wide. Jordan was sure she was thinking about her planned proposal tonight. She leaned over and bumped Sarah's shoulder, drawing her from her musings. "You're going to rub a hole in your hand. Relax, she'll say yes. I have no doubt about it."

Jon turned his head and looked at them. "What's the question?"

Jordan snickered. "Blondie here plans to ask my sister to marry her tonight."

Sarah punched Jordan. "Don't make fun. I'm nervous enough."

Jon laughed at them. "You'd think you two were already related the way you go back and forth. God help your sister if she has to put up with both of you."

The truck tires hummed along the blacktop, taking them back to the dock where they'd met Jon that morning. They helped him return the gear to the boat. Standing on the ramp, Jordan shook Jon's hand. "Thank you, Jon. We'll see you in a bit with Mom and Dava. I'll enjoy watching you make Sarah nervous about revealing her secret." She winked at him and laughed when Sarah's face blanched.

Jon patted Sarah's shoulder. "Relax, I'm in no mood to get tossed off my own boat. Go. I'll see you in a bit."

***

Their party enjoyed Jon's antics as he dove under the boat. The live video fed back onto a big screen at the front of the boat. Mini-Jon helped everyone scale items and creatures he found on the bottom. He brought lobsters and sea cucumbers to the surface so that everyone could have a lesson in marine life. At the end, he released the sea creatures back into the ocean before they headed for the dock. Jordan carried the wheelchair off the boat, while Sarah carried Dava in her arms. The love Jordan saw between the couple was as tangible as what she'd witnessed between her mother and father. She watched as Dalia wiped away a tear.

"She's okay, Mom. Sarah loves her."

At the top of the ramp, Sarah gently put Dava into her chair and kissed her briefly before walking behind to push her to the van.

Dalia wrapped an arm around Jordan's waist. "These are tears of happiness, Jordan. They're in love, and it's a glorious thing to see. I only hope Dava won't push her away."

Jordan smiled as she leaned over to kiss her mother's temple, wrapping an arm around her shoulder. "Don't worry about that. I've been grilling Sarah on all Dava's possible objections."

Dalia stopped abruptly and looked at Jordan, eyes wide.

Jordan quirked a grin and put her finger to her lips. Dalia's eyes grew wide and glinted with understanding. The pair joined Dava and Sarah at the vehicle. "How about lunch, ladies?"

Dava spoke up, "I say we grab something then hike up Cadillac Mountain." She turned to Sarah. "Didn't you say we have dinner reservations at that place? What's it called?"

Jordan's eyes met Sarah's in the rearview mirror. Jordan almost laughed as Sarah cleared her throat.

"Uh, yeah. Jordan's Pond House at seven thirty tonight."

"Well, let's get a milkshake and a sandwich to go. Then we can make our way to the trailhead."

After picking up their chosen lunch, they traveled to Cadillac Summit Road. The trail from there was a leisurely path that allowed Dava to use her motorized chair to reach the top. The vista was truly beautiful, and the group talked about making the trip back to see the sunrise. They all felt it would be worth getting to the trailhead around four in the morning to fight the crush of others wanting to do the same. Jordan stepped to the trail edge near the rock barrier. "This place is gorgeous."

Dalia stepped up beside Jordan and folded into her open arm. "Your dad would have loved this."

"He would have, no doubt." They watched as Sarah and Dava traveled ahead of them. "So, going to tell me what Sarah's up to?"

Jordan pursed her lips and used her fingers to pantomime locking them and throwing away the key.

"Spoilsport."

"Telling you would be the actual spoilsport part. This is Sarah's gig. I was merely the sounding board. Trust me, she'll be fine. It's what you've always wanted for Dava, someone to love her unconditionally."

Dalia reached up and held Jordan's hand that was draped over her shoulder. "I want that for you, too, not just Dava."

"Mom, we've been down this route. I'm not in the market for love. I have my research, and right now, this quest to find Professor Scott. I don't have any time for love."

"Be careful, my child, love will find you when you least expect it. Just when you're sure you don't need it, don't want it, and have sworn it off, it will bite you in the backside. It's the universe's greatest act of defiance. I only want you to be able to recognize it when it presents itself."

The trail looped back to their vehicle, and everyone wanted to go back to the hotel to look over the clues and the diving video. Jordan had promised herself to be in the moment on this trip, and she was trying to do that. *Especially tonight.*

***

Condensation ran down the walls of the greenhouse and into a tray that led to a storage tank. The water would be recycled into an irrigation system for the plants. Noeul had been logging data on the growth and heartiness of her plants for almost two hours. Each lot had similar conditions with one or sometimes two variables from Jordan's research. Disease was always something she had to watch for. She kept conditions as close to optimal as she could with her primitive surroundings. Noeul wondered about upgrading the greenhouse to eliminate more of the unknowns in her research. She closed the fanless computer and secured it in the moisture-free cabinet.

Kyo lay outside, so she joined the dog on the stoop, running her hands over the sun warmed fur. "What do you think about it, Kyo?" The dog lifted her head and wagged her tail at Noeul.

"If only you could talk back." Noeul rose and went to her chair where the journal sat. Pen against the paper, she let her thoughts free.

It's another sunny day here on Topside. The breeze makes the temperatures more than tolerable. Thor and Athena are grazing along with the goats, and Rico and Kyo are laying in the sun soaking it all up. All seems right with the world, except it's not.

I'm accumulating volumes of data and am even making great progress in the research. Without someone to share it with, it's little more than busy work. I'm going off the mountain tomorrow, down to the girls for a few days of company. They're probably getting sick of me invading them. I can't explain it. The days grow longer, and the nights alone are nearly insufferable. How I've done it for this long, I have no idea.

I feel like something inside has been dormant for a long winter's nap. Now it's breaking the surface, struggling for air and light. Maybe my heart is finally accepting Aggie's death in a way well beyond the physical. I don't have the answers, and I don't know where to find them. I know I must do something different before I lose what little bit of sanity I have left. The sound of my own voice, and to be honest, the touch of my own hand, isn't enough anymore.

***

Jordan sat in her room, looking over the clues she'd written out and the video Sarah had given her. She recognized the pigpen cipher and decoded a sort of poem.

most southern of the northern,
most northern of the southern,
most western of the eastern,
most eastern of the western

A sudden tiredness overtook her. She stretched and yawned, while she rolled her neck left and right. Jordan rubbed her own neck to relieve the tension. She stood and walked to the windows to watch the day fade into evening. The waves crashed into the shoreline, pounding rocks smooth and opening crevices into wide yawns.

Lately the quest had overtaken everything in her life. Taking this vacation with her family was breathing life back into her soul. Living vicariously through the list Aggie had created for Noeul was feeding Jordan, and yet part of her soul still felt raw. She was alone, experiencing these incredible things. Tina had taken, no stolen, something from her that she had yet to find again.

Jordan put her hand over her heart. *In this single organ lies the alleged center of our ability to connect to someone on a level beyond outward appearance. Beauty is skin deep, but love? True love is supposed to be molecular, something so deep we feel it in the marrow of our bones. Love isn't perfect. I only hope that true love is honest and will rise above the din of life, above the noise and the doubts.* She was watching what she was sure was true love grow between Dava and Sarah. She wished for them a long life full of adventure, good health, and children if they wanted them. *I'd totally rock at being an aunt.*

Jordan stepped back to the computer and the other clues. One looked like it might be in German, and another was likely a letter shift that would definitely take Dava's skills. Her cellphone rang. "Come on over to our room," Sarah said. "Dava has most of your clues worked out."

Jordan wanted to check on Sarah first. "Am I on speaker?"

"Nope."

Jordan laughed and proceeded to try and help settle Sarah's nerves. "Take a deep breath. She's going to say yes. Dava loves you. I'll be right over." She heard Sarah take a deep breath, and then laugh.

Jordan tried hard not to smirk as she walked through the door Sarah opened. "Whatcha got, Watson?"

"Get over here, smartass. Figure any of it out by yourself, Sherlock?"

Jordan squeezed her sister's cheek. "I did. I used that pigpen cipher to come up with that bizarre saying about north, south, east, west. I haven't looked it up yet. The symbol...I haven't been able to check out. There's something familiar about it."

"Well, it's far from the current logo that it's associated with." Dava pulled up the symbol. "That," she pointed to her screen, "is the logo for the Metropolitan Museum of Art from 1958. It's been through a few renditions, most recently in 2016 when they adopted the red logo."

Jordan watched the screen flip through various renditions of the logo. "Ok, so I also translated the Roman numeral code ninety-seven point five. Any idea about that?"

Dava shook her head and reached out for Sarah's hand. "Some. Sarah actually figured out a little of this with some firsthand knowledge. There is a reference to a Gustave Jacob Stoeckel that came into play."

"We worked that out in Morse code. My mom is a classical pianist who studied at both Yale and Julliard. I remembered his name from one time when we went to her performance at Yale." Sarah pointed to the screen. "This guy was Yale's first music professor. We had to figure out what connected him to a place called, 'The Music Shed.' It was his son, Carl and his wife, Ellen, that founded the music venue. In the next clue, Dava found a word shift that gave us Thomas Hovenden. He was commissioned by Gustave's daughter-in-law, the same Ellen Stoeckel, to create a painting called, *The Last Moments of John Brown* which..."

Dava continued, "The Met just happened to assign the ascension number 97.5 when they took it into their collection. That painting depicts the abolitionist John Brown's last moments before his execution. You remember what he did right?"

Jordan nodded as she sat at the desk. "I do. He was the abolitionist who seized the federal armory in Harpers Ferry, West Virginia, although it was Virginia at that time."

Sarah pointed to Jordan. "Bingo."

Jordan furrowed her brow. "What?"

Dava turned the computer to her. "Remember that phrase you said you decoded? Most southern of the northern, the most northern of the southern, the most western of the eastern, and the most eastern of the western?"

Jordan indicated that she did. "Yes."

"Well, you can't do much of a search for it in modern day. Try to think about the time period of the Civil War. West Virginia became a separate state in 1863, four years after John Brown was hung. The final reference I had was in a shift, Fredrick Douglas, Storer College. My dear sister, I think you are headed to Jefferson County, West Virginia. More than likely the national park at Harpers Ferry."

Jordan looked at Dava, and Sarah sitting beside her holding her hand. In a few more hours, she had every confidence that they would take their relationship to the next level. She welcomed the addition to their family and couldn't wait to congratulate them.

Jordan stood up and hugged Dava and Sarah. "Okay you two, I'll start doing some research on that...tomorrow. Tonight, we have dinner plans. I'm going to go get ready. I'll see you guys in twenty minutes."

***

Jordan saw Sarah wipe a bead of sweat off her upper lip. Sarah's bouncing leg was hitting the back of the driver's seat. The reassuring smile Jordan tried to send in her reflection didn't seem to bring any comfort. If Sarah couldn't find some control Dava would soon notice.

"Is the tag in your shirt bothering you, Sarah?" Dava reached over and pulled slightly at the crisp collar of the light-blue, button-down shirt Sarah was wearing with a matching tie.

"Uhm, maybe a little, I'm warm." Sarah leaned up, meeting Jordan's eyes in the mirror. "Can you turn the AC on? I'm sweating like a gambling addict in front of his loan shark."

Jordan couldn't stifle a laugh. There was little doubt in her mind that Sarah's sweating had more to do with the small velvet box in her pocket than the temperature of the van. "Sure, we're almost there. A few more minutes."

Dava used a magazine to fan Sarah. "Are you sure you're feeling okay? Your face is flushed, and your ears are beet red. Why'd you dress up so much anyway? I didn't think dinner outside constituted a state affair. I'm not complaining, because you do look sexy as hell. That robin's egg blue has always been my favorite on you."

Jordan bit her upper lip and, without moving her head, shifted her eyes briefly to her mother, who was biting her own lip. *Little sister you are going to be blown away.*

They arrived at the restaurant and were shown to a semi-private table with Jordan's Pond and the Bubble Mountains clearly in view. Jordan knew that Sarah had made special arrangements with the restaurant to provide them with a modicum of privacy for what she had planned. The manicured lawn looked like carpet, as Sarah pushed Dava's companion chair up to the teakwood table and took a seat beside her on the hunter-green bench.

A waitress brought menus and glasses of water to their table. "You all are in luck. With these unseasonably warm temperatures, it's comfortable enough to sit outside at night. I'll be back in a minute to take your order."

"So, tell me about the clue you found. I watched the dive video and it was spectacular. It's hard to believe the world that exists below the waves." Dalia picked up her water glass and sipped.

Jordan winked at Sarah. "I'll let Dava and Sarah tell you since they figured out the majority of it."

Dava proceeded to lay out the clues, with Sarah adding commentary. She was unable to stay away from a physical connection to Dava. The gentle touches, the way she held Dava's hand, even the way she turned herself so as not to miss even an accidental touch, was truly a beautiful sight to behold.

Jordan's mind was so lost in her thoughts, she missed what had been asked. "What?"

Dava's amusement made Jordan's face flush. "I asked you what your plans are for Harpers Ferry?" Dava turned to Sarah. "I think that cold water froze both your brains."

"Very funny." Jordan took a sip of her water. "I honestly don't know. Should be an easy trip once we get back to D.C. I've never spent much time there, other than a research trip over to West Virginia University's orchard. I did some long-distance projects with Dr. Kallie Nelson."

Dava raised an eyebrow at Jordan.

"Don't start. Here comes our waitress." Jordan was glad for the interruption. Dr. Kallie Nelson had never made any secret of her interest in Jordan. The two had graduated together and gone their separate ways after receiving their doctorates. The brief relationship had burned hot and quickly incinerated.

The group placed their orders and looked out over the tranquility before them. Diners carried on conversations that drifted on the evening air. "So, have you talked to Kallie lately?" Dava asked.

Jordan sent a piercing look Dava's way that seemed to only increase her sister's persistence. Dava narrowed her eyes at her. "I know we share a brain sometimes. Right now, I'm having trouble reading anything in your head other than the daggers you're throwing my way."

Jordan sighed. "No, I haven't. The last time Kallie called was an invitation to her wedding, as much to show how her life turned out without me as it was to have me there as a friend."

"She was crazy about you, JJ." Dava reached out and held her sister's forearm.

"I know. We wanted different things and were completely incompatible in most of our choices, Dava."

"Well, at least you had fun while it lasted."

Their meals arrived, but Sarah barely touched her food. Even the delicious dessert menu didn't seem able to tempt her. Dava placed a hand on Sarah's cheek. "Are you feeling ok? You're not getting sick, are you?" She put the back of her hand on Sarah's forehead.

Sarah clasped the hand and kissed the fingers she held. "I'm fine."

Dava's brow creased. "Well, something must be wrong with you. You didn't eat even half your dinner. Scallops are your favorite."

Jordan decided it was time to help Sarah out with a small push. "Maybe she has something important on her mind."

Dava looked over at Jordan, missing the shocked expression on Sarah's face. "What's going on with you two?" Dava waved her finger back and forth between the women. "I know that look, and it means you're up to no good and you..." she turned to her girlfriend, stopping midsentence at the ring held between Sarah's thumb and index finger.

One glance at their mother had Jordan pulling Dalia close and reaching for her hand. They watched as Sarah got up from the bench, turned Dava's chair to face her, and dropped to one knee.

"Dava, I've searched my whole life for someone who accepted my head for what it is, a giant jumble of thoughts and ideas. The day we met, my heart stuck in my throat. I thought you were the most beautiful woman I'd ever seen. I knew I'd met my equal when you showed me a possible enhancement to my program I hadn't even considered. Ever since that day, I've dreamed of a life with you by my side. Now, before you lay out all the objections as to why this can't work on a permanent basis, save it. I've thought of every one of them, and my answer is still the same." Sarah pointed to the wheelchair. "This doesn't matter. It doesn't define who you are. Your mind and heart aren't confined to this method of mobility." Sarah placed her hand on her own heart. "This doesn't need you to stand, for me to love you." She touched the side of Dava's head. "All it needs is this to believe that I'll love you unconditionally for a lifetime, no matter what's to come." Sarah held up the ring again. "Dava, will you marry me?"

Jordan held her breath, as she watched her sister bring her hand up to rest against Sarah's cheek, their gaze unbreakable. Slowly, Dava shook her head up and down, while quietly mouthing, "Yes." Sarah leaned forward to kiss her and slipped the diamond ring on her finger.

Dalia couldn't contain herself anymore and rose to hug and congratulate them both. Jordan followed suit and put her arm around Sarah's shoulders. She leaned close and whispered into her ear. "Told ya."

***

The next few days, the group continued to tour Bar Harbor and the surrounding areas. Jordan was beyond ecstatic to see the love and happiness between Dava and Sarah. Dalia had already gone into wedding planning mode, thrilled to finally see one of her daughters engaged. Jordan's memories of a marriage proposal no longer revolved around the disaster of her own. Now she could see how they were meant to be, full of love and promise.

They were enjoying lunch at the Terrace Grille before their afternoon flight. A bright yellow umbrella flapped in the breeze coming off the harbor, where sailboats of every size glided through the water and provided quiet entertainment.

Jordan speared a forkful of her lobster salade Niçoise while the others enjoyed similar light fare. She chewed and wiped her mouth with her napkin before taking a drink of her iced tea.

Dalia was looking out into the harbor. "I'm going to miss having my whole family around every day. This has been wonderful."

Jordan reached out and squeezed her mother's hand. "And now you have a wedding to plan, along with all your playground designs."

Sarah beamed at the comment and leaned over to kiss Dava's cheek. "Now that I've got the girl on the hook, what do you think about a rainbow tux?" Sarah wagged her eyebrows up and down.

A resounding *no* came from the other three seated around the table, sending them all into fitful laughter. Dava patted her arm. "Honey, if you want to actually get me down the aisle, you'll settle for your rainbow bow tie."

"And so, the compromises begin." Sarah smiled, leaving little doubt her intention had only been to get a rise out of Dava.

Jordan's phone rang, with Sam's name and picture displayed on her screen. She'd talked with the couple less than a week ago. Icy fingers of fear gripped her throat in a choke hold. She swiped to answer. "Sam?"

"Jordan, I'm sorry to call you on vacation." Sam's voice sounded thin and worried.

"No, No. You're not bothering me, what's wrong?" Jordan's heart began to pound in her chest.

"It's Max, he apparently got confused this morning and walked away from the house. He fell over the hill at the neighbor's house."

Jordan stood quickly and pushed her hand into her hair. "Sam, is he okay?

"He's alive, Jordan. We're at the hospital. He has a skull fracture. He isn't conscious right now, and things don't look good. I knew you would want to know. Bandit was with him. It's the only way we even knew something was wrong. He kept running up and down the hill, barking until someone noticed. If it hadn't been for that dog, who knows how long it would have been. Max's got that bracelet that tells us where he is with the machine. To do that, I had to know he was missing and I didn't." Sam's voice broke.

"Sam, we are leaving Maine today. I'm changing my flight, and I'll be home as soon as I can." Her heart was frozen with fear, her limbs grew numb, and her lips tingled. Her mother had come to stand beside her and wrapped an arm around her waist. "You tell him to hang on. I'm coming, and you give Bandit the biggest treat you can find from me. I'll be there as soon as I can get a flight. I'm coming, Sam." Jordan hung up the phone and covered her mouth with her hand, momentarily unsure of what to do.

Dalia's voice broke through her haze. "Jordan, what happened? Sit down and talk to me."

Jordan allowed herself to be guided back to her chair, while she relayed the details of the phone call. Dalia picked up Jordan's phone and found the airline contact. Dava pulled out her own and arranged a rental car for Jordan, as her Jeep would still be in D.C. Within minutes, flight arrangements had been made.

Dalia held her hand out to her daughter. "Come on, let's pay for our lunch. We need to get you to the airport for your flight back to Boston. After that, you have a small layover and a flight to Ithaca. It's all arranged. We just need to get you there."

Jordan started to protest until she saw the no-arguments look on her mother's face and acquiesced. Within thirty minutes, they were pulling into the airport. She hugged Sarah goodbye, and then leaned down and held on to Dava for a few extra seconds. "I'm so happy for you, Watson."

Dava's hug belied the weakness others expected of her. "I love you, JJ."

Dalia walked Jordan to the gate, handing her the ticket she'd printed off at the kiosk. "I love you, honey. Hug Sam for us and tell him we are all pulling for Max." She took Jordan by the shoulders. "Before you start playing the 'what if' game, stop. This wasn't your fault and you couldn't have prevented it. You could have easily been there in New York and at work. Concentrate on being strong for Sam. He's going to need you." Dalia hugged her again, looked her in the eye and released her.

Jordan waved at all of them as she slung her backpack over her shoulder and handed her ticket to the gate attendant.

***

A few hours later, Jordan walked into the third floor of the Cayuga Medical Center. Sam sat in the waiting area outside the critical care unit. She took a good look at him before he saw her. His normally perfectly combed blond hair was ruffled, as if he'd been running his hand through it continually. Sam's ever-present chef's coat lay wadded up beside him. Eyes closed, his head was tipped back against the wall. She didn't want to startle him, choosing instead to softly call out to the obviously distraught man.

"Sam?" Jordan watched as he opened his eyes, recognition immediate. He jumped to his feet and nearly melted in her arms. Engulfing him in a tight hug, she choked back her own anguish and allowed him to release his. They stood there for a long time before he pulled away and wiped at his eyes.

"Jordan, you came."

"I wouldn't be anywhere else. I'm sorry I wasn't here from the beginning." Jordan led him back to his seat and sat down beside him holding his hands in hers.

He tilted his head back to look at her. "Jordan, don't take this on yourself. It's no one's fault. Max wanted to be as independent as possible. If it's anyone's fault it's mine. Trying to keep the restaurant going and keeping track of Max hasn't been easy. Thank heavens for Bandit. If he hadn't been with him, it would have taken longer to find him, because we would have needed the Sheriff's department. Bandit left him to get help."

Jordan murmured to herself, "Timmy fell in the well." She shook her head at the *Lassie* reference and vowed to find Bandit the biggest steak she could. "What are they saying about his condition? Any changes since I talked to you?"

Sam fisted his hair and leaned forward on his elbows. "They're watching the pressure in his head with that bleed. The prognosis is pretty grim, Jordan. Even if he survives the bleed, they think he may have had a stroke."

Jordan watched as the anguish in Sam overcame him. He rose from his seat and began to pace. She followed him up and put her hands on his shoulders to stop him. "Sam, this isn't your fault either. Max wouldn't want either of us taking blame for this."

Sam's pained expression nearly broke her. This was the time for Jordan to be strong, to give Sam someone to lean on. He collapsed into her again, his face in his hands against her shoulder. They stood there for a long time, until Max's doctor approached.

The younger gentleman carried a stethoscope and wore a white coat over scrubs. "Sam, let's have a seat." He motioned them back to the chairs.

Sam made introductions. "Nathan, this is Jordan, a close family friend. Jordan, this is Dr. Nathan Phillips."

Nathan updated them on Max. "I'm sorry to meet you under these circumstances, Jordan. Max is holding his own. His intracranial pressure is still higher than I'd like, and he still hasn't regained consciousness. Everything else is within normal ranges for his age. There was a bleed involved with the skull fracture. I won't have any idea if a stroke occurred until we repeat his scans and even after that, not fully until he wakes up. He's breathing on his own. His brain just needs time to heal."

Jordan wrapped a protective arm around Sam. "When can we go in to see him?"

The doctor put his hand over Sam's. "Visiting hours start in about twenty minutes. You both look like you could use some coffee. Go get a cup and come back. I'll talk with the nurses about letting you in together. Do you have any other questions?"

Jordan watched Sam's shoulders heave. "I'll try to help him write some down. Thank you, doctor."

As Jordan watched the physician walk away, she could only say a small prayer asking for a miracle for her friends. She knew Max's beautiful mind drifted away every day. She hoped the rest of him didn't follow suit.

Chapter Thirteen

SATURDAY MORNING, NOEUL PULLED out of Miranda and Kelly's place with the back seat of her truck full of goat's milk lotion and soap. She sold her surplus from a booth at the Marlington Farmers' Market. Making money wasn't the issue. Lately, she craved the customer interaction. Whatever she didn't sell, Noeul would donate to the local women and children's shelter, as well as one of the local service organizations that gave hygiene products to the homeless. Mr. Anderson would likely stop by to trade a basket of the herbs he grew in exchange for some soap. *Such a kind man.*

He always protested and Noeul always refused to let him pay. He preferred to barter, and she realized it helped him keep his dignity. She was sure he'd never taken anything for free in his life. His generation rarely did.

Kyo hadn't protested too much at being left behind. Noeul was pretty sure her dog loved Miranda as much as Miranda loved Kyo. When Noeul returned, Kyo would be lazily sleeping after a full day of activities.

Green fields rolled beside the two-lane road, eventually giving way to the edge of Marlington's corporate limits. Billboards with advertisements for local businesses and safe driving messages dotted the landscape among the pine, oak, and maple trees. The American flag hung from the fronts of many of the shops that lined the main street. The red, white, and blue stripes were constantly in motion, moved by the breeze. It was truly small-town Americana nestled into the Appalachian Mountains.

Noeul pulled in beside Mr. Anderson's rusted out Ford F150. Body putty, flashing, and rivets held it together as much as any weld joint made on the assembly line twenty-five years ago. Stanley Anderson stood barely an inch taller than she did, even in his cowboy boots. She stepped out and wrapped him in a hug. "Good to see you, Stanley. How are you?" Noeul took a good look at the rail-thin man dressed in worn jeans and a plaid shirt with pearl snaps.

Stanley's dark eyes glinted, his smile deepening the lines in his sun-weathered skin. He took off his dusty John Deere hat, turning it round and round in his hands. "Fine as frog hair. How's life up on your mountain treating you?"

Noeul matched his smile with one that bubbled from deep inside and warmed her throughout. He was the kindest man she'd met in many years—always polite, always respectful. "The growing season has been good. I saved you some seeds from those heirloom tomatoes. They have incredible flavor. I think Martha will love them."

"I've got some herbs for you. Them graft tomatoes you gave me are doing good. Craziest thing I ever seen, roots from one, stem from another." Stanley put his hat back on and pushed his hands in his pockets.

Noeul loved talking to Stanley. He'd been a farmer his whole life. His sons had taken over caring for the beef cattle, while he and his wife grew herbs and flowers that they dried for sale. Stanley also kept a small vegetable garden using seeds Noeul provided. "Science is an amazing thing. The Mayans and the Aztecs were creating an edible corn by selective cross breeding over four thousand years ago. We're putting a new twist on making stronger, more resilient plants."

Stanley helped her set up her small stand, and for the next four hours, they greeted customers, answered questions, and referred other venders for things they couldn't provide. Shoppers meandered past the tables full of vegetables, crafts, homemade breads, and sweets. Some stopped, some passed by. When they didn't have customers, they caught up with each other.

Stanley pushed his hat back on his head and scratched at his thinning hair. "You're tellin' me you're taking weeds and puttin' 'em together with somethin' else?"

Noeul nodded her head. "I've been doing some trials. Sometimes it works and sometimes not. There's another professor working on this back at my old university. It could revolutionize how we grow food in places of severe famine."

"I've spent time graftin' different kinds of apple tree's together, trying to get one Martha likes for cookin'. She's particular 'bout her apples. Just never heard tell of it in something like what you're a doin'. The West Virginia University's Ag Department's got a research facility over in Kearneysville. Breed all kinda apple and other fruit trees. Ever been over there?"

"My old university and WVU have a pretty good relationship. We used to share research. I think a few of my former students work there.

That's the good thing about the type of research I enjoy doing. You don't mind collaborating with others. It helps further the science. Don't get me wrong, we're competitive. The difference is the research makes its way into the field and into other programs. Everyone wins in the end."

Stanley's dark eyes twinkled. "Kind of like farmers. We might have the prize bull, but if our neighbor's in trouble we'll cross a hip-deep river to get there to help."

"Exactly." Noeul enjoyed her afternoons at the market with Stanley. Sitting with this gentle soul always made for interesting stories about his family. "How's little Tyler doing?"

"That boy is full of piss and vinegar. He went with his daddy over to Moorefield to the sale. Got himself a new pair of boots and we can't get him outta them. He'd sleep in 'em if his momma'd let him. Tried to tell me they'd make him run faster if I'd let him wear them at T-ball practice the other day. That boy is ate up with them boots." Stanley's laughter started him coughing, and he fingered his shirt pocket in a long-practiced manner of reaching for the nonexistent pack of cigarettes. "Aw thunder, gotta get a drink. Haven't smoked in ten years, and I still can't lose this daggone cough."

A few more hours passed as they attended to customers and made small talk. All too soon, everyone started packing up their tables. She hugged him and kissed his cheek, as she climbed back into her truck. Arm resting on her opened window, Noeul made sure Stanley got in and started his truck. "See you next week. Tell Martha hi. Let Tyler know I missed him."

"I sure will. I'll bet he'll be back with me next time. He's sweet on you. Be careful, Noeul. I'll see ya." Stanley tipped his cap and put the truck in drive.

The truck rattled and squeaked its way out of the lot and back out onto the main street. For as beat up as the truck looked, Noeul knew the mechanics were solid. She also knew that as frugal as Stanley was, he was financially secure, and his great-grandchildren would be too. His farm sold prime beef to some of the east coast's top restaurants, and his breeding skills were second to none. Stanley was a millionaire in patched blue jeans and shirts made for him by his wife on her own sewing machine. Noeul turned her truck toward the women's shelter and dropped off the few bottles of lotion and several cakes of the goat's milk soap she hadn't sold. It had been a good day, and she headed back to Green Bank and the girls' house.

***

Jordan leaned against the wall, her eyes closed, the sounds of a monitor steadily beeping out Max's heart rate. Max hadn't regained consciousness yet. The doctor assured them his brain was trying to heal itself. Sam sat close to Max's bed and rested his forehead on their joined hands. She thought he might be asleep. He needed it badly, if the bruised look of his eyes was any indication of how much rest he'd been getting. Even though Jordan knew she needed to call her family and update them on Max, something told her leaving them right now wasn't the right thing to do.

Her friend lay still on the bed, his skin as white as the bleached hospital sheets. Tubes and wires tethered him to medical equipment and reminded her of the root system of a plant. Jordan ran her hand across her face and walked over and knelt beside Max's bed.

At a whisper, she spoke to him in hopes of reaching through his injury-induced coma. "Max, it's Jordan. I know you're tired. It's really important that you wake up. Sam needs you, and so do I. I didn't get to tell you about the dive in Acadia. You would have loved it."

She spent the next twenty minutes kneeling beside him. She spoke in low tones, relaying details of her adventures since they'd last talked. When the pain in her knees was more than she could bear, she rose and rubbed the sore spots. Jordan picked up Max's hand and held it to her body. Her brow furrowed in confusion. She wasn't sure that her mind wasn't playing tricks on her out of pure appeal to a higher being. She looked up at Max to see his eyes fluttering.

"Sam, look." Jordan reached out, shaking the sleeping man.

Sam stirred, then looked to Jordan and up to his partner. Sam rose and went to the head of Max's bed. "Max, honey?"

Max's eyes slowly opened, unfocused at first, finally zeroing in on Sam. A smile slowly formed. Sam clasped his hand tighter and bent over to kiss him. Jordan left them to alert the nurse at the desk and followed her back in, as the older woman began to attend to Max.

"I'm going to wait outside and call Mom while they check him over. Come get me if you need me." For the first time since her boots hit the ground in Ithaca, Jordan let out the emotional breath she'd been holding.

Once the doors to the critical care unit closed, Jordan reached for her cellphone, hitting her speed dial for Dava. After a few rings, she heard their familiar greeting.

"You guys get back okay?" Jordan hated jumping ship before she made sure everyone got home safe.

"Quit worrying. Your future in-law took charge and captained us all the way home. How's Max?"

Jordan took a deep breath and slowly let it out before answering. "He opened his eyes a few minutes ago." Jordan watched Max's doctor pass through the closed doors. "Sam is with him, and his doctor recently went in. It's pretty touch and go. At least they know what's wrong. Between his age and his condition, there are too many variables to his recovery to know anything definite yet. He seemed to recognize Sam, so I take that as a good sign."

"How's Sam holding up?"

Remembering the way Sam looked when Jordan first arrived made her heart hurt. "He's tired. I don't think he's slept since they brought Max in. He looks like he's been through the ringer. Seeing Max open his eyes made him perk up. I know he's worried sick."

"How long are you going to stay? Need us to bring your vehicle up? Sarah and Mom can drive it up and come back on a flight. You know we'll do whatever you need, JJ."

Jordan smiled, realizing Dava always knew when to throw out the childhood nickname like a warm hug. "No, there's no need for that. When things settle down, I'll fly back down and get it. I'm waiting to see what Sam needs. He shouldn't be alone trying to handle this and the restaurant."

"What about the search for Noeul?"

"Low on my priority list until we figure out the extent of Max's injuries. Someone has to watch Bandit, or he'll destroy the house and there won't be anything for Sam and Max to come home to." Jordan moved out of the way, as the doors opened and Max was wheeled out on the hospital bed, Sam holding his hand. "I'll call you in a bit, they're moving Max."

"Kiss them both for me and don't forget to take care of yourself, Jordan. You can't help them if you get down. At least grab a jar of Nutella and some Teddy Grahams. I know eating is another thing that won't be high on your priority list, and I doubt Sam will be cooking much."

Jordan laughed softly. I love you, too. Hug Mom and my future sister-in-law. Tell her thanks for me."

"For what?"

"For being brave enough to believe in love and not let you weasel your way out. I told her you'd say yes. She just had to get past that stubborn streak."

"Hey pot, this is kettle. Love you, now try to get some rest when you can. Call me if there's anything you need or if there is any change. Hug them both for us."

They disconnected, and she and Sam took a seat outside of radiology. According to Sam, they wanted to run another CAT scan.

***

Over the next few days, Max was moved to a step-down unit, allowing Sam to be with him around the clock. Jordan had asked the nurses for a sleeping chair so that Sam could get some rest while he sat with Max. The latest scans showed the swelling had receded considerably. The doctors warned he wasn't out of the woods yet. They did say the test results were promising. He'd managed a few words for Sam and had welcomed Jordan home.

Forcing Sam to go home for the night to get some sleep in a real bed had been a battle. He hadn't left the hospital for more than a few hours in the last two days. Jordan offered to spend the night, reassuring Sam that Max wouldn't be alone. She'd pulled out her laptop to check on emails and transfer the latest decoded clues out of her journal into her database. The lines of the Excel file started to blur, and she sat back and closed her eyes. She felt Max touch her arm.

She turned to him and covered his hand. "Hey, you. You're supposed to be sleeping." She laughed when he rolled his eyes. She closed her laptop and turned to face him more. "You feeling a little better?"

Max used his hand to indicate so, so.

"I sent Sam home to get some rest, he'll be back in the morning at six. I had to threaten him with bodily harm to accomplish that." Jordan smiled, hoping to lighten Max's spirits.

She watched as he smiled and shook his head that he agreed.

"You gave us quite a scare. Good thing you took Bandit on your walk. Did you lose your balance?"

His shoulders shrugged.

"You don't remember?"

He shook his head no.

"Well, that's okay. It will come."

He shook his head no again.

Jordan didn't say anything else and held the hand of the man she considered family. She closed her eyes as guilt over her absence washed over her.

Max squeezed her hand and narrowed his eyes. He shook his head again.

Jordan smiled at him. "Are you reading my thoughts?"

Max nodded his head yes. He raised a shaky finger and pointed to himself. He shook his head yes, then pointed to her and shook his head no.

Jordan closed her eyes. He *was* reading her mind. She was sure he was telling her it was his fault, not hers. "You trying to tell me to stop feeling guilty?"

Max nodded his head again and closed his eyes. Jordan watched as he slipped into sleep. Her friend was absolving her. It was her own mind that couldn't stop being angry she hadn't been there. He squeezed her hand once more, as his breathing evened out into the cadence of sleep. Maybe someday Jordan would forgive herself. Today was not that day.

Over the next several days, she stopped in at her office to check on her assistants and the research projects she'd left behind. Most seemed to be doing well, in general. Unfortunately, others were not. Certain plots of her grafted superfood weren't thriving.

Jordan sat in her office and massaged her temples trying to relieve the growing headache. "Deena, was there anything that seemed to preempt the failure? Change in light or humidity?" The tall, redheaded grad student was her most trusted lab assistant. If there was anything that could be pinpointed, she would have some theory about it.

"I've run every calculation three times. There were no variances. The same soil, the same irrigation or lack of, and the same growing conditions." Deena turned her laptop around and displayed the data for her.

"Okay, keep recording everything. None of it's your fault, it's part of research and why I need to find Professor Scott."

Deena made a few more notes in the computer. "You still believe she's the key?"

Jordan leaned back and pulled her hair into her hands. "I've mimicked her grafting techniques as much as possible. Something's missing. Which means, until I find her, we're likely to continue to have random failures."

"When are you heading out again?"

"Max has been moved over to the rehab center to work on getting him up on his feet. Sam and I are worried this injury will accelerate his dementia. In a few days, I'm headed to Harpers Ferry, West Virginia after I stop by D.C. to pick up my Jeep at my sister's."

A knock behind them drew their attention to the door. "About that." A petite, silver haired woman in an impeccably tailored navy suit, leaned against the door frame with her arms crossed.

Jordan rose and walked over to Dean Elaine Bell and bent to hug her. "Hey, Elle."

Elle hugged her back and slugged her arm. "You could have told me you were here."

Jordan blushed, shrugging her shoulders in response. "I came back to help Sam with Max. When he called and told me what happened, I was getting ready to leave Maine to go back to D.C."

Elle narrowed her eyes at Jordan. "You're on sabbatical, Professor Armstrong. You aren't even supposed to be here."

Deena closed her laptop. "I'm going to head back over to the test patch. It was good to see you, Professor A."

Jordan scowled at her about the formal title. Deena widened her eyes and pointed her chin at Elle, grinning as she waved and exited.

"I know I'm on sabbatical, but that doesn't mean I don't care. Please, Deena, keep me from going crazy. Throw a dog a bone and send me an email update."

Deena shook her head, laughing as she went back down the hall.

Elle hooked her hand through the crook of Jordan's arm. "Walk with me." Elle led her outside. "I have a favor to ask."

Jordan ran her hand through her hair that was desperately in need of a cut. "I know, leave the research to my assistants."

Elle squeezed her arm. "That too. This is more of a personal favor. I heard you say you were going to Harpers Ferry. Is that correct?"

"It is. That's where my next set of clues leads me."

"Dr. Henry has had an unfortunate accident, while skiing in Canada. He's broken both his legs."

"That pompous ass, I didn't even know he could ski." Jordan scowled.

"Thus, the two broken legs. The problem is he was supposed to be in Kearneysville on Tuesday, as part of a workshop on grafting. You know our relationship with West Virginia University. It's an important one for both institutions. I need a replacement and since you're already going that way, how about I finance your little adventure there?"

Jordan slowed down, realizing her legs were much longer than her companion's. "Elle, I'm not so sure that's a good idea."

"I know where your apprehension lies. Kallie's happily married and has two children. The circumstances are vastly different. I need you on this, Jordan." She held up the index finger of her right hand. "One, you're going that way." She held up another finger. "Two, you're one of the nation's premier experts in a field in which you've written three books about. And three, it's a small workshop of less than sixty people. I'd consider this a personal favor to me."

Jordan shook her head while she chuckled. "Elle, this isn't something I want to do. Because you are always so good to me, I will. Can you send the particulars to my email? Who's my contact?" Elle grew quiet and looked at her, a small grin on her face.

"Elle, personal favor or not, you're going to owe me big time." The two women laughed as they walked back to Elle's office.

***

Three days later, Jordan sat by Max's bed, filling him in on the parts of her journey their short phone calls hadn't fully described. He was improving slowly, more alert each time she visited. She used their time to tell him about the guidance she couldn't explain.

"Jordan...not everything...has explanation. Some things, take on faith." Max drew in a breath and his eyes closed. "Serious moment, Jordan. I'm not going to be around forever...a given." His speech was slow and slightly slurred.

Jordan put her hand on his arm. "Max, don't wear yourself out." He lay there for several minutes, not speaking. Jordan thought he might have gone to sleep.

"Seventy-two years old...dementia.... I have...loving husband...good friends. I've had a really good life."

"Max please, you're going to be fine. Just rest. We'll have plenty of time to talk when you're feeling better."

Max coughed. Jordan held a large thermal cup and directed the straw to his lips. He drank and reached up to push the cup away. "Not checking out...promise. Stating the facts. There is something that I need you to do."

Jordan couldn't imagine what she could do for him that she wasn't already doing. If it was within her power, she would deny him nothing. "What's that?" Long moments passed as she watched him appear to gather his strength and his thoughts.

"I want you to find happiness and love again. Put Tina in past...get back to land of living."

"Max..."

"Don't Max me. You need someone...besides two old men with a dog...your mother, and sister." Max took a few deep ragged breaths.

"You're tired Max. Sam will be here soon. I'm going to go home and take care of Bandit."

Max grabbed her arm. "Take Bandit. Needs run and play. Can't sit by my side...rest of my life. He needs to be with you."

Jordan watched as he relaxed into the pillow, obviously worn out, his color ashen.

Max opened his eyes wide. "Please?"

Jordan closed her hand over his. She leaned in and kissed his forehead. "Sleep, Max, he'll be in good hands."

"Thank you...Jordan. Now...work on the rest." He patted her hand.

***

Noeul rubbed Kyo's ears and kissed her nose. "Now you be a good girl for Auntie Miranda and Kelly."

Kelly hugged and released her. "Quit worrying. Leo has your place covered, and Miranda has plans to run this girl every day until she's good and tired. Now get on the road."

Noeul reached for Miranda, embraced her and climbed into her truck. She looked at her friends. This would be the first time in years that she'd slept anywhere other than her own home or theirs. Something Stanley mentioned at the farmers' market about the research facility in Kearneysville had peaked her curiosity.

A quick search had found the website and a list of staff members. There were a few names she recognized from reading research and one she recognized from her teaching days. What had really caught her eye was a notice for an upcoming workshop with an announced change of speaker. Professor Martin Henry was being replaced with none other than Professor Jordan Armstrong, the one name that seemed to be finding its way into her life over and over.

Sometimes she worried that her research into Jordan was becoming an obsession. The fact that this talented scientist was coming so close to Noeul proved to be a temptation too strong to resist. It was a chance to add to her research knowledge and see the woman who had been fueling her curiosity for months.

A few clicks had confirmed there were still seats available at the workshop. After registering, she'd booked a room in nearby Shepherdstown. She couldn't bring herself to stay in Harpers Ferry. Memories of her time there with Aggie and the day she'd placed the memorial, were too close to the surface. Shepherdstown was small and full of quaint specialty shops and restaurants. Her dreams that night were filled with melodious tones she'd spent years enjoying and years missing. As she drove away from Green Bank, she could recall every word as if they had been a goodbye.

"Two hundred eight minutes and one hundred seventy-three miles".
"What?"
"Two hundred eight minutes and one hundred seventy-three miles lead to your future."
"Aggie?"
"The seeker draws close. The distance between you seems like a giant leap. In reality, it's a single step."
"You're leaving me, aren't you?"
"My sweet Noeul, I've been gone a long time. I came back to remind you of the fact that you are still very much alive and not the one who died. My life was cut short and as a result, you put yours on pause. It's time to push play. Carry me in your memory for as long as you need. It's time for another to heal your heart, feed your soul, and hold your body. Two hundred eight minutes and one hundred seventy-three miles and the story of the phoenix will be revealed."

The dream had caused Noeul to sit straight up in bed, covered in sweat, her heart pounding out of her chest. She was drawn back to the computer in the study. Pulling up a map to Kearneysville left her little doubt she was being directed to the workshop. The screen showed the research farm was two hundred eight minutes and one hundred seventy-three miles away.

Chapter Fourteen

JORDAN CHECKED INTO THE trundle suite at Lily Garden Bed and Breakfast in Harpers Ferry. When she'd looked online for a place that could accommodate her and Bandit, she'd found this small gem with great reviews. Without knowing exactly where the quest would lead her, she wanted a place where they would be comfortable for more than a few days. There was a yard, and almost everything in Harpers Ferry was within walking distance. It was a good set up to allow her to explore the area and give Bandit a 'job' to keep him occupied.

She was grateful for Elle's brother-in-law, who happened to be a private pilot. He was able to fly her and Bandit to Reagan National, where Sarah picked them up. After a few hours with her family, she'd made the drive to West Virginia.

The call she'd made to Kallie to confirm her participation in the workshop had been surreal. Talking to a former lover felt a little awkward. It wasn't unpleasant like most would expect. Kallie had made Jordan promise to come to dinner with her family at their farm. Jordan had argued, feeling like it could be a disaster.

"If you can survive dinner with a three-year-old and a seven-year-old, I'm sure my wife will provide you with a meal second to none. I promise, it'll be worth the trip. Please join us?" Kallie's voice was almost pleading.

Jordan resigned herself to the visit and planned to make the best of it. "As long as I can bring my four-legged companion, we'll be there."

Kallie's place sat outside of Winchester, Virginia. As she made her way up the drive, the white clapboard farmhouse was far from what she expected to see of the Kallie she'd dated. A wide, wraparound porch surrounded the large, older home, and the yard held a wooden play structure littered with children's toys. A horse and a small pony grazed in a paddock near the house. The woman on the front porch stood with one hand on her hip and the other shielding her eyes against the sun.

Jordan pulled up and put the Jeep in park. Bandit whined from behind her and leapt out as soon as she released him. He promptly relieved himself against a tree and followed Jordan to the wide porch steps, where Dr. Kallie Nelson—correction—Dr. Kallie Nelson-Allen, stood with a wide smile and open arms.

Jordan couldn't help but laugh, as she walked into those arms and hugged her.

Kallie kissed her cheek. "Hey, stranger."

"Hey, yourself. This place is fantastic. Not exactly what I pictured for you."

Kallie dropped her head and laughed. "Yeah, the things we wanted in our youth don't always translate into what we need as an adult. The mansion didn't mean a thing when I didn't have true love to go along with it." Pointing to Jordan's sidekick, she asked. "Who's this?"

Jordan put her hand on the top of the dog's head. "Do you remember Max Keller?"

"I do."

"Unfortunately, he fell and ended up with a skull fracture. Bandit belongs to Max and his husband, Sam. With Max out of commission, Bandit wasn't going to get enough exercise. His energy has a tendency to become destructive without a job. So now, I'm his job."

Kallie dropped down to pet Bandit. "I'm sorry to hear about Max." She looked at Jordan and laughed. "That's a pretty big job for such a little guy."

"Trust me, he's up to it. You look good, Kallie."

"And you're too thin."

The screen door creaked, and a tall woman with short, wavy, brown hair and stunning blue eyes came out carrying a young girl, the spitting image of Kallie.

Kallie stretched out a hand and took the child from her, settling the young girl on her hip. "Jordan, this is Paula, my wife, and this," she tickled the young girl, "is our daughter, Ariana. Her brother, Ben, is washing up for dinner. Can you tell mommy's friend, Jordan, how old you are?"

The child held up three fingers. Jordan laughed and squinted one eye at the child. "You sure?" Ariana vigorously shook her head, and Jordan reached to shake Paula's hand. "Paula, I hear you are quite the chef. Nice to meet you. Don't believe anything this one's told you." She pointed to Kallie and bit her lip.

"I promise, she only told me you were an old friend, and don't believe anything she tells you about my cooking. Although we aren't starving around here." She patted her stomach, as she casually put an arm around Kallie's shoulders. "It's great to meet you, too. Welcome to our little slice of heaven."

Jordan turned around and eyed the large maple trees in the front yard. The sunlight streaked in and out of the verdant branches, as a swing swayed lazily in the breeze. "It is that."

"Come on in. Dinner's almost ready."

Paula held the door for Jordan and stopped to look at the young boy descending the stairs. "Let me see." She inspected his hands and smiled. "I'm pretty sure I said wash your face too. There's more dirt there than in our garden. Try again, buddy. Once you're done, meet us in the kitchen." The young boy grinned and climbed back up the stairs.

Kallie and Paula looked at each other and shook their heads. Paula offered Jordan a beer, as she put the rest of the food on the table. Kallie put Ariana in her seat and made sure Ben was pushed up to the table when he returned, clean faced.

Watching Kallie, Jordan saw the picture of domesticity. Gone were the designer suits and high heels, replaced with jeans and flip flops. Her nails were still as manicured as ever, down to the pink polish on her toes. Kallie's smile was different too. For the first time, Jordan was sure the happiness was genuine and focused purely on her wife and children.

The meal was delicious. Before long, the dinner plates were empty, and Kallie was dishing out cherry pie with vanilla ice cream. Jordan snickered, making Kallie look up at her.

"What?" Kallie's grin widened, as Jordan continued to chuckle. "What are you laughing at?"

"You." Jordan turned to Paula. "I'm sorry, Paula. You are obviously a miracle worker."

Kallie put her hands on her hips. "What's that supposed to mean?"

"It's nothing bad, Kallie. You have completely turned into the picture of wedded bliss. Ten years ago, I'd have never been able to picture you with a ketchup stain on your shoulder, slicing up cherry pie for guests. The change is fantastic. The best part is, you look happier than I ever imagined." Jordan raised her coffee cup to Paula. "My bet is that it took meeting the right woman. You're good for her. I can tell you make her happy."

Paula ruffled Ben's hair. "I think she's the best thing that ever happened to me. When we met, I'd never have guessed she wanted a life like this. She took to it like a duck to water. She's a wonderful mother and still an active researcher. That's where we met. I was doing research on pest and disease management for the apple trees. She knocked me over, literally. I was bent over, looking at an unknown fungus, when she backed into me. I went ass over tin cup and looked up into the most beautiful face I'd ever seen. I was gone from that point. Took me two years to get her to say I do." She put her hands behind her head. "The rest is history. I'm a lucky woman."

Jordan watched Kallie smile and set a bowl down in front of Paula. "I tell that story a little differently. The ending is the same." She bent over and kissed her wife. "What about you, Jordan, have you settled down yet?"

Jordan shook her head and accepted a bowl from Kallie. "No. You know me, married to my research."

Kallie looked at her skeptically but didn't call her out.

After dinner, the group went outside to the porch where Ben spent the next hour throwing the tennis ball for Bandit. Ariana was sitting on the porch floor with some blocks, while Paula and Kallie swayed in a wooden swing suspended from the ceiling. Jordan relaxed in a glider beside them.

"You know we're going to have to get a dog now. We've been putting him off. Somehow after this," Paula pointed to Ben and Bandit, "I don't think a hamster is going to cut it."

Jordan watched Kallie run her hand through Paula's hair like she'd done it a million times. "I'm betting not, and I'm blaming you." Kallie shoved Jordan's shoulder. "Remember that, when I make you house break the new puppy."

"Somehow if you can housebreak two kids, a dog will be a breeze. Tell me about the workshop tomorrow."

Kallie pushed the swing with her foot as Paula did the same. "Well, we put this on every year. Fruit trees are big business around here. Winchester has an apple blossom festival at the end of April. Anything we can do to help the orchards, helps the economy. We tap our university partners to bring in subject matter experts from several specialties. Having you come to speak with us is a real treat. I only wish we'd had more time to advertise your session. I'm almost positive we'd have had a much larger crowd than was expected for Professor Henry."

Jordan and Kallie both murmured, "Pompous ass," and Jordan shook her head. "I wouldn't go so far as to say your crowd would be larger."

Kallie sat forward. "You still don't know what a big deal you are, do you? Jordan, you are the top expert on grafting research. You've achieved every top accolade in your field. They're using your research everywhere, and it's quoted in a dozen other research studies and text books."

Jordan waved her off. "And yet with all that, my main goal still eludes me." Jordan put her hands behind her head and squeezed the back of her neck.

Paula shifted. "The superfood?"

Jordan rolled her head toward her, surprised to realize Paula knew that much about her research.

Paula shrugged her shoulders. "Jordan, even in my field, you're a big deal. You work in disease abatement by using controlled cross breeding, and your genetic research is, well, legendary."

"A legend I'm not. Driven is a better descriptor."

Kallie's laugh resonated across the yard, causing Bandit to perk up his ears. "Can you say understatement?"

"On that note, I think it's time I let you get that little one to bed." Jordan watched as Ariana crawled up into Kallie's lap and laid her head on her mother's chest. "Thank you for a wonderful evening. I'll see you tomorrow morning at the workshop. Paula, it's been great to meet the woman who finally tamed Kalista Nelson."

Paula rose and took Ariana from Kallie. "Trust me, Jordan, it was much more the other way around." She leaned over and kissed Kallie.

Kallie reached out and hugged Jordan, who accepted it with genuine affection. "There's someone out there who's going to see what I used to. More importantly, someday you're going to see it."

Jordan kissed her cheek and waved to Paula. "Ben, thanks for playing with Bandit. He'll sleep well tonight."

Ben shook her hand. "Thank you for letting me play with him, ma'am."

Jordan bent down and whispered in his ear. "He had a great time. I can tell. I'd start reading about how to train a puppy. Once you study up, start leaving hints." She winked at him. The grin he returned made her night. She watched as he ran back to the porch to wave at her with Kallie. Paula, shifted a sleeping Ariana, so she too could wave, and Jordan watched them go into the house as a family.

Bandit jumped into the Jeep, and Jordan turned toward the bed and breakfast. She needed to review her notes. Kallie told her the handouts she'd emailed were ready. Her PowerPoint presentation was a visual for her audience. She rarely even glanced at one as she spoke. It had been interesting to spend an evening with a woman she'd once known intimately. *I barely recognize her now.* Jordan could tell Kallie was truly happy and wondered, had she known this version of her, could they have been something more? No, the Kallie she'd met tonight didn't exist until she'd met Paula. It was all about meeting 'the one.'

***

Noeul slipped into the bathtub in her room at the Thomas Shepherd Inn. When she'd been with Aggie, they'd always preferred to stay in smaller, quirky accommodations. Traveling on her own, she sought out the same type of places. Occasionally, she'd stay where she and Aggie had as a couple. Some places were too hard to revisit.

Her room was tasteful. The comfortable, queen-sized bed was balanced with a mixture of antique furniture and oriental rugs. She'd been happy to find that her room had a private bathroom. She turned on the hot water to fill the tub, while she unpacked a few of her toiletries. After shedding her clothes, she slipped into the scalding water and groaned as the knots in her shoulders started to release. Driving long distances had never been a favorite activity. Noeul had always enjoyed being able to take in everything on the journey, riding in the passenger seat and singing along with the radio. *Aggie had...*She let the thought drop.

The hot water lulled her senses, as she settled with her head against the back of the tub. She'd poured in the fragrant bath crystals she'd found on a shelf beside the tub and luxuriated into the smell of lavender. Noeul's thoughts strayed to the woman she'd traveled to see. It had been a long time; Noeul remembered Jordan as a student with extreme intelligence, able to grasp and understand concepts well above her educational background. She was a sponge in Noeul's class, soaking everything up. Her research papers had been extraordinary. Noeul had known she was bound for incredible achievements. By all the research Noeul had read, she'd done just that.

Her skin nearly pruned, she rose from the tub and dried off with a soft, cotton towel. A thick, terry cloth robe hung in the closet. After moisturizing with her homemade lotion, she slipped into a tank top and boxers. She was tired, and the queen-sized bed was too inviting. She'd stopped for dinner and shopped in some of the smaller stores around her lodging before retiring to her room. In the morning, she'd take advantage of the complimentary breakfast and make the short drive to

Kearneysville. If not for the bath, her nervous anticipation would have kept her awake. She was grateful. For once, loose muscles and a quiet mind allowed her to slip into slumber easily.

***

Jordan took Bandit for a morning run along the Potomac River, her four-legged companion happily bounding beside her, mouth open wide as his tongue lolled slightly out of his jowls. After an hour run, they turned and headed back toward town. The smells from one of the shops up ahead made her stop. She pulled her wallet from her shorts and told Bandit to stay. Inside the Guide Shack Café, the smell of good coffee and baked goods filled her senses. The café sported kayaks on the walls as decorations, while patrons sat in colorfully painted chairs. Shelves were lined with local goods from preserves to apple butter, while another wall contained books and magazines.

Jordan stepped to the counter and ordered two large Black Dog coffees and a selection of blueberry muffins and some banana bread. She stepped out and signaled Bandit to follow, as they made their way back to their lodging. She could have had breakfast delivered to her suite from the offerings the owners included with her stay. The time schedule she'd laid out for herself required she be gone before the offered delivery time. Jordan drank one of her coffees, saving the other for the drive. She fed Bandit and went to shower and clean up. Before seven, she was on her way to the venue. It wasn't a long drive, and she enjoyed watching Bandit stick his nose out the window, taking in all the smells of new territory. It had been a long time since she'd been to the facility. When she pulled up, she noticed it hadn't changed much. The tan, sheet metal building housed the offices, labs, and other necessary facilities. She'd cleared it with Kallie to bring Bandit with her. There were some areas he needed to stay clear of, like the research area. The rest he was free to travel with them.

An intern showed Jordan to her host's office. Kallie's eyes sparkled, as Jordan leaned in her doorway. "Good morning. I see you survived your evening with my brood."

Jordan's smile emanated from deep inside. "You have a great family. Not something I was expecting from the woman who used to like fast cars and faster women."

Kallie leaned back in her chair and let her own laughter bounce off the walls of her office. "The only fast things I do now are to microwave macaroni and cheese and run for the bathroom when Adriana tells us she has to go." She laughed. "Potty training, not something I ever thought about. I wouldn't change a single thing."

"Motherhood looks good on you, Kallie. It really does. You seem happier than I ever remember, and it's obvious Paula is head over heels for you. I'm happy for you."

"A far cry from my days at Cornell with you, for sure. I'll admit, you're right, I've never been happier. So, now that I have you to myself without little ears around, how the hell are you? And I don't mean your standard 'I'm fine' answer."

Jordan took a seat in the chair in front of Kallie's desk, and Bandit lay down beside her. "I'm on sabbatical right now. I'm missing a piece of my research for the grafting process of the superfood. I've tried everything. That damn thing still eludes me." She stopped and rolled her head sideways to try and release the tension that always built up when she felt the answer slipping through her fingers like the sand she wanted to grow her plants in. She leaned forward and steepled her hands, as she rested her elbows on her knees. "Do you remember Professor Scott?"

"I do. I remember she dropped out of sight after her wife died, right?"

"That's her. I've been on this sort of quest to find her. I think she's the key to my research. I've been following a trail of breadcrumbs across the country. Each location building on the next. I have no idea where she is. I'm doing my best to look in all the places she's been. I tracked her to Acadia, which pointed me to, believe it or not, Harpers Ferry. Before I could get there, Max fell, and I went home to check on him. Elle found out I was home. Before I knew it, she asked if I could take care of this while I was down here."

Kallie rose. "Well, whatever brought you here, I'm glad. If I can help in anyway, let me know." She walked around the desk and drew Jordan into a hug. "If it's possible to grow your superfood where you want to, I have all the confidence in the world you'll do it. Now, on a more personal note, I know we didn't work out. I also know what that bitch after me did to you. I'm telling you, the real thing exists and it's going to jump up and bite you on the ass when you least expect it. My life is living proof. My advice is when it happens, don't let your past throw up a roadblock. Life's too short, Jordan."

Jordan melted into the embrace. "Looking at you now, I can almost believe that, Kallie. Maybe someday, when this quest is done." A strange sensation came over her as her tattoo chose that moment to start in with that irritating tingling again. *Strange.*

Kallie wrapped an arm around her waist. "How about we go see where you're going to set up."

"Lead on."

***

Noeul sat in a session, absorbing the information. Climate change was near and dear to her heart. The book she and Aggie had authored, years ago, was more relevant than ever. Long recorded norms in temperature, rainfall, and shifting weather patterns, were becoming less predictable. California was drying up with the persistent lack of rain. Severe flooding in the Midwest jeopardized food crops in the United States' bread basket, and Florida's record low temperatures were playing havoc with the nation's citrus crops. It was snowing in places where, historically, it never did, and the polar ice caps were melting. The misconceptions about global warming were rampant, along with the attacks on science. Government officials had rolled back years' worth of legislation designed to cut carbon emissions. Watchdog government agencies had been gutted in the name of progress and prosperity, even dropping out of agreements that every other nation in the world was signing. Noeul often wondered if anyone read the acknowledgement in their book. She still remembered the entire Theodore Roosevelt quote, verbatim.

"We have become great because of the lavish use of our resources. But the time has come to inquire seriously what will happen when our forests are gone, when the coal, the iron, the oil, and the gas are exhausted, when the soils have still further impoverished and washed into the streams, polluting the rivers, denuding the fields and obstructing navigation."

Noeul glanced around the conference room. It was like some of the classrooms she'd taught in. Tables and chairs, white boards and screens, all the familiar trappings of her former profession filled up the space. Sometimes she missed the classroom and the interaction with colleagues. Even those fresh, and sometimes hungover, faces of the students she'd tried to impart her knowledge to. She wondered what some of them had become. Noeul looked at her watch. In about another ten minutes, she was about to see, live and in person, what kind of impact she'd had on one of her star pupils. Regretting that she hadn't been around for more of Jordan's discoveries, she was excited to listen to her talk. Maybe after, they could even go get a cup of coffee. The speaker wrapped things up, and the facilitator called for a fifteen-minute break. Noeul decided to step out to the displays and make a call back to Miranda and Kelly.

***

Jordan entered the classroom from a door off to the side, avoiding the crush of people headed for the displays in the hall. Bandit was on her heels. Jordan had visited with Kallie while the other speakers carried on their sessions. Now, it was her turn to impart her pearls of wisdom. These smaller, intimate speaking engagements were more to her liking. In larger venues, the bright lights shining in her eyes had prevented her from seeing a single face in the audience.

Her back turned to the room, she pulled up her presentation and wrote a few things on the white board, including her name. People were meandering back into the room. Jordan waited off on the side for Kallie to introduce her, shuffling from foot to foot and looking at her shoes.

After announcing Jordan's current title and accolades, Kallie held out her arm. "And with that, I give you, Professor Jordan Armstrong of Cornell University."

Jordan told Bandit to stay and stepped up to the front and addressed everyone. "Thank you, Kallie. For those who were expecting Dr. Martin Henry, my apologies. Let's say, he's on the mend." She clapped her hands together. A bright light from a video camera was forcing her eyes down a bit. "So, let's talk about grafting for disease and pest management." She began to write on the white board. "Bottom line is this." With a dry-erase marker, she wrote the words *resistant rootstock*. "You have to pick a rootstock with natural properties that will fight against the diseases which could potentially destroy the crop." Jordan drew a grafting illustration with a crosscut view. "There's a hundred-dollar scientific word for this that I'll spare you from. All you really need to know is that it's the process of combining the DNA from one plant to that of another. One part, the root stock," she circled that part of the illustration, "has the disease and pest resistance we desire. We'll combine that with a shoot," she pointed to the other drawing, "containing the desired properties of an apple tree suitable for either the climate, soil conditions, or for the particular fruit we seek to produce." Jordan wrote a number on the white board. "Apples alone are a 1.7 billion-dollar industry in this country." She turned completely and faced her audience, pointing to the number. "Disease and pests drive down production, and in turn, the profitability." She advanced the PowerPoint. "If we can take the properties of a very hearty and resistant apple tree rootstock and combine it with the canopy of a desirable apple tree, profitability goes up, because we reduce loss at the most elementary level. Which means more apples for me." She smiled and bit into an apple she had sitting on her podium.

Jordan started chewing, as she scanned the faces in the room. A few looked familiar. Her eyes were drawn around the room and to the back, left corner. Time stopped and her hearing blunted. She grabbed the podium to steady herself. Sitting there, looking back at her, was the woman she'd traveled hundreds of miles to find. Before her sat Professor Noeul Scott.

A burning tingle started in her side, the same sensation she felt every time she thought about Noeul and this insane quest to find her. Jordan's hand went to her side. She forgot to breathe. Within seconds, her body screamed for oxygen and she sucked in a ragged breath, along with a chunk of apple. Violent coughing made her eyes water, and she turned away from her audience to bring her hand to her mouth. Jordan tried to pull in the air her body desperately needed. Unfortunately, the chunk of apple was lodged tight. Jordan's eyes watered as she struggled to bring her body under control.

Kallie jumped to her side and turned to the audience. "Let's take a break and come back..."

Jordan coughed one more time and managed to yell, "Wait!" She was terrified Noeul would leave the room and disappear completely. She couldn't let that happen, not when she was so close.

Jordan stood, seeing the concern in Kallie's eyes. She wiped her own eyes and tried once again to bring herself under control. With all she had left, she turned and locked eyes with Noeul, willing her to stay in place until she could get to her. Walking around the podium, she coughed again and went directly to Noeul and bent down at her side.

"Professor Scott, please don't go anywhere until I have a chance to talk to you. I can't explain how important this is to me and maybe to the world in general. Please, stay until we can meet. I'm begging you."

Noeul's eyes were wide, as she shook her head up and down. Jordan squeezed her hand and noticed her holding her side. "Are you okay?" Again, she watched Noeul shake her head. Jordan coughed again, still trying to bring herself under control.

Noeul furrowed her brow. "Are you?"

"Aside from almost choking to death, better than I've been in a long time. We'll take a break here in a bit. I know this is going to seem like a crazy request. Please, please don't leave without talking with me."

Noeul finally laughed. "I promise. Believe it or not, I came here for you. So, I'm not going anywhere. It's good to see you, Jordan. Now," she looked around, shifting in her seat, "I think everyone else is wondering what the hell's going on and is looking to you to finish your presentation. I'll be here. Go."

Jordan took her first clear breath and let a smile escape as she shifted her eyes around. "Right."

Once she returned to the front of the room, Jordan continued her presentation. Her mind raced with the need to finish her session. Part of her brain was talking about grafting apples, while the other calculated the odds of running into Noeul at this workshop. Grateful beyond all things for her ability to multitask, she allowed the analytical part of her brain to focus on the task at hand, while the emotional side concentrated on Noeul. The action wasn't new to her even if the subject matter was. Jordan's eyes flitted frequently to Noeul to quell the overwhelming fear that she'd look up and find her gone.

Leaving time for a question and answer session at the end, Jordan began to wrap up her thoughts. After ten minutes and a few above-average questions, she thanked everyone for their attention and fought the urge to leap over those who stepped forward to speak with her. She looked up and caught Noeul covering what appeared to be an amused smile. She did her best to focus her attention on those in front of her, while she graciously answered their specific questions and took the time to pass out business cards for those who were looking for reference material. Ten minutes later, she called for Bandit to come and found Noeul leaning up against the wall.

Noeul shook her head. "Professor Armstrong. God that makes me feel ancient since you were a student when I stopped teaching. It's been a long time." Noeul extended her hand out for Bandit to smell. Rewarded with a lick and a tail wag, she scratched behind his ears.

Jordan scowled. "It's Jordan, only Elle makes me use that title." Jordan extended her hand. "Professor Scott, it's a pleasure, one a long time in coming."

"Well, if you want me to call you Jordan, you'll have to agree to call me Noeul. Fair is fair. Besides, I haven't been Professor Scott for a very long time." The two women stared at each other for a few minutes before both spoke at once.

"Do you…"

"How about…"

Both laughed, and Jordan bit her lip. "I was going to ask if you wanted to go have a cup of coffee or maybe some lunch? That was the last session until one thirty."

"I've seen what I came for, Jordan. Lunch sounds good. Is there someplace we can go that will let us bring this guy?" Noeul reached down and patted Bandit's head.

"I'm not sure, let's go ask Kallie. Maybe she'll know of a place with some outdoor seating." Jordan started to walk off. Instead, she turned back as if concerned Noeul would walk away.

Noeul laughed. "I'll be right here." Jordan took two steps and ran into Kallie, literally, bringing even more laughter from Noeul.

Kallie rubbed her head.

"Sorry, Kallie." Jordan grabbed her hand and led her back to Noeul. "Kallie, you remember Professor Noeul Scott, right?"

Kallie extended her hand. "Of course, I do. It's an honor to have you Professor Scott. If I'd known you'd be here, I'd have had you as a speaker as well."

Noeul accepted the proffered hand. "Good to see you, Kallie, and it's Noeul. I'm pretty far from being a presenter these days."

Jordan stood watching the two women, both superb researchers in their respective fields, both a part of her past. One whom she hoped she could convince to be part of her future. Her musings were broken by the sound of Kallie's voice.

"I still can't believe you're here. Jordan has been on a mission to find you. Instead, you find her. I'd call that destiny."

Jordan blushed as she looked up to see Noeul grab her side. "Anyway, Kallie, Professor…I mean Noeul and I, are looking for a place to go grab some lunch that has outdoor seating, because I have Bandit." Jordan pointed down to the black-and-white border collie that had taken up residence on her foot.

Kallie shrugged her shoulders. "Why don't you let him stay here with me for now? Actually, Jordan, I know you have a lot you want to talk to Noeul about. Why don't you let me take him home to play with Ben for the evening? I know I'm going to regret it, because he's going to be insufferable until we get him a dog now. What do you say?"

"Are you sure, Kallie?"

"I am." Kallie looked to Noeul. "If you can stand to spend a few hours with the seeker here?"

Jordan looked anxiously at Noeul, silently saying a prayer she would be receptive.

Noeul raised an eyebrow. "I'm game if you are."

Jordan looked at Kallie with overwhelming gratitude. "Well then, let's go find a place where I can tell you a tale you're not going to believe."

Chapter Fifteen

NOEUL SLIPPED BEHIND THE wheel of her truck and took a deep breath. Kallie had called Jordan 'the seeker,' the exact term Aggie had used as a moniker for the one who was coming. Her dragon tattoo was itching or tingling, something. The rearview mirror showed Jordan following her. They'd decided on a restaurant in Shepherdstown. They parked the vehicles at Noeul's bed and breakfast. The Blue Moon Café was well within walking distance. Soon they were seated at a set of metal table and chairs, situated on a flagstone patio surrounded by trees and greenery.

Their waiter set down the beers they'd selected. He waited for them to look at the menu and took their order. Noeul held the icy mug near her lips and asked the first question. "Okay, want to explain to me why you almost had everyone dialing 911 today when you saw me?" She drank of the smooth, amber microbrew they'd both ordered. She watched Jordan take a sip of her beer and pause for a moment, as if contemplating an answer.

"First, I need to tell you why I was looking for you. After that, I'm going to tell you a story that'll be hard to swallow for those with an analytical mind. No matter how open you are to things you can't explain, this one will leave you scratching your head. I don't know how much of my recent research you've read. My main focus, for the last few years, has been creating a superfood by grafting a species that resembles quinoa, onto a root stock that can grow in almost any condition. The hardiest and most resilient things on this earth, besides cockroaches are..."

"Weeds."

Jordan pointed her finger at Noeul, emphasizing her correct conclusion. "Exactly. I want a root stock that can basically thrive in almost any soil condition, a wide variety of climates, and for the *pièce de résistance*, with little to no rainfall."

"Lofty goal."

"And damn near impossible, because I'm missing something from the grafting process. All my trials have failed to produce consistent results. My end game is to be able to grow a food, rich in nutrients and protein, in the African desert. If I can find a way to do that, we could significantly impact world hunger. Which leads me to why I wanted to find you. I've read everything you've ever written, even the obscure essays you wrote while you were a university student, long before you were a PhD. I can quote every single word, verbatim."

Noeul stopped her with an upheld hand. "How in heaven's name did you even find any of those papers? That was over two decades ago."

Jordan took a deep breath. "I'm a researcher and a scientist, like you, Noeul. I dig for answers and, with the help of a good memory, I have every bit of your research up here." She pointed to her own head in emphasis. "All along I've had this," Jordan stopped and shook her head, "obsessive belief, that what I'm missing from my research can be found there." Jordan leaned up and held her finger a fraction from Noeul's forehead. Noeul's shocked expression must have concerned Jordan, because she withdrew her hand and looked down into her lap.

"Jordan, I've been out of the scientific research business for a very long time."

Jordan smiled at her. "You mean to tell me, since you left Cornell, you've done no research and have been traveling the world looking at ancient ruins?"

Noeul's face heated. As a fellow scientist, Jordan would know that the need to experiment and test theory was an integral part of who they were on an elementary level. "I didn't say that. I said I've been out of the business. There are always questions to answer. I've spent a bit of time studying your research of late, too."

"If you've done that, you know I'm missing something. No matter what I try, I can't find it. I believe, with every scientific bone in my body, you and your research are the key."

Noeul closed her eyes and listened to the sound of muted conversation, silverware clinking against plates, chairs scrapping against the stone beneath them. "I don't know if I can help, Jordan." She watched, as Jordan scooted back in her chair, then leaned forward to rest her elbows on her knees. Her hands were steepled at her mouth, and Noeul could see the gears grinding behind her eyes.

"That's where I'm going to argue with you, Professor Scott. The fact that you aren't working in a lab at Cornell doesn't mean that your mind doesn't have the answer. You might not know it yet. I, on the other hand, don't have any doubt about it. I believed it so much that I took a year's sabbatical to find you." Jordan straightened and moved to the edge of her seat.

Noeul was shocked. "What do you mean, to find me?"

***

Jordan knew that what she was about to say could make or break her chances with Noeul. Would Noeul be angry that she'd been actively seeking and opening the memorials that had been left in tribute to her dead wife? Would the woman before her feel violated, or would she understand the desperation to find her at any cost? Would she believe that something beyond the physical world was guiding and leading her to each memorial? There was only one way to find out. She steepled her fingers and began.

"About a year ago, I started trying to find you. I sent letters to every address that had ever been listed for you. I sent emails to every known electronic address that had ever been recorded. I talked to former colleagues, friends, and anyone else I could find who even vaguely remembered you and..."

"Aggie."

Jordan dropped her eyes. "Yes. I kept running into brick walls at every turn. After Professor James died, you basically dropped off the face of the earth." Jordan stopped and looked up at Noeul. "I remember what happened, and I'm so very, very sorry."

Noeul sipped her beer again. "My world dropped out from underneath me when she died. I couldn't take the sadness I saw in others, like what I'm seeing in you now."

Jordan dropped her eyes again. When she'd gathered her thoughts, she sat up straight and looked directly into Noeul's eyes. "About two months ago, I was in the library at Cornell, looking for the book you both authored." Jordan reached down and pulled a file folder out of her messenger bag. Before she'd left her vehicle, she'd collected several things from her quest, hoping to convince Noeul of the unbelievable. She pulled out a folded, yellowed piece of paper. "When I found the book, I also found this." She handed Noeul the paper. She watched as Noeul's eyes squinted to a thin line. Seconds later, they grew wide as they looked back up to Jordan.

The paper in Noeul's hands trembled. "How...how did you get this?" She pointed to the paper.

"When I leafed through the book, this fell out. I thought it was some student's notes, until I saw this." Jordan pointed to the heart with the initials in it. "That led me to believe one of you had written it."

Noeul's hand covered her mouth as she looked at the paper. The waiter returned with their lunch.

"Noeul, do you want to get this to go?"

"Yes, I don't think I can eat right now." Noeul continued to stare at the paper.

Jordan asked the waiter to box the meals up and turned back to the woman who sat slack jawed in front of her. "Noeul, I know this is a lot to take in. I honestly do. I have a great deal to tell you and to explain. I promise, if you'll give me the afternoon, I'll lay everything out. Once I've done that, if you ask me to leave you alone, I'll go and never contact you again. All I ask is that you give me the time to tell you everything."

She watched as a kaleidoscope of thoughts played in Noeul's eyes. Jordan's heart drummed out of control. She felt slightly light-headed, as she waited for an answer. The seconds that ticked by seemed like hours, before Noeul finally nodded her head.

Jordan paid, grabbed their lunch, and reached out to steady Noeul, who nearly stumbled when she rose. Noeul cleared her throat and shook her head. "Let's go back to the bed and breakfast I'm staying at. There's a porch and backyard with seating."

"Sure."

They walked back through the small town that was home to Shepherd University. Pedestrians ducked in and out of small eclectic shops and cafés, while vehicles crawled through town past them. Once they'd reached the Thomas Shepherd Inn, Noeul asked Jordan to wait for her out back while she went to her room for a moment.

Jordan chose a table in a cool area of the yard under shade trees, away from the main house. She wanted some privacy for their discussion. In all the times she'd imagined finding Noeul, at no point had her thoughts run through what she would say to explain all that had come to pass on her quest. To any normal person, her tale would sound completely insane. At the last moment, Jordan decided she needed to hear a supportive voice. She hit speed dial and called Dava. After their typical greeting, Jordan took a deep breath.

Dava plowed forward. "Okay, what's up, Sherlock? You didn't call me to be some perverted heavy breather. Did you flub that presentation or did Kallie hit on you? Something has you tongue tied. Did you already find the next clue?"

"Dava, stop."

There was silence on the line for a moment. "I found her. More accurately, she found me." Jordan slid down in the chair and let her head fall against the wicker back.

"You what? She what? Explain immediately, or I'm coming through this phone and putting smelling salts under your nose. What the hell, JJ?"

Jordan shook herself. "Professor Scott, Noeul, came to the workshop to hear my presentation. She saw the announcement about a change of speaker on the website and decided to come and hear me. I looked to the back of the room and there she sat."

"You're fucking kidding me!"

"As I live and breathe, Watson. Even that was touch and go. When I saw her, I choked on a piece of apple and nearly passed out."

Dava's laugh rang out, and for the first time since finding Noeul, Jordan laughed too, releasing the tension that had been building since her unexpected discovery. "I showed her that original piece of paper with the codes down to the falls at Cornell."

"How'd she take it?"

Jordan rubbed her side that was tingling again. "It shook her up pretty bad. We were getting ready to have lunch. We ended up getting it to go, and we walked back to where she's staying. She went upstairs for a minute, so I took the opportunity to call you."

Dava sighed. "JJ, this has to be pretty shocking to her, and I'm betting you haven't even gotten to the parts that really have no explanation."

"No, and that's what I'm afraid of. What if she thinks I'm a total whack job?"

"Well, you are a whack job, my dear sister. That's beside the point. Just lay it out as simply as you can. Remember, whatever it is that's been guiding you didn't lead you to her only to have her run away. Try to be sensitive to the fact that she lost her wife tragically. This is going to stir that all up again, no matter how long ago it was. Call me tonight and let me know how it goes. I love you, JJ."

"I love you too, Watson, with all my heart. Hey call Mom and—"

"Sarah and let them know the latest. You got it."

"Beautiful and a mind reader. That's why I love you, little sister. Call you tonight."

After they signed off, Jordan held her phone in both hands up to her mouth. She slid it back into her pocket, as she watched Noeul approach. Jordan stood.

"Sit down, Jordan. I think it's time you tell me exactly what's going on." Noeul took a seat across from the one Jordan had been sitting in.

"Like I said before, give me the opportunity to tell you everything, and if you ask, I'll go and never contact you again. If you hear everything I've got to say and can dispel your disbelief, you'll see why I was seeking you out.

"Well, start talking."

Jordan shifted in her seat to fully face Noeul, then leaned forward and clasped her hands together. "Okay, when we left the restaurant, I was getting ready to explain the note I found."

***

Noeul listened intently, as Jordan explained finding the note in the book she'd helped author with Aggie. Hearing that Jordan's sister was a cryptologist and had been the one to help decipher the clues was plausible. What didn't make sense was how Jordan had been able to find the individual memorials she'd placed.

"So, let me get this straight. You found this list," she pointed to the bucket-list paper, "and your sister decoded it. You went down to the glade and stumbled across the memorial I placed there." She took a deep breath. "All that's believable, for the most part. Next, you say she decoded the clues to Havasu Falls. Somewhere in that process, you took a sabbatical to follow our bucket list in hopes it would lead to me or the next check box. Am I understanding that correctly?"

Jordan looked up and nodded her head.

"Jordan, what I don't understand is this. I never put the clues to the next location in that memorial. For that matter, I didn't put the clues in *any* of them."

Jordan's head shot up and disbelief filled her face.

"What do you mean? I took a picture. Look." Jordan got up and thumbed through the gallery on her smart phone. She turned the screen to show her the pictures of the two notes she'd found inside. "In every memorial, there was a personal note from you and a list of the next clues. In everyone! Without them I wouldn't even have had a clue where to begin looking."

Noeul sat quietly, trying to remember if by chance, she'd accidentally included them. *No, it wouldn't have even been necessary, because I knew where I was going next. I'd already put the memorials together when I placed them. This doesn't make sense...or does it?* "Go on."

Jordan ran her hand across the back of her neck. "At Havasu Falls, I met a woman on the trail. Her mother and grandmother led me through a cleansing ritual to rid me of any negativity. When that was complete, they took me to the cave. After I read the next set of clues, I heard a voice telling me to seek the highest point. We figured out I was headed to Moose Lake in Sequoia National Park. When I got to the lake and climbed to the highest point, I heard a whistle that led me to the tree. I heard a voice tell me to follow my heart. I found the rocks, Noeul. I don't have an explanation for any of it. I never found the source of the whistle. I know what I heard."

"Is that all?"

"Not hardly. I followed the next clues to New Orleans and ended up staying across from a bar called Lafitte's Blacksmith Shop Bar. The bartender hadn't worked there for years. She was called in as an emergency backup. A bartender that just so happened to recognize your book, which I had with me. She showed me a picture of you and Aggie with her. You can guess where all that led me. Last, but not least, was my trip to Acadia with my family. My soon-to-be sister-in-law and I stumbled across a brochure." Jordan pulled it out of her bag and handed it to Noeul. "That version never went to print, because there were major errors." She showed Noeul the dive adventure pamphlet and pointed out the errors. "I had no clues at all other than Acadia, and by some miracle we find this," she pointed to the brochure, "with your picture on it that leads me to..."

Noeul spoke so softly, she could barely hear it herself. "Diver Jon's."

"Yes. My family never accompanied me on the other adventures. I found out Acadia has decent wheelchair accessibility on several trails and adventures, so I brought them along. My sister has spina bifida and is confined to a wheelchair because of her condition. We chose the boat adventure, because the owner figured out a way to make it accessible for..."

"His son, Jon Jr." Noeul covered her mouth as her voice broke.

Jordan got up from her chair and knelt beside Noeul. She held her hand out, and Noeul clasped it in her own. She was silent, not allowing Jordan to say anything else for a few minutes while she tried to collect herself.

Jordan put a finger under Noeul's chin and lifted it until they were eye to eye. "I don't understand it all. I know that some force has been leading me to you. I think we are meant to solve this grafting problem together. Even the fact that we're here right now is a miracle. I wasn't originally supposed to give that presentation. Henry broke both legs skiing. I know you've met that man. What in the hell was he doing skiing? I happened to be back at Cornell to check on a mutual friend, Max Keller, after he fell. I was headed to Harpers Ferry, looking for the next clue to find you. Elle overheard me and asked me to do this as a personal favor to her. I need you to find it within you to trust that I mean you no harm. I'm sorry that I had to invade your privacy, that I disturbed those memorials. I promise I put them back exactly as you placed them and ensured they were water tight. If you have a better explanation for all this, I'm all ears."

Noeul's mind was spinning. She felt sick. The only stabilizing force was Jordan's hand in hers. *What in God's name does this all mean?* This couldn't be clocked up to coincidence. The odds were astronomical. After Aggie's death, her life had been upended and completely off the tracks. Completing their 'bucket list' was her way to heal and pay tribute to the woman she'd loved for so long. She'd revisited the places they'd been together and ventured to the places they'd never gotten to. *I know I didn't put those clues in with her ashes. I know I didn't.*

"Jordan, I think I need a strong drink. How about we walk down to the pub at the corner? I need a shot of Irish whiskey."

Jordan offered a small smile. "My sister has told me, more than once, I've driven her to drink. I think I can accommodate you. Can you stand?"

Noeul nodded and allowed Jordan to help her to her feet. She needed to calm her nerves and process all this. Right now, she felt like she was on overload. She needed to put her analytical mind to work. Mentally, she started columns in her mind, filling in the data from all Jordan had told her.

As they walked to the pub, a million thoughts bombarded her. Jordan was quiet, seemingly content to let her process everything and ready to answer questions when asked. Noeul didn't say anything, as she watched Jordan throw away the now cold lunch. They entered the bar and headed outside to the small tables. After they were seated, Jordan asked her what she'd like.

"Bushmills if they've got it. Three fingers, neat."

"A woman after my own heart. Coming right up." Jordan went back inside to order their drinks.

Noeul's mind spun. The feeling reminded her of being a child on the swings and twisting the chains together tightly, then picking up her feet to spin as the chains unwound. At the end, the forceful jerk always brought her to a dizzied stop. *Years of research and I can't even begin to analyze this with any solid footing. What the hell am I supposed to do with this?*

After a few minutes, Jordan returned with two glasses, placing one down in front of Noeul and holding her own as she sat. "Seek and ye shall find. This quest has been a winding path to find you." Jordan clinked their glasses.

Words floated through Noeul's memory, as she took her first sip. The smooth, amber liquid burned away disbelief as it slid down her throat. A dozen phrases bounced around in front of her eyes, words appearing as if written by an invisible hand. Words that she'd recently heard in different conversations and dreams.

Seeker...Seek.

Words hovered, quick and blurred, like a hummingbird's wings. Phrases drifted in and out of her vision.

...A seeker's heart is destined to find you.

...A seeker will appear.

...The rider is your future and she walks your path.

...Her journey brings her closer to what she seeks.

...You are part of her quest.

...The seeker draws close.

...The distance between you seems like a giant leap. In reality, it's a single step.

Noeul gripped the glass so tightly, her knuckles were turning white. She brought it to her lips, nearly spilling with her shaky hands. Jordan reached out to calm her as she downed a third of the whiskey.

"Oh...my...God..." Noeul whispered.

***

Jordan watched the fear and confusion cross Noeul's face. She knew it was a lot to take in and make sense of. She looked away, trying to give Noeul time to collect herself. The day was warm, and Jordan pulled at her shirt, trying to release the heat that had built up under the collar of her button-down.

Part of her wanted to ask about Noeul's distress, to confirm she was okay. The other part knew that what Noeul needed, more than anything, was time. She used the silence to process a few things of her own. *Noeul said she didn't put the clue sheets in with the memorials. If that's true, how did they get in there? Did Noeul accidently include them?* Somehow, she doubted the woman would have forgotten that detail. *Had someone else found the memorials before her and placed them in there?* That didn't make sense either. Why would anyone do that? Besides, at least two of the memorials required an escort to get to them. There was no logical explanation, and yet she'd taken a picture of the first one and had Sarah's video of another. She slowly sipped her drink while sneaking glances to check on Noeul. She looked up as Noeul spoke.

"I don't understand this, Jordan."

"Well, that makes two of us. I'm willing to try and find the explanation if you are."

"I know I didn't put those clues in Aggie's memorials. I have every one of them she wrote in a keepsake box at my home. I didn't make any copies, and I deciphered the codes before I ever set out. I had pictures on my phone for convenience while I was traveling. Jordan, I can say with surety that I did not put those in there."

Jordan paused and swirled the liquor in her glass before taking a sip. The liquor was certainly calming her nerves. Unfortunately, on an empty stomach, it was going straight to her head. The buzz wasn't unpleasant at all, but it was distracting at a time when she needed all her faculties. "Noeul, I'm going to go order us some food. I know you might not be hungry. I still want you to try. I don't know what you had for breakfast. I've only had a muffin and the apple I almost choked to death on." She grinned and finished the rest of her drink. "I'm going to have another drink. I'm not done numbing my frazzled nerves yet."

"You don't have to do that, we've already thrown one lunch away."

Jordan smiled at her and pointed to her glass. "How about this? I'll let you get the next round to make it up to me. I'll be right back."

The waiter stood near the bar, so she placed an order for them of burgers and fries. Jordan watched Noeul from a distance, the confusion on her face so evident it made Jordan take pause with what she was doing. *Maybe this was a terrible idea. I asked her to give me the afternoon to explain, and she has. If she walks away, I'll have to live with it.*

Jordan walked back to the table and sat down. The urge to say something was creating continual pressure in her chest. She actually coughed and pounded on it with her fist, as if to expel the compulsion from her body. Noeul sat in front of her, staring blankly into her drink.

When she raised her eyes to Jordan's, those eyes didn't seem any clearer.

"I'm at a loss here, Jordan." Noeul put her hands up to her face and rubbed her eyes, shifting nervously in her seat. "I've had some strange things going on of late. Things I can't explain. For the last month or so, I've been having conversations with Aggie."

Jordan's eyes widened.

Noeul shrugged. "I know what you're thinking, and yes, I'm fully aware that Aggie has been gone for years."

"I'm not doubting you. After what I've seen and experienced on this journey, nothing surprises me. Noeul, something has been leading me to you. Something I can't explain no matter how many ways I look at it. There's no logical explanation for those clues, no logical reason for the coincidences that have presented themselves to me. I am sure, beyond a shadow of a doubt, that I've been destined to find you since the very beginning of this. I'm not trying to invade your life. I have a goal to eradicate hunger, if I can. I believe I have the superfood to accomplish that. Unfortunately, it's not hardy enough to survive where I need it to, in places that have little to no rainfall. I'm missing something, and everything tells me what I'm missing...is you."

Noeul didn't reply. The waiter placed their lunch on the table. They ate in silence, not speaking again until they'd consumed at least half their burgers.

"Talk to me, Noeul."

Jordan watched, as the pale woman signaled for the waiter to bring two more drinks. She slid the glass she had back and forth with the thumb and middle finger of her right hand.

"I'm trying to put this all into some kind of logical scenario. It's like looking at Salvador Dali's *The Apotheosis of Homer*. Your mind can't settle on any one thing in the painting, your eye is constantly drawn to something different. Just as you start to settle on the broken bits of Homer, Pegasus catches your eye. Suddenly, you're drawn to Gala. You can never settle, never analyze any one piece."

"Like walking through a carnival funhouse."

Noeul threw her head back and laughed, and Jordan watched some of the tension melt out of the woman right in front of her.

"Yeah, something like that. It's all distorted and disjointed, out of place and context."

Jordan wiped her mouth with the cloth napkin and relaxed back into her chair. "Will you let me help you try and work through it?"

"To be honest, Jordan, I don't think I have a choice." Noeul closed her eyes and shook her head side to side. "I've been listening to my dead wife tell me my future is about to change, that a seeker who walks my path is about to appear. I can name a dozen different phrases you've used or that I've heard in the last three hours that I've dreamed about, had conversations about, and can't seem to get the hell away from. Personally, if you're not a figment of my imagination, I have to believe you've been sent here by the only person in my life who has ever talked to me from beyond the grave."

Jordan wasn't sure how to respond to all Noeul had said. She closed her own eyes and tried to clear her mind, to allow any help from places unseen to guide her as to how to proceed. If only she'd hear the voice, a whistle, anything to try and ease Noeul's distress.

"Noeul, I don't have all the answers. I promise, I'm not a figment of your imagination. I'm very real and well...I need your help. It must be your decision. All I can say is that everything in the marrow of my bones is telling me you are the key."

***

The waiter set down another glass of Bushmills and took their empties and the plates. Noeul looked up to the young man. "Thank you."

He smiled. "Do you need anything else right now?"

Noeul shook her head and pulled her eyes back to Jordan. Her brain was spinning. *Aggie, I need a sign. I don't know what I'm supposed to do.*

Beside them, a woman began furiously digging through her purse. Faint music drifted up from the duffle-bag-sized catchall. The refrain was soft at first, growing in volume as the woman brought out her phone and fumbled with the case around it. The woman swiped at the screen over and over with her finger, unable to answer the call or silence her phone. Noeul heard the entire chorus.

Noeul threw back her head and laughed so loud, all the diners around them turned their heads to her. The attention had no effect on her laughter. She looked at Jordan who seemed alarmed. "Jordan, I'm fine. Aggie has her own way of driving home a point."

Jordan's eyes grew as wide as saucers. "She spoke to you just now?"

Noeul was nearly hiccupping from the boisterous laughter. "Not in the way you think, although it wouldn't be the first time. I asked her for a sign." She nodded to the table where the phone sat on the tabletop, now silent. "In one of our conversations," Noeul made air quotes with her fingers, "Aggie recited the lyrics to a song." Noeul discretely pointed at the table across from them. "That song, 'Turn, Turn, Turn' by the Byrds. Aggie even added a few lines of a time to this and a time to that." Noeul picked up her drink and sipped. "I asked for a sign, and she gave me one. Something I could understand. The fact that the owner of the phone couldn't get it to shut off clearly tells me Aggie's hitting me over the head with a sledgehammer, while wearing a set of velvet gloves."

Jordan sipped her own drink. "You're kidding."

"I couldn't make that up if I tried."

They sat there for a while with their drinks. Twenty minutes later, they paid and began to make their way back to Noeul's bed and breakfast. They walked slowly. Noeul could feel the pleasant stupor from the liquor. She needed to sleep. Jordan's tension was palpable to her. They hadn't discussed where they went from here. Noeul needed to sleep on it and try to process it all somehow. The streets were still busy with people walking in and out of shops. She peered into them as they passed, watching the shoppers peruse the merchandise and make purchases. It was a pleasant evening.

"What are you going to do now, Jordan?"

"Well, I'd say a great deal of that answer depends on you. If you agree to help me, we work out a plan on how to proceed."

Noeul wrapped her arms around herself. "And if I decide not to?"

Jordan put her hands in her back pockets and kicked at a pebble in front of her with the side of her shoe. They'd reached the entrance to Noeul's stop. "Well, if that's your decision, I guess I go pick up my dog and we stay the night. After that, I'll head back to Cornell. I took the sabbatical to find you. I've accomplished that. If you choose not to help me, I'll go back to teaching and researching on my own until I figure out a way to accomplish my goals. I'll help Sam take care of Max and, at some point in the future, I'll be walking my sister down the aisle to marry her fiancé, Sarah. Beyond that, I don't have any plans."

"How are Sam and Max?"

Jordan sighed. "Sam still has the restaurant. Unfortunately, Max has developed signs of dementia."

Noeul reached out and rested a hand on Jordan's forearm. The look on Jordan's face told her Sam and Max meant a great deal to her. "I'm sorry to hear that."

"I appreciate that. We've been doing all we can to hold it at bay."

Noeul crossed her arms. "Other than those two, no one special waiting on you back at Cornell?"

Jordan sighed. "Uh no. I haven't been very lucky in that regard. This morning, you talked to one of the few girlfriends I've ever had. I spent last evening with Kallie, her wife Paula, and their two great kids. I'm married to my research, Noeul. I'm well aware that it can disappoint me. The other side to that is it won't rip my heart out. What about you?"

"I've had opportunity. I've never pursued anything so, no. There is no one special in my life. I have two best friends that run a cabin business. I grow vegetables, make goat cheese, sell soap and lotion at the farmers' market, and enjoy a quiet life with a dog and a one-eyed cat."

Jordan ran her hands through her hair. "Aren't we a pair?"

Noeul wrapped her arms around her chest. "I don't know, Jordan. I don't know. Let me sleep on this, and we'll figure something out tomorrow."

***

Jordan made a call to Kallie and asked if there was any way she could arrange a ride for her. She'd had too much to drink to drive back to Harpers Ferry. She'd thought about getting a hotel there in town for the night. She had Bandit to think about. Kallie said it would take her about twenty minutes to reach her.

After leaving Noeul with her cellphone number, email address, and other pertinent contact information, Jordan went back and sat in her Jeep to wait. She'd turned down Noeul's offer to find her a room, using Bandit as an excuse. There was nothing more she could do right then to convince Noeul to work on the research with her. If she decided to help, Noeul had all the necessary information to contact her.

As Jordan put the seat back in the Jeep and closed her eyes, she thought about the striking woman that she'd spent the evening with. Jordan knew how old Noeul was. Nothing she could see disclosed Noeul's age other than a few stray streaks of silver in her long, black hair. Jordan shook her head and let that thought settle to the bottom of all the things she had on her mind.

Twenty minutes flew by, and soon she heard a vehicle pull up beside her. Jordan sat up and looked out her window to an eye roll and a wave from Kallie. Jordan got out of her vehicle and slid into the passenger side of the Dodge Ram club cab. As she was buckling her seatbelt, Jordan started to laugh.

Kallie furrowed her brow at Jordan. "What?"

"The days when you used to pick me up certainly have changed. Bye-bye Corvette convertible, hello diesel monster truck."

Kallie laughed too. "Shut up, jackass. It's hard to hook up a cattle trailer to a sports car. I'm taking you back to our place. We have an extra room, and Bandit is already comfortably snuggled up with Ben. We can talk about today, and Paula will feed you dinner."

"I'm in no shape or mood to argue. Honestly, I'm not really hungry, though I'm grateful for the offer, so put it in gear."

They didn't talk on the ride back to the farm. Apple groves slid by the window, as her conversation with Noeul repeated, over and over, in her mind. It was obvious Noeul believed her that some higher power was guiding Jordan to the memorials. It appeared that Noeul was also being contacted and affected by something that defied conventional explanation.

They pulled into the gravel drive of the farm, and Kallie parked the truck. "Come on, let's go have a seat on the porch."

Jordan crawled out of the truck and made her way up the steps. She sat down heavily in the swing and pushed off with one foot to start it rocking. Kallie went in the house and got them something to drink. She sat down and matched Jordan's rocking motion. "So, tell me what the hell is going on."

Jordan rolled her head to face Kallie and laughed. The buzz from the whiskey was still pleasant like the breeze blowing across the porch, warm and sweet. The sounds of the farm softly called out all around her, crickets in the background, the horses nickering and whinnying in the pasture.

"Kallie, I'm not sure you would believe it if I told you. Hell, half the time, I don't believe it. I'm a scientist. I believe what I can see, test in the lab, and duplicate repeatedly. I don't believe in luck or coincidence. I've never believed in heaven or hell, and I never believed you could talk to the dead."

"But?"

Jordan took a deep breath. "But, in the last few months, I've been led around the country by deciphering clues apparently being revealed by a ghost, guided to the next set by something unseen, and unexpectedly directed to be at the right place at the right time, like

231

today. I wasn't supposed to be the speaker at all. Martin breaks both legs, Elle asks me to fill in, and Noeul shows up. I don't have explanations for any of it. All I can tell you is, it all happened."

Kallie took a sip from her glass as they rocked back and forth.

"And your conversation with Professor Scott?"

Jordan rubbed her eyebrows with her thumb and forefinger, trying to rub through the alcohol haze to find a coherent description of the conversation. "The short version is, she's been visited by her wife who, as you know, died years ago. She's been telling Noeul that someone was looking for her and that it's time for her to get back to living."

Kallie shook her head. "And it all came together today, here?"

"Exactly."

"That's a lot to process, Jordan. I'm not sure how I'd handle it. I do believe there are forces outside of our control that are at work. I can tell you it's a pure miracle that the woman you knew from our past met a down to earth woman like Paula, fell madly in love, and moved to this farm. That same woman has two growing children and..."

Kallie's words drifted off until Jordan finally turned to her. "And what?"

Kallie put her hand on her stomach. "And one on the way."

Jordan grinned as she looked at Kallie, who was smiling shyly. "Oh, Kallie, that's wonderful!" She sat her glass down and hugged the blushing woman. "When?"

"I'm only two months along. We haven't told anyone yet." Kallie wiped at tears. "Damn hormones."

"I feel privileged you chose to share it with me." Jordan kissed her forehead.

Kallie pulled back, still wiping tears and laughing. "I figure if anyone could appreciate the pure miracle of my life, it would be you."

"Certainly feels like an alternate universe. If you'd have given me the choice of scenarios with you being a scientist working in a huge corporate lab, or you being a researcher, a wife, and mother to three children, I know where my money would have been. The reality is much better, trust me. I've never seen you happier."

Kallie shook her head. "Jordan, I was a different kind of happy when we were together. I wouldn't trade my life now for anything. Know that the one I had with you wasn't so bad." She looked around. "You deserve this kind of happiness. Maybe it's not a farm, wife, and three kids that's in your future. I can tell you it can be something more than research and a dog."

Jordan scooted over and put her arm around Kallie. For the first time in a very long time, Jordan wondered if there really was more to life than microscopes and scientific process.

***

Noeul lay turned on her side, watching the shadows bounce around the room. It felt like she was floating in dim light. She'd asked for a sign and Aggie had provided one, in spades. Across the room, a wooden clock hung on the wall, the second hand loudly ticking off each moment of time in the quiet room. She could hear people passing by in the distance, laughing and talking.

Life continued to roll on. Nothing stopped it. No amount of hiding up on a mountain, no amount of cutting off contact with every part of her previous life, prevented life from moving forward, one second at a time. Over a decade ago, Noeul had pushed the stop button, built herself a castle in the sky, and walled off her heart and her emotions. In one afternoon, her perfectly ordered life had been tossed in the blender. *That's not true and I know it. The reality is my life is far from perfect.* Noeul couldn't say she was truly happy, contented yes, happy no.

Her journal lay on the table. She sat up and wiped her face, then found the pen that lay tucked inside.

All I ever wanted to do was teach, research, and spend my life with Aggie. Fate and an unknown heart condition threw a monkey wrench into my plans. Now, I find out the woman I loved with all my heart, has been leading someone right to my door. Well close enough. How am I supposed to make sense of any of this? I feel like I'm standing in the middle of a minefield, and someone has handed me a connect-the-dots picture for a road map. Do I accept this for what it appears to be on the surface? A student turned brilliant researcher, reaching out to a former professor for help with a project? Or do I see this for what I think Aggie has intended it to be, a new day with new possibilities?

This morning I sat in a classroom and watched one of the most brilliant minds I've ever seen. Jordan is dedicated to her field and her cause. She reminds me of who and what I used to be all those years ago.

What the hell do I do now?

Noeul shut the journal and walked into the bathroom to turn on the hot water in the bathtub. She poured in fragrant bath crystals and began to undress, her mind rolling over and over. The steam rose off the surface, as she allowed her body to sink into the water. She slid down until only her head was above the surface. Noeul chuckled, as she locked her knees under the water. The tub was not large by any stretch of the imagination and yet, she could stretch completely out because of her diminutive status. Noeul smiled. *That was always one of Aggie's biggest bitches when we traveled.* Her wife had loved soaking in the tub. With Aggie's height, she always complained that either her knees or her toes were above the water line.

The tension began to leave Noeul's body and float away on the steam. Tight muscles relaxed, as she was lulled into a stupor. Not quite asleep, yet she was certain she was not in the conscious world either. Pictures flashed on her eyelids...Aggie...her primitive lab. Sunset, sunrise, and the sensation of running. Running while digital numbers of a clock flipped forward like a deck of picture cards, each a little different, giving the illusion of movement and time passing. She watched her life flash with each card, right up to the minute Aggie collapsed on the running trail in her arms. After that, blank cards flipped, one after another. No movement, no change, nothing at all. Card after card, exactly the same, until they weren't. The change was subtle at first; a seed that grew into a sprout. The sprout grew into a sapling, then progressed into a tree with a broad canopy. Emerging branches reached to the sun, forming shapes.

Noeul jerked awake, cold water touching her chin. She shook her head, shivering, as she pulled the plug and drained the water as she rose. She dried off and slid into her pajamas, her side tingling as the vivid dream replayed in her mind. Once under the covers, she picked up the journal again.

Enough blank cards. Life's too short as it is to have blank moments in time.

***

Jordan held the Cornell University mug in her hand, sipping rich, dark coffee. She watched, as Bandit sniffed around the edge of the yard. He dropped and rolled around in the grass to scratch his back, while he made noises of complete happiness. *Simple pleasures of life.*

Kallie sat down on the swing beside her. "How's your head?"

Jordan smiled and accepted the two pills Kallie held out for her. "Better soon, I'm sure."

"Thought you could use those. How'd you sleep?"

"Restless, even with that amount of alcohol in my system."

Kallie sipped from her own coffee and stared out into the yard. "What are you going to do now?"

"No clue. That'll depend a great deal on Professor Scott. At this point, I have no idea what she's going to do. I'm going to hang around until I hear from her, one way or another. Once I have that answer, I'll figure out which way I'm going."

"Well, I hope you find your way back here for a visit. You ready for me to take you back to your Jeep?"

"I am. I could use a run with Bandit and a shower."

Once they pulled up to Jordan's Jeep, Kallie put a hand on Jordan's forearm. "Keep the faith, Jordan. I'm betting there are still a few more miracles to come in your life."

Jordan leaned over hugged Kallie and kissed her cheek. "Thanks, Kallie, for everything." Jordan's phone dinged with a text message. She pulled it from her pocket and looked at her friend with a raised eyebrow. "I'm about to see if one of those miracles might happen today." She held up her phone. "She wants to talk."

"Let me know how it turns out. I love a good mystery."

"Let's hope it doesn't turn out to be a tragedy."

"Come back and visit, Jordan, please?"

"I will. Take care. Come on, Bandit." Jordan climbed out of Kallie's truck and typed out a quick message.

"I'm downstairs at my Jeep, want some coffee?"

"Meet me in the backyard in fifteen minutes."

"Okay."

"And bring coffee…lots of it."

Jordan laughed and signaled Bandit to follow, while she made her way down the street to pick up coffee and some pastries. Once she'd made her purchases, she walked back to the bed and breakfast and returned to the same chairs they'd occupied the night before.

"Good morning." Jordan handed Noeul a cup of coffee and set down the carrier holding three more cups and the bag of pastries.

Noeul accepted the cup. "Thanks. Your head hurt as much as mine?"

"It did. Thankfully, Kallie gave me some Motrin. I can go get you some if you need something."

"No, I'm good." Noeul gestured with the coffee. "This will do the trick. They serve good coffee here. I'm guessing this is some high test. I'll be fine."

Jordan pulled a flakey pastry out of the bag. She tore part of it off and tossed it to Bandit, who sat beside her licking his lips. "Don't tell Sam. Got it, Bandit?"

The dog lay down at her feet, as she sipped her coffee. They were silent for a few moments, the air still and damp with morning dew on the ground around them.

"I've made a decision, Jordan. I honestly don't know where this is going to lead us by any means. Somehow, I think collaborating is important. I'm not even sure I can help you, but I'm willing to try."

Jordan let out the breath she'd been holding. She had no doubt Noeul was the key, and she was beyond grateful her former professor was willing to step out of her self-imposed exile.

"I don't know either. Thank you, I'm grateful for the opportunity."

Noeul sat back and sipped the coffee. "Come back to Topside with me and look at what I've been doing there. I have a small lab that we can do some basic things in. I've got animals I have to care for, and I've been away enough. Actually, this is the longest period I've been away in years."

Jordan thanked whatever spirits had led her to Noeul and smiled over the rim of her cup. "I'm on sabbatical. I'll go wherever you need me to."

Chapter Sixteen

A LITTLE OVER THREE hours later, Noeul looked in her rearview mirror to see if the black Jeep was still following. She could see Jordan behind her, driving with the windows down, her arm and Bandit's nose sticking out the side windows. Noeul had released her hair from the silver clasp and let it whip around her in the breeze. Soon, they would be at Kelly and Miranda's. She'd already called to advise them she was bringing company. They'd been full of questions. Noeul held them off by telling them she would fill them in when they arrived. Jordan had retrieved her belongings and checked out, and they'd met up at a small gas station.

The closer they got to home, the more relaxed Noeul was. Home was where she could find her balance. The minute her tires hit the gravel road, Noeul was filled with peace. The comfortable home came into view and her world found its center again. The smiling faces that greeted her warmed Noeul from the inside out.

Miranda came off the porch and immediately threw an arm around Noeul's shoulders as she stepped from the truck. "Welcome home." Miranda nodded her head toward Jordan's Jeep. "And you brought friends I see."

Jordan let Bandit out and stood by her Jeep, as if waiting for permission to approach. Noeul waved her up and introduced them, while Kelly made her way over to the group.

"Jordan, these two are my best friends, Miranda and Kelly Standish, former Green Bank scientists, now owners of this fine lodging establishment." She turned and motioned to Jordan. "This is Jordan Armstrong, a former student of mine and now a professor at Cornell."

The initial greetings left Noeul feeling secure that her friends were open to having a new face join their merry group. It was confirmed shortly after, as Jordan sat at the table laughing and joking with Miranda as if she'd been with them for years.

"Kelly, this is the best kale soup I've ever had." Jordan held up her hand. "Please don't tell my mother I said that."

Kelly held up three fingers. "Scout's honor."

Miranda began to clear the dishes. "What're your plans?"

Noeul smiled. "I thought we'd saddle Thor and Athena and head up the mountain. I'm sure Leo would like to head home, and I'll show Jordan around my primitive lab."

Kelly laughed. "Jordan, don't let her fool you. Her lab up there is far from primitive, even if It might not have everything you're used to at the university. I won't be surprised if you enjoy it more than any lab you've ever been in. The view is incredible."

Jordan shook her head. "What I'm really looking for can't be found in a lab. It's what she has in here," Jordan pointed to Noeul's head, "that I'm really in need of. She was an outstanding professor, and her research was ahead of its time. Primitive lab or not, I believe with everything in me, she's the missing piece."

Noeul shook her head. "If we don't get up the mountain, we can't even begin to get started. Jordan, anyone you need to contact? Once we leave here, you're in the land of no cell service *and* no internet."

Jordan nodded her head. "Yeah, I need to call my sister, if I can use your phone for a minute?"

"There's a phone in the office so you can have some privacy." Miranda pointed to a door down the hall.

After Jordan left the room, the inquisition began. Miranda's protective nature was immediately front and center. "You not only went to see her, you brought her home? And you're taking her up on the mountain. Noeul, this isn't like you."

Kelly stood at the sink, her hands on her hips. "Miranda, Noeul's a grown woman. I don't think Jordan forced her into this. Besides, it's none of our business what she does."

Noeul glanced up at her friends, grateful for their support and protectiveness. "Thank you both. I love you to the ends of the earth for everything you do for me. I'll try to explain this as best I can. Do you remember me telling you that Aggie has been talking to me off and on the last few months?" She waited for their acknowledgement. "Apparently, I'm not the only one she's been talking to. It seems, she's been leading Jordan through our bucket list to find me."

Miranda sat back and folded her arms. "She what?"

Noeul proceeded to relay to them everything that had happened in Harpers Ferry, including Jordan's revelations. "Apparently, Aggie's been facilitating Jordan's quest to find me." Noeul proceeded to explain the peculiarities involved in Jordan's quest and how she'd ended up in West Virginia.

Kelly set another cup of coffee down in front of Noeul. "Honey, I'm not beyond believing in things I can't see. I'm trying to wrap my head around something that doesn't make sense."

Miranda furrowed her brow. "None of that explains why you'd bring her here. She could be a stalker for all we know."

Kelly smacked Miranda on the back of the head, eliciting a shocked ow from her wife. "I think Noeul is smart enough to make this decision. Let her finish."

"The kicker to all this is that in each of the memorials, she found a set of coded clues to the next location."

Miranda fended off another blow from her wife. "Okay, okay. Geez. Did you leave a memorial to Aggie at the Kearneysville Research Center?" Miranda rubbed the spot on the back of her head where Kelly's point had been made.

"Not exactly. I left one in Harpers Ferry. She hadn't had time to find it yet. I found her instead."

Kelly covered Noeul's hand. "I get the feeling that's not the interesting part is it?"

"No." Noeul explained the supernatural elements related to the capsules and watched her skeptical friends try to digest the information. "You can stop worrying about Jordan's character. I called Cornell last night and talked with my former colleague that sent her to Kearneysville. She gave Jordan a glowing recommendation and vouched for her character. Elle is the dean and a very old friend. I have no concerns about my safety."

"Are you sure about this, Noeul?"

Noeul took a deep breath and blew it out. "I'm not sure how to answer that, Kelly. I asked for a sign for what I should do. I got one that related to that scripture I told you Aggie quoted me. It's too much for coincidence. For now, I'll follow my gut instinct and see where it goes. Aggie never led me down a path I regretted."

✳✳✳

Jordan sat at the desk and waited for Dava to pick up, realizing that her sister wouldn't recognize the number. She hoped the location would be enough for her to answer.

"Hello?"

Jordan smiled at the sound of her sister's reassuring voice. "Hey, little sister. Calling to check in."

"Are you at Noeul's yet?"

"Close. We're at her friend's house, getting ready to go up the mountain...on horseback."

"You're kidding right?"

"After everything on this journey, this is the least weird thing I've called to tell you about. Noeul lives in the Quiet Zone near Green Bank, West Virginia. There's no passable road up to her place and once we get there, no communication."

"I beg to differ, big sister. The fact that there is a place with no roads and no communication sounds way too weird for me. How am I supposed to get in touch if I need you?" Dava's voice had turned from teasing to concerned.

"I'll give you Miranda and Kelly's number. From what she's told me, it's a short ride up to Noeul's place. I'll do my best to come down and make contact as often as I can. I'll talk with her friends to see if they'd be willing to run an emergency message up if needed. We're going to Noeul's soon to start work. This is what I've been searching for, Watson. I've got to take a chance."

Dava whispered into the phone. "What if she's an axe murderer?"

"Dava!"

"Well?"

Jordan laughed. "I love you, little sister. Tell Mom and Sarah hi for me, and I promise, I'll check in with you in a few days." She gave her sister the number that was printed on the business cards that sat on the desk, then said a final good-bye before walking back out to the kitchen. She stopped short when she heard voices. After hearing the concern from Noeul's friends, Jordan wondered if this was a good idea. She knew she'd been drawn here. At this point, it would be impossible to deny her excitement at finding Noeul. There was no doubt that Noeul agreeing to help had fueled Jordan's spirit. She leaned against the wall, trying to come up with something that might ease Miranda and Kelly's concerns. *Maybe some humor.*

Jordan was smiling as she entered the kitchen, her hands in the pocket of her jeans. "My sister is concerned I'm going off with an axe murderer. I told her I'd ask you to make sure." The comment sent roaring laughter reverberating off the walls of the kitchen, and Jordan watched as Noeul shook her head.

Noeul pointed to her friends. "These two are in agreement with your sister, although I think they are more concerned about you wielding the axe."

Jordan tried to make sure her smile revealed everything about her. "I can promise you that the only thing I intend to take from Noeul is the knowledge she's willing to pass on to me. I have great hope that she's the missing link." Jordan looked at a red-faced Noeul and stammered a bit. "I mean, her research, that's what I've been missing. Not to say...I'll shut up now and go pull some of my gear out of the Jeep to take with me." Jordan stood to leave the kitchen, her face burning.

Miranda tipped her coffee cup at Jordan. "As long as she doesn't go missing. If that happens, Lord help you."

Jordan slowly shook her head up and down. "Noted."

***

Bandit was lying on the porch with Kyo as if they'd been friends forever. Jordan had watched them playing through the window, while she was on the phone with Dava. The dogs had made fast friends as soon as they'd arrived and now seemed inseparable. Both followed her out to the Jeep, rough housing along the way, chasing and play fighting behind her. Occasionally, they'd dart right in front of her, nearly causing her to trip.

"Okay, you two. I see you." She stopped and scratched them both under the chin. She sorted through her belongings. Clothes she could wash, and from the sounds of where they were going, she was sure that fashion would quickly lose out to function. Her backpack could serve to carry plenty. Some things would have to wait for a second trip if she stayed very long. Jordan wondered, as she flipped through her selection of paperbacks, if Noeul had a library. She stuffed her worn copy of the complete works of Henry David Thoreau and two of her favorite Nevada Barr's Anna Pigeon series in her bag.

Once she had her items sorted, she set the bag beside the Jeep and looked up to see Noeul leading two beautiful horses in her direction. "Our Ubers I presume?"

Noeul patted the side of each horse's neck, as she stopped by Jordan. "Meet Thor and Athena. Thor is a good bit bigger, but he's gentle in nature. He'll be your trusty steed. I usually use one or both horses to pack goods in and out. Fortunately for you, I brought them both down with me. We'll come back down in a few days, so you'll be able to bring more of your things. You ready to go?"

Jordan raised an eyebrow and tilted her head toward the house. "Have their fears about my intentions been sufficiently assuaged?"

241

"For now. If we don't show up back here in two days, the cavalry will be coming in force." Noeul kicked at the gravel under her feet.

"I promise not to give them anything to worry about. I'm ready if you are."

Noeul handed her the reins. "Will Bandit be okay to walk?"

Jordan nodded her head. "He's an excellent trail dog. I've had him on day hikes with me before. As long as there's water along the way, he'll be fine. And he'll sleep tonight."

"I'm sure, once we get there, he'll catch his second wind and want to explore. We'll see how it goes." They mounted the horses and rode up to the house where Miranda stood with her arms around Kelly.

"You two be careful riding up," Kelly said. "We'll see you in a few days."

"Or sooner." Miranda grumbled before Kelly could jab her with an elbow. "Ow."

Twenty minutes had gone by when they stopped to let the horses and dogs drink. Jordan looked around at the dense forest. Oaks and maples made broad canopies and offered cool shade from the summer heat. The temperatures weren't unbearable, given their current altitude. She looked around and it gave her little doubt about the season. Green was the predominate color, complimented with splashes of white in the occasional flower on the forest floor.

"How long have you lived up here?"

Noeul stopped to think about it. "About nine years I think. The house was finished in 2010. I didn't move in right away. I was still traveling."

Jordan decided to keep the conversation going. "What made you decide to build here?"

"Aggie and I had started thinking about retirement, so we looked for property in a place where we could do the things we enjoyed, hiking, biking, and exploring. Some of Aggie's family is from the area, and she had a distant relative that owned this property. We worked out a deal with him for a down payment and hunting rights. After her death, I went forward with our plans."

Jordan thought about the daunting task of building up here in the mountains. With no road, she wondered how they'd done it. She decided to hold that question until they reached the house.

Everything around them on the journey up the mountain harkened back to a simpler time. There were no cellphone towers, no power lines, and no skyscrapers spoiling the view. Other than the trail they were on, there were no visible signs of human existence anywhere. The trail was worn earth, probably created by the years of travel Noeul did back and forth to Kelly and Miranda's, and them to her.

Jordan looked up to see Noeul holding up her hand for her to stop and silently pointing off to her right. Three deer stood grazing near the creek bed. Jordan smiled at their seemingly disinterested postures. A few yards past that, Noeul pointed again to where a red fox dug at the earth beneath its paws. They watched the fox stick its nose into the earth, stop and dig some more. Eventually, the fox came up with a field mouse in its jaws and sprinted off.

Jordan looked at Noeul's smile and thought how beautiful the woman was. Her dark hair cascaded down her back, pulled back from her face in a silver clasp. The tiny crease lines at the edges of her eyes were a small sign of her age. *Get a grip, Jordan. Focus.*

After about two hours, Jordan found herself approaching an opening from the forest they were exiting. The sun was reflected off the glass front of a house set back into the hillside. The roof was covered in greenery that hid most of the structure. Off to one side, there was a paddock. A man was walking out of some type of shelter with a bucket in his hand. He threw up his arm in greeting, as he passed through the gate and walked closer to the house.

Noeul called out to him. "Hey, Leo, you just milk her?"

"Yes ma'am. Got some this morning too. I put it in the glass jars and labeled them like you said."

Noeul climbed off Athena and made quick introductions. "Leo, this is Jordan Armstrong. Jordan, this is Leo Tiggs, Kelly and Miranda's ranch hand. He helps keep things running down there and occasionally helps me up here."

Leo set the bucket down, took off his hat, and shook Jordan's hand. "Pleased to meet you."

Jordan felt the strong grip and the rough texture of his hand in hers. *Working hands.* "Pleasure to meet you too, Leo."

Leo put his hat back on, picked up the bucket, and began walking toward the house. "Glad to see you made it home. I enjoy coming up here and staying, so don't ever worry about that. I'm sure Miranda and Kelly miss me fussing around the place. I'll admit, a stay up here is like a vacation. I'll put this away and be on my way down the mountain before dark. I've got an appointment with the eye doctor in the morning. This getting old sucks."

Noeul called out thanks and pulled her bags off Athena, setting them by the door. Jordan took hers off too and placed them nearby. She followed, as Noeul led the horse through the yard and over to the paddock. Once there, Jordan watched her remove the saddle and start to brush down Athena. Following suit, she pulled off Thor's saddle and patted the horse's neck while she stroked his nose. Noeul finished, and Jordan led Thor over to her.

Jordan reached for the brush. "If you tell me how, I'll be happy to do it. I watched you take care of Athena. Do you have any suggestions about anything I should avoid?"

"Anyplace bone runs close to the surface, be gentle, there isn't much padding on those spots. Other than that, they generally like it. Be careful. When you have your back turned, he'll nose you unexpectedly to watch you jump."

Jordan began brushing him down the way she'd watched Noeul. She'd done trail rides on horseback before. In those cases, she was a tourist and not a caretaker. Determined to do this right, she used broad firm strokes, removing the dirt, mud and debris from his coat. When finished, she took off the bridle and let him wander over to his mate, while she leaned on the fence near Noeul to watch them.

"Come on, I'll introduce you to the rest of the inhabitants." Noeul took her hand and pulled her toward the barn. She seemed to realize what she was doing and quickly dropped Jordan's hand and looked at her own.

Jordan felt the spark and looked at Noeul, whose blush was apparent. "Was that me?"

Noeul looked at her own hand. "I don't think so."

Jordan rubbed a hand around the back of her neck. "Lead on."

***

Noeul rubbed her palm. The shock still tingling through her hand. Most likely it was nothing more than built-up static electricity from currying the horse's coats. She continued to walk over to the barn area with Jordan following behind.

"This is Pip, who provides me with more goat's milk than I can use. Maybe with you and Bandit here, we won't have to turn so much of it into soap and lotion. I have a few more goats out in the pasture and a small number of sheep I keep for meat and wool. I have chickens for the eggs and..." Noeul held her finger to her lips. "Shhh, don't tell them, they are my poultry supply too. Out this way is the walipini, the greenhouse and my lab area. I do grow some vegetables outside. It's challenging, because it's hard to keep out the scavengers that live around here. Don't touch the fences, they're always electrified to keep the predators back. Coyotes are a problem, so the electric fence is a must."

Jordan scratched her head. "I can imagine. If you don't mind, I need to ask one thing. How in heaven's name, did all this get built without a road up here?"

"They flew everything in by helicopter. The crew stayed onsite for almost six months. I know what you're thinking. It did cost a fortune. Thankfully, money wasn't an issue because of Aggie's foresight. I'll let you figure that part out on your own. Welcome to your new lab, Professor Armstrong."

Jordan stepped through the door Noeul held open. Warm, moist air met them as they moved further in. Raised beds held leafy greens, and other plants grew on elevated tables. Vegetables and fruits of every color hung heavy on vines all around them.

"This place is fantastic. I've been in some of these over in Bolivia. They're rare in the United States. High tunnels are becoming more and more popular."

Noeul smiled and was strangely pleased to be talking with someone who understood everything around them without having to explain the basics. "For my purposes, it's a lot more practical. Saves me from replacing plastic since I went with heavy duty panel design for the roof. My snow load here is substantial. I needed it to be sturdier than plastic sheeting. I can harvest root crops all through the winter when I can't get off the mountain to get to a store. I had them bring in the supplies to do this while they built the house." Noeul watched, as Jordan walked through the structure examining the plants like a scientist. It wasn't long before Jordan spotted her experimental grafting plants.

The shock and joy on Jordan's face caused Noeul's heart to jump. Obviously excited, Jordan dropped down on her hands and knees to examine the grafts. The smile Jordan displayed warmed Noeul in strange ways, and once again, her side had that irritating tingle.

"These look great. What else do you have grafted?" Jordan gently examined the plant.

"Follow me." They walked to an area where Noeul had her experiments set up. "This is what I've been working on. Even before I started reading your research, I'd been working on some simple cross grafts, perfecting technique and testing them out on different soil mediums and environmental settings. I think, if you look at lot twenty-seven, you might find something interesting."

Jordan moved down the rows of grafted plants until she came to the wheat stems crossed with another root stalk. "Noeul, if anything ever told me I was on the right track when I decided to find you, this proves it to me. If you can do this, we'll be in the right ballpark with what I'm trying to do."

Noeul walked to where Jordan stooped, and bent down beside her. "It's not Cornell with all its resources. It can't hurt to give it shot."

Jordan's smile lit up her face. "That's all I can ask."

"Come on, let me show you the house and your room."

"Great."

The pair made their way into the house, and Noeul watched with amusement as Jordan looked around. The younger woman made a beeline for her bookshelves, examining the titles with her head tilted.

Jordan pointed to the books. "You've got quite the collection here."

Noeul nodded. "With no TV option, it's my main form of entertainment. I do have plenty of movies and TV shows on DVD. It's never been my thing. Most evenings, you'll find me curled up right there with a book." She pointed to the leather couch in front of the fireplace.

"I'll be joining you. I brought a few of my favorites with me, because I wasn't sure about options."

"Feel free to read anything on the shelves. The movies are in that cabinet, and your room has a combination TV/DVD player. I didn't put one in here." Noeul shrugged her shoulders and clapped her hands. "Let me show you to your room. Bandit is welcome inside. Kyo sleeps with me at night."

They walked down a hallway, and Noeul pushed open a door. "All the creature comforts of home." She flipped on the light and moved across the room. "Bathroom is attached."

Jordan looked around and set her bag on the floor. "This place is as nice as any hotel. Thank you."

"It's my pleasure. I'll let you get settled in. I'm going to get some supper started. You know where to find me."

"Let me put my stuff away and I'll come and help. I'm serviceable in the kitchen. Even my mom lets me help when I'm at her place. I have a few recipes she and Jida taught me."

Noeul looked back at Jordan. Her smile was broad and almost

enchanting. Leaning against the doorframe, Noeul smiled back. "Jida?"

"Oh, sorry. Grandmother. My family is Jordanian, thus my name."

"Ah, I can see the Middle Eastern features. Well, I'm grateful to her if your cooking is even close to edible. Living up here alone, I get pretty sick of my own cooking."

Jordan laughed and shook her head. "We won't starve, as long as I have my stash of Nutella and Teddy Grahams. I don't travel anywhere without them." She went back to unpacking.

Noeul stood silent in the doorway, then turned and walked to the kitchen. She thought about the supply of the chocolate hazelnut spread she too indulged in. *Coincidence, it has to be a coincidence. Then again, nothing about this whole thing seems to be coincidence.*

After their meal, Noeul and Jordan sat outside and watched the dogs play in the yard. Jordan got lost in the words of Thoreau, while Noeul absorbed the warmth from the big rock and wrote in her journal.

There have only been a few times when I've felt like I was not completely in control of what was going on in my life: when I lost my parents, when Aggie died, and now. The fact that Jordan's even here is testimony to the uncertainty I feel. To be honest, she's like someone opened a window and let in fresh air. I've been comfortably stagnated in this world I've created. Her presence is like a tidal wave coming in and taking everything that existed on the shore back out to sea. What the wave leaves behind is either treasure or destruction.

I thought having someone here in my very orderly world would cause an uneasy feeling. The reality is the exact opposite. It's like tasting food while cooking. If you stick to the recipe, you know exactly what you'll get. The magic happens when you throw in an unexpected ingredient and the dish takes on a whole new flavor.

Just the short period of time she was in the greenhouse breathed new life into the space. Jordan is determined and seems to have an untamed spirit. It's been a long time since I looked forward to a change of pace. I'm thinking this pace might be more like a sprint.

Noeul put the journal down and silently watched Jordan sitting there with a book that Noeul knew well. She turned her face to the sun and offered up a silent thought to Aggie. *I hope you know what you're doing, because I'm following your lead here.*

CJ Murphy

Chapter Seventeen

THE NEXT FEW DAYS, Jordan followed Noeul around as she explained her scientific process. With access to all Noeul's most recent research, including pictures and specimens that had been catalogued, Jordan had months' worth of data to pour through and match up with her own. Their processes were slightly different, and Jordan began to recognize something. Because Noeul wasn't surrounded by technology or distracted by the shiny things of a busy life, she could see things with a much clearer eye. Her senses, no longer dulled by the hum of electronics or the trappings of a world bent on immediacy, seemed much sharper and more attune. *Remember the 'KISS' principle, Jordan. Keep it simple, stupid.*

Jordan enjoyed letting Noeul lead their daily run through the wooded trails that crested in and out of the forest around the house at Topside. The pounding of Jordan's trail runners set a rhythm for her heart and cleared her mind. Bandit and Kyo ran ahead of them, darting on and off the trail to chase chipmunks and squirrels. Noeul slowed when they came to the falls with the deep swimming hole at its base.

Hands on her hips, Jordan drew in some deep breaths. "I need to come back here for a swim. This place is gorgeous." Both dogs leapt into the water and swam out to the center. They turned and made their way to shore only to shake off right in front of the women.

Noeul put her arms up to ward off some of the water. "You two, go play."

Jordan sat down at the water's edge and tossed a rock. She watched the ripples make their way out in ever widening circles. She closed her eyes and listened to the sounds around her. Off in the distance a woodpecker drummed out a repetitive rat-a-tat-tat that echoed off the trees, as leaves fluttered on the breeze. "Nothing like it in the world."

Noeul sat down beside her. "What's that?" She began drawing geometric shapes in the sand with a stick.

"The pure lack of mechanical sounds. Most people can't do without that kind of noise. This kind of quiet drives them crazy. I, on the other hand, lose my way in it." She picked up another rock and tried to skip it across the surface. It didn't get very far, given the angle of her throw.

Noeul stood and sailed a rock that skipped five times. She grinned at Jordan. "It's all in the wrist."

Jordan laughed and rolled to her side. "Well done." She accepted the hand up that Noeul offered and brushed the sand from her shorts. "Come on you two, time to go." Balling her hand into a fist, Jordan tried to dispel the spark she felt every time they touched. It was a peculiar feeling. She rubbed at her side which tingled without reason.

"Tomorrow, we'll take the horses for a trail ride, if you're up for it."

"That sounds great. I'd love to go for a ride. I rode occasionally when I worked for the national parks. They were some of my favorite jobs. I chose those jobs so I could tell my sister all about the wonders she was never going to be able to see in person. There's not much that she lets stop her. Unfortunately, most of the parks are inaccessible. I'd send her pictures and tell her stories about my travels."

"I imagine she appreciated that a great deal. It sounds like you were an amazing big sister."

"I tried to be. Dava was one of the greatest gifts my parents ever gave me. I wouldn't be who I am today without her. She drove me, made me better than I'd ever have been without her."

"I'll bet she'd say you did the same for her."

Jordan laughed at that. "I'm not so sure. My best guess is she'd say I'm a big pain in her ass." Jordan noticed that Noeul's smile didn't seem to reach her eyes. "You're an only child, aren't you?"

Noeul shook her head. "Yes. My mother miscarried when I was five, and they told her it would be dangerous to try again. They poured all their love and attention into me. I had incredible parents."

They walked slowly back along the moss and fern lined trail to the house. "I'm sorry, Noeul."

Noeul shrugged her shoulders. "It's okay, that was a long time ago. It would have been nice to have a sibling left after my parents passed. I can't complain, I had a good life. Your bio mentions the foundation your parents started. That's incredible."

"They truly wanted Dava to experience everything she could. I loved pushing her around the baseball diamond. It's still one of my fondest childhood memories."

"I get the feeling you're still a pretty big kid."

Jordan's grin crept out. "Excellent observation, Professor."

They eventually made it back to the house, where Noeul decided she was going to go take a shower. Jordan wanted to do some cultivation work in the outdoor crops that were growing near the house where she'd seen some weeds. The tools were stored in a small shed and easily accessible.

Within minutes, she was using the hoe around a row of corn, sweat pouring down her back. The sun was bearing down on her, giving her cause to strip down to her sports bra for comfort. She ran her hands through her wet hair and pushed it out of her eyes. Her muscles ached pleasantly, as she worked the soil around the edge of the stocks, stopping the weeds from taking hold. She'd forgotten how much she enjoyed simple manual labor. *I could get used to a life like this.*

***

Noeul stood in her bedroom, drying her long hair with a towel. Movement out the window drew her to see what it was. Jordan was standing with her back to her, wearing nothing except shorts and a sports bra. Her skin shimmered with sweat, as she worked her way down the row. Noeul squinted at something on Jordan's back, as she stood and wiped at her brow. When Jordan put her hands on her hips, Noeul had a better view of her back. Noeul could now see a phoenix with wings of crimson, the tail curving around Jordan's left side. The tattoo was beautiful against her bronze skin.

The more Noeul watched, the more her own dragon tattoo tingled. Her hand went to it automatically, as she recalled the dream she'd had in Shepherdstown, the phoenix and the dragon wrapping around each other. *This is crazy.* Noeul shook herself out of her reverie and dragged her gaze away from the window to look in the mirror.

She finished combing out her long, black hair and pulled it back, gathered it with the clasp, and pushed the pin through. Noeul stood at the sink, staring at her own reflection, and shook herself again. She moved through the house and gathered up a pair of well-worn leather gloves on her way outside. Her guest had almost completed the second row, as Noeul came up beside her.

Jordan greeted her with a blazing smile. "The corn looks great. How about we roast some ears over that open fire pit? I could grill up some vegetables to go with it for supper tonight. What do you think?"

"Good idea. By the way, we haven't even had lunch yet. Are you hungry?"

"I want to finish the other two rows. I figured I'd do that before I showered. Anything else you want done while I'm already dirty? I'm not afraid of heights or hard work, so think about anything that might need done while I finish this."

Noeul shook her head and couldn't help staring at where the tail of the phoenix wrapped around Jordan's side and climbed up toward her breast, disappearing under the sports bra. *I'd like to see where that tail ends up.* Her eyes were transfixed on Jordan when she heard her name as if from far away. She felt a touch on her arm.

"Noeul? Are you okay?"

Noeul startled. "Hum? What did you say?"

"I asked if the animals need to be turned out into the field?"

Noeul wrung her gloves in her hands before answering. "Uh, I'll take care of it." Her eyes were still glued on Jordan's side.

Jordan looked down where Noeul's eyes were trained and smiled shyly. "It was a gift to myself after a pretty rough time in my life."

Noeul felt her cheeks heat, and she dropped her gaze. "I'm sorry."

"No need to be sorry. I'm not embarrassed. The tattoo has a lot of symbolism for me, a rebirth of sorts."

"Oh?"

"That's a story for a glass of good whiskey and a crackling fire. It's safe to say that the Jordan you see now was born out of the ashes of another one."

The bleating of the sheep cut the tension between them. "I'm going to go, uh…" Noeul's words died before she could find them. "Uhm, I'll let them out. I'm going to head to the greenhouse if you want to join me. I have a few things I wanted to show you."

Jordan's smile lit up her face. "I'll finish this up and be there in a minute."

Noeul rubbed her side and waved with her gloves in hand. "No hurry, you know where I'll be."

The rest of the afternoon, the two women worked together. They tended the animals and worked in the greenhouse lab. Noeul enjoyed teaching Jordan her grafting techniques and showing her the progress of an experiment that was showing promise. Jordan added her own knowledge and suggestions. Noeul was enjoying working side by side with someone, something she hadn't done in years. She found herself frequently turning to Jordan to bounce an idea off her or work through a concept. The conversation was easy and productive. They'd started a few new experiments together. It felt like they'd been research partners for years even though the reality was far from that.

Early evening, Noeul called out to Jordan who was cleaning vegetables in the kitchen. "I'm going to go get a fire started so it can make good coals to cook on."

"Great. How about I make us a drink? I got a good look at your liquor cabinet, and I think I can make about anything with what's in there. Do you have a request, or do you want me to surprise you?"

Noeul muttered under her breath. "You've been doing that since you got here."

"What, I didn't catch that?"

Noeul could feel the heat rising in her face and quickly moved toward the door, calling behind her. "Surprise me."

Outside, Noeul placed small kindling in the bottom of the fire pit and followed that up by stacking larger pieces around it. She lit the fire and waited for everything to catch. Slowly, she added more substantial pieces until she had a nice fire going. She sat back watching the red and yellow flames lick at the wood, slowly consuming it. Glowing coals were lining the bottom, and she used a long wooden stick to move them around. Heat radiated off the fire, and she pulled at the open work shirt that covered her tank top. The sliding glass door slid open, and Jordan handed her a glass of white wine.

Noeul sipped from her glass. "Thank you, this is perfect."

"I figured we'd save the Jameson's I found for later. Those coals look great." Jordan had soaked ears of corn in water, and she laid those directly onto the fire. The corn sizzled, and rising steam mingled with the small wisps of drifting smoke.

Noeul helped her move a small grill over the pit, and Jordan pulled vegetable kebabs off a plate, sliding them onto the surface. Red, yellow, and green bell pepper, chunks of onion, and cherry tomatoes lined the skewers. Within seconds, a delicious aroma filled the air around them. "Oh wow, that smells wonderful."

"This is pretty simple. I've never been much of a cook, not for lack of trying on Mom or Jida's part."

"I'm happy to have someone to share dinner with. Kyo is a great companion. She's pretty sparse on the conversation side though."

"Well then, I'm honored to fill that role." Jordan turned the kebabs and the corn that sat down in the coals.

The wine and the fire brought Noeul's blood to the surface, warming her skin to an uncomfortable level. She set down her glass and leaned forward to remove the work shirt. She looked up in time to see

Jordan's piercing dark eyes looking at her, more accurately her shoulder. Noeul smiled, "What?"

"Your tattoo."

Noeul looked at her right side, where the dragon head crawled up from her back to lay across her shoulder. She looked over at Jordan with a question on her lips. "What?"

"It's like the one I saw in my vision during the cleansing at Havasu. I'm not asking you to show me. Can you at least tell me about the dragon, does the tail end with roots that penetrate the earth?"

"Jordan, I'm afraid to ask how you know that. I know for a fact this is as much skin as I've ever exposed to you."

Jordan blushed and turned their meal again. "I promise, Noeul, I haven't been a peeping Tom. If you can bear with me, I'll explain. I don't want to let this dinner go to waste, because I'm starving. There is an explanation for my question."

Noeul concentrated on Jordan's face, trying to detect any kind of subterfuge. There was none that she could see. She relaxed only a bit and raised an eyebrow. "Please don't give me a reason to doubt you or your purpose, Jordan.

"Noeul, I assure you, my reasons and purpose are above board. I haven't told you one thing that hasn't been the truth, and I never will."

Noeul took a deep breath and held out her hand for the plate Jordan was offering. "I'm counting on that. Don't make me regret it."

***

Jordan's stomach flipped. She felt dizzy remembering the vision at Havasu, when she was somewhere she couldn't explain with Maiah in that out of body experience. She needed to be able to explain this to Noeul in a way that didn't seem fabricated.

They ate in near silence. Once they'd finished, Jordan took their plates into the kitchen and poured them both a generous portion of Jameson's. Walking back outside, she sat down beside Noeul and offered her the tumbler. She sipped her own, leaned forward on her elbows, and collected her thoughts.

"Noeul, when I was searching for you, things happened all along the way. Some things I've told you about in detail and others, I only skimmed the surface. I told you that when I was at Havasu I met up with the same medicine woman you did, Maiah. She told me during my vision that I had to seek the rooted dragon to find balance." Calling on her uncanny memory, she relayed the vision to Noeul, exactly as she remembered it.

Jordan turned to Maiah "Where am I?" She watched, as a breeze blew back the silver strands of hair that surrounded the older woman's face.

"You are in between earth and sky."

Jordan watched Maiah draw something on the ground with a stick. A crude bird hovering above what seemed to be a dragon. The dragon wasn't one she recognized from any depiction she'd ever seen. Most in her recollection appeared dangerous and imposing. This one seemed gentle, fiercely protective, and strangely female as both figures came to life.

The bird shifted above the dragon, and Jordan saw it transform into a fiery phoenix, studying the ground beneath it. The dragon found a branch and held it up for the phoenix to land upon. Talons closed tightly around the wood, and the dragon brought the branch down where it could look eye to eye with the phoenix. The dragon reached out and sliced through the ground with a great claw, peeled back the sandy earth, and planted the branch. A great tail swept the soil back in place and rested near the base of the branch that had sprouted green leaves. Jordan watched, as the great tail began to grow roots that entwined with those of the branch beneath the soil. The phoenix wrapped its flaming wings around the dragon.

The branch grew into a great sequoia, as the phoenix and the dragon grew with it, an integral part in the heart of the trunk. The great tree reached into the sky, and a blinding light caused Jordan to raise her hand in front of her eyes. After a few seconds, the light turned into warm sunlight, and she stared at the massive tree. Something niggled at her conscious, something she couldn't explain. She looked for Maiah and found a small red wolf that lay quietly alert beside her. Jordan grew sleepy and lay down, pillowing her head on the small wolf's side, as she drifted into sleep.

Jordan finished her story. "After that, Solanya and Kelea took me to the cave where I found the memorial leading me to Sequoia National Park." She watched for any reaction from Noeul and was willing to wait out her silence. There was nothing more she could say that would explain it. If there were questions, she would answer them. If Noeul wanted her to go, she wouldn't fight it.

"Jordan, I don't know what to say."

"You don't have to say anything. I wanted you to know why I asked about your tattoo. I don't know if the dragon she was talking about is you, or if I'm yet to meet that person. I only know that when it comes to you, I take nothing as coincidence anymore."

They sat around the fire and watched the flames dance without much discussion for a long time. Noeul finally broke the tension. "Tell me about your life back in Ithaca."

Jordan smiled, thinking about the university. "Well, the university itself hasn't changed much. The labs have been expanded and updated." She chuckled. "The students are, well, students. Brilliant and juvenile all in one. It's the same as when you were teaching there. Occasionally, you find one that hangs on your every word. I love that moment when you see that flash of understanding and gears that start turning. The next thing you know, they're your research assistant, and they far surpass every expectation you ever had and some you didn't even think to expect."

"I remember students like that. One of them is sitting in front of me right now. Although, I never had the pleasure of having you as my research assistant."

"A loss for both of us." Jordan sipped her drink. "Many things are the same. Friday night bonfires and Saturday football games still exist and for those less sports minded, Friday night chess club."

"Chess club?" Noeul's smile was as wide as the sunset that was beginning to paint the sky in streaks of pink and yellow.

Jordan shook her head and smiled. "I'm an advisor. We've ranked a few times, and I've had the privilege of coaching a student that beat a Grand Master."

Noeul's eyes widened. "A Grand Master?"

"Yes, and a biochemical engineer student at that. Eighteen and so smart he made my brain hurt."

Noeul's laugh was genuine and filled the night air. "That's hard to believe, given what I know of your IQ and accomplishments. I could see that even back then."

Jordan looked at the woman beside her in the firelight. Noeul was truly beautiful. Her Asian features were stunning, and Jordan felt her heart skip a beat. *Stop that. It's not why you're here.*

"How about your home life?"

"I live in an apartment above Max and Sam's place. It's small and fits my needs perfectly. I've never been one for material possessions. I don't need much."

Noeul furrowed her brow. "Max and Sam Keller, right?

"That's them. Max said he knew your parents well and always spoke of you with deep affection."

"I love them both. I worked with Max, and Aggie and I were frequent guests of the restaurant Sam worked at, Il Frantoio. His alfredo sauce was to die for. I can still taste it if I think about it." Noeul closed her eyes and shivered visibly. "He was always so particular about everything food related. I loved watching him cook."

Jordan visibly puffed up with pride. "Now he owns his own place. They bought a small bistro that's a big hit. He's always busy." She pointed to the dogs that were snoring near the fire. "Bandit used to bring me my dinner every night. Sam knew if he didn't send that guy up with leftovers every evening, I'd have a meal that he couldn't stand."

Noeul got a faraway look and rolled her head on the chair back where she leaned, more directly in line with Jordan. "The only thing I enjoyed more than watching him cook, was watching him dance with Max. They used to do this swing-dancing routine, pure poetry in motion."

Jordan grew quiet, as she remembered when she'd first met the two men, before the dementia diagnosis. Max was a mathematician, and Sam, an artist when it came to food. Sam had told her once, age difference be damned, he knew what he wanted. He wanted a life with Max. "On their tenth anniversary, they hired this band and entertained the crowd for hours with dance routines and lessons. I can't tell you how many times Max would drag me into an afternoon of dancing while Sam worked. At least I had some idea what I was doing. Mom and Dad used to entertain me and my sister with their own moves." She chuckled. "So, when Max decided he wanted to practice, guess who he chose to step on his toes?" Jordan raised her hand.

Noeul's laughter was infectious. "That sounds exactly like Max. He and my parents were good friends."

"You're right about watching them dance. Sadly, it was one of the ways Sam started recognizing something was wrong. Max started missing steps, forgetting routines they'd perfected years before. It wasn't long before he started forgetting simple tasks and names of longtime friends. He was diagnosed with the early symptoms of dementia. They're doing everything they can to slow the process. I frequently give him complicated irrigation calculations to keep his mind active." As if he heard Jordan talking about his dads, Bandit came to stand at her side, placing a paw on her knee. "It's also one of the reasons they got this guy. Bandit gave Max something to focus on, to take care of. When I went back home after Max fell, they asked me to bring Bandit with me, said he needed a job and I was the biggest job they knew." Jordan dropped her head, shaking it side to side. "My mother might agree with them." Bandit stood on his hind legs, with his paws on her thigh, and licked her face.

The women sat watching the crackling fire. Occasionally, Jordan leaned forward to poke around in the coals. The shadows cast by the flames grew long on the ground.

"You haven't really said much about the vision I had at Havasu."

Noeul sighed. "I'm trying to process it. First off, yes, my dragon's tail ends in roots firmly embedded below the surface. That part is a tribute to my love of agriculture. The dragon is more a symbol of my Korean heritage. My mother, Mi-ya, was born in Soeul and met my father, Finnegan Scott, on an expedition to the South Pole."

"Ah, so you too have an eclectic heritage. I can relate. I told you part of my family is Jordanian. My mother was born there and came to the United States to study at Princeton. She met my dad, James, in a sociology class. The rest was history."

"I do have interesting DNA. A tall, dark-haired man with Irish blood and a short, dark-haired Korean woman produce..."

"A dark-haired beauty with stunning green eyes," Jordan whispered, reverent and smooth like aged whiskey.

Noeul blushed. "Not sure I'd agree about the beauty part. The dark hair and green eyes are accurate though."

Jordan returned the blush and chastised herself for thinking out loud. "I apologize, no disrespect intended."

Noeul reached out, resting her hand on Jordan's forearm. "None taken."

Jordan noticed the warm fingers lingering. The sensation felt like the tingles that ran over her back whenever she thought about Noeul. The tiny, pinpoint shocks reminded her of the electric stimulation therapy she'd had on her shoulder, years ago. The sensation was not unpleasant and caused a gentle thrum. When Noeul removed her hand, Jordan instantly missed its warmth.

"So, tell me about your tattoo. It's beautiful, by the way. What I could see of it."

Jordan sunk back into the Adirondack chair and ran her hands through her hair.

Noeul stammered. "You don't have to tell me if it's too hard."

"It's not hard, just uncomfortable. In the same token, talking about it doesn't make it hurt any more than usual." Jordan proceeded to tell her about Tina and the betrayal. It was a hard memory to bring up, and she cursed that part of her brain that recalled the smallest detail.

Jordan narrowed her eyes, as she flipped the ring again. She looked up, wondering why Tina's answer was taking more than a breath.

Tina closed her fingers around Jordan's and the ring. "Jordan, you know I love you."

Jordan's breath stopped in her chest. "And you know I love you. Is there a problem?"

"I can't marry you."

The words struck like a blow from a sword: sharp, deep, and fatal. "Why? What have I done?"

Tina reached out to touch her, flinching when Jordan pulled back. "I can't. I just can't."

Jordan's shock was turning to anger, and her tone dropped dangerously low. There was some piece of the puzzle left out of the box, and she was now able to see that it was missing from the whole picture. "That's not an answer, Tina. Why won't you marry me?"

"Jordan, let's just leave things as they are. We're good like this. We can still have everything we already have."

"Are you saying you won't marry me?"

"I told you, I can't."

"And why can't you? It isn't like you're already married or any..." She stopped as Tina looked away. Jordan stood and walked to the water's edge, a million thoughts bombarding her synapses. The weekends Tina went back to Massachusetts to see her family. Funny, in more than a year, Jordan had never met any of them, even though she and Tina spent weekends visiting Dava or her mother together. The week Tina went back to MIT, she hadn't wanted Jordan along, because Jordan would only be bored while Tina was at work. The trip with her friend once a month. It all started to make sense. "You can't marry me because you're already married, aren't you?"

"Jordan, I..."

Jordan walked back to the small picnic and gathered her things. She rummaged in her bag until she found her phone, then texted Sam to meet her at the trailhead in three hours. "I've got to get out of here." She looked at the woman she thought she knew inside and out, the same woman she'd fallen for and wanted to marry. "I don't even know you. I've been sleeping with a woman I thought was the love of my life. In reality, I've been sleeping with a stranger. A married woman, for God's sake." Her words were loud and foreign sounding to her ears.

"You're still the love of my life. I can't change mistakes I made almost twenty years ago. I married him right out of high school, and I can't undo that. He doesn't deserve that."

Jordan was astonished. "He? He doesn't deserve that?" Jordan jumped away as Tina tried to grab her arm. "Don't touch me. Who the fuck are you? The woman I thought I knew and loved is a complete fraud." She laughed out loud. "Unfuckingbelievable. This certainly isn't how I planned this day. Don't follow or worry about me. We're done. Goodbye, Tina." She stopped, reached into her pocket, and found the ring she'd thought would be on Tina's hand by then. Looking at it, she muttered, "God, what a fool I was." She reared back and threw the ring as hard as she could into the falls. Tina was still calling out to her as she walked away without even a glance back.

It had been a long time since she'd relived those moments. That day had single-handedly led to her inability to connect with anyone, and in turn, caused her to pour herself into her research. "After Tina, I sort of took a scorched-earth policy. I'd walked through the fire and emerged. I promised myself I wouldn't give my heart until I figured out what I wanted, including what I was capable of giving and receiving. Somehow, after that dark time, I found a way to live a productive life. The phoenix is reborn out of the ashes. To me, it's very symbolic of that time of my life and what came after."

Noeul shook her head. "I'm so sorry you had to go through all of that. What a bitch."

"You have no idea."

"How about now?"

Jordan furrowed her brow. "What do you mean?"

"Have you figured it out? What you can give and what you can receive?"

Jordan blew out a long, slow breath. Light flickered across Noeul's face, her striking beauty completely bathed in firelight. Noeul was watching her. Jordan's pulse raced a little faster, and her breathing became a little shallower. The corners of her mouth lifted. "I guess you could say I'm a work in progress."

Chapter Eighteen

WHEN NOEUL WOKE, SHE heard the wind and the pitter-patter of rain against the windows. She loved listening to rain first thing in the morning. It washed away all the dust and greened up everything around her. The rain always made her surroundings seem fresh and new. It ruled out the trail ride she'd wanted to take Jordan on, for sure. That could always be rescheduled.

She yawned and pulled in the enticing aroma of coffee through her nose. After washing her face and brushing her teeth, she dressed in a soft pair of tan shorts and a sleeveless, camp shirt. She brushed the tangles from her long hair and reached for the silver clasp she held it in place with. The metal was cool in her hand as she ran her thumb over the pressed design. The memory of Aggie giving her the gift, all those years ago, slid through her mind. She shook herself and gathered her hair back away from her face again.

The mirror in front of her hid no secrets about the lines at the corner of her eyes or the frown lines between them. With no conscious thought, she pushed up at her temples and pulled out the lines that she had long since stopped worrying about. *Stop being ridiculous, Noeul. You're fifty-five years old and no spring chicken. Why does it matter now anyway?*

She knew why. Jordan's words from last night came roaring back. *A dark-haired beauty with stunning green eyes.* Looking at herself with those same eyes, all Noeul could see were crow's feet. She shook her head and smoothed down her clothes, then turned left and right to check the fit. *What the hell are you doing?* She put a hand on her forehead and turned to the doorway.

Jordan handed her a cup of coffee. "Good morning."

Noeul readily took the cup and drew in the smell of the strong brew, closing her eyes at the delicious aroma. "Thank you. I needed this."

Jordan frowned. "Rough night?"

"Not really. I don't function at peak performance without coffee."

"Ah, that I totally understand. I hope I didn't make it too strong for you."

"The stronger the better." Noeul blew across the top of her mug, taking a cautious sip. She groaned in appreciation and watched as Jordan appeared to shudder then turn away from her. *Interesting.*

Jordan cleared her throat and ran a visibly shaky hand through her sleep-styled hair. "So, what's on tap today?"

"A little work in the barn and maybe some lab work. The trail will be far too muddy for a ride."

"I'm up for that. Can I fix you some breakfast?" Jordan pointed to the stove.

"You made coffee, I'll cook breakfast. Omelets okay with you?"

"Perfect."

Breakfast was uneventful, and soon after they went about the chores of the day, milking being first up. Noeul moved her milking stool beside the snow-white goat. "Hey Pip. How are you this morning?" She ran her hand down the goat's back and over her sides, before beginning the rhythmic pull and squeeze motion that streamed milk into the stainless-steel bucket. Jordan seemed entranced by the action. "You want to try?"

Jordan smiled shyly and kicked at the straw in the pen. "I've never done it."

"Well then, let me be your teacher one more time. Come here and sit on the stool." Noeul stood and patted Pip's side. Once Jordan sat, Noeul pulled Jordan's shaky hand down to the udder and positioned it around the teat. Within minutes, she removed her hand and watched the childlike wonder cross Jordan's face as she was able to direct a steady stream of milk into the bucket. "Want to make Rico happy?"

The question obviously disrupted Jordan's concentration, as Pip raised her leg in protest. Jordan patted her side. "Sorry, girl. Rico?"

Noeul pointed to the cat sitting a foot away from the goat. Confusion passed over Jordan's face. Noeul bent down and directed Jordan's hand back to the teat. She closed her hand around Jordan's and directed a stream of milk toward the one-eyed cat.

Jordan's laugh resonated around the barn, and Noeul smiled as the cat bit at the line of warm goat's milk streaming toward his mouth.

"That's the funniest thing I've ever seen." Jordan tried it on her own and was less accurate than Noeul, hitting the cat in the head. Rico went away to clean himself. "Sorry buddy. Geez, I think I'm ticking off the animal life around here."

Noeul shook her head and crossed her arms. "I've done worse. You should have seen me when I started."

"I would've liked to see that."

Noeul blushed, as Jordan rose from the stool, allowing her to finish the job. Noeul soon had Pip milked and was carrying the bucket back into the house, where she showed Jordan how to label and store what they had gathered.

"What do you do with this when you can't drink it all?" Jordan picked up a glass jar with a date from when Leo had been there.

"Rico, Kyo, and now Bandit, get to have a treat." She pulled out an old-fashioned ice cream maker. "Later, we'll make some blackberry ice cream."

Jordan's eyes widened. "Really? You know how to do that?"

"Of course I do, silly. It's not hard. A little goat's milk, sugar, fruit, ice, and salt. Oh, and a lot of cranking."

Jordan flexed her bicep muscle. "The cranking I can handle."

"We'll see. Okay, off to the lab with us. I wanted to look in on test plot nineteen today. I saw something yesterday that was pretty promising." Noeul looked up to see the enthusiasm she was beginning to associate with Jordan and couldn't help smiling. *A bright mind and the spirit of an adventurer. Tempting combination.*

The rest of the afternoon and evening was spent in the greenhouse, recording data for growth and diagnosing potential issues. Noeul was fascinated with the way Jordan's mind processed, collated, and systematically categorized information. She watched, as Jordan bent looking at each plot and recorded her observations in a leather-bound notebook with a pencil. Jordan frequently held the pencil to her forehead, as if memorizing the words documented.

"Noeul, can you come here for a moment?"

Noeul shook herself from her admiration and walked over to the broad shoulders and strong thighs that knelt near plot number nineteen. "What's up?"

"Is this what you were concerned about?" Jordan used the pencil to point out some symmetrical rings that were forming near the graft.

"Yes, I've never seen those. The graft and the plant look healthy, I'm not sure if those rings are a good sign or a bad sign."

Jordan pushed the pencil behind her ear. "Certainly worth keeping an eye on and recording the data every day on any adverse findings we see."

Noeul stood behind Jordan. Not for the first time, she admired

Jordan's arms and the way her shorts hugged her ass. The muscles in Jordan's triceps rippled, as she reached forward to examine another plant, and her broad shoulders pulled the tank top she wore tighter across her back. Noeul felt butterflies in her stomach, as Jordan turned to her. The blood rushing to her face made her feel like she was doing something she shouldn't. Jordan's small smirk told her she'd been caught.

Noeul smiled back at her, turned, and walked over to her research bench. Nothing about their smoldering looks felt wrong. The rest of the afternoon passed in companionable conversation. Data had been entered, lunch fixed, and the normal chores completed. The dogs played in front of them, as they all walked back to the house for the evening.

Noeul looked at the tank top Jordan wore. A prominent v-shaped perspiration mark showed between her breasts. Small beads of sweat ran from the hollow of Jordan's neck and disappeared down the front of the shirt. Noeul shoved her hands into her pockets in an attempt to keep from reaching out to trace that same line down the front of Jordan's shirt. She closed her eyes and shook her head, as a shiver traveled through her body when her thoughts turned to licking that bead of sweat off Jordan's neck. *What in God's name am I thinking? It's been too damn long since I've been in the company of anyone other than a close friend. Liar, admit it. She's a stunning woman, and you are attracted to her.* Her internal monologue followed them into the house as the rain started again.

"I was thinking about a big salad for dinner, what do you say?" Noeul reached for the handle on the refrigerator, as Jordan pulled a glass from the drainer and filled it with water. She held the glass to her forehead a few seconds before she drank it down.

"Salad sounds great. Can I help?"

Noeul shook her head. "No, I've got it. Why don't you go shower, and I'll get it ready. When you're done, I'll take my turn. *Or I could shower with her.*

Noeul watched as something passed over Jordan's face. A look of mischief was plastered there. *Oh my God, did I say it out loud? No, impossible. Or maybe she read my mind?*

Jordan tilted her head and laughed. "A shower sounds good. Whatever you need me for, don't hesitate to ask." Jordan reached for the hem of her tank.

Noeul swallowed hard as the shirt slipped up Jordan's torso, exposing her chiseled stomach muscles and the tan skin that glistened with sweat. Noeul's eyes traced the line the feathers took around her left side, where they disappeared under the sports bra near her breast. Her mouth went dry, as she forced her eyes down before the tank cleared Jordan's head. Try as she might, she couldn't calm her racing pulse. She raised her eyes to the devilish smirk Jordan wore as she stood there for a moment. She smiled and walked away. *I think I'm losing my mind. I should not be having these thoughts. Worse, I think that little shit knows I am. Lord, help me.*

***

Jordan's center clenched, as she thought about her eyes meeting Noeul's seconds ago. She'd watched the pulse point in the beautiful neck bound under the creamy skin. For an instant, she'd quirked an eyebrow, as she let her own dark eyes meet the cool green ones that had looked down, then locked on her own. Instinctively, Jordan knew Noeul was attracted to her, and the feeling was very mutual. She turned on the shower and allowed steam to fill the bathroom, as she shucked out of the rest of her clothes. Jordan chuckled at her attempt to be sexy. Stripping her tank top off in front of Noeul had the desired effect. She'd watched Noeul unconsciously lick her lips. Her own attraction to Noeul was palpable. *She's so freaking hot. This is crazy.*

Jordan scrubbed her body, then stepped from the shower. She dried off and dressed in a pair of snug, cotton gym shorts and a faded T-shirt bearing Cornell's mascot, Big Red. She'd finger combed her hair back off her forehead, and strands near her neck left dark droplets on the shirt. She slid her feet into a pair of worn Birkenstocks and made her way back to the kitchen. Noeul faced away from her, stirring the salad and swaying to a beat that existed only in her head. There was no music playing in the room. Jordan cleared her throat and watched Noeul stiffen and halt the gentle sway of her hips before she resumed stirring the salad.

"Okay, your turn. What's left to do?"

Noeul turned, a slight blush rising from under the collar of the shirt she wore. Jordan watched her pull at the collar uncomfortably, before she dropped her gaze from Jordan's face.

Noeul cleared her own throat. "I haven't seen a red Cornell T-shirt in years."

Jordan laughed. "I have a whole drawer full of them back home I'd

265

be happy to send you."

"Can you make salad dressing? I'm not picky. There are plenty of ingredients here in the spice cabinet. The olive oil, vinegar, and other items are there in the pantry."

"You're in luck. Sam taught me to make his signature vinaigrette. Do you have any honey?"

Noeul bit the side of her cheek. "I do. It's in the pantry. Okay, I'll leave you to it and go take a shower. I'll be out in a minute." Noeul's hands shook, nearly causing her to drop the salad.

Jordan quickly went around the bar and took the bowl from her. "Noeul, are you okay?"

Noeul raised a shaky hand to her forehead and looked Jordan in the eyes. Jordan set the salad down and tentatively reached out to grasp Noeul's hand, entwining their fingers. She watched, as Noeul tensed, then took a deep breath and visibly relaxed into the touch.

"I'm okay. I'll be back in a minute."

Jordan tilted her head and looked Noeul in the eyes, willing her voice into a whisper. "Take all the time you need, I'm not going anywhere."

Noeul shook her head. "Good to know."

Seconds later, she disappeared down the hall and out of sight. Jordan stared at the spot for a long time, before she turned to the cabinet to pull down ingredients for the salad dressing. She heard the water turn on and shivered at the thought of Noeul naked. *Get a grip. It's attraction, pure and simple. She's a beautiful woman. A beautiful, intelligent, sexy-as-hell woman.*

Jordan finished most of the dressing, leaving it on the counter while she got out plates and silverware. Searching Noeul's wine rack, she selected a sauvignon blanc from a winery she recognized. She rummaged around to find the wine key, uncorked the bottle, and placed two glasses on the table. In the stack of CDs beside the stereo, she found several of her own personal favorites and laughed. She loaded three albums to shuffle and pushed play, filling the space with the bluesy sounds. Stevie Ray Vaughn's "Double Trouble" had been one of her father's favorites, and he'd taught his children to love the sound of the guitar played as only Stevie could. After cycling through one song, the gravelly voice of Bonnie Raitt crooned.

Back in the kitchen, she added the final ingredient to the dressing that had been marinating. She drizzled the honey into the mason jar and stole a taste of the smooth, sweet, gold-colored liquid, as James Taylor started into "Something in the Way She Moves." One of the lines about going where no one else can go moved her to sing along, and soon she was dropping her smooth alto through the chorus. She washed off the drizzle stick in the sink and turned, only to be startled by a grinning Noeul leaning cross-armed against the door jam. Jordan stammered before she bent over in laughter at being caught.

"Bravo, bravo. Encore." Noeul clapped.

Jordan's entire body heated, and she turned from Noeul to the salad dressing, mixing it while she licked some honey off her thumb. She looked up in time to see Noeul swallow hard as their eyes locked. She cleared her throat, found a spoon, and poured out a small amount. She beckoned Noeul to come closer to taste. Noeul walked forward and covered Jordan's hand with her own, as the spoon was raised to her mouth. Jordan watched as the silver cutlery disappeared between the pale, pink lips. Her eyes slammed shut. Without realizing it, she put voice to her thoughts. The words slipped out quietly, almost reverently. "Holy shit."

"Indeed." Noeul took the spoon, turned it over, and licked the remnants before placing it in the sink. She passed incredibly close by Jordan, nearly touching her, as she headed for the table. Jordan was left grasping for the counter to steady herself, as she watched Noeul step up to the table. Jordan rushed around the counter to pull the chair out for her. After Noeul sat down, Jordan scooted it in after her. Jordan's smile crept across her face, as she poured the dressing and mixed it in with the salad. "May I serve you?"

"Please."

Jordan dished out half the salad onto Noeul's plate and the other onto her own. They ate while they talked about the research and Stevie Ray's guitar filled the room.

Wine glass in hand, Noeul pointed to the CD player. "Nice selection you put in."

Jordan sipped her own wine and smiled. "My dad was a big blues fan, and my mom loves James Taylor and Carol King, so your stack over there was a lot like the collection on my own play list."

"I have a lot more music in digital form and even vinyl." Noeul wagged her eyebrows.

Jordan's laugh almost made her choke on her wine. "Vinyl? You know that's making a big comeback?"

"I like the sound of the pops, crackles, and clicks in with the music." Noeul topped off their glasses again. "Mom and I used to dance in the kitchen. She and Dad taught me. I can say, without prejudice, that I was never as good as Max and Sam." Noeul shook her head. "Mom was a good dancer."

Jordan set her glass down and went to the CD player. She sorted through until she found what she was looking for, the CD that had made her smile earlier. Once she started it, she walked to Noeul and held out her hand. "Dance with me?"

* * *

Noeul looked at the strong fingers extended toward her. There was a choice to make, take Jordan's hand and open Pandora's box, or say no and drive a nail deep into the lid. Her eyes slid to Jordan's fathomless dark pools, liquid with heat. Noeul reached out and rose from her chair. Melissa Ethridge's voice floated around them. It wasn't a slow song by any means. The tempo would still be one that would put Noeul inches away from the woman in front of her. When she allowed Jordan to pull her close, her breath stopped in her chest. The heat between them slowly grew as they moved to the beat. Jordan's hand rested lightly on the small of Noeul's back, the touch streaking through her like lightening.

"Jordan…"

Jordan bent down and murmured close to Noeul's ear. "Shh, it's just a dance."

Noeul forced herself to relax, as she allowed Jordan's hand to enclose hers with a soft but firm touch. The gentle direction from the press of Jordan's body against hers had them easily gliding across the small, empty square of hardwood beside the kitchen table. The beat was light and playful, as Jordan swung her out before pulling her back in and spinning them around. The dogs lay at the edge of the room, heads tilted, eyes on them. Jordan increased their pace, as the chorus rang out declaring unrequited need, desire, and longing. The next song slowed down and Jordan pulled her closer, so close she could smell hints of laundry soap on the faded, red T-shirt. Noeul closed her eyes, as Jordan expertly swayed and stepped them from one corner to the next.

Noeul shuddered at the touch. "I haven't done this in a very long time."

Jordan looked down and pulled their clasped hands to her chest. "That makes two of us."

Their legs entwined as they swayed to the music. Noeul felt herself melting into a soft touch, her hand slipping from Jordan's to lie flat on her chest. Without conscious thought, her hands moved to Jordan's neck, while Jordan's moved to her waist. The sensation was overwhelming, and panic started to rise within her. She stiffened and felt Jordan slow.

"It's ok, move with me. One step at a time."

Noeul once again forced herself to relax and move with Jordan. On one particular step, Jordan's leg brushed her center, causing a gasp to escape her throat and her arms to tighten around Jordan's neck. She raised her head, her lips inches from Jordan's. Warm breath wafted over her cheek from the taller woman's head bent close to hers. The first touch of their lips was tentative, sweet, tasting of the lingering wine and honey. Jordan didn't chase her when she pulled back. Noeul tried, without success, to slow her breathing. It felt like all the air had left the room.

"Hey, hey. I'm right here. Noeul, look at me." Jordan drew her hands up to Noeul's face, forcing her to stare into eyes that scorched her skin and seared into her soul. Noeul felt her breathing even out and her pulse slow, her heart no longer threatening to leap out of her chest.

"Hold me, please. Hold me until I'm not afraid anymore, because I'm terrified, Jordan."

"I can do that. How about we move over there?" Jordan nodded her head.

Noeul allowed Jordan to lead her over to the couch and turned to allow the taller woman to hold her. Drawing her legs up, she melted into the strong arms that held her tenderly, as soft kisses rained down on her temple.

"What are we doing, Jordan?"

Jordan rested her cheek on the top of Noeul's head. "Noeul, I've driven from coast to coast, hiked down into canyons and up mountains. I sat in a pirate's bar and swam into an ocean cave to find you. I've talked to spirits, followed whistles, voices, shadows, and visions, all to be where I am right now. I don't have all the answers. All I know is I'm willing to take the chance and that's a lot for me."

Noeul felt her chin lifted until, once again, she was staring into two dark, burning embers that threatened to incinerate her. "Why?"

"Because in all my life, the only thing I've been more driven to do, is show my sister how much fun she could have. From the moment I set out to find you, I've been driven...no pulled is a better explanation, by things I can't even begin to understand. The second I saw you, it became much more than figuring out how to graft a plant." Jordan pointed to her chest.

Noeul reached up and rested her hand against Jordan's cheek, only to have her turn and kiss her heated palm. "What did it become?"

Jordan shook her head and chuckled. "A study in masochism looking at you in those tank tops. Noeul you're gorgeous, sexy, and funny. You're also driven, all the things that leave my insides humming."

"Jordan..."

"I wouldn't lie to you. I'm only so strong, and you're quickly breaking down every barrier I've carefully put in place over the last several years."

"It certainly hasn't been my intention, Jordan. I'm not the only one wielding a sledgehammer. Although what you're doing to me is more like driving a bulldozer through me. It's been a really long time since anything has remotely reminded me I have a pulse." Noeul traced Jordan's lips with her thumb. She gasped as Jordan drew it in and sucked it lightly. Noeul physically shivered, as she pressed her mouth to the lips a whisper away from hers. She parted her own when Jordan's tongue sought entrance.

Noeul felt Jordan's arms tighten around her body, as Jordan held her in a way that calmed the jitters and lit a fire. It burned deep within the place where only cold, gray ashes had existed. Noeul moaned into the kiss and threaded her fingers through Jordan's hair. "Jordan, I feel like I'm ready to self-combust."

"Like the phoenix."

Noeul deepened the kiss, pressed hard into Jordan's mouth, and whispered into her kiss. "Rising from the ashes."

***

Noeul wasn't the only one close to going up in an inferno of lust. Jordan's center spasmed, clenched, and released. *Fuck, I'm ready to come and she hasn't even touched me yet.* She wanted Noeul, wanted to lick down her neck, suck the pulse point, and run her hands all over the beautiful body in her arms.

Jordan drew back and placed her forehead against Noeul's. She could feel her own chest rise and fall quickly. "God, Noeul, I'm on fire."

"Glad to know I'm not in this by myself."

"Not by a long shot." Jordan nuzzled Noeul's ear and tilted her chin so she could draw the soft lobe into her mouth. Noeul physically shivered in her arms.

Noeul ran her hand down Jordan's arm and back up to her neck. "You're so beautiful."

Jordan laughed and traced Noeul's fine features. "Looked in the mirror lately?"

"Jordan, I'm over fifty. My days of being beautiful are pretty much behind me."

"Your mirror is broken, because what I see is a gorgeous woman with incredible green eyes and luscious, kissable lips." Jordan paused and pushed an escaped lock of Noeul's hair behind her ear. She kissed her, nipping and biting softly on her lower lip.

Noeul drew in a deep breath and lowered her head.

Jordan closed her eyes for a moment, doing her best to calm her racing pulse. "Don't hate me for what I'm about to say. I'm going to slow this down. It's been a long time since I've wanted more. My body is telling me to push the accelerator. Unfortunately, my head and heart say it's time to pump the brakes." Jordan tipped Noeul's chin up until they were looking eye to eye. "And I think you are a hair's breath away from running far away from me. If not in body, in heart and mind. I'm not going anywhere unless you tell me to. So, let's take our time. We know the attraction is here." Jordan closed her eyes and drew in a ragged breath. "Let's see if all the rest is too, at your pace. Okay?"

Jordan felt Noeul stiffen slightly, before she relaxed against her and released the breath she'd been holding. Noeul shook her head affirmatively.

"Now, let's have some fun. I spied something else to test your dance skills."

"Jordan, I told you I'm not much of a dancer."

Jordan walked over to the CD player, loaded up her selection, then turned and grinned as the unmistakable tinny, guitar riff began. She crooked her index finger toward the laughing woman and extended her hand. By the time Van Morrison reached the chorus about his brown eyed girl, Noeul was following Jordan's lead as she pulled the shorter woman in and out. As they slid around, Jordan spun them in a tight circle, holding her close. She leaned back and extended her arms, while she harmonized the sha la las. Noeul's smile swallowed her face. *Time. We just need time. I'll give her all she needs and the chance we both need.*

***

Noeul lay in her bed, staring at the shadows shifting across her ceiling. Her mind wouldn't settle, and her body was a long way from quieting. Her center pulsed and thrummed with need. Kissing Jordan was unlike anything she'd ever experienced. Maybe she was fooling herself. She reached for the journal she'd basically abandoned since Jordan's arrival. As the words began to pour out of her, she felt a heavy weight being drawn from her shoulders. It was as if each word was so heavy on her soul, that the only way to relieve the burden was to put it to paper.

I have no idea what happened tonight.
Dammit.
That's a lie. I do know what happened. An attractive, charming, and engaging young woman looked at me with eyes that saw right through me. With each look, each touch, she reached through the solitary sadness I've lived with since Aggie's death.

What the hell am I doing? I'm twenty years older than she is. For that matter, what in the world does she see in me? I've seen at least one of her previous girlfriends, and I am nowhere in that class.

There's something about her though. To be honest, I felt ten years younger tonight. She even had me swing dancing in the living room. I thought I'd forgotten all those steps Mom taught me. Dancing with her took me right back there.

Her playfulness made me smile more tonight than I have in ages, and it's been years since I've laughed that much. Every time I grew fearful, she felt it and soothed me. God love her. She stopped what would have led us down a road right into this bed. Of that I have no doubt. I was hanging on each kiss, and my God, those eyes! Deep pools of molten desire. I never imagined wanting anyone else to touch me again. I know this, if she'd not cooled us down, I would have spent the night with her. In the morning, I'd have hated myself. It's too fast, too soon. Maybe the worst mistake I might ever make. Why am I so indecisive? I loved Aggie, still do.

But that kiss. I can still feel it. My whole body is on fire thinking about it. I'm still wondering if there will be another and dammit, when? I think about everything she's told me she went through to get here. None of that can be happenstance. Can it? The dreams, all the things Aggie said to me, it must be Jordan she was talking about. Aggie confirmed it with that ringing phone in Shepherdstown. I asked for a sign and she gave it to me without words.

Am I ready to take a chance on this, on Jordan...hell, on me? This place isn't Jordan's home or her dream. At some point, she'll walk back into her life at Cornell, and where will that leave me? Is it worse to be lonely with a loss I've long since learned to endure, or risk facing another loss in a month, six months, or a year if she stays her whole sabbatical? And then what?

Questions, questions, questions and no magic eight ball to shake for answers.

Noeul closed the journal, her shoulders lighter. Her heart still felt like lead in her chest being pulled straight to her stomach. Her hands pressed against her pounding temples. She walked to the bathroom for some aspirin. Filling a small glass with tepid water, she threw back the pills and raised the glass to her mouth. Noeul looked into the mirror and caught a glimpse of something she hadn't seen in years. Her eyes gleamed with what looked like hope.

*** *** ***

After a fitful night's sleep, she rose and started to the kitchen, pausing outside of Jordan's bedroom door. Noeul startled, shocked that her knuckles were inches from the smooth wooden surface. She pulled her hand to her side and covered it with the other, while she moved quickly into the kitchen. It was still very early. She was surprised when Kyo didn't greet her. Kyo had been sleeping side by side with Bandit since he'd arrived. Kyo normally wished her a good morning with a wet nose to her palm when Noeul's feet hit the kitchen floor.

A spoon lay on the sink, a tea bag pressed to it and a mug missing off the hook above the coffee pot. She let her fingers touch the teabag and felt the lingering warmth. Noeul looked around the empty living room, noticing for the first time that both dogs were missing. She stepped to the glass wall looking out into the yard, daylight barely visible. What she could see, was the figure of a tall woman sitting in a chair facing a small fire in the pit, two dogs at her side.

Guess I wasn't the only one who couldn't sleep.

Noeul turned on the coffeepot, stepped to the sink, and splashed some cold water on her face. Droplets ran off her jawline, as she stood there looking at the teabag.

I'll bet she didn't make coffee because she didn't want to wake me with the smell.

Thoughtful, but futile. She pulled eggs, cream, and butter from the refrigerator and a cast iron skillet from the cabinet. The crisper contained bell and hot peppers and onions that she gathered, along with some goat cheese. Noeul cooked the breakfast burritos and assembled two plates. She poured them both a cup of coffee and loaded everything on a tray. She slid the door open with her hip and closed it with her foot.

When she got to Jordan, she saw relaxed features and a death grip on an empty mug held in her lap. Noeul allowed the smell of the strong brew to announce her presence. It didn't take long, and she watched as Jordan opened one eye and looked in her direction. A small table sat between the chairs, and Noeul put the tray down and traded Jordan a cup of coffee for her empty mug.

"Brought you some breakfast. I was trying to be quiet and not wake you. I noticed the tea bag in the sink and realized you must have slept about as well as I did. Thought you could use some high test."

Jordan grinned and closed her eyes. "You're now my hero."

Noeul watched her pull in a deep breath, inhaling the aroma. She enjoyed watching a contented smile cross Jordan's face as she took her first sip followed by an appreciative groan.

"Oh yeah, definitely my hero."

"I take it you are happy with the coffee?"

"God, yes. I didn't want to wake you, so I settled for some tea."

Noeul nodded, as she reached out and grabbed the poker to stir the coals while taking a sip from her own mug. "You could have made coffee. I wasn't sleeping either."

Jordan tapped the arm of the chair with her free hand. "I'm sorry if I did anything that made you uncomfortable last night, I apologize. I won't lie about my attraction to you. If I pushed it in any way, I'm sorry."

Noeul sat back and took a bite of her burrito, indicating Jordan's plate to her. She covered her mouth. "Oh wait, I forgot the salsa. I'll be right back."

Jordan reached out and gently caught her wrist. "I'm fine unless you need it. Thank you." Jordan picked hers up and took a bite. She chewed and laid her head back with another groan. "This is delicious. Thank you."

"You're welcome." Noeul let the silence sit for a few minutes, while they ate and sipped coffee and she found her courage. "Jordan, you didn't do a thing last night that I didn't want you to. I'm sorry if I wound you up and left you hanging. I'm not a tease, or at least I didn't used to be. It's been a really, really long time since I even thought about kissing someone."

"I can understand that. You're the first person since Tina that I've even gone past a moment of casual flirtation with. Never wanted to open myself up to the possibility of betrayal again. I got my trust shattered the last time and was in no mood to travel that path ever again."

Noeul noticed the phrase included was instead of am. "That's not anything I would ever do to you, Jordan. I mean it."

"I know that. I think that's why it was so easy to open the door to the possibility. That and you're a beautiful woman." Jordan took another bite of her breakfast, chewed, and stared at the flames in the fire pit. "I wrapped myself up in my work and buried that part of my heart."

Noeul sat back, her breakfast forgotten. "And now?" Jordan turned those dark eyes on her, causing her to feel her pulse skip as they glinted with firelight.

"Now, the earth has been pulled back and someone turned on the sun."

They sat there for a few moments before Noeul spoke again. "That shovel apparently gets around."

Chapter Nineteen

JORDAN DECIDED SHE REALLY needed a friendly ear to bend. A call to Dava, or maybe even her mother, was in order. Her emotions were so jumbled up, they resembled those bent-wire puzzles her dad used to make for her. You had to really move the pieces around and look at them from every angle to see how to take them apart or put them back together. To make that call would require a trip off the mountain. She also needed to check in on Max. His condition had been improving when she'd last called. Unfortunately, things could change in the blink of an eye.

After the sun finally came up, she approached Noeul in the kitchen. "Hey, do you think I could borrow one of the horses to go down to Miranda and Kelly's? I need to check on Max and pick up a few more things from my Jeep. If not, I can walk down. It's not a problem."

"Jordan, you don't have to walk. The horses can always use a workout. I'll go down with you. I need to take a fresh supply of soap and lotion for the cabins. Give me a few minutes to get things settled here and we'll ride down. We can stay or come back up, that makes a difference in how long it will take me to be ready."

"If it's okay, we can come back. I only need to make some calls and check on my research plot with my assistant. When I was up there last, she had an issue. What needs to be done with the animals? I'll do that while you get things ready."

Noeul gave her a list of small tasks, which she quickly accomplished. She saddled the horses and called the dogs, who were playing under the shade trees.

Noeul stepped to her. "Okay, I'm ready."

Jordan looked back at the barn. "Do you need to check on what I did before we go?"

Noeul stared at her and grinned. "No, I trust you. Let's go."

With a small smile, Jordan shook her head and mounted Thor for their ride down, appreciatively noticing how good Noeul's ass looked in the saddle. *Stop it. Concentrate on getting down the mountain without falling off by becoming distracted.*

They talked about the research on the way down the mountain and arrived, dogs in tow, in under two hours. Greeted by a smiling Kelly, who exited the house wiping her hands on a dishtowel, the pair dismounted near the porch. Jordan led the horses over to the corral, while Noeul carried in the saddlebags loaded with lotion and soap.

Miranda greeted her with a wave and a handshake. "How goes it?"

Jordan put on a smile that masked some of her trepidation. "Good, we've made some progress working on the grafting research. That place is great. I was completely blown away by everything she's done up there. It's like no place I've ever been."

"I didn't expect you guys today. Everything alright?"

"Yeah, I need communication devices." Jordan laughed. "I need to check on my friend Max. He was being moved to the rehabilitation center when I left. I want to make sure he's still on the mend. I also need to touch base with my research assistant at Cornell to check on some progress. Lastly, if I don't call my sister every few days, she gets twitchy...with Noeul being an axe murderer and all."

Miranda laughed. "I'm sure it's hard being out of touch with the world. "Though it's one of the reasons we stayed here after we retired. It's nice being out of the fray sometimes."

Jordan shook her head in agreement. "Very true, I didn't miss it while I was up there, per se. Even though so much was going on when Noeul found me, the chance was too good not to come. Like it or not, the world still spins around after we step off. Anything I can help you with?"

Miranda waved her off. "Nah, I'm good. I'm sure Kelly and Noeul are in there cooking something up for lunch. I've got to go to town for a bit. Feel free to use whatever you need. We've got an extra data cable you can use if you need to hook up a computer or anything."

"That'd be great. I'll need to borrow your phone if my satellite phone won't get out, if that's ok. It didn't work the other day when we were here." She held up her phone. "I thought I'd give it another try."

"Anything you need, Jordan. See you later."

Jordan waved as she watched Miranda head into the house, only to come back out, hop in her truck, and drive off. She was pleasantly surprised that service on her phone was better. She punched in Sam's cellphone number and waited as it rang through.

"Jordan."

"Hey, Sam. How's Max?"

"Crankier than normal, if you can believe it. Chomping at the bit to come home. Trying to get him to understand that the doctors say he's not ready has been difficult. He's settled in at the rehabilitation facility. His pain is under control with meds. Unfortunately, they add to his confusion."

"Oh, Sam, I'm sorry. Do you need me to come home? Because I will. I can be on the road by tomorrow morning. You say the—"

"Jordan, as much as I'd love to have you home, there is nothing you can do. Nothing at all, other than visit. His bones have to heal, and we need to get him off the meds to try and clear his mind. How's our boy?"

Jordan laughed as she looked up to see the dogs flying around the corner and into the field chasing some unknown foe. "Having the time of his life. Noeul's dog, Kyo, is his new best friend. It's like they were separated at birth and are making up for lost time. He goes to bed tired every night."

"Kiss him on the forehead for us. Now, how are you?"

"I'm good. Working with Noeul is as amazing as I thought it would be. We're making good progress in only a few days. You should see her place. It's incredible. Do you think Max would be up to a call? I don't want him to think I've forgotten about him."

"I left there not more than a half hour ago. They had brought him back to his room after therapy. He was wiped out, but I will make sure I tell him you asked about him."

"I'll send an email with everything going on, and you can read it to him when you go back. I'll include some pictures I took of Bandit and Kyo playing. You can show him those."

"How long do you think you'll be there, Jordan?"

"No idea, Sam. Why, is something wrong, something you're not telling me?"

"I promise, I'm telling you everything. The reality is, I don't know what is going to happen when the rehabilitation center tells me he can come home. He's tired, Jordan. This took the wind out of his sails. I have no doubt he'll come home. My only concern is that he'll need more care than I can give with the restaurant schedule, at least initially. I'm trying to keep you informed."

"Sam, I will be home tomorrow if you need me. If anything changes, you call immediately. I gave you the number. It will take a friend a horse ride up the mountain to deliver the message, two hours in good weather. You call, and I will be on the next plane home, okay?"

"We love you, Jordan. I promise to let you know."

The friends ended their call. Jordan tried hard to hold in the tears that threatened to escape. She bit her lip and ran her hands through her hair as she paced. She was terribly worried about Max, not only his current condition, but about losing him. Without noticing his arrival through her closed eyes, she felt a wet nose nuzzle her palm. She slid down against the side of her Jeep, holding Bandit and allowing his soft tongue to bath her face and kiss away the tears. "I'm okay, boy, really I am." She buried her face into his black-and-white fur, while she worked to regain her composure. When she felt she could make her next call, she pulled the phone back up while Bandit settled his head on her thigh.

"Atchawhay antway eengray umbthay?"

Jordan's voice was a choked a whisper. "Hey."

"Jordan, what's wrong?"

There was a long pause, before Dava's voice became demanding and urgent.

"Jordan, what the hell is wrong? JJ, you're scaring the shit out of me. Where are you?"

She cleared her throat and pulled herself together enough to croak out a reply. "Uhmm." She cleared her throat again. "I'm okay. I called Sam before you. I promise, I'm alright."

"Is Max okay, has something else happened?"

"No, he's at the rehab center. It was the conversation with Sam about his fears. They have other friends that can help until I go back. I feel guilty not being there. Max and Sam are family."

"I know. It's not easy being that far away. I can attest to that with the heart attack you just gave me. I can't remember the last time you didn't reply in kind to that greeting. If you're ever kidnapped, fail to do that and I'll know something's wrong."

Jordan heard her sister take an audible breath. She tried to laugh at the comment but failed in the attempt. "I'll try to remember that."

"Other than that, what's going on? I can tell that's not all."

"God, with all your other talents, are you clairvoyant too?"

"When it comes to you, yes. So spill."

"I kissed her."

"Her who?"

"Noeul, you dumbass. I kissed Noeul. I haven't been anywhere else." Jordan rose quickly, startling Bandit so badly he swung his head left and right looking for what might be a threat. "I'm sorry, Bandit. It's okay boy. Go find Kyo." She knelt and ruffled his ears. "I promise. Go play." He slowly walked off, his tail down, his eyes constantly returning to hers. "It's okay."

"Jordan, talk to me."

Jordan walked over to a large oak and put her back flat to it. She drew up a foot against the tree. "I'm sorry. Last night after dinner, we were dancing. You know, like Mom and Dad used to? The swing dancing?"

"Okay, yes, I remember. That doesn't explain why you sound like you've been crying. That's an occurrence rarer than me making a coding error."

"I'm getting there." Jordan growled with frustration.

"Okay, lips are zipped."

Jordan took a deep breath and started to explain everything that had happened. She shared Noeul's responses and her own sleepless night. Dava was quiet, prompting Jordan to check the display to see if they'd been disconnected. "Are you still there?"

"I am. I'm listening for what the real problem is."

"God, you're such a little pain in my ass."

"Yes, but I'm your pain in the ass. So again I ask, what's the real problem?"

Jordan looked out at the corral. The horses grazed lazily, their tails moving in the breeze. Bandit and Kyo were on the ground beside her, their heads on their paws looking up at her. "The real problem is I have feelings for her, Dava. And before you say it, I know. I haven't spent that much time with her. I don't know everything about her, and yes, it's all too fast."

"First off, don't put words in my mouth. Second, you do know her. You've spent over a year looking for her. You've spent how many months driving across country to find her, learning about pieces of her life few will ever know. You know she trusted you enough to take you back to her home, and as far as the too fast part, Mom and Dad married after knowing each other for six weeks. And, might I add, they didn't even know half as much about each other as you do her. Having feelings for someone is not a crime, Jordan. I'm ecstatic that you've let someone that fucking close. You haven't let anyone that near your heart since that bitch Tina ripped it out and put it through the industrial wood chipper."

There was a pause in Dava's diatribe long enough for Jordan to close her eyes and absorb the sounds around her.

"I'm going to give some of your own advice back to you. Take a chance, Jordan. I don't think you'll regret it."

Jordan laughed, remembering their conversation in Acadia. "God, our ability to recall every single day of our lives is coming back to bite me in the ass."

"Pot, say hi to kettle. Jordan, if this is something you want, go for it. Give her time and space when she needs it, reassurance, and not a single reason to doubt you. That's a two-way street, Sherlock, so tell her what you need to. All the small stuff will work itself out. You found the needle in the haystack, use it to sew a plant or two together. While you're at it, maybe your broken heart too. If it doesn't work out, part as friends. It's that simple, JJ. Don't make it harder than it has to be."

"I love you, little sister, you know that?"

"Of course, you do. What's not to love? Now go, load that needle up with thread. Call me when you can. I'll call and check on Sam and Max for you. I know you won't always have service. How about you try taking that satellite phone up there with you? Maybe we can use a text burst. It's worth a try. You never know, it might work if you hold your mouth right and cross your eyes. JJ, few other than me, know how incredible you are. Now, I swear, if you tell anyone I said that, I'll deny it."

"Love you, Watson."

"I love you too, Jordan, with all my heart. Now go buy some fifty-fifty tickets and take a chance."

"I think I'll do that, Dava. I'll go do just that."

***

Noeul watched out the window and it took all in: Jordan's pacing, the running her hands in her hair, her near collapse against her Jeep. Noeul was a whisper from running out the door, as she watched the younger woman's body heave in sobs while holding onto Bandit's neck. The only thing that stopped her was Kelly's hand on her arm.

"Noeul, honey, what's going on? You haven't said five words since you got here. You both look like you're ready to jump out of your skin. And unless I miss my guess, that woman is out there crying. Why?"

Noeul wrapped her arms tightly around herself and hugged her own body. When she raised shaky fingers to her mouth, Kelly took matters into her own hands and led Noeul away from the window and into the living room. She parked Noeul on the couch.

Kelly knelt in front of her. "You'd better tell me what happened, because when Miranda gets back from town and sees you like this, she will likely kill that woman out there with no explanation."

Noeul tried to explain what had happened the night before. She couldn't keep the emotion from her voice.

"Kelly, I'm scared to death. There is no doubt in my mind Aggie led her here. I know that every time she said the seeker, she meant Jordan." Noeul touched her fingers to her lips, remembering the feel of Jordan's mouth on hers. "I feel something, Kelly, and I'm terrified of making a mistake. Jordan isn't here long term, and I can't lay my heart out on the line for someone who is going to go back to another life. I've already lost one lover and it nearly killed me. I can't do that again."

"How do you know she's going to leave? Have you asked her?"

"My God, no." Noeul rose and began pacing the small living room.

"Tell me how it felt."

"What?"

Kelly rose and leaned against the arm of the couch. "Tell me how it felt to be held in her arms and kissed."

Noeul turned, a million thoughts were running through her mind. The words, descriptions, and feelings were all jumbled up. She lifted her hands, dropped them, and lifted them again to hold her head. "Magical."

"And?"

"Almost orgasmic." A laugh bubbled up, and she held her mouth with her hand.

"Well, that's saying...something."

"Kelly, if she hadn't pumped the brakes, we'd have been in bed. I'd have ripped our clothes off to touch her and be touched."

"She put a stop to it, not you?"

"No...I mean, yes." Frustrated, Noeul pulled at her ponytail. "Yes, she put a stop to it and not me."

"If that's the case, I think you need to see where this goes. You can't say she won't stay if you haven't asked her to. Right now, I think you need to go outside and offer the support and comfort she looks like she could use. And frankly, that you look like you need to give."

Noeul wiped under her eyes and shook her hands, trying to cool her heated cheeks. "I'm probably a mess. If Miranda sees me like this, she *will* kill Jordan and it's not her fault."

"I'll head off Calamity Jane, you go check on Jordan. Honey, the effort she put into finding you should count for something." Kelly stepped forward and pulled Noeul into her arms.

"Thank you."

"That's what family is for."

Noeul wiped her face on the hem of her T-shirt and went to find Jordan.

After searching around the Jeep, she spotted Jordan sitting on a rock near the creek. The dogs were chasing after a stick she'd thrown into the water. "This seat taken?"

Jordan squinted up at her, her eyes shaded with her hand. She patted the ground beside her. Noeul sat down and drew her knees up to her chest to hug them with one arm, while she rested her head on the palm of the other. She looked at Jordan. "You okay?"

"I will be."

Noeul released her knees and inched her hand over until their fingers touched and Jordan intertwined them. "What's wrong? Is Max okay?"

Jordan sighed and used her free hand to throw the stick again. "He's in the rehab center. There's not much change other than that he's getting cranky. Sam's worried about him."

Noeul squeezed Jordan's hand. "Do you need to go back? I can ship what you have up at the house if you do."

"No, no. Sam says there's nothing for me to do there. Max is medicated. Sam will let me know if, and when, he gets to take Max home. Right now, Max wouldn't even know I was there."

"I'm so sorry, Jordan. What can I do?"

Jordan looked at their joined hands and held them up. "You're doing it."

"We need to talk about something else."

Jordan nodded her head. "Us?"

"Yes." Noeul's heart was pounding out of her chest. The rhythmic pulse swished in her ears.

"Noeul, the ball is in your court with this. I will respect whatever you want to do, and I mean that. I know what I feel. I will follow your lead. You will have to take the first step. I can't make it any clearer."

"What happens at the end of your sabbatical? Let's say we start this, and eight months passes. What do we do at that point?"

"What happens if I give you my heart and two months from now, you decide you can't do this? I've had my heart shredded before. I'm not relishing the thought of that ever happening again."

They sat looking at each other for a long time, until they were showered with water from two shaking dogs. "Ewww, you guys. Go play." Noeul threw the stick for Kyo and Bandit, causing both dogs to streak back into the wide creek and carry it back to shore together.

Jordan tipped her chin to the masses of fur and teeth biting down on the stick as they swam. "They seem to have it figured out. How about we see if we can too?"

Both women turned their heads at the sound of a truck. Noeul heard the screen door slam and saw Kelly walk out to the driveway, smoothing back her hair as she went and put her hands on the truck door.

When Miranda stepped out, she turned to look toward the creek where Noeul sat, still holding Jordan's hand. Noeul watched, as Miranda put her hands on her hips, shook her head, and began to pull boxes out of the crew cab.

"I'm going to go help." Jordan stood and dusted off the back of her cargo shorts.

"Jordan, Miranda is going to grill you. It's in her nature. She means well, so please don't take offense. Kelly will try to cool her off, I'm sure. Unfortunately, there's no way to hide that we've both been crying. It's not your fault, but Miranda will see it that way."

"Ah, the protective big sister, huh?"

"Sort of."

"Well, I guess I'd better head to the woodshed."

Noeul swatted her arm and casually looped hers through Jordan's, as they walked to the truck. She let go when they reached Miranda, whose eyes were scrutinizing them both.

"I'll help carry this stuff in with Kelly. I'll be back to help get the animal feed." Noeul grabbed a box and pulled it from the truck.

"I'll help her with that, you and Kelly go ahead. We got this, right, Miranda?"

Miranda narrowed her eyes. "Sure, it'll give us a chance to talk."

Noeul caught the hard emphasis spoken through gritted teeth. "Hey now, banty rooster, cool your jets. Whatever is running through your head didn't happen." Noeul hugged her. "I'm fine."

Miranda looked at her. "You don't look fine."

"Maybe." Noeul turned to Jordan and watched the trepidation and concern pass across her studied features and dark, expressive eyes. "Somehow, I think that's about to change."

***

Jordan watched Noeul walk back toward the house with Kelly, their heads bent close in conversation. "She's an incredible woman."

Miranda sighed. "Why has she been crying?"

Jordan straightened her back after she picked up a bag of feed and hefted it to her shoulder. "You'd need to ask her that."

Miranda picked up two salt blocks, balanced them on her hips and started walking toward the barn. "I'm asking you."

"Look, Mirand—"

"Don't you 'look Miranda' me. She's been through hell. Carved a life out for herself, alone, I might add. Your presence here is not only affecting her, but making her cry? That's fucking great." Miranda threw down the salt blocks, put her hands on her hips, and faced Jordan.

Jordan set the bag of feed down and spread her feet a bit to find her balance in case Miranda decided to let her fists do her talking before listening to reason. She was sure the woman could pack a punch, given those biceps. "Miranda, I've driven from coast to coast to find her. Last night we danced, and we got close, so close we almost got carried away. I could tell she was scared to death, so I told her nothing would happen unless she wanted it to. I said it, and I meant it. A few minutes ago, when you drove up, we were openly discussing those fears. And again, I told her the choice is hers. If she tells me to go, I will. If she tells me to stay, I will. Not you, me, my sister, Kelly, and not even my mother, will make this decision. Noeul will. If you have a problem with that, it's your issue not mine. If you're going to take a swing at me, have at it, because I've done nothing wrong and absolutely nothing to hurt her. Whatever you're going to do, you're doing it for yourself and not her."

Miranda stood there like a bull close to charging. She laughed and shook her head with her hands still on her hips. Jordan was confused, completely unsure of what to say or do.

"Well, I'll give you this, you've got a backbone. You're going to need it when it comes to that one. Come on, let's get that truck unloaded. I need a beer, and from the looks of you, I'd say you need something a little stronger. After that, we'll talk." She held up her hands. "Just talk."

Jordan took a deep breath, relaxed her hands that were balled into fists, and picked up the feed bag. She was still a little leery of being within arm's reach of Miranda, although fairly confident they'd turned a corner.

Twenty minutes later, they were sitting on the porch, beers in hand and a fifth of Jim Beam between them. Kelly and Noeul came out with plates of sandwiches and chips. Jordan smiled at Noeul and gratefully accepted the offered lunch.

"You'd better slow down on the shots if we're riding back up the mountain here in a bit. I don't need you falling off Thor."

Jordan bit into the sandwich and smiled. She chewed and held up a finger so as not to talk with her mouth full, a rule her mother strictly enforced. "Don't worry about me, I haven't had a single one." She pointed at Miranda "Although, I wouldn't let that one over there operate anything more dangerous than the lever on a recliner."

Noeul reached over and used her thumb to wipe something off the corner of Jordan's lip. She placed it in her own mouth to clean it off. "Mmm, hot pepper mustard."

Jordan stopped chewing. Her slack jaw drew a sly smile from Noeul. Jordan closed her eyes and prayed she could avoid groaning out loud at the sight. She took another bite of her sandwich and accepted the shot Miranda handed her.

With a grin, Miranda threw back her own and said, "I'll bet you need that shot now."

Jordan's hand trembled as she clasped the short tumbler. She downed the whiskey in one gulp and visibly shivered as the bourbon slowly burned all the way to her toes.

Noeul picked up the beer beside Jordan's foot and handed it to her. "You'd better chase that."

Their fingers brushed, and Jordan felt like she'd stuck a screwdriver into an electrical outlet. A slow, smoldering smile crossed Noeul's lips, and Jordan's body heated as if she was surrounded by molten lava. It wasn't the whiskey. If they didn't get out of there soon, she'd have to tie her own hands together to keep from ripping Noeul's clothes off, laying her down on the wooden porch under her feet, and fucking her senseless. She drained three quarters of the beer, as Noeul got up to get something. She returned with a bottle of water.

"Thanks."

"You're welcome. Now, I will assume you two found some common ground other than what comes in a bottle from Kentucky?"

Miranda chimed in. "We have. You're a big girl, Noeul. I'll still drown her in the creek if she hurts you." She looked at Jordan, who nearly snorted water out of her nose. "And I've got two hundred acres to bury you somewhere they'll never find you, along with owning a tractor big enough to dig the hole." She tipped back her beer again and took a bite of the sandwich Kelly held for her.

Kelly rolled her eyes. "Oh, shut up and eat. Good lord, Jim Beam isn't going to back you up when Jordan kicks your ass, or Noeul for that matter. Nor is it going to put a heat pack on your back when you throw it out with all that chest puffing you're doing. I'm positive it's not our business." Kelly kissed her cheek. "I love you, you old fool, now eat and soak up some of that liquid courage that's thinning out the blood trying to reach your brain."

Jordan and Noeul both laughed, and Jordan sighed contentedly as an arm wrapped around her and a warm hip touched her shoulder. She melted into the embrace and felt her world right itself.

"If I hurt her, you won't have to drown me in the creek, I'll do it myself." Jordan stood and helped Noeul off the chair's arm, "Lunch was delicious. Thank you for your hospitality. Time for us to make the trek back up the mountain. Pip will need to be milked, the eggs gathered, and Thor and Athena will need brushing out."

"And those two," Noeul pointed to Bandit and Kyo, "will need baths."

Jordan agreed, wrinkling her nose at the dogs that lay panting on the porch. "Maybe I'll take a bar of your soap and take them out to the falls when we get back."

***

It was past noon when the group said goodbye, as Noeul and Jordan mounted the horses and turned for home. The return trip was uneventful. Jordan brushed down both Thor and Athena and stored the tack, while Noeul did the milking and gathered the eggs.

Noeul watched Jordan trot off with both dogs at her side and a towel over her shoulder. She smiled at the sight that seemed as natural as if she'd witnessed it a million times before. Deciding she would put together a stir-fry for their evening meal, she appropriately labeled and put away the eggs and milk. She headed outside to gather items for the dish.

Noeul could hear a raised voice coming from the direction Jordan had gone. Not a fearful or an angry tone, by any means, it sounded like frustration and carried through the woods more than she would have expected for the distance. It seemed strange, though she'd never had anyone around other than Miranda and Kelly to have even thought about it.

The dogs have to be doing something to make her crazy. Noeul moved up the trail and through the woods. She stopped right at the tree line, out of sight of the woman trying very hard to scrub down a wiggling Kyo, as Bandit ran back and forth tormenting her.

"Just wait you little jack in the box, you're next. Kyo, stand still and stop walking. Bandit, go lay down. Stop, both of you."

Noeul had to cover her mouth with her hand to keep the laughter from revealing her hiding place.

"Kyo, go swim. Bandit, get over here now." Jordan stood, one hand on her hip, the other pointing to a spot in front of her, as she tried an authoritative voice to get the black-and-white dog to obey. Bandit chased after Kyo in the water, and Jordan threw her hands up.

Noeul was nearly doubled over with laughter, as both dogs came out of the water and shook off all over Jordan. Kyo hadn't completely rinsed the soap off her and patches of white foam now covered Jordan.

"Ugh, you two." Jordan reached out and grabbed a crouching Bandit and pulled him by the collar as she began to lather him up. Kyo was now the instigator, and Jordan snapped her fingers, ordering her to sit and stay.

Noeul's sides were hurting from watching the tableau before her. Bandit tolerated the scrub down much better than Kyo had. Before long, both dogs were swimming out in the deeper area where Jordan had thrown a stick. The tall woman stood with her hands on her hips, her T-shirt dripping. Noeul watched as she tried to brush off wet dog hair that clung to her arms and legs, spitting as she tried to wipe hair away from her mouth with the back of her arm. This only made it worse.

Noeul's eyes widened, as Jordan reached down and stripped the T-shirt off her body, then slid down her shorts. Noeul licked her lips at the sight of Jordan in her jog bra and boxer briefs. She could hear the blood rushing through her own body. She expected Jordan to dive into the pool after the dogs. That wasn't what happened.

Holy...shit!

Time crawled. Noeul heard the slow ticking of a clock, each second drawn out into two or three before the next ticked by. Jordan pulled the jog bra over her head and threw it down with her T-shirt and shorts. Her thumbs hooked the waist band of her briefs and pushed them down her long legs. The dark triangle at the apex of Jordan's thighs was visible against the tanned flesh of her body. Lean muscle and flawless skin stood on display for Noeul, as Jordan raised her arms over her head in a sun salutation.

Noeul reached out a hand and placed it against the tree to steady herself. Her other hand was clamped firmly over her mouth. Jordan assumed the warrior pose, drawing one leg back, the other leg bent at the knee, her arms stretched out in front and behind her. As Jordan turned into another pose with arms raised, the full view of the phoenix tattoo was now on display. The tail feathers traveled around Jordan's side and wrapped her breast.

Noeul was unable to draw a breath, as all sound, save the beating of her own heart, ceased to exist. Triceps and biceps were clearly defined, and Noeul admired Jordan's toned obliques, abdominals, quads, and calf muscles. Jordan was a female Adonis standing in all her glory.

A shocking revelation hit Noeul. "Young, beautiful, intelligent...and wants me." The words left her throat in a whisper, as fleeting as a snowflake landing on warm ground. Noeul watched Jordan stand upright and turn toward where she was standing. The tall woman spun back around and walked into the pool to disappear under the water.

***

Jordan broke the surface and whipped her head around to shed the water from her hair. She used her hand to wipe her face and enjoyed the feeling of the stray dog hair being washed away in the water. Both dogs swam around her and brought their stick to her in invitation. She pushed off the bottom and launched herself out of the water to throw the stick across the deeper part, near the falls.

The cool liquid felt good on her heated skin, as she dipped her head back under again. Her eye was drawn to a fleeting movement near the tree line. More than once, she'd felt like she was being watched. The flash of royal blue told her exactly who'd been watching. She dove back under and emerged to grab her clothes. She gathered them up and took them back into the water to divest them of the dog hair that clung to them. Her shoulders were above the water, as she dunked the clothes and swished them around.

She dressed sans her jog bra, choosing her John Muir shirt over struggling with a wet bra. When she exited the water, she made sure to keep her eyes down, partially to not embarrass Noeul and partially to keep her libido in check. Knowing that Noeul had seen her completely naked was a huge turn on. The dogs swam around a few more times before she whistled, calling them out of the water.

"Come on, you two, let's go!" Jordan called more for Noeul's benefit than for the dogs. She used the towel to somewhat dry herself and her clothes before signaling her four-legged companions to follow. She stayed far enough away so that when they shook, she would not be covered in dog hair again.

Drag your feet, give her enough time to get back and under control, Jordan. After a few minutes, she made her way back to the house with the clean, yet still wet, dogs at her side. Watching them play fight and chase each other was entertaining. The walk back had given her time to calm her own raging hormones. This whole letting Noeul set the pace thing was going to force her to take matters into her own hands soon, literally, if her mind continued to fantasize. The throbbing in her center grew more intense all the time. Even the cold water hadn't settled her. *Well of course not. How could it, knowing she was watching?* Jordan shook her head to clear her lustful thoughts.

What she needed to do was go work in the greenhouse for a while, check on the plants' progress and try a few things that had come to her last night while she was *not* sleeping. When she cleared the edge of the trees, she could see Noeul over by the vegetable patch. The path led near Noeul, so Jordan kept walking. She turned her attention to a lagging Kyo and Bandit.

"You two, go lie in the sun and dry out. Take a nap. I swear you'd better not get dirty again, or you'll be sleeping outside." Noeul's eyes met hers. It was clear something was now present that hadn't been there when they'd parted ways. It looked very much like desire. "We're back. I think they're tired enough to go to sleep and dry out. Bathing Kyo is like trying to nail Jello to the wall. It doesn't stay where you put it."

Noeul's laugh came out almost as a bark, and both dogs lifted their heads before groaning and lying back down. Jordan watched, as Noeul's eyes traveled up her body, stopping at her breasts where her nipples stood out starkly against the clinging wet T-shirt. She watched the woman blush.

Noeul dropped her eyes and picked zucchini and crookneck squash off the vines. She cleared her throat. "Uh, I hope you like stir-fry, because that's what I'm fixing tonight."

"I do. I'm going to work in the greenhouse for a bit. I'll do some weeding, and I'll take care of the animals before I grab a shower while you fix dinner. I don't think my dip at the falls removed all the dog hair." She held up the wet, wadded up jog bra. "Do you need me for anything?"

Jordan watched Noeul's eyes rise and settle on her breasts once more, before she shook her head and visibly swallowed hard.

"No, no I've got this."

"Okay, see you in a bit." Jordan moved past her, a huge grin covering her face, as she felt Noeul's eyes on her. *Just how strong are your roots, dragon?*

***

Noeul stared at the retreating form in front of her. She shivered at the frisson of desire that jolted through her. Jordan had obviously noticed the blatant ogling of her breasts. The wet T-shirt clung to her body like a second skin and starkly displayed her erect nipples. Noeul shook her head, causing wisps of her hair to escape her ponytail and hang loosely in her face. *Just looking at her is driving me crazy. I can't imagine touching her.* She closed her eyes and allowed Jordan to pass from view, before she pulled at the cuff, gathered her hair back, and shoved the pin through.

She stood, weighed down with produce bursting with the colors of the summer growing season. She loved the yellow squash, purple eggplant, red tomatoes, and white scallions adorned with long, green tops. The basket looked like she'd walked through the farmers' market. She was pleased to know, all of it had been grown with her own two hands. Noeul decided that she could shower before she fixed dinner. She walked in the house and left the basket in the kitchen. As she headed to her room, she stripped off her clothes. Her fingers brushed her own taut nipples, eliciting an unintentional gasp from her lips.

This is ridiculous, I'm like a horny teenager. God! I've got to get myself under control. Angrily, she turned the shower knob, then pulled clean clothes from her drawers while the water came to temperature. She removed the silver cuff and held it in her hand. It was still one of her prized possessions. On her way to the shower, she passed the dresser and caught a glimpse of her naked reflection in the attached mirror.

For fifty-five, Noeul knew she was in good shape. Her heritage had a lot to do with that. Her mother had aged beautifully, and Noeul was the spitting image of Mi-ya Scott. She stopped and leaned heavily on the dresser with both hands, as she examined herself critically. Small lines were starting to form. Her green eyes were still bright and, not for the first time, she offered up a few words to her father. *"Thanks for my eyes, Dad."*

Her hair bounced against her back, as she stepped into the hot spray. She turned the jets to a fine, hard stream and allowed the needle-like pulsations to penetrate tired muscles. *Tired, that's all this is. No sleep last night has put me on an emotional roller coaster.* She squeezed a small ribbon of shampoo in her hands and lathered her hair, as she enjoyed her favorite coconut and almond scents.

They were like an aromatherapy for her, something that calmed and soothed her. She applied a light layer of conditioner and worked it in. After a few minutes, she rinsed the long strands and luxuriated in the feel of it. Her hand reached for the bar of her homemade soap. She rolled it in her palms to create a thick, creamy lather that smelled of rich vanilla from the essential oils she'd added to her special mix. Her hands traveled over her body, washing away the sweat and grit. The soap also removed the smell of Athena from the trail ride home.

One errant brush across her nipples and they were instantly pebbled, standing up at her heightened state of arousal. Noeul groaned, as she lathered her hands again. Her eyes shut tightly, and flashes of Jordan's naked body played across her closed lids. *Oh God, I wanted to touch her.* Jordan's skin glistened from the water that shed off of her.

Visions of the fiery tattoo that covered her triangular back and the tail that caressed her breast flashed through Noeul's memory. She saw those dark, fathomless eyes turn on that power to peel away every wall and barrier erected. Noeul dropped a shaky hand to her center and stopped short of circling her clit to relieve the agonizing pressure building between her legs. The temptation was too great, and she ran a gentle finger through her own wetness, gasping at the copious moisture she found. Startled, she withdrew her hands and placed them on the cool, tile wall. Her cheeks flamed at the thought of being aroused by anyone other than Aggie. *My God, what am I doing?*

Leaning her body against the cool tile, she cried. Cried it all out, the loss, the loneliness, and the longing. Noeul cried for what would never be again and what might be if she could only let go. What could happen if she took a chance and allowed Jordan into all the places that had lain dormant for so long? She cried until no more tears would come. She turned her face to the spray and let it all slide down her body, onto the floor, and circle the drain until it disappeared. Only then did she hear the music, the unique sound of Sophie B. Hawkins singing expletives over an unrequited desire to partner up.

Wow, that's how I'm feeling. I couldn't have nailed that sentiment any better if I'd written that myself. Even with the pulse-pounding desire she felt for Jordan, she wasn't yet ready to commit her body. Her heart still teetered on the edge of yesterday and today. Climbing out of the shower, she dressed and made her way to the kitchen to start dinner. She passed by Jordan's room and stopped. She rested her hand on the doorframe and listened to the chorus. She smiled when she heard Jordan singing along. She had an excellent voice, pleasant in that gravely Carol King-Bonnie Raitt way.

A quick turn and Noeul was walking toward the kitchen, rubbing her sweaty palms on her shorts. *Sophie, you're not the only one. I wish I was her lover.*

***

Jordan wandered into the kitchen, her nose in the air. "My God, that smells incredible." She enjoyed watching the smile envelop Noeul's face at the compliment. "Ginger?"

"Good nose, it's one of my mother's recipes."

Jordan sat down at the bar in front of Noeul's prep station. She reached out and stole a long slice of red bell pepper.

"Hey you, you'll spoil your dinner. It will be ready soon."

"Can I help?"

Noeul quirked a smile. "Sure, if you come chop these crookneck squash into chunks, I'll get the rice."

Jordan went to the sink and washed her hands. Noeul handed her the knife, and she went to work on the vegetables left on the cutting board. She watched, as Noeul seasoned the boiling water and poured the rice out of a cloth bag.

Jordan threw a piece of broccoli in the air and caught it in her mouth. "How about we make that ice cream tonight? I've got a craving."

Noeul shook her head at her. "You are such a kid. Yes, we can make the ice cream. Although, I might have to go back out to the garden if you keep eating the ingredients before we make dinner. Come over here and stir this while I cook that in the wok."

Jordan traded her places, her hands resting lightly on Noeul's hips as she passed by. As her pelvis brushed Noeul's back, she felt the smaller woman shudder against her and heard a sharp intake of breath. As much as she wanted to explore the moment, she moved past Noeul and grabbed the wooden spoon to stir the small white grains around in the boiling water.

"Go ahead and turn the heat down and cover the pot."

Noeul poured canola oil into the hot wok and added the fresh ginger. The sweetly pungent aroma filled the kitchen, as Noeul deftly stirred the aromatic root around the wok. She added the carrots and broccoli first, followed by the squash, peppers, and onions. She finished with the eggplant, sprouts, and tomato. The wave of delicious scents hit Jordan and made her mouth water. Both women laughed at the loud rumble that emanated from her stomach.

"At least I know you're hungry." Noeul pointed with her stirring sticks. "Grab a fork and fluff that rice a bit. I'll get bowls." Noeul removed the wok from the heat and grabbed two wide, shallow bowls. She handed one to Jordan and opened a sealed jar.

Immediately, a tangy smell hit Jordan's nostrils. "Is that kimchi?"

Noeul smiled. "It is. If Mi-ya Scott served rice, we had kimchi. I think she'd have served it with every meal, because that's how she grew up. Dad and I drew the line when she tried to serve it with spaghetti."

Jordan couldn't help but laugh as she screwed up her face.

Noeul pointed to the expression. "Exactly."

The pair sat down at the table. Noeul brought over a bottle of white wine and filled a glass for Jordan, who accepted it with a grateful smile. Dinner conversation was light, as Jordan regaled Noeul with tales of cooking with her jida and her mother. They decided that the next night Jordan would cook dinner with some lamb that Noeul had frozen and some of the goat yogurt sitting in her refrigerator.

Once dinner was over, the pair set to making homemade ice cream. Jordan stirred the cream, sugar, and goat's milk in a saucepan until she was sure the sugar was dissolved, following Noeul's instructions to the letter. Once Noeul was satisfied with the consistency, she poured the mixture around the beater into the metal cylinder, while Jordan added the berries. They closed it up and placed it in the larger bucket, poured ice around the can, and added a little salt to the top. Noeul attached the cranking mechanism and they headed outside with the ice cream maker and the rest of the wine. Noeul fed the docile canine members of their menagerie, while Jordan began cranking the mixture with the bucket on a small table held between her knees.

"That kimchi was outstanding. I haven't had that in years. Although I will say I'm glad you had some mouthwash available or you wouldn't want to be within three feet of me." Jordan watched Noeul's pleased smile and vowed to compliment her as often as possible. She stopped cranking with her left hand and turned the bucket, so she could use her strongest arm, as the mixture started to thicken. Noeul added more ice and salt.

"I'm glad you liked it. Mom taught me to make kimchi, and it was always heavy on the garlic. Getting tired? I can take over."

"Nah, I'm good. I started lefty so I can finish out strong. I can feel it getting thicker. Can I get a little more wine?"

"Absolutely. Tell me more about your adventure looking for me. Did you enjoy the places on the list?"

Jordan took a sip of her wine. "Havasu was one of the most beautiful places I've ever been. The water was gorgeous. Moose Lake was a challenging hike. Bandit would have loved that trip. I didn't have him with me. The lake looked like glass, calm and serene."

"It had to be freezing, given the time of year."

"Oh yeah, I froze my ass off." Jordan watched, as Noeul's eyes traveled down her body. The sensation was like a caress, and her skin warmed. "New Orleans, that was an adventure. The food was unbelievable." Jordan went on while she cranked the ice cream, describing her brush with the ghost in the guest house.

"I can't imagine doing the list one right after the other. I took a bit more time in between. It had to seem like an Indiana Jones adventure."

"I prefer Laura Croft, personally. You're right, it was an adventure. The best part was finding you...made every blister and callus worth it."

Noeul quirked a grin and blushed. She stood and reached out for the ice cream crank, "Let me see what the consistency is, we might be done."

"I suspect it's time to put the calories I cranked away back on."

Noeul shook her head. "Let me take this in and go get spoons. I'll be right back. Want to start the fire while I'm gone?"

"Sure." Jordan watched Noeul rise and carry the ice cream maker back toward the house. She whispered to herself, as she watched the gentle sway of Noeul's hips, "I hate to tell you, that fires already started and you're the one who lit the blaze."

***

Noeul looked out the window as Jordan moved around preparing the fire. She knew she'd been lonely, that was no secret. She hadn't fully understood the depth of her isolation until she had Jordan here every night to share a meal and to go about her day with. *Hell, having someone to say good morning to and having them say it back feels like the first warm day of spring after a frigid winter.* Simple things like that were making her realize how much she missed being with someone.

Her relationship with Aggie had never been all rainbows and unicorns. They'd fought, disagreed, and downright argued at times. The point was that they'd been there for each other, for better or worse. She and Jordan had fallen into such an easy companionship. Noeul enjoyed turning around to see Jordan working close to her. And having someone to bounce an idea off immediately was completely invigorating. *I certainly don't mind the incidental touches or being close to Jordan.* She wasn't sure she was completely ready to admit what it was doing to her body...*or my heart.*

The ice cream maker pulled apart easily, which allowed her to remove the beater and scrape the ice cream back into the metal cylinder. She reached into the drawer and pulled out two spoons, shutting it with her hip as she headed to the door. At the last second, she looked at the two spoons in her hand and set one on the table by the door. Without giving herself a chance to second guess her actions, she walked out to the blazing fire and took a seat by Jordan.

Jordan's face was full of anticipation. "Well, how'd it turn out?"

Noeul smiled. "You be the judge." She slid the spoon into the creamy, frozen confection and held the utensil up to let Jordan take the first taste. Her eyes met Jordan's, and she swore the fire she saw there had nothing to do with the flames licking at the wood in the pit.

Jordan wrapped warm fingers around her wrist, bringing the spoon to her lips. Noeul watched, as she tentatively stuck out her tongue for the first taste, her eyes never leaving Noeul's. When Jordan accepted the spoon, Noeul watched those same eyes flutter shut, open, and roll back. A pleasure-filled moan escaped Jordan's throat. Noeul swallowed hard and tightened her thighs against the deep clench and pulse of her center.

Jordan pointed to the ice cream. "That is one of the most incredible things I've ever tasted. No pint of Ben and Jerry's could ever compare."

Noeul's throat felt like an arid desert, her lips as parched as if she'd been lying in the sun. She tried to wet her lips with her tongue, instantly liking the wide-eyed reaction Jordan gave her. "Really?"

Jordan dipped the spoon into the ice cream and scooted close, holding it out for Noeul. As she drew it into her mouth, she watched Jordan visibly shudder and close her eyes. She nearly dropped the spoon. Noeul was enjoying this little impromptu seduction scene. She rose and sat down in Jordan's lap, snugging her ass into Jordan's crotch and enjoying the very tiny whimper that escaped the taller woman's throat. Noeul spooned up another bite and held it for Jordan, as she felt tentative hands settle on her hips.

They sat there like that taking several more bites, until Jordan signaled she'd had enough. Noeul turned the spoon upside down and cleaned off the last remnants of the ice cream. She fixed her eyes on Jordan's. "Did you enjoy that?"

"Utterly intoxicating." Jordan's head dropped against the back of the chair.

Noeul leaned over and placed a soft kiss on Jordan's lips, the taste of blackberries and cream still present. Noeul could feel the body beneath her nearly vibrate with tension. When she pulled back from the kiss, she rested her forehead on Jordan's, their chests heaving in almost perfect rhythm. "I'd better get this in the freezer before it goes to waste." Jordan held her hips firmly in place.

"Please, don't move."

"I promise, I'll be right back. I want to put this in the freezer." Jordan continued to hold her tight, and Noeul searched her eyes. There was no fear, no anger, no hurt. "What's wrong?"

Jordan drew in a slow breath, ragged and anything but smooth.

"Jordan, you're worrying me. What's wrong?" Noeul placed a tentative palm against the heated cheek. "Do you have a fever? You're very warm." Her hand automatically went to Jordan's forehead, only to be captured and pulled to Jordan's lips, the knuckles kissed reverently.

"Noeul, I feel fine. Actually, better than fine. It's just..."

"Just what?"

Jordan closed her eyes, and Noeul saw a small smile form on her lips.

"I'm so turned on right now that if you move your ass, even a little bit, I'm going to embarrass myself."

Noeul's confusion cleared in a flash. Her face heated and she shook her head, slightly embarrassed. "Feeling a bit like a fourteen-year-old boy watching Jamie Lee Curtis dance in *True Lies*?"

Jordan snorted, laughter rolling off her until she had to wipe her eyes. Noeul joined in and the two sat in a futile attempt to bring themselves under control. Finally, Noeul looked into Jordan's eyes and saw composure and smoldering need.

Jordan shook her head. "That description is pretty accurate. Give it a few more seconds, and I think you can get up without incident."

Noeul sat there, perfectly still, admiring Jordan's stunning features and the dark, chocolate eyes that glinted in the firelight with a lingering look of desire. Jordan shifted and released Noeul's hips.

The sight of the beautiful woman, visibly struggling to rein in her desire, had Noeul's center pulsing. "I'll be right back. Hold that thought, okay?" Noeul briefly touched her lips to Jordan as she rose. When she walked away, she realized there was little she wouldn't give to see that look in Jordan's eyes again and again and again.

***

Jordan watched Noeul enter the house. Without a doubt, she only had a few minutes to bring her libido under control. She took several deep breaths and adjusted her uncomfortably damp shorts. Her fingers brushed across her tingling lips, and her side burned like never before. *Holy shit what that woman can do to me with just a kiss.*

She'd vowed to take this at Noeul's pace, and she meant it. The problem was, Jordan was no saint. One more session of Seduction 101 and she wouldn't be responsible for her actions. The exquisite feeling of Noeul sitting in her lap, feeding her ice cream from a shared spoon, had been as arousing and erotic as anything she'd ever done in her life. The storm that raged through her center had her on the edge of climax. If she hadn't stopped Noeul from moving when she did, Jordan would have orgasmed with even the most accidental stimulation of her swollen clit. She heard the sliding glass door and took a deep breath. Using the poker, she moved some of logs around in the pit. It appeared that Noeul had outdoor speakers, because the distinctive voice of Carol King came floating out onto the night air.

Noeul stood less than two feet from her, her hand outstretched. Jordan rose out of her chair and joined Noeul in an embrace followed by gentle kiss, as the two swayed together to Carol's voice singing into the darkness.

"Remember, I'm right here and we take this one day at a time, side by side," Jordan whispered. She felt Noeul draw in closer. Jordan wanted to shelter her, body and soul, in the safety and comfort of her arms. Loss had been too much a part of this beautiful woman's life for far too long. Noeul deserved to be worry free, and Jordan knew that it would take time to believe she wasn't going anywhere.

They danced to a few more songs, before Jordan added logs to the fire. She sat and drew Noeul into her lap. She used her long arms to hold Noeul close to her body, as the tiny woman drew her legs up and nestled in the curve of Jordan's neck.

Jordan tightened the circle of her arms and looked up into the night sky. "I love the way you can see every star up here on a clear night. It reminds me of the night I spent at Moose Lake. That place was amazing."

"I will admit, it was pretty incredible. Cold but incredible. I toyed with putting the memorial in the lake. It was too damn cold. I looked around and climbed to the highest point. Once I did, that tree where you found it, called to me. It reminded me of how I felt, all alone, rooted in a place I couldn't change. Not really living, merely surviving from one season to the next."

"Maybe you don't recognize the most important part of that statement. You were surviving. I know that doesn't tell the whole story. The reality is, it's the most critical element. You could have curled up and refused to move forward. That's not what you've done."

Noeul sighed and entwined her fingers with Jordan's. "When I hear you say it, it sounds so different than what it felt like going through it."

"Our perception is always skewed. You've traveled to amazing places and pushed yourself to limits you didn't know possible. You built this place and have done more than exist. Noeul, you've thrived. That's a fact."

Jordan didn't say anymore, letting her words sink in. She prayed that simple sentiment had helped Noeul see that her life didn't stop because Aggie died. The fire crackled and popped in front of them. Off in the distance, an owl hooted and another one answered. Noeul's fists tightened their grip on the T-shirt Jordan was wearing. Jordan's eyes closed as she leaned down and gently placed her lips against Noeul's warm forehead. She rested her cheek against the silken strands of hair. The touch elicited something that sounded much like a sigh from Noeul, who had yet to speak.

"Noeul, I don't claim to know everything. Hell, I'm not sure of most things at this point. What I am sure of, is being with you is like nothing I've ever done, like nothing I've ever felt. With you, there's more to life than research, facts, and figures. For the first time in a long time, I feel something."

Seconds passed as Jordan held her, firelight flickering off everything around them. Bandit yawned and Kyo followed. Jordan stroked Noeul's cheek and was pleased to see sleepy eyes turn up to her. "I think the children are telling us that it's time to go to bed."

Noeul snuggled into Jordan's chest. "I know. I'm finding it hard to move from this spot."

"I know the feeling." Jordan paused and tightened her arms around the small frame that sat encircled inside her arms. "If we fall asleep like this, you'll be sitting on my full bladder all night." Jordan stood, still cradling Noeul.

"Jordan, you'll hurt yourself, put me down."

"The only thing that would hurt me right now is if you made me follow your wishes. Let me enjoy this for a few minutes more, okay?"

Noeul shook her head, and Jordan felt the nod go straight to her heart. Several strides later, she whistled for the dogs and laughed as Noeul reached out and slid the door open with a free hand, while the other clung tightly to her neck.

Once inside, she slid the door shut with her foot, barely noticing the weight of the very petite woman in her arms. Kyo and Bandit went to the living room and turned around several times, before they settled into a pile. Bandit's head rested on Kyo's shoulders. Jordan carried Noeul back to her bed and set her down on it, kissing her head which she held tenderly between her hands. "Good night."

When she stood to leave, Noeul grabbed her arm, entangled their fingers, and pulled Jordan's head back down. Soft kisses touched Jordan's lips, and she fought to prevent a groan of pleasure from escaping.

Noeul words were soft and feather light. "Can you..."

Jordan looked deeply into Noeul's eyes. "Can I what?" She watched emotions cross Noeul's face like an approaching storm cloud rolling over a mountain top. "I told you, there's nothing you can't ask of me, Noeul."

"Can you hold me tonight? I mean, just hold me?"

Jordan dropped to her knee so that Noeul didn't have to look up at her. "I can do anything you need. Let me go take care of a few necessary things and I'll be right back. Will that be okay?" She watched doubt fall across Noeul's face and vowed to drive it away. "As much as I want to crawl in there right now and draw you into my arms, I'm not sure how comfortable we'll be sleeping in our current attire. And to be honest, I need to pee and brush my teeth." She was pleased to see a small smile cross Noeul's face. She kissed her forehead and quickly exited to her room. After taking care of the must dos, she shed her clothes and pulled on another faded, red Cornell T-shirt that lay sitting on her bed and a loose pair of cotton boxers.

Stepping on the wood floor, she walked quietly back to Noeul's doorway, tentative and fearful that Noeul might have reconsidered.

When she saw the covers pulled back on the vacant side of the bed, Jordan stepped forward and lay down on her back. In invitation, she opened her left arm.

After a few seconds, her eyes adjusted to the soft moonlight illuminating the room as she gazed around. A photograph of a sunset view adorned the wall closest to her. She was sure that view was right outside the door. A bit further over, a pencil drawing of a fern leaf was framed in dark wood, and across the room, a pastel water color too muted for her to distinguish, hung in a place of pride. She pulled up on an old-fashioned quilt that covered the queen size bed and settled her head deeper into the soft, feather pillows that lined the headboard. She felt, more than saw, Noeul move into her arms, her head coming to rest above Jordan's left breast. She felt fingers tent a piece of the shirt she was wearing.

Noeul's words were still no more than a whisper. "I like this shirt on you. You wear it like a second skin."

"I'm surprised it's survived all these years. It was the first one I bought when I got to Cornell. It's followed me through every research project I've ever worked on, through my PhD. and more hikes than I can remember. It carried me through…"

Noeul sat up, her eyes searching Jordan's face. "Through what?"

"My search for you."

Jordan felt a hand smooth the T-shirt over her skin. That movement alone was arousing enough. Add in the hand that tightened and clenched the shirt in a ball, and she was in sensory overload as the fabric pulled tight against her erect nipples. Biting her lip, she stifled a moan. Jordan brought her hand from behind her head and wrapped it around the small body lying at her side.

Tension vibrated and rippled through her, as she fought to control the onslaught of arousal coursing low in her center. She clasped Noeul's hand and rested her cheek against the sweet, coconut smelling hair beneath her cheek. Jordan rarely prayed, a fact not lost on her as she offered up a silent request to anyone listening. *Please don't let her fear this, let her trust me.*

***

Noeul lay with her head tucked below Jordan's chin. The rise and fall of the soft skin beneath her cheek was nowhere near as relaxed as someone trying to sleep should be. A sixth sense told her Jordan was trying to lay still and doing a poor job of it. She felt the waves of stress roll off her.

Noeul was uncomfortably warm from her own rising desire. She couldn't force herself to separate from the muscled body she was curled up next to. She lay there and listened to the prestissimo beat of Jordan's heart, quick, steady and unerring. Years ago, she'd crawled into a hospital bed to be close to Aggie in her final moments, praying for a miracle.

The machines had been turned off at Noeul's request so that those last moments of Aggie's life wouldn't be filled with beeps and shrill sounds. As Noeul's ear lay pressed to the cooling skin of the once vibrant woman, she strained to hear one more beat. The room was eerily silent for a long time. Aggie's doctor, Rita Hamilton, placed a hand on Noeul's shoulder.

"Noeul, can I listen for a minute?" Rita held up her stethoscope.

Noeul slowly shook her head as the numbness crept in, leaving her feeling empty. She already knew what Rita would find. There would be nothing to listen to. Noeul felt the loss the moment Aggie left her. Never again would she hear that voice or feel her embrace. Aggie was gone, and no medical intervention could ever bring her back.

"Noeul?"

The sound of her name pulled her from the memory. Noeul was startled to feel moisture on her face and was embarrassed that those same tears had dampened the shirt beneath her cheek. "Oh, Jordan, I'm sorry." She attempted to sit up, only to be held fast in place by the strong arms that embraced her.

"There's nothing to be sorry about. Have I done something to make you uncomfortable, something that's made you cry?"

"No, Jordan, you've done nothing except be wonderful. These tears don't have anything to do with you. I'm sorry I've gotten you wet." Noeul felt a small chuckle beneath her, and a hand cupped her cheek. She recognized the double entendre and lightly smacked Jordan's tight abdominal muscles. "You're so bad."

"Guilty as charged. Honestly, I wanted to make you smile. Mission accomplished, I'd say."

"Yes, well done. Now, calm your teenage hormones and let's go to sleep. I'm exhausted."

"As you wish. Thank you for trusting me to hold you and for feeling like you could let go."

Noeul rolled over and felt Jordan spoon in behind her. Soft breath drifted across her neck.

"Is this okay?" Jordan kissed her shoulder as she asked the question.

Noeul drew the arm wrapped around her tighter against her body. She pulled Jordan's hand into hers and cradled it to her chest. The feeling was so incredibly right that it soothed her frazzled nerves. At the same time, it scared her. "It's more than okay."

She kissed the knuckles she held in her hand and closed her eyes, reveling in the warmth of another body against hers. Not just *a* body. Jordan's body. It was different than Aggie's, leaner and in many ways, more defined, and radiating warmth and need. She could tell those feelings were being tempered, allowing Noeul to take comfort without the demand for more, right now. *It feels like we've done this thousands of times.* Noeul marveled at the feeling and allowed the lateness of the hour to draw her into a blissfully dreamless sleep.

Chapter Twenty

THE NEXT MORNING, NOEUL found herself curled into a warm body. Initially startled, she flushed, realizing that her hand was snaked under the soft cotton T-shirt of the woman she was half covering with her own body. She lay there, not moving, enjoying the incredible feeling of waking up with someone. For years, she'd climbed from sleep to awaken in an empty bed. She was surprised that at no time did she ever forget that it was Jordan's body beside her. This felt different than the countless times she'd experienced the dawn with Aggie. Her first clue was their position in the bed.

Rarely had she woken up without Aggie literally sprawled out over top of her, frequently pinning her, while she clung to a very small portion of the bed. The fact that Noeul was resting so naturally, near the middle of the bed with Jordan, wasn't lost on her. It was as if they were meeting in the imaginary middle, giving and taking from each other in a balanced way.

Jordan's arm was around her shoulders, protectively sheltering her. The other arm lay on the leg Noeul had thrown across Jordan's thighs. Unable to see Jordan's face, Noeul could tell she was still deep in sleep, as her heartbeat repeated a slow, gentle cadence. The sun was filtering in, and Noeul snuggled in closer. She could feel the moment when Jordan came into conscious thought; a slight stiffening gave her away.

"Good morning."

Noeul tilted her head up to meet the smiling, chocolate eyes that greeted her. "Good morning."

Noeul focused on lips only inches from her own. She watched, as Jordan's tongue snaked out to wet them. The tantalizing view of that second's worth of tongue peeking out was too strong. The attraction was like the gravitational pull of the sun. Noeul drew closer until her lips met with Jordan's, the first few seconds tentative before dissolving into a bone-melting fusion that ripped through her.

Jordan's hands slid into her hair and held her in place as their kiss deepened, until too soon, they both pulled back, Noeul dizzy from lack of oxygen, Jordan still holding her inches from where she'd been.

Noeul knew she was about to step beyond the boundary she herself had drawn. It wasn't fair to tease Jordan. For that matter, it wasn't fair to deny her own body what it so clearly was begging her for. Fear suddenly welled up in her chest, and she closed her eyes, biting her lip in an attempt to bring her emotions back to center and firmly under control.

"Please, Noeul." Jordan's voice broke midsentence, her eyes pleading.

Noeul heard the desperation and her own heart broke at the sound. Swirling emotions flooded her system: sadness, joy, and overwhelming desire. Quietly, she tried to explain, "I'm trying, Jordan. You must remember, it's been a long time since I've had these feelings. I'm completely overwhelmed with the need to touch and be touched."

"You're not in that boat alone. I'm flat out on fire with want, not only for sex and the physical aspect of it. I need the connection to you. I've been fighting it ever since I came here. With you in my arms, that want has grown into something else completely. I need much more than a one night stand."

Noeul watched Jordan struggle to calm the mounting inferno that threatened to leap across the firebreak and scorch everything around it. Noeul had no idea how Jordan was controlling the desire that played out with each shallow breath. She tried to help temper it, while failing miserably to keep her own conflagration from burning out of control. Trying to find a safer topic, she asked, "How'd you sleep?"

Jordan shivered as if someone had dumped a bucket of ice water over her head. She took a deep breath. "Better than I can remember in a long time. You?"

Noeul suddenly realized her hand under the hem of the T-shirt was probably stoking the fire she was trying to temper. She attempted to nonchalantly withdraw, only to have it held in place with the hand that had released her thigh.

Jordan spoke in quiet tones. "It's been years since I've gone to sleep wrapped around a beautiful woman. I slept fabulously."

Noeul ducked her head in embarrassment, and again, tried to move her hand.

Jordan held her in place. "I'm sorry, that was uncalled for. I apologize."

Noeul rose up enough to be able to look into the depths of those dark eyes and pulled her hand free in order to cup Jordan's cheek. "You have nothing to be sorry for." She couldn't let Jordan think she was in this completely alone. She placed a soft kiss on the lips so close to her own, she could see each line and indentation. She could see the small scar in the upper lip and traced it with her index finger.

The dark eyes locked onto hers, the clench of Jordan's abdominals a physical sensation under her hand. Pleading eyes searched Noeul's face, as if Jordan was trying hard to memorize every detail without the benefit of broad daylight. Placing her forehead against Jordan's, she made a decision. "I need you to hold that thought I saw pass through your eyes." She dipped her head and flicked her tongue across Jordan's lips. "I'll be right back."

Noeul moved a fraction of an inch and felt Jordan tighten her hold with a near growl. Noeul laughed softly. "I need to get up. The body insists. I promise that's the only reason. I'll meet you right back here in a moment."

Jordan groaned out loud. "Noeul, I'm close to self-combusting here."

She smiled at Jordan and gently kissed her with promise in her eyes. "Without risking killing this moment, I'll meet you back here in under five minutes. Go do whatever you need to make yourself comfortable, because when I kiss you next, I don't want anything standing in my way of hours of exploration." She bit and pulled at Jordan's lower lip, eliciting a moan of pure need from the woman she drew away from. Noeul tried to smother a laugh, as Jordan, legs tangled in sheets, nearly fell out of bed in her rush to complete necessary measures. Decision made, Noeul rose and made her own way into the bathroom.

***

Jordan had never relieved herself or brushed her teeth with such urgency before. Terrified that in those brief minutes Noeul would change her mind, she attempted to set a land speed record to complete the required tasks. Moments later, she rounded the corner and watched, as Noeul stepped to the bed and held out her hand.

Later, she would have no memory of taking the steps across the floor to meet the beautiful woman. All she knew was she felt a warm hand in hers pulling her closer. Her temperature rocketed, as their lips met in a fury. Jordan felt hands push her back until her knees met the bed. She sat down in an uncontrolled descent and stared up at Noeul, who crossed her arms and drew the T-shirt up and over her head, before dropping it to the floor. The sexy imp stood before Jordan in only a pair of jade-green bikini briefs. Her mouth went completely dry, as Noeul stepped forward and directed that mouth to her breast.

Soft, pebbled skin met her lips, and she closed her eyes. Jordan rolled her tongue across a nipple, provoking a moan from Noeul. Heart pounding, she wrapped her arms around the slender waist, pulling soft flesh against her body. Noeul's fingers tangled in her hair and held her tightly to the breast she lavished. Noeul's head fell back, a whispered oh God escaping her lips.

Jordan let her teeth close gently around the swollen flesh, and blunt nails dug into her scalp encouraging her to continue. And continue she did, until she felt urgent hands pull at her T-shirt, roughly dragging it up and off her body. Within seconds, the fingers of one hand dug into her shoulder, while Noeul's other hand brought her mouth back to the position it had been forced to relinquish while she was divested of her shirt.

Jordan palmed the soft, round ass she held in her hands and pulled Noeul even closer, until the woman collapsed on top of her. Noeul supported herself above Jordan on all fours, knees apart and straddling Jordan's hips. Soft, round breasts loomed tantalizingly close to Jordan's lips, as she leaned up to capture what she'd lost in the move. The sound Noeul emitted forced the blood out of Jordan's head and straight to her center. Their brief separation had done nothing to quell Jordan's desire, instead it ratcheted up the fire within her.

Flipping Noeul over, Jordan pushed them up the bed as she slipped her own leg between taut thighs, raising her knee until it made contact with the radiating heat of Noeul's center. Jordan felt hands release her head and slide around her body. Divine pleasure bordering on pain sent Jordan into overdrive, as nails dug into her back and clutched her tighter. Noeul's hips rose and the small of her back left the bed and bound her to Jordan's flesh. Tongues battled for dominance when their mouths crashed back together, each engaged in the dance.

Jordan could stand no more and hooked her thumbs into the sides of Noeul's bikinis. She dragged them down and over soft flesh. Immediately, the intoxicating scent of Noeul's arousal filled Jordan's senses. The need to touch sensitive flesh overcame her, and she threaded her fingers through soft black curls, her palm finding wet heat from the body beneath her struggling to maintain contact.

"Please, Jordan, please...nothing between us."

Jordan heard the desperate plea. She struggled out of her own boxers and climbed up Noeul's body, joining flesh to flesh and heat to heat. "I'm here, baby. I'm here. Hold on."

Jordan once again found the soaked curls at the juncture of Noeul's legs as they wrapped around her. She shifted until she could access the places her own body longed to touch with desperate need. Sliding two fingers deep within Noeul's heat awakened exquisite pleasure that immediately sent Jordan dangerously close to her own climax. She held back, focused on bringing her lover endless pleasure. "Let go, baby."

Noeul's sensual moans threw gasoline on an already white-hot inferno. Pure animalistic desire and passion flooded Jordan's overloaded senses. She'd watched as Noeul's closed eyes shot open when she slid her fingers through liquid desire and into Noeul's heat. Gently at first, Jordan pushed deep inside. She was urged on by the rise and fall of Noeul's hips, followed by a powerful shudder that overtook the body submitting to her touch. They rocked and arched into each other, the erotic climb rising ever higher, as the pair charged toward the precipice. Each thrust of her fingers bottomed out her knuckles against Noeul's hot flesh. She looked up to see Noeul palm her own breasts, pinching and twisting the nipples roughly. Jordan felt electrified as she heard Noeul scream out.

"Jordan, don't stop!"

Jordan felt the spasms start to clutch at her fingers that were buried deep inside her lover. Her eyes were drawn to Noeul's lush gaze. Those green eyes latched onto her own and never closed, locking them together as Noeul spiraled over the edge in a keening, guttural release.

"Jordan!"

Jordan rode Noeul's thigh and tumbled with her until she was left spent and panting. She collapsed into Noeul's neck and kissed the skin that pulsed beneath her lips.

Jordan lay there, ripples of pleasure still coursing through her, as sweat tricked down her back and around her side, igniting the area of her tattoo like molten lava. She felt transformed in an elemental way that she couldn't explain. What it meant for her future, she had no idea. For now, Jordan forced herself to enjoy the glory of the moment. *Whatever happens from here on out, I'll do anything to stay by her side.*

***

Noeul lay on her back, covered by Jordan's body, the scent of their shared pleasure hanging in the air. They were both panting from their mutual exertion. She was sated, and yet not completely fulfilled. Noeul needed something more. What she needed was to touch Jordan, to connect on another level. *I need to be inside her.* Though she was sure she'd felt Jordan climax with her, the desire to touch and taste was still strong. She rolled over and stretched out on top of the long, lean body. Her fingers traced a small bead of sweat rolling down Jordan's neck and into the hollow at the base of her throat. Noeul let her fingers glide gently across the collar bones, toned muscles, and tanned skin. "Perfection." She kissed the tail of the phoenix that wrapped protectively around Jordan's left breast.

"Oh God, Noeul."

A smile formed on Noeul's lips, as the nipple became more pronounced and swollen every second she teased it with her tongue. Jordan cupped her face, pulling on her and bringing their mouths together. Noeul felt a warm tongue delve into her mouth. When she broke the kiss, she pulled back to look at Jordan's swollen lips and traced them with her index finger. "You're so beautiful, baby." The tip of her finger rested in the center of the bruised lips.

Noeul shivered when Jordan gently sucked the digit into her mouth. Her center clenched at the sensation of her lover slowly tonguing that finger. The sight of Jordan drawing it in and out caused her pulse to race. Noeul began planting slow, wet kisses along Jordan's jaw, and continued to let Jordan suck her finger. When she could stand it no more, she moved her hand and began to pepper the heated flesh beneath her lips with light kisses.

Noeul lightly grazed her teeth over skin, as she moved down Jordan's body. She stopped to run her tongue around a nipple and moved lower to kiss more of the vibrant ink that trailed down Jordan's side. Once she'd nestled herself between Jordan's spread legs, she marveled at the woman beneath her. Fine wisps of velvety soft hair covered her intended destination. Noeul dropped her head to kiss and taste Jordan with the tip of her tongue, delighting when the lean woman's hips surged. Noeul met the dark embers that stared down at her over heaving breasts and used her hands to expose the swollen flesh. Slowly, she dipped her head once again to taste the sweet evidence of Jordan's arousal. *So soft.*

Jordan moaned and reached for the headboard, her knuckles white with strain. Noeul sucked her swollen clit into her lips and marveled at how wet Jordan was as she drank her in. Noeul felt as if she were a thirsting woman being given her first drink after being lost for years in an arid desert. The taste of Jordan's need was exquisitely sweet. *She tastes like honey.*

Noeul shifted her body to drive fingers into Jordan's depths. The instant she did, she had to wrap an arm around Jordan's hips to keep from being dislodged. The arching of the taller woman's back brought her off the bed, as Noeul felt an intense orgasm rip through the body she clung to. Noeul's mouth was flooded and she drank greedily, as if nourishing her soul with all things Jordan. Great gasping heaves of breath from Jordan's chest and a full body jerk worried Noeul. She blocked it out because she couldn't stop feasting.

Feeble hands reached for her, desperately drawing her up and into Jordan's waiting arms. "Baby, stop...come...up...here."

Noeul was alarmed by Jordan's tone. "Oh God. Are you okay, did I hurt you? Jordan talk to me!"

Jordan clutched at Noeul's head, continuing to jerk. "I'm okay..." Jordan's chest heaved, "Shattered into a million tiny pieces. Ask me again in a few minutes."

Noeul relaxed and held Jordan's face in her hands, lavishing kisses on salty cheeks and eyelids. They lay there enjoying quiet moments after the intensity that had exploded around them.

"Holy...Shit..."

Noeul chuckled. "I'll second that."

Jordan's hand visibly shook as she ran it through her hair. "What did you do to me?"

"I think it's more like what did we do to each other."

"Yeah, I think you're right." Jordan panted. "I have one question."

Noeul raised her head to look into Jordan's eyes. "What's that?"

"When the hell can we do it again?"

They both laughed as they struggled to catch their breath. While it was still early, the morning light slanted in through the skylight, illuminating their bodies. Noeul raised up onto an elbow, and as they rolled slightly to her right, she let her eyes wander to admire more of the phoenix tattoo. Her eye caught something interesting. She pulled Jordan back down and made her lie flat on her back, then aligned their bodies. Noeul noticed how the dragon tattoo on her own body visually related to Jordan's phoenix. The claws on her dragon nearly "held hands" with the phoenix's talons. She tried to mentally lay one tattoo on top of the other and realized they would wind around the other in almost perfect symmetry. It was startling. She remembered Jordan's story of her vision dream. Maiah had said that Jordan *had to seek the rooted dragon to find balance.*

Noeul sat up, her shaky hand covering her mouth as imagery filled her mind. Her own dream of the flipping cards came back with vivid clarity. The sprout with its root system, visible below the soil line, became a dragon identical to the tattoo on her side, entwining with a bird. Tails and wings interlaced with roots and limbs until the blank outline of the bird filled in, distinctly forming a phoenix. It wasn't any phoenix. It was the one Jordan had permanently inked into her skin. The wings wrapped protectively around the dragon until the two were no longer distinct. They were completely one, without a starting or a stopping point. The roots from the tree grew into a sprout that was completely different than any she'd ever seen. The sprout grew until the limbs intertwined to form a bowl that filled up and ran over. Not all of it made sense to her. One thing was clear, her joining with Jordan had been predicted in her own dream.

Jordan rose beside her. "Hey, what's wrong? You're white as a sheet and trembling. Noeul, look at me."

Noeul felt Jordan's arms surround her and draw her into a warm embrace. She melted into the feeling of complete safety, suddenly able to visualize Jordan's arms as wings. Tears began to flow, and Noeul peered up into terrified eyes that looked as if they were desperate to find the source of the pain or discomfort. She reached up and cupped Jordan's cheek in her hand, as she brought their lips together. If she had any doubt about the rightness of this moment, it disappeared like a wisp of smoke from the previous night's fire. Whatever the future handed her, she would face it wrapped up in Jordan's arms for as long as she was able. Today, she would revel in this feeling. For once, Noeul wasn't alone.

***

They cuddled for another hour, quietly sharing thoughts and concerns before Jordan tugged Noeul from bed. "Pip will need milking, and I'm hearing a lot of toenails on the hardwood floor. I'm betting two dogs need to go out." They looked toward the door to see four eyes staring back at them, as tails wagged against the doorframe.

"Must you be so responsible right now?" Noeul looked at her with one eye closed.

"Somebody has to be the grown-up. I will do you one favor though,

I'll go start the coffee and let them out if you start the shower."

"I'm not sure that's going to lead to Pip getting milked anytime soon." Noeul couldn't help the grin that welled up from her chest.

Jordan bent over with laughter. "I think I've created a monster."

Noeul dragged herself out of bed and wrapped her arms around Jordan's neck. "No, you've made me very happy. Happier than I've been in longer than I can remember." She kissed Jordan. "Go, before we have to clean up more than one mess in this house." Noeul bent over and picked up Jordan's T-shirt and threaded it on over her own head.

Jordan eyeballed the only other shirt in the vicinity and realized it was never going to fit over her shoulders. A smile crept over her face, as she shook her head and quickly stepped into her boxers. She watched Noeul walk to the bathroom, looking absolutely delicious in the pilfered Cornell T-shirt. On her way by the room she'd been staying in, Jordan snagged a thermal Henley and pulled it on. A brief thought crossed her mind as she looked inside. *I hope I've spent my last night sleeping in there.*

The dogs were dancing around, as she let them out and flipped the switch on the coffee maker. As she made her way to the bathroom, she swiped the hair off her forehead, and Noeul's unique smell on her hand caught her attention. A thousand memories of making love that morning flashed behind her blinking eyes, as she quickened her pace. Noeul stood inside the open-style, tile shower, her back turned to the door. Jordan watched unnoticed, as Noeul placed her hands against the wall and allowed the water to cascade across her magnificent body. The black dragon ran in a bold swath down Noeul's right side. Every time her muscles stretched and contracted, the dragon swayed as if it were alive. Mesmerized, Jordan didn't notice Noeul had turned her head and was studying her.

"Like what you see?"

"Like is not a strong enough word."

Noeul raised an eyebrow. "You have too many clothes on."

Jordan nearly tore the Henley from her body, as she fumbled to pull off the aging cotton boxers. They ripped down one side, and Jordan shook her head and looked up at Noeul. The ferocity she saw there made her physically shiver.

Noeul licked her lips and reached out her hand to Jordan. "You won't be needing those much anyway."

Jordan's mouth went dry when Noeul turned to her, water sheeting over her breasts and plastering her long, black hair against her back. After she stepped into the shower, Jordan melded her body to Noeul's, as she reveled in the feeling of slick skin against her own. "It's been so long since my showers weren't solo."

"If you know what's good for you, you'll forgo mentioning any thought of anything before this moment." Noeul's face grew serious. "It's what I need Jordan, and if we have any chance of this being more than sex, I need you to do the same."

"Not a hardship, given how much I want you. Believe that."

For the next several minutes, they caressed and bathed each other. Lingering glances so full of heat they could have boiled water, danced between them. Jordan was sure they were melting the polar ice caps. They touched, in the most sensual ways possible, as they explored every inch of the other's body. Jordan trailed fingers down to the small of Noeul's back, kissed her shoulders, and nuzzled at her jaw line, right behind her ear. As she held Noeul close, her own breasts pressed tightly to the smaller woman's back. She reached down and dipped into Noeul's center, while she held the warm body to her chest.

Noeul's arm extended back and wrapped around Jordan's head, holding her mouth tightly to her skin. Jordan felt muscles stiffen in her arms as the grip on her neck tightened. Noeul cried out her release and nearly collapsed in Jordan's arms. Noeul gasped as she caught her breath. "You are way too good at that."

"I've never been like this. You bring something out in me, a need or hunger that's all new. I don't have an explanation. I know when I'm with you I feel desire at a different level."

They were quiet for a few moments, before Noeul reached back and turned off the water that had started to cool against Jordan's back. "As badly as I want to take you back to bed and start all over again, we've got a few things we've got to do today."

Jordan didn't mean for the childish whine to be audible as it left her throat.

"Be a good girl now, and later, I'll see about taking care of why you're whining." Noeul kissed her.

"Are you sure we can't go back to bed?" Jordan's heart warmed at the broad smile forming on the face of the naked woman in her arms.

"My turn to be the adult now. We'll see how much work you can get done, and how fast."

Jordan almost fell down, as she tried to get the towels off the rack and dry off at lightning speed. Noeul's laughter echoed in her ears.

***

Noeul recorded several pages worth of notes on their experimental progress. Twice, Jordan had tried a different technique under the microscope, calling her over to view the results. It took a steady hand to manipulate small cells on plates of glass with very fine tools, and Jordan had that kind of touch. More than once, Noeul had looked over to see Jordan bent over, glued to the microscope, while her own eyes were taking in the shorts-clad ass on display. Her center clenched at the memory of how she'd melted into Jordan's arms that morning. A pleasant shiver moved through her, as hands found her hips and warm lips grazed her neck.

"Hey, you're supposed to be working over there."

"I *was* working over there. I took a break, and when I looked over here at you, it was like steel to a magnet. I couldn't resist."

Noeul turned in her arms and settled in against Jordan's chest. They'd stopped earlier for a lunch that had dissolved into feeding each other pieces of fruit, interspaced with spontaneous bouts of kissing. She was finding it harder and harder to concentrate on her work. They'd managed to get a solid six hours of research in along with a few hours where they'd tended to the animals, the vegetable garden, and some maintenance issues that needed Jordan's brute strength.

"How about we call it a day and I fix you dinner?" Jordan offered.

Noeul smiled against Jordan's chest. "What do you have in mind?"

"Well, we pulled out that lamb yesterday, so I thought I'd make you one of my favorite dishes Jida and Mom taught me. It's called mansaf. Remember when I asked if you made yogurt?"

"I do."

"Well I took some of it this morning and dehydrated it in the oven. That's the smell you asked me about that I said you'd have to wait and see. It's going to be a poor substitute for jameed, but I think you'll get the idea."

"Did your jida teach this dish to you?"

Jordan's smile lit up her face, something that Noeul was coming to look for and enjoy.

"That's what you called your grandmother right?" Noeul stared intently at Jordan's mischievous eyes.

"Yes, good memory."

Noeul watched those chocolate eyes grow molten and began to sparkle, as Jordan bent down for a kiss. The kiss was soft at first, the intensity growing as Jordan lifted Noeul up onto the workbench. Noeul wrapped her legs around Jordan's waist and pulled their lips together again. The kisses teased and their tongues explored, as they lost themselves in the moment.

Noeul put a hand on Jordan's chest and pushed her back. She had no doubt they were minutes from ripping each other's clothes off. She threaded her fingers in Jordan's hair and pulled their foreheads together. She gently pulled a fistful of hair in order to get Jordan to look directly at her. "As much as I want this, and I do want this, let's put it on simmer. Cook me a delicious Jordanian meal, and let's see where it goes from there. You go on in, and I'll finish up a few things out here, take care of Pip and the horses. I'll meet you inside. Okay?"

Jordan bit her lower lip and displayed the saddest puppy dog eyes Noeul had ever seen. "Always the sensible one," she grumbled.

"Somebody has to be the grown-up here, remember? Since I'm twenty years your senior, I'm steering the ship right now." Noeul dropped her eyes after hearing her own words. *Twenty years her senior.*

Jordan tipped her chin up. "Hey now, feel free to steer the ship any time you want. All I ask is that you do me one favor."

Noeul tried to meet Jordan's eyes. She couldn't do it. The lump in her throat was weighing her head down.

"Noeul, believe it or not, I can read your mind right now and can hear your thoughts."

"How's that?"

"Age is a number. My entire life, my brain has never matched the age of my body. Stop using this so much." Jordan pointed to her head, as she placed her hand over Noeul's heart. "Listen more to this."

The hand Jordan placed on her chest was warm, and she pulled it to her lips to kiss the knuckles. "I'll try to remember that. Now go fix dinner. I'll be in shortly."

Jordan leaned forward and kissed her, as she helped her off the bench. "Hmm, demanding little thing. I like it."

Noeul smacked her arm. "Go." She watched, as the shapely legs carried Jordan to the door, where she was met by two excited dogs who were banished from the interior.

The equipment they'd been working with needed to be shut down and stored away. Once Noeul was done, she fed the animals and milked Pip. The minute she stepped in the house, she was greeted with mouthwatering smells coming from her kitchen.

"Oh my God. I have no idea what that is. All I can say is it smells heavenly."

"Jida might not agree, since I don't exactly have all her requirements. Mom would applaud my innovation. I'm grateful that you keep so many different varieties of rice. It's got about another twenty minutes to cook."

Noeul wandered into the space and wrapped her arms around Jordan from the back, resting her cheek against the strong muscles that rippled through the tank top. Each time she was this close to Jordan, she had an overwhelming need to make contact, to feel the heat emanating from her. The sensation reminded her of walking up to a fireplace and allowing the warmth to spread throughout her body. Noeul soaked up that heat as if she had been frozen for a long time.

Jordan turned and rested her chin on Noeul's head. "Hey, are you okay?"

Noeul grew quiet and took a moment to formulate an answer. She grabbed Jordan's hand and led her to the couch.

"Should I be worried?"

"There's nothing to be worried about. I just..."

Noeul let Jordan pull her down and into her arms, where she curled into Jordan and drew those arms more tightly around her.

"Just what?"

"I shouldn't feel this much this fast. I'm afraid that it's only the joy of not being alone—on connecting at a level that I haven't felt for years. I'm afraid of grasping at something that isn't mine to hold."

Jordan lay quiet for several minutes. Noeul started to worry that she'd said something wrong and pulled back to look into Jordan's eyes. "Are you okay?"

A deep breath slowly released was the only answer. Noeul was prepared for almost anything, except what she saw staring back at her. Fear lingered in the dark pools, making them seem liquid. "Hey, hey, what's wrong?"

"You're not the only one who's scared, not the only one who's worried she's feeling too much, too fast. I get it. I also know more about me than you do. I don't trust easily, and I don't give my heart easily. I've loved exactly twice, if you don't count my seventh-grade crush. I wish the people who know me best were here to tell you about the Jordan they know. I can't give you back the years you've spent alone. What I can give you is the promise to be my most honest self. I have no plans of going anywhere. Do I have it all worked out? The honest answer is no. Do I want to? You bet I do. Now, are you willing to take a chance with me to see what tomorrow brings? Only you can answer that, and I'm willing to wait for you to figure that out."

Again, Noeul relaxed into Jordan's touch, as she fingered the hem of Jordan's tank top. Her fears hadn't been completely put to rest. The words spoken had meaning and held promise. Time would be the ultimate test. Noeul's concerns lay in the part of Jordan's life she wasn't an integral part of and what would happen when it came calling.

Chapter Twenty-one

TWO WEEKS WENT BY, with Jordan enjoying the feeling of waking up to a warm body wrapped up in her arms. Their experiments were doing well, and the couple had spent almost every waking moment together. Long hikes in the woods, trail rides, and even a few trips to the farmers' market together had brought them even closer. Jordan met Mr. Anderson, and the two hit it off immediately. They were headed there again, another load of handmade soap and lotion filling the back seat. After the market, they would drop off supplies at the various shelters Noeul helped support.

They parked in their usual spot, and Jordan lifted a case of the lotion in her arms. "Do you want all this out, or just a selection?"

Noeul was setting up the small table off the tailgate of the truck. "Probably five of each. The lavender has been pretty popular lately."

Jordan stopped when she looked up to see the blazing smile Noeul sported. Genuine, not forced and not out of obligation, the smile reached right into Jordan's soul.

"What?" Noeul furrowed her brows and looked at Jordan.

Jordan shook herself back to the here and now and out of her musing but couldn't stop her own smile. "Nothing."

Mr. Anderson cleared his throat and chuckled. He pointed to Jordan, as he spoke to Noeul. "That one there looks like the cat that got the cream."

Jordan felt her face flush, as she looked at the woman who had captured her so completely. Noeul's raised eyebrow and lascivious smile made her body heat as a direct result of desire and not embarrassment. She cleared her throat and pulled five lavender lotions out of the case and handed them to Noeul, while shaking her head at both of them.

Two hours later, they each hugged Mr. Anderson who held on to Jordan long enough to whisper a few words. "I like the smile she's sportin'. See that you keep it there." He patted her on the back and released her, to climb into his truck.

Noeul handed him two bars of her new fragrance of lotion and soap. "Tell your lovely wife I said thank you for the herbs. We'd almost run out."

"I'll be bringing a fresh batch next week, you can be sure. Now you two be careful. I'll see ya."

Jordan watched his creaky truck make its way out of the parking lot, as she folded up the table and slid it into the truck bed. "Are we staying off the mountain tonight?"

"No, I really want to go home. That one test crop looks really promising, and I want to check the graft's ability to draw up the nutrients we've been analyzing."

Jordan watched Noeul look her body up and down. Her center clenched so hard, it nearly doubled her. "And?"

"And, I want to be alone with you. We spent last night with the girls. Tonight, I want to be home in our bed."

Jordan walked up to Noeul and bent over so she could whisper in her ear. "We've got to get out of here, and I mean now, before I throw you down on this tailgate and let you know exactly what I think about when you say *our bed*." She watched Noeul's eyes grow large before dissolving into a smoky heat.

"We have one more stop. I need to drop the rest of this at Haven House before we can go home."

"You driving, or am I?"

Noeul's smile spoke volumes, as Jordan felt her discretely run a fingernail up the zipper of the shorts she was wearing. She shook herself and laughed, as the keys were handed to her. Jordan climbed in the driver's side and watched, as Noeul slid into the passenger seat. Once they'd dropped off the hygiene items, they left the city limits.

When Noeul lifted the center console and unbuckled her seatbelt, Jordan began to sweat. Noeul slid over and used the center seatbelt to buckle herself in.

"Your left knee is bouncing out an interesting rhythm over there."

Jordan cleared her throat, anticipating what was about to happen. Noeul had teased her mercilessly on their last trip in the vehicle. She felt a warm hand land on her bare thigh, below the edge of her shorts. She took her eyes off the road for a moment and locked on the fingers that were drawing lazy circles on her skin.

A low voice broke the silence in a quiet, controlled tone. "Watch the road, Jordan."

Jordan tried not to jerk the wheel, as she raised her eyes back to the road. "You're killing me."

"My suggestion is you find somewhere very quiet, and very private."

Jordan groaned. "Holy shit."

Noeul's laugh filled the cab and Jordan's heart. Her mind was racing trying to think of somewhere she could pull the truck over that would offer them a modicum of privacy. Nothing would come to her, and her leg bounced harder, as Noeul's hand inched farther up her shorts. "I could use a little help here. I've made this trip with you exactly twice. At this point, I'd settle for a side road. My luck, I'd park us in someone's driveway."

Noeul turned and leaned over enough to pull Jordan's earlobe into her mouth. The groan Jordan released had her struggling to concentrate on the road.

"Take the next right, then the next left after that." Noeul continued her assault on Jordan, who nearly missed the turn she'd been told to take.

After following Noeul's directions, Jordan pulled the truck into a grove of pine trees. She'd no more got the truck put in park and killed the engine, when Noeul unbuckled her seat belt and leaned across Jordan's body. She pulled their lips together in a furious kiss. The seat began a slow decent backward after Jordan dropped her hand to the side and found the controls.

"Go ahead and move it back too. I don't want to hit the horn with what I'm about to do."

Jordan felt Noeul turn in her seat until she was completely facing her. She watched as delicate fingers opened a button on the shorts she was wearing. Her pulse raced, and she felt herself grow wet. "You are driving me crazy."

"Seems to me, I'm accomplishing what I set out to do. I want to touch you and feel you in my hands."

Jordan reached up and cupped Noeul's face. She kissed her and drove her tongue between waiting lips, the passion and impatience building quickly.

Noeul drew the zipper down slowly, click by click, until Jordan thought she'd rip her own clothes off to feel Noeul's hands on her. When the fly of her shorts lay open, she felt Noeul skim the waistband of her boxers until soft fingers threaded through her center, a thumb landing on her clit.

"Oh God, Noeul."

"That's it, lift those hips for me. Let me in."

Jordan did as instructed and felt the exquisite slide of fingers deep inside her. Noeul's thumb began working back and forth across her clit, and she felt Noeul's breath hot against her cheek.

"Does that feel good, Jordan? Tell me what you want."

Jordan felt the fingers stroke in and out, before the pad of Noeul's thumb stroked across her clit. Her mind blurred, as another stroke made her tense every muscle in her body. A voice broke through her haze and it was that voice, Noeul's voice, that demanded she answer. "Tell me."

"I want another deep stroke, oh God. Please, Noeul, don't stop."

A tongue snaked along her jaw, tremors building with each thrust. Again the voice, smooth like honey laced with fire, whispered in her ear.

"And what else, Jordan what..." another stroke along with a nip to her bottom lip was followed by a deep tongue that entered her mouth and danced with her own.

Jordan cried out in desperate need. "Noeul, please, don't tease. Please!"

"Your wish is my command."

The strokes, however restricted from the shorts still in place, became faster, more forceful, and the circling on her clit became harder, with more pressure. Jordan could feel the heat rising off her body as her orgasm approached. She was holding on to the armrest so tightly it creaked. "Please!" Jordan sought a connection with Noeul's eyes.

Noeul stared at her. "Feel me touch you, Jordan. Feel me deep inside of you. Come for me."

At the last three words, Jordan felt the dam break. Everything inside of her let go as she climaxed at Noeul's command.

"Noeul!"

Jordan felt an arm circle her neck and grip her tightly, as her chest heaved and her body trembled. Noeul's fingers were still inside her, as she spasmed around them.

Noeul kissed her face and nuzzled into her. "Baby, you okay?"

Jordan's breathing hadn't settled yet, and words were still hard to come by. Noeul rose up slightly and kissed her softly. "Jordan?"

"What did you do to me?"

Noeul's soft chuckle bounced against her chest. "I think I took you to another dimension if your scream was any indication."

Noeul slowly withdrew her fingers and smiled when Jordan jumped at the brush of fingers against sensitive flesh. When Noeul drew them into her mouth, Jordan's pulse raced again and her center pounded. "I swear, you're trying to kill me."

Jordan noted Noeul's eyes blinking in rapid succession. Noeul started to sit up, and Jordan held her close to her chest. "Hey, what's wrong? Please, don't pull back from me. What you did to me was nothing like I've ever experienced. I didn't even make out with a girl in a car as a teenager." She fingered dark strands of hair that escaped Noeul's ever-present cuff and pushed them behind her ear. She cupped Noeul's face with her free hand. "The life I have with you right now is unlike any I've ever known. Nothing has ever compared to this, not one touch, not one kiss, not one night in your arms."

Jordan stopped and forced Noeul's eyes to hers, fearful that what she was about to say could easily send Noeul running. Not breaking eye contact, she spoke the words that had rattled in her chest and threatened to come out every time they made love. Without knowing what the reaction would be, she spoke the words she'd wanted to say since that first kiss. "Noeul, I'm falling in love with you." Jordan watched for the rejection she hoped wouldn't come. She was holding her breath in expectation of the pain she feared.

"Jordan, I..."

Jordan closed her eyes and breathed deeply. She pulled Noeul to her and kissed her forehead, as she raised the seat back. Noeul didn't move away, but she wouldn't meet Jordan's eyes. Jordan could feel the bitter disappointment rise in her throat like bile, and she tried to swallow it as she zipped her pants.

"Jordan, it's not that easy for me." Noeul's voice trailed off.

"I know. It's okay. Come on, let's get back." Jordan kissed her softly. "If we don't get going, we won't make it back up the mountain in daylight."

Jordan felt Noeul pull away and move back into her seat. She tried hard not to act disappointed, not wanting to put any undue pressure on the woman she was fast growing to care about more than anyone she ever had. She needed to talk about this and there was only one call she could make. She needed a few minutes at Miranda and Kelly's before they started up the mountain.

***

Noeul reached up and turned on the radio to break the silence that had settled in between them. A few miles before they reached their friends' house, the growing need to explain started to pound through her heart. Jordan's words about killing her, had caused Noeul to flash to the last time she and Aggie had made love, the night before that fateful trail run. Noeul was connecting with Jordan on a different level and that scared her to death. When Jordan spoke about feeling something she'd never known, it frightened Noeul. Believing in those feelings, allowing this connection to become a reality, would mean her whole world would change. The question of what Jordan would do at the end of her sabbatical still hung between them without a definite answer.

Jordan's voice broke the silence. "I need to call Dava before we go back. I checked in with Sam and Max last night. I couldn't reach Dava and Sarah, because I forgot they were at a benefit. I'll saddle up the horses while I'm doing that."

"Jordan, we need to talk."

"I know. We will, after we get back to Topside."

Noeul smiled at Jordan's reference to the name she'd given her home long ago. It rang of a familiarity that felt very natural. Maybe what she needed to do was talk to Kelly, have her help sort it all out. "Okay, when we get ba—"

"We'll talk, I know. Let's take care of what needs to be done and take time to gather our thoughts on the ride, okay?"

Noeul nodded her head, feeling the chill in Jordan's voice. She didn't voice any disagreement. Once they turned into the cabins, Jordan dropped Noeul at the door and took the truck near the garage where it was stored. Noeul watched her go, before she stepped into the house. From the sounds of it, Kelly was in the kitchen. Miranda's truck was gone, and the dogs were on the porch, asleep in the sun. They barely raised their heads when she went inside. Noeul walked to the bathroom to wash her hands and splash water on her face. As she stared into the mirror, only one word came to mind. It was written all over her. *Coward.* She flipped off the light and left the room.

Once inside the kitchen, she saw Kelly with her hands covered in flour and a smear of the same across her forehead. "Hey hon, how was the market?"

"Good, we sold more than half of what we took. We dropped off the rest at Haven House."

Kelly had a look of concentration on her task. "Wonderful, they can always use that stuff. I took a load of bedding by there the other day. They are always in need."

Kelly looked up and met her eyes, and Noeul saw the immediate concern. She fixated on watching Kelly form the dough into a ball and place it, fold side down, in a pastel ceramic bowl that she covered with a moist towel. Kelly turned, washed her hands, and grabbed two beers from the fridge.

She handed one to Noeul. "What's going on? When you left here today you looked like you were on cloud nine. Now you look like someone stole your birthday."

Noeul chuckled, as she twisted the top off the beer she was holding. Before she spoke, she took a deep draw and swallowed. "I think I hurt Jordan today, badly."

Kelly's brows drew together. "What? That doesn't sound like you. How?"

Noeul pursed her lips and blew out a long breath. "We, uh...well let's just say we took a little side road getting here on the way back."

Kelly's laugh filled the warm kitchen, as Noeul's face heated.

"And this turned out badly how?"

Noeul shut her eyes and shook her head. "When the moment," she made air quotes, "passed, she made a comment that I was trying to kill her." Noeul raised an eyebrow in Kelly's direction.

Kelly made a rolling motion with her hand. "And?"

"I flashed a bit. The last time Aggie and I made love, she made that comment. The next day, she collapsed during our run."

"Oh honey, I'm sorry. Did you explain that to Jordan?"

"I couldn't. I'm pretty sure that's not what hurt her." Noeul was trying to put everything into perspective and find a way to explain what she was feeling. "Right after that, she told me she's falling in love with me."

"Wow, and I'm guessing you didn't return the sentiment?"

Noeul could only shake her head.

"Is it because you don't feel that way, or something else?"

Noeul shook her head vigorously. "I'm terrified, because I do feel that way. I'm a coward. I'm scared that she'll decide what I have to offer isn't enough. Hell, Kelly, I'm twenty years her senior. What do I even have to offer her? She's in the prime of her life, and I've crossed over that hill." Angry now, she stood, her chair scraping back on the tile of the kitchen floor. "I'm too fucking scared to tell her I'm falling in love with her too and scared to death she'll wake up one day, tied down to someone she realizes is old enough to be her mother."

"Does she have any say in this?"

Noeul was stunned as she looked at Kelly. "Of course, she does. I'm not sure she's looking at this from all sides."

"Noeul, how do you feel when you're with her? Does she leave you in the dust when you run? Does she complain about your age, how you look, or the few strands of silver in your hair?"

"That's not..."

Kelly raised her hand and stopped Noeul midsentence. "I'm not done. Does she complain about you not keeping up with her in anything? How about in bed?"

Noeul's mouth fell open. "Kelly!"

"Don't Kelly me. You're making excuses. If you really want to know what I think is unfair, consider the fact that you're making decisions for her. You're telling her how she should feel and not taking into account what she has to say about it. You've been alone a long time. I'll be honest with you, Noeul, you've been more alive since the day you dragged her home than you've been since I've known you. Your eyes sparkle. You smile when you hear her voice. Stop being a self-fulfilling prophecy and start seeking your own destiny. I think she's incredibly good for you. Stop throwing out roadblocks on the life you could have so that you can safely stay in the life you've settled for."

Noeul was shocked at her friend's frankness. Kelly had always been the gentler of the two women. Miranda was fiercely protective and frequently voiced her emotions without thinking about how the words would sound. Kelly was thoughtful and weighed her words, balancing the fiery temper of her wife with her own reasoning and tact. To have Kelly talk to her this way was like experiencing an earthquake in her carefully planned life.

"Kelly..."

"I mean it. Don't Kelly me! You built your dream home up on a mountain and have done very little in the way of allowing the outside world to be part of it. Before you say it, I know exactly where we live and the challenges of living in the Quiet Zone. I worked in the business for thirty years. You parked yourself up on a mountain that's inaccessible to anything other than visitors by foot, horseback, or fucking parachuting in from a plane!"

Kelly walked to the sink, then turned and crossed her arms over her chest. "You built the home your deceased partner planned with you. The problem is Aggie isn't here to be a part of it and never will be. Honestly, Noeul, I'm proud of how you've gotten out of bed every day and put one foot in front of the other. But dammit, you haven't been living. What you've been doing is merely existing. What you've been doing for the last few weeks is *living*. You should try it more often, it looks good on you." Kelly walked back to the table and pulled Noeul up into her arms.

Noeul was stunned to silence. She was scared and confused. Her best friend had gutted her. Her body felt like a walnut shell that had been cracked open only to see that the flesh inside had turned to dust. She clung to Kelly holding on for dear life for fear of the ground opening to swallow her whole. It felt good to bury her face in the neck of a woman who'd only showed her kindness, befriended her, and formed one of the few attachments she had to the outside world. She held on to Kelly's shelter in the firestorm that was blazing around her.

"I don't know what to do, Kelly. I'm terrified of having her and even more terrified of losing her now that I've opened myself up. All this time, I've kept my heart safe. Aggie's loss nearly killed me, and I was much younger back then, much more secure with my place in the world. Now I don't know what I am or how I fit, especially when it comes to Jordan's world or her in mine."

Kelly took Noeul by the shoulders and pushed her back enough that they were staring at each other. "And you never will if you don't try. You must give her a reason to stay, honey. Only you can figure out what that is. I'm going to say this...don't wait too long. You, of all people, know that life is too short to be indecisive. It can change in an instant."

Noeul collapsed back into Kelly's arms, as she fought to take a breath through her sobs. "What am I going to do?"

***

Jordan saddled up the horses while her thoughts bounced around inside her skull like bumper cars at a small-town carnival. Her hand stroked Athena's soft nose, and she leaned into the warm neck. Thor nickered beside her. She shifted to him and grabbed for the saddle that sat near her on a sawhorse. The barn smelled of warm straw and manure. Thor backed up as she threw the saddle on top of the horse blanket she'd placed there a minute before.

Her eyes closed at the memory of Noeul's kiss, her touch, and the words she'd longed to hear coming from her lips. They hadn't come, and it was possible they never would. Jordan feared she'd pushed too far and opened herself up for rejection. *You knew better. Noeul lost the only woman she'll ever love. Beyond all that, you aren't built for long-term relationships. Tina proved that. Even Kallie was able to find her happy ever after once you were out of her life.* She pulled the girth strap through the loop and cinched it down, making sure the saddle was secure. It had to be snug and avoid discomfort for Thor.

Dark-brown eyes with long lashes turned to her, and Thor rumbled next to her shoulder. "Good boy. We'll be ready to go in a bit." She patted his neck, as she tied his lead rope over the fence, giving him enough length to reach the water trough.

Jordan pulled the satellite phone from her saddlebag. Pleased she had service, she dialed the familiar number and waited for her sister's voice. Their typical greeting failed to bring its normal smile. She answered in kind in an attempt to hide her sadness. "How was the benefit?"

"Really good. We brought in some top talent for the entertainment and raised a boatload for the implementation of the software we designed. It's going to make such a difference in the lives of so many who would never have access to this technology."

Dava's voice held all the excitement Jordan expected from her vibrant sister. "I tried to call Mom last night. She didn't answer, and her phone went straight to voicemail."

"Uh, she was, uh...out."

"What are you not telling me?"

"Well, let's just say she was out with the colonel."

"Colonel Margo Bishop?"

"The one and only. Don't freak, Jordan. She looks happy."

Jordan thought about her mother and how lonely she seemed at times. Once Margo had come on board with the foundation, Dalia's smile had returned. Jordan knew how much her mother had loved her father, and it saddened her to see such a vibrant woman alone when there was so much life left in her. The few times she'd interacted with the colonel, Jordan had seen how smitten she was with her mother. Her sky-blue eyes would track Dalia's every movement.

"I promise, Dava, I'm not freaking out. I'm rooting for them. Dad's been gone a long time now. It's not good for her to travel this world alone. We aren't meant to be solitary creatures."

"And now that we've traveled down this road, tell me what's going on with you and the professor."

Jordan's pause must have been longer than she realized, because Dava quickly followed up her question with another.

"Tell me you haven't shut down. Jordan, I haven't met this woman. The one thing I can tell from what you've shared is she's not Tina. Take a chance."

"It's not me that put the parking brake on. Hell, not only the parking brake, she pulled the emergency stop."

"Explain, in detail. Don't feed me any bullshit about not knowing, because I know you can remember exactly what happened."

Jordan tried to explain everything, only divulging that she and Noeul had made a leap she hadn't anticipated. Intended or not, it was a leap she'd been very willing to take.

"So, you fucked, am I getting this right?"

"Dava Grace!"

"Well, the way you are describing it sounds like a business transaction. I know you, Jordan, you don't just sleep with women. You need the connection. The last time you tried, it didn't go well. Thus, you have opened up to this woman in a way you haven't for years. I'm not afraid to say it, intimately. Now why do you sound like a herd of wild boars ran through your experimental plots?"

Jordan took in a deep breath to gather her thoughts into a coherent explanation. There was no way to explain without laying it on the line. "I told her I was falling in love with her."

The line was silent, so silent that Jordan was afraid the call had dropped out. It wouldn't be the first time she's lost service in the Quiet Zone. They'd tried text bursting and calls up on the mountain with no success. The digital display indicated Dava was still on the line.

"Watson, you still there?"

"I am, Sherlock, just uncharacteristically speechless. I wasn't sure I'd ever hear you utter those words again."

"You're not the only one. I'm pretty sure I fucked up. I should never have said it."

"Were you being truthful?"

"Dava, of course I was. I don't say things I don't mean, period. You know that."

"That's what I mean. Does she understand what a big deal this is for you?"

Jordan rubbed her eyes. "Probably not, it doesn't matter. She doesn't feel the same, and I'm not going to force her to try."

"And you know she doesn't because..."

"She didn't say much at all. I know, I know, before you say it. We don't know each other very well. I realize it hasn't been that long, and yes, it's probably more of the fact that I've been alone a long time."

"Jordan Moriah Armstrong, stop! God, you drive me crazy when you put words in my mouth."

Jordan kicked a bale of straw on the barn floor and closed her eyes to quell her temper. "Dammit, Dava. You know what, never mind." Jordan shrugged and threw her arm out as if she was clearing off a table. "I wanted to check in with you and tell you I talked to Sam last night, Max was asleep. They moved him home yesterday, and the adjustment has him agitated. Sam said he's pretty confused. I'm beginning to wonder if I need to head home to help. Anyway, I'll call in a few days to check in. Tell Mom I'll catch up with her next time. I—"

"Shut the fuck up, Sherlock."

Dava's abruptness caught Jordan off guard. "Hey, don't talk to m—"

"Have you gone deaf up on that mountain? You seemed to have lost your ability to hear me. I said, shut the fuck up. Listen and shut your lips."

Jordan took a few deep breaths and paced back and forth between the water trough and the far end of the barn. She took a few seconds to release her growing anger. Dava wasn't the source of her frustration and didn't deserve her ire. "I'm listening."

"First, I love you. Second, I don't care about the length of time you and Noeul have known each other, or how *well* you know each other, or even how long it's been since you've been in love. None of that has any bearing on how you feel right *now*. If your heart and soul is telling you that you're falling in love, I suspect you are. It's also very possible that Noeul feels the same. She may be too frightened or confused to do anything about it other than what she's been doing. She let you in. The woman took someone home that was a virtual stranger, and in less than a month, let you share her body. She's been alone a long time too. Maybe, just maybe, if you're patient enough, she'll tell you what's in her heart. She's not Tina, and whether you say it or not, this feels an awful lot like when you asked Tina to marry you."

Jordan violently punched the air. "This has nothing to do with T—"

Dava nearly growled into the phone. "Stop! You're getting ready to say this has nothing to do with Tina. I beg to differ. It has everything to do with her. Back then, you opened up your innermost feelings to someone who used your body for her pleasure. That bitch used your heart as a doormat. When you gave her all you had, she was holding something back. Something so big that it was an impossible obstacle. What you did, walking away from Tina, was justifiable. That bitch didn't deserve you."

There was a long pause on the phone, and Jordan could hear Dava breathing quickly.

"Now, I don't know Noeul. I do know you, JJ. If you told this woman you were falling in love with her, my gut tells me you have a deep and binding connection. Give her time for her heart and mind to catch up to her body. You searched for this woman all over the damn country, and in the end, she found you. That must count for something. You were patient as we deciphered each clue, and you drove, walked, and swam to reach your goal. Now that it's right there in front of you, isn't it worth giving her the time you gave the quest to find her, Jordan?"

Every one of Dava's words rang true. The arrows found their target and released the anger and hurt Jordan was harboring. Noeul deserved time to process and analyze everything that was happening. Jordan knew she was willing to wait until Noeul had all the facts to come to the conclusion, like any good scientist would. "You're right."

"Of course, I'm right. I'm a freaking genius, need my references?" Dava's laugh rang through the satellite phone.

"I love you, Dava, more than I can ever tell you. You're the only person I know that can kick my ass and never leave a seated position."

"Imagine what I could do if I could walk?"

Jordan rubbed the back of her neck, trying to relieve some tension. "I do every day. Part of me is scared to death that might be the only thing that keeps you on this planet. Otherwise, you'd likely be an astronaut on her way to Mars or something."

"Very true, big sister. Now, deep breaths. Cool your jets and give her some time. I get the feeling you won't have to wait long to see what her intentions are. I'm a phone call away, JJ. Well that and apparently a horse ride. I love you."

A chunk of the boulder broke away and slid off Jordan's back. "I love you right back."

They signed off with promises of another call, and Jordan stored the phone. She wasn't sure she felt completely better. What she did have, was a different perspective. She led the horses out of the shaded area and over to the house. It was time to try and focus on the main reason she'd originally gone looking for Noeul, her research project and how Noeul's work fit in with her own theory. If something else happened before her sabbatical was up, she'd welcome it. On the other hand, if Noeul was unable to take the next step toward a deeper connection, Jordan would have to find a way to close Pandora's box and get back to work finding the answers to her own problem.

Chapter Twenty-two

THEY WERE BOTH QUIET on the trip back up, only stopping to allow the horses and dogs to drink from the cool streams they passed. Noeul could feel the dark eyes firmly on her back. Her thoughts were back in the truck, remembering the feel of Jordan's hard clit under her thumb and the powerful climax she'd brought her lover to. It took all she had not to moan out loud. *I'm not even sure how to go about talking to Jordan tonight.* Noeul was completely exhausted from the emotional turmoil. Everything seemed simpler when she had a predictable life. Predictable wasn't passionate. *Predictable doesn't wear a faded Cornell T-shirt like a second skin and it doesn't spoon around my body in the middle of the night.*

The shadows were growing long on the tree-lined trail as they reached Topside. There were things to do before they could call it a day. The horses need to be brushed down, fed, and watered. Pip needs milking, and everyone tucked in for the night. Kyo and Bandit need supper, although she suspected Kelly had been slipping them her homemade dog biscuits all day. *I don't think I could eat if I tried. I'll check with Jordan and see if she wants anything.*

The light was fading, as she let Jordan take Athena's reins. There was little discussion about the division of labor. The nightly jobs had become routine and were accomplished with almost a symbiotic rhythm. Noeul watched Jordan carry the saddlebags into the house. When Noeul made it in, there were no lights on in the kitchen. She noticed the bowls for the dogs had fresh water and food. There was no fire in the fireplace, and she couldn't hear anything from the bedroom area. She sat down on the couch and dropped her head against the back.

I'm guessing that means she isn't hungry either. Noeul threw her arm across her eyes. *What am I doing? She has to know I drug my feet outside. What message did that send?* A thought crossed her mind to try and put it down in her journal, but she was too tired to attempt that.

How much time had passed when she made her way to bed, Noeul didn't know. Jordan lay on her side, a gentle rise and fall to her shoulder. She noticed that the woman lying there wasn't naked as she'd been the last few nights. Instead, she was wearing that threadbare Cornell T-shirt. Noeul went to shower, grateful Jordan was in her bed and hadn't fled to the guest room.

When she was cleaned up, she crawled in beside Jordan and spooned in behind her. A wave of relief washed over her, as Jordan pulled her arm around her own body. The welcome was a lifeline tossed to someone adrift on the vast ocean during a raging storm.

Noeul found herself reaching for Jordan over and over throughout the night. If she woke and didn't immediately feel Jordan against her, she rolled and sought her out, always to be welcomed with Jordan's answering touch. She watched the clock tick by. The iridescent, blue numerals kept changing until sometime around four in the morning, when she drifted off, wrapped around the body next to her.

The next time she woke and reached for Jordan, she found the bed cold and empty. Panic rose in her chest until the smell of coffee wafted through the room. Noeul sat up and scrubbed her eyes to try and see the clock. It was barely seven, later than she usually slept. Last night had rendered little sleep, or rest for that matter. She rose and pulled on a pair of soft, cotton shorts to accompany her tank top. She stopped to comb out her long hair and draw it back in Aggie's gift. She'd stopped wearing her wedding ring when it became an excellent conductor against the electric fencing one night. The scar on the top side of her finger served as a permanent reminder of what used to be there, growing fainter every year. Noeul would always know, even if someday she wouldn't be able to see it.

Come on Noeul, it's time to face the music. You broke it. You must be the one to fix it. She washed her face and brushed her teeth before she stepped out into the hallway. The kitchen was quiet, and no dogs greeted her. The missing cup above the coffee maker told the story. Jordan was outside and had chosen not to wake Noeul when she got up. Noeul needed to make this right, find a way to bridge the gap that was forming.

After she poured herself a cup of coffee and slid into her Birkenstocks, she pulled on a worn, zippered hoodie. Coffee in hand, she made her way out to the fire ring, where she found two sleeping dogs and Jordan.

"Why didn't you wake me?"

"You were finally sleeping."

Noeul sat in the chair beside Jordan and stretched her feet out toward the fire, while she sipped her coffee. "Didn't feel like you got much sleep either."

Jordan's mouth quirked at one corner.

Noeul stretched out her hand. "Is it time to talk?"

Jordan took Noeul's hand. "In the words of my sister, I need to shut the fuck up and listen more."

Noeul chuckled. She wanted to meet the infamous Dava. "Okay, are you sure?"

Jordan's head fell back against the chair, and she rolled her head in line with her body. "All I'm going to say is this. I'm sorry. I probably got ahead of myself, or at least ahead of you. My sister reminded me that although we may be in the same place physically, we might not be on the same level emotionally. I understand that now."

"Jordan..."

A noise drew them to the clearing, as both dogs leapt to their feet barking. The pinto horse and rider passed by the last line of trees and trotted toward them.

Noeul stood quickly. "It's Miranda."

Her horse was lathered and steaming in the morning chill, as Miranda dismounted. "Jordan, we need to get you off the mountain and over to the observatory. Your sister has a plane on its way to meet you."

Noeul's head turned to see Jordan's panicked expression, as the shaking woman stepped closer to Miranda.

"What's wrong? Is my mother okay?"

Miranda shook her head. "It's not your mother. It's your friend, Max."

Noeul watched, as Jordan dropped her coffee cup and ran. *Oh no.*

***

Jordan's chest constricted, as she sprinted into the house to throw a few things into her bag. She didn't need to know what was wrong. The only thing she needed to know was that Sam and Max needed her and she was going to be there for them. Her hands trembled as she grabbed her satellite phone and journal that lay on the bed. She put everything into her duffle along with a few pieces of clothing. *The rest Noeul can send to me if I need it.* Her mind raced as she turned a circle in the room, Bandit under her feet. "Come on, boy, Daddy needs us." She jammed her feet into her hiking boots and ran to the front door, not taking even a moment to look around.

When she saw Thor saddled up and Noeul holding the reins, a wall of gratitude hit her and released the emotional turmoil she'd held at bay since yesterday. She sprinted to their location, Bandit hot on her heels. She slipped the duffle strap over her shoulder and across her chest and came to an abrupt stop by Noeul's side. As she put her foot in the stirrup, Noeul stopped Jordan and forced her to look at her.

"Jordan, I know it's important for you to get down there quickly. Please be careful on the way down. If you push Thor too much, he'll make a mistake and you'll both go down. Take a few deep breaths, he's going to feel the anxiety and adrenaline coursing through you."

Jordan felt Noeul's hands on her face, as she struggled to see through the tears.

"I'm sorry, I've got to go."

Noeul met her gaze and planted a soft kiss on her lips. "I know. I'll take care of things here and head down the mountain as soon as I can. Call me when you know something. Give them both my love."

Jordan pushed up into the saddle and grabbed the thick leather. "I will. Thank you, Noeul, for everything." Before Jordan allowed herself to say anything more, she pulled sharply on Thor's reins to turn him toward the trailhead and used her knees to urge him on.

All the way down the mountain, she had to remind herself to go slow, to not push as the trees zipped by. Part of the trail was rocky, and she forced herself to get off and walk to avoid injuring them both in her blind need. She wouldn't push Thor that hard. His flanks and haunches were lathered, and she stopped at the first streambed to allow the beautiful animal to drink. She filled her canteen with cool water and poured it over his powerful shoulders.

"Calm down, Jordan," she told herself. She hadn't even thought to ask what was wrong. It wouldn't have changed why she needed to go. *It's simple, they need me.* Miranda had quickly told her that she'd used her influence to get landing permission at Green Bank airport. She was to show her identification to the guards who would hold her Jeep until Miranda and Kelly could retrieve it.

Jordan climbed back on Thor's back and tried, without much success, to slow her own pulse rate and anxiety overload. Thor was feeding off her emotions and had fought her directions more than once. Over an hour had passed when Jordan finally got her heart rate under control and she knew she had at least another fifteen minutes of riding. Bandit seemed to feel her anxiety too and constantly looked up at her as he ran beside her mount.

What do I do about Noeul? Maybe this is a sign that I'm not where I need to be. Her sleepless night had been rough on her emotions, as she lay there in the dark, sometimes being held by Noeul and at other times doing the holding.

Sun was beginning to burn off the morning mist, as she finally broke through the trees at the edge of Miranda and Kelly's property. Bandit was lagging at this point. They galloped through the gate to see Kelly standing by her Jeep, a small brown bag in her hands. Jordan practically leapt from Thor's back before they'd even come to a stop, the dust catching up with them a minute later.

"Slow down, Jordan, you can't drive the way you rode Thor in. Let me drive you and bring the Jeep back here. Your eyes are wild, and there is no way you can be thinking straight. Go ahead and get in. You can call your sister while I put Thor in the paddock. I'm sure it will be a while before Miranda gets back down here, as hard as she rode up the mountain. That horse has to be tired."

Jordan could barely stop the shaking in her hand long enough to hit the speed dial for Dava. When she answered, there was no pig Latin greeting. Her sister got right down to explaining Max's condition, as Jordan stowed her duffle in the Jeep and let Bandit grab a drink of water.

"Jordan, take a deep breath. He's still with us. His blood pressure spiked, and he passed out on Sam. There was a nurse with them, and they were able to get the ambulance to transport him within ten minutes of the episode. He's at CMC and being monitored. They aren't sure if he's had a stroke or not. Sam asked me to call you. There'll be a driver waiting for you at the airport that will take you to the hospital and take Bandit over to the house. Calm down and don't worry about anything."

Overcome, Jordan screwed her eyes closed. Her hand covered her mouth. The attempt to bring her emotions under control was failing miserably, and she could only whisper an okay to her sister.

"Jordan, hang in there. Sarah pulled some strings and got a private plane to get you back home. They've sent you their best pilot, so all you have to do is get your ass to the airport and you'll be back in Ithaca before you know it. I love you, JJ. I wish I could be with you. Sarah says we'll fly up tomorrow, after we clear from our appearance with the First Lady."

Jordan tried to choke out her question. *"The* First Lady, as in The

337

First Lady of the United States?"

"That would be the one. She's a huge literacy advocate. She was at the benefit the other night and wanted to meet with us privately. She also wants to talk to Mom about Unlimited Fun! Her niece is wheelchair bound and had the opportunity to play on one of the special baseball fields. At this moment, none of that is important. I'll fill you in on all the details later. Right now, get your ass to the airport."

Jordan let out a huge sigh of relief. "I love you, Dava. Thank my future sister-in-law, will you?"

"You bet, call me when you're wheels down okay?"

"Will do."

They ended their call and Jordan wiped her face with her T-shirt, as Kelly slid into the driver's seat and started the Jeep.

Kelly turned in her seat to maneuver around the tractor right beside them. "It'll take us about twenty minutes to get to the observatory, another few to get through security."

"Thank you, Kelly, for everything. What time did Dava call?"

"It was after four thirty this morning when the phone rang. I wouldn't let Miranda ride up that mountain in the dark. As soon as light broke, she took off like a shot and I started arranging permissions with our old connections. Pays to have worked at the place for thirty years." Kelly shot her a smile. "And to be their go-to lodging for visiting scientists. They know we'll take care of their people."

Jordan turned quickly in her seat to see Bandit sprawled out on the back seat. "Oh my God, did you put him in the Jeep? I don't remember doing it."

"Calm down, Jordan. We wouldn't have left without him. He was waiting by the driver's door after I took care of Thor. You were on the phone. Any update on Max?"

Jordan ran a hand through her disheveled locks. "Only that he's at the hospital. There's a driver waiting for me in Ithaca to take me to the hospital and take care of Bandit."

Kelly patted her shoulder. "Sounds like you've got a lot of people who care about you back there."

"It's mostly my sister, Dava, and her fiancé handling the travel details. Sam will be at the hospital, and I'll go spell him when I get there."

Kelly glanced away from the road and at Jordan before returning her eyes front and center. "I hate to ask you this, Jordan, and if it's none of my business, tell me. How did you and Noeul leave it this morning?"

Jordan took a deep breath and ran her hands through her hair. "We didn't really. We were starting to talk when Miranda got there. She avoided me last night and came to bed well after I'd lain down."

"You slept in the same bed last night though?"

Jordan looked out the window at the apple orchard they were passing. "We did. Nothing happened. We held each other. She didn't fall asleep until about four."

"And I'm gathering that you didn't sleep at all."

"I tried, unsuccessfully. I couldn't get my brain to shut off. I think it's possible I screwed up. What's done is done. You can't unring a bell."

"Do you want to?"

Jordan met Kelly's eyes for a second, before the older woman returned hers to the road. "No, I meant what I said to her. Something tells me, though, that hoping for that isn't going to be enough. She's not ready, and I have no idea if she ever will be."

Kelly tipped her head from side to side. "Time will tell. All I ask is that you don't count her out. Still waters run deep with that one. She's been alone a long time, and you have to admit, you've taken a pretty strange path to get here."

Jordan laughed without humor. "Understatement."

A few more miles passed before Kelly spoke again. "I rarely speak for someone, Jordan. You know Noeul's story, and I'm sure, by now, you can guess what some of her issues are. There is a twenty-year difference between you, for one. That might not mean much to you. She's the one with the gray hair and the insecurities. Right now, through no fault of your own, you're scaring her to death because of what she feels for you. For the first time since she became a widow, she feels something. Noeul believes that Aggie foretold your coming in a few appearances that she can't explain, and I certainly won't try to. If you want this, you're going to have to be made of some extraordinarily tough stuff. That sawed-off spitfire is more stubborn than the blue mule my dad had when I was a kid. The harder you tried to push or pull that beast, the more it dug in. It moved when it damn well wanted to and not a minute before."

Jordan shook her head. From the moment she'd seen Noeul at her presentation, she'd never paid attention to their ages. Age didn't matter to her, no matter how much of an issue Noeul tried to make of it. She'd dated younger women and women her own age. Truth be told, she had always been older than her physical age, which made it difficult to connect with her own generation. What she had with Noeul, in her mind, was perfect.

"Kelly, we enjoy the same things. We can talk on a level I can't with anyone else other than my sister. My brain works differently, has since the day I was born. Physically, I'm thirty-five, mentally I've always been much farther along. Our connection is much more than physical, and I'll make no excuse for how incredibly sexy I find her. Right now, I can't think about any of it. I need to get back to Max and try to help my family through this. As much as I care for Noeul, this is something I have to do. If she can't understand why I must go, then maybe I've been fooling myself and what I feel is nothing more than a pipe dream."

"Just care for her?"

Jordan turned to her and let her ire rise. "Much more than just care for her. I'm in love with her, and when I admitted that, it spooked her. I'm willing to wait, to give everything I've got to make it work. Unfortunately, something else has precedence, and I can't do it this minute."

Kelly shook her head. "Fair enough. We're here. Find your identification."

The process went quickly from there, and they made their way to the plane. Jordan picked Bandit up and placed him inside, followed by her duffle.

Kelly handed her the brown bag and gave her a hug. "Breakfast, which I'm pretty sure you didn't get."

"Watch over her, Kelly. I know I don't have to say that to you. I'll feel better knowing I don't have to worry about her being alone."

"Don't worry about that. We've been watching over her for years, and she does the same for us. Safe flight and call us when you can." Jordan climbed in and secured the door as the pilot finished his check list. Minutes later, they taxied down the runway and lifted off into a cloudless morning.

***

"Miranda, I'm okay, go on down. When I've finished up here, I'll saddle Athena up and follow. I'll even stay the night."

After very little sleep, Noeul was at the end of her patience and completely irritated with her friend. Miranda's hovering felt like someone trying to force her to wear a woolen sweater in the summer heat—scratchy, oppressive, and unnecessary.

Miranda raised both palms in front of her. "Hey, don't bite my head off. I'm trying to help. I thought you'd like some assistance to be able to get down the mountain quicker. You want to be alone, fine by me. I've got work to do and half the day is gone. Since you're coming down later, I'm taking Kyo with me. I could use a run when I get back, and that pup looks like she lost her best friend." Miranda swung her leg up and over the red and white pinto, as she whistled for Kyo. "I'll see you for supper. If you're not there by that time, expect a visit from my wife."

Noeul raised her hands to her head. "Miranda, wait. I'm sorry." It was too late. Miranda and company were already headed for the trail at a trot. "God, I'm such a bitch. What's gotten into me?" Noeul knew the answer to her own question, and it was fifteen thousand feet in the air, headed to New York.

Miranda had filled her in on what she knew of Max's condition change and the arrangements that had been made for Jordan and Bandit to fly back. Miranda was trying to be helpful by gathering the eggs and offering to milk Pip. When she'd bumped into Noeul for the third time, Noeul's patience snapped and she'd told Miranda to go home. The hurt in Miranda's face was quickly replaced by a flash of the Slovakian temper Noeul knew existed below the surface. She also knew that temper was kept in check by Kelly. Noeul had some apologizing to do. *And not only to my best friends.*

After Miranda's abrupt departure with Kyo, she was left alone at Topside. One-eyed Rico rubbed up against her bare leg and startled her. She reached down and picked up the once sick stray, luxuriating in his warm, black fur. His purr had a small hiccup, as if his motor suffered from a miss. It was one of the quirky things about her chief rodent control officer.

"You want some cream? I'll bet Pip would be happy to fill a saucer for you." She carried him back to the barn and set him on the floor, as she positioned Pip to milk. It delighted her how he would catch the stream of milk in his mouth ninety percent of the time. The other ten percent, milk would find its way across his cheek and result in an impromptu bath with his tongue. When he'd had enough, he curled up in some fresh straw, his one good eye closed to a slit. After she finished the milking, Noeul headed to the house, her pail in hand and her mind scattered in a thousand places.

"*It's the dash in between, Noeul. The dash in the middle is what counts.*"

The words startled Noeul. She turned too quickly and lost her balance and her grip on the pail in her hand. Warm goat's milk covered her feet and legs, as she sat down hard on the ground.

"Aggie, don't." She started to cry and fought not to. She knew, once she did, she'd never get stopped. Noeul's quiet, orderly life was turning into a complete mess. She'd once loved that voice. Now it was like Rico's tongue, rough sandpaper on tender skin. She sat there looking at grass dull with the summer heat, lacking the bright green of spring. A trail of ants marched by her foot and into the edge of the spilled milk. Athena neighed off in the paddock, no doubt missing her partner in crime. Thor had carried Jordan away, exactly as Noeul had feared. As she stood, she brushed off her backside and felt the pull of the milk drying on her legs. She needed a shower anyway and started toward the house.

She left her shoes outside, as she strode through the house noticing the subtle changes since Jordan had arrived. Two plates sat on end in the drainer, and two wine glasses were perched on the bar, waiting for the deep rich wine to flow into them. Two dog bowls sat at the base of the counter. *Two.* Two of everything, where before there had been only one.

Noeul stopped in the guest room and noticed the bed was no longer pristine from the first few days Jordan had slept there. A pair of socks lay near the chair, and a ball cap was hanging off the closet door handle. She turned away and headed to the master bedroom. The sheets she'd crawled out of in search for Jordan lay rumpled and twisted. A pair of her jeans were lying on the hope chest. Two towels and two wash cloths hung in the bathroom, two toothbrushes sat on the sink. *Two where only one has been for so long.*

The sight was too much for Noeul. She crumpled at the side of the bed, her hand landing on something soft. She pulled out Jordan's faded, red, Cornell T-shirt and held it to her face, pulling faint hints of Jordan's cologne into her nose.

That was all it took for the damn to break, and the tears flooded forth. Great sobs of anguish escaped her body. Jordan was gone. She'd been there such a short period of time. None of that mattered. Her brief stay had left her imprint everywhere. Aggie's words brought back the memory associated with them.

Noeul lay with her head in Aggie's lap after their hike up Cadillac Mountain. "I've enjoyed this vacation. I'm sorry about the other day. Work will always be there." She picked up Aggie's hand and kissed it. "Our time alone is always too short as is."

Aggie smiled down at her. "We need to remember something my

grannie used to say. There are two dates that will be written in stone, the day we're born and the day we die. The thing that really matters, is the dash in the middle."

It had become a running joke between them whenever they lost sight of the important things. One or the other would throw out the line, it's the dash in the middle, as a reminder to live every day to the fullest. The emptiness of the house was oppressive. Noeul was once again alone, and this time, the sorrow cut like a dull blade, tugging and pulling everywhere it touched, leaving a jagged tear. Jordan was gone, and Noeul had no idea if she was coming back or how she would survive if she didn't.

She climbed onto the bed to wrap herself in Jordan's lingering scent. She held Jordan's pillow and shirt, as she cried herself out. Her eyes felt like she'd been swimming in the ocean without goggles, full of sand and burning from the salt. Noeul rose and walked to the bathroom. After splashing some water on her face, she stood there looking at the bruising under her own eyes. Jordan hadn't even been gone three hours, and the loss was bone-marrow deep. The quick smile, the spontaneous bouts of laughter, being held close during a slow dance, these and a dozen more memories played out in quick succession, as she stared into the mirror. The longer she looked, the less she liked what she saw.

***

Jordan hopped out of the plane and clipped a lead to Bandit's collar. She waved to the pilot and walked to the terminal. Her eyes scanned the crowd for a familiar face or a sign. When she didn't see one, she reached into her bag to grab her satellite phone. Unable to find it, Jordan walked over to the pilot who'd joined her. "Hey, you didn't happen to see a satellite phone on the floor in there did you?"

The pilot indicated he hadn't, and she tried to remember where she'd put it. Jordan smacked herself in the forehead. She could see it now, sitting in the center console of the Jeep. She'd been too preoccupied with thoughts of Max, and Noeul, on her ride to the airport. With so few payphones in existence, she couldn't even call Dava without finding someone to loan her a phone. Her brain was trying to sort through the options available, when she looked up to recognize her grad assistant, Deena, as she pushed through the crowd.

"Hey, Deena. Did they send you to rescue me?"

"Something like that." The tall sandy-haired woman bent to accept kisses from Bandit. "And to take this guy home after I drop you off. Your sister called Dean Belle, and I volunteered to be your chauffer and," she pointed to Bandit, "his human for the day. Max is okay. I checked in with the number Sam gave me right before I came in here. Not much change."

The band of anxiety that had been squeezing Jordan's heart backed off, if only a fraction. No matter what happened, she'd made it to be by Sam and Max's side before it was too late. She drew her first deep breath since Miranda had come up the mountain.

"Do you have any bag other than this?" Deena pointed to the duffle sitting at Jordan's feet.

Jordan shook her head. "No, I grabbed a few things and caught the plane. I can go to my place later. For now, can we head to the hospital?"

"My car's this way. Come on, Bandit." Deena took the lead from Jordan and walked them both back toward the exit doors. Once they'd made their way to the parking lot, Jordan handed Deena a ten-dollar bill to pay for the parking. The small Subaru made its way out into traffic on NY 13 south. Jordan slid on her sunglasses, regretting that she'd left her ball cap at Noeul's.

Deena changed lanes. "The good thing is that you got here after the noon rush. As you know, this trip would be a little longer if that happened. Not much has changed."

The force of Deena's words cramped Jordan's stomach and the pain in her chest was almost disabling. *Everything has changed for me.*

Within fifteen minutes, they were pulling up to the hospital entrance. "Thanks, Deena." Jordan pulled out her spare key from her wallet. "If you need to put Bandit someplace, here's the key to my apartment. He's used to being there, so he won't mind. I appreciate you taking care of him for me."

Deena held up a hand. "Professor A, it's the least I can do and one way to take something off your plate. Hey, if you get a chance stop by the lab. I have a few interesting things to show you. I won't even tell Dean Belle."

Deena's smile was infectious, and Jordan let out one of her own for the first time in hours. "Will do." She scratched Bandit's ears and kissed him on the head. "See you later, buddy." Bandit's bark gave her another reason to smile, as she exited the car and walked through the doors. Dava hadn't given her Max's room number, so she checked with the small woman in the pink smock for visitor information.

Jordan hated hospitals, the smell of disinfectants and sickness made her skin crawl. She'd endure it for Max and Sam. She punched the button on the elevator and rode to the third floor. The walk from there to the waiting room was like déjà vu. Sam sat with his head leaned back against the wall, his eyes shut tight, and his leg bouncing. Sam looked a mess and that was saying something. Dark shadows lay beneath his eyes, and he looked thinner.

"Hey."

Sam's eyes flew open at her voice and he leapt from the chair into her arms. His embrace was so tight, Jordan couldn't draw a normal breath. She could feel him as she held him.

"Oh, Jordan, thank you for coming home."

She rested her cheek against his head. "I'm sorry I haven't been here. I wish you'd let me know you needed help when I've called. You look exhausted."

Sam sighed deeply, as Jordan drew him back to the seats. "It's been difficult since I brought him home. I thought it would calm him, give him a sense of the familiar. More than anything it seems to have exacerbated the condition. Then this." Sam's countenance was that of a broken man. He looked like a man worried about a battle he had no chance of winning. "I'm going to lose him, Jordan, and I'm not ready for it. We've had twenty good years together, and it's not enough."

"It never will be, no matter how long he has left. The important thing is, he's not gone yet. Your love will pull him through this."

"You know, he fought me tooth and nail against getting serious. Kept telling me he was too old for me, that I had too much living to do for settling down with an old man like him."

Jordan gripped the top of her thighs. "That sounds a little familiar."

Sam ran his finger over his wedding band and twisted it around and around. "From the moment he stepped into Il Frantoio, I thought he was the most dashing man I'd ever met. Max was so charming and moved with an elegant grace. I tell you, I was smitten from the first hello."

Jordan smiled and placed a hand on Sam's back as he leaned forward. "I remember him telling me that you took his breath when you came out in your chef's coat. Told me it was sexier than anything he'd ever beheld. I think his actual wording was breathtaking."

Sam covered his mouth. "What am I going to do without him, Jordan?"

Jordan quieted the voices of loss that screamed through her head. She was having a hard time answering him, because she still wasn't sure how she was going to cope if she had to live without Noeul. The next move belonged to the woman living at the top of a mountain.

***

Noeul paced the front porch of Miranda and Kelly's. She'd tended to everything at Topside and ridden down the mountain, her heart in her throat the entire time. It was well into the afternoon, and she was sure Jordan would be with Max. Kelly told her she'd received a call from Dava, telling them Jordan had arrived and was making her way to the hospital. Dava told her Jordan hadn't called the girls because she'd accidentally left her satellite phone in the Jeep. With everything on her mind, Jordan had turned the task over to her sister to make contact.

"You're going to have to replace those boards if you wear a hole in them with all that pacing." Miranda leaned against the doorframe, her gruffness still present.

Noeul knew she needed to apologize and make things right with her. "I'll build you a whole new one if you'll forgive me for being such an ass. I'm sorry, Miranda, I really am." Noeul's shoulders slumped, as she sat in a chair Jordan had occupied on one of their visits. She put her head in her hands.

"Nothing to forgive. I let it go the minute I rode off."

Noeul looked at her skeptically, not doubting the forgiveness for one second. Forgetting was another thing.

Miranda threw her hands up in defense. "Alright, I won't lie. I was mightily pissed."

Noeul shook her head up and down to indicate she knew the truth of the statement. "It wasn't you. I was angry about a lot of things. Our stepping on each other was the match that lit the fuse. Jordan and I were getting ready to have a really serious conversation when you showed up."

"I wondered about that. What's going on? And before you say it's none of my business, you're family to me, so that makes it my business. Regardless of what you and my lovely wife think."

Noeul chuckled at that sentiment. "You're family to me too, and I can't tell you exactly what's wrong. Before you get your dander up, it's not Jordan's fault. The blame lies squarely with me. She told me she was falling in love with me. And I freaked."

"Ah."

Noeul sat back and closed her eyes. "Yeah. I keep trying to justify in my head why I couldn't say it back. I go through a checklist that tells me all the reasons why I can't, and they pale to the one box on the other side."

"And that box says what?'

"That not only do I miss her, but I *am* in love with her."

Miranda came to sit beside her, as Kelly came out and gave each of them a glass of iced tea. Kelly kissed the top of Noeul's head and sat in the rocking chair on the other side of her. She reached out a hand, which Noeul readily took and threaded their fingers together.

"So, what are you planning to do about this revelation?" Miranda took a deep drink of the glass dripping with condensation.

Noeul rolled her head from side to side. "I have no idea, and she's not here even if I knew what I wanted to do."

Kelly squeezed her hand. "And?"

Noeul drew her brows together. "And what? I can't make it right. Jordan's not here. She's back in Ithaca trying to help Max and Sam."

Miranda let out a huff. "Bullshit."

Noeul turned to Miranda. "What?"

"You heard me, I call bullshit. Not a thing holding you here except your own damn, stubborn determination to be a fucking martyr. I have a really hard time believing this is what Aggie wanted, and yet you hole yourself away up on that mountain, hiding from the world and any possibility of love. Not a damn thing holding you here, and yet you wallow in self-pity with the means to be able to fix it. Now are you going to sit here on your ass, thinking about what might have been, or are you going to get on a fucking plane and fix this, so you can start living again? I wanted to kick her ass when I thought she'd hurt you. About now, I'm thinking it's your ass I should kick." Miranda rose and took up the pacing across the porch.

Kelly jumped up and pulled her up short, pinning her against the rail with her back to Miranda's front, pulling Miranda's arms around her own waist. "Settle down you ole grump. I love you."

"Well!"

"Well nothing. You're not her mother or her keeper. Last time I checked, Noeul's old enough to vote, buy beer, and order from a menu that doesn't come with crayons." Kelly turned and kissed her.

Noeul watched the exchange between the two women. They were a balance of fire and ice, sugar and spice, sweet and salty. They weren't the perfect couple, and their differences numbered as many as their similarities. They made it work. She loved to watch how Kelly could quiet the savage tigress into a mewling kitten. Differences and similarities, balance and counterbalance, all working side by side to provide a life full of love, for better or worse.

Noeul rose before she had a chance to change her mind. "She's right, someone should kick my ass. If I can borrow your computer, I'll see what I can do about changing why Miranda has cause to...with a plane ticket."

Miranda pumped her fist in the air. "I'll call Leo. He can watch your place for a few days. You know he loves doing that."

Kelly drew Noeul in under one arm as she walked her into the house. "I knew you had it in you."

"I'm not on the plane yet." Noeul shuddered in relief.

"If love had wings, you'd already be there." Kelly kissed her temple.

Miranda clapped her hands together hard. "Now, let's get your ass to New York."

Chapter Twenty-three

JORDAN HAD SENT SAM home and stayed the night in the waiting room, not wanting Max to be alone. She was waiting for her chance to go in for the morning visit with him. Her back was stiff, and her last cup of hospital tar was setting up in the paper cup she held in her hand. Sam came back looking like he'd actually accomplished a little sleep.

He smiled and kissed the top of her head. "Thought you could use this."

She took the offered coffee in the travel mug and the small bag that she hoped held one of Sam's amazing breakfast sandwiches. Jordan pulled the still warm biscuit creation from the bag and took her first bite, followed by an appreciative groan. There was a reason Sam's restaurant was always packed. With a grin, she swallowed and took a sip of coffee and let her eyes roll in pleasure. "Marry me?"

Sam's face lit up and he chuckled. "Sorry." He held up his left hand, indicating his wedding ring. "I'm taken."

Jordan watched the smile slowly fall away and the sadness return. She put her sandwich down and pulled him into a hug. "We will get through this, and Max will come home. We've got to get him through this crisis and get you some help. I'm home now. I should have never left. I'm sorry, Sam."

Sam pulled back from her embrace. "Jordan Armstrong, Max wanted you to go. He knew how important this was to you. And the fact that you found Noeul? Well, he was thrilled about that. Max adores you and thinks of you much like a daughter. You've done nothing other than make him proud. Although, he's likely to kick your ass for coming home. I, for one, am more grateful than you'll know. It's so hard. Everyone feels bad and wants to help. That starts to fade when he can't remember something they've done together, or something that was a private joke between them. Their feelings get hurt. They want to remember him as he was. For me, I want him to still be here, however I can have him. Those moments when he remembers our wedding or a touch..."

"Sam, he remembers because your love is what tethers him here. "

Sam wiped his eyes. "What a queen I am."

"A queen that can cook like nobody's business." Jordan picked up her sandwich and took another bite, savoring the buttery biscuits with layers of egg and cheese in between.

"They talked about moving him today, somewhere to a floor where I can stay with him. He gets so confused when I'm gone."

Jordan reached out and covered his hand with hers. "Like I said, you are his tether."

Sam looked up to see Max's doctor approaching. Jordan chewed furiously to clear her mouth, wiping buttery fingers on her worn jeans when the doctor extended his hand.

"Dr. Tennant, this is Jordan," he looked at Jordan with a wink, "our daughter."

Dr. Tennant looked tired. "Jordan, I'm sorry to meet you under these circumstances. The good news is, Max is markedly improved. His pressure is down and none of the scans show any sign of stroke damage. It appeared to be an isolated spike with no long-term consequences. I'd like to keep him another day for observation, to be on the safe side. I think you can take him home tomorrow. "

Sam nearly collapsed in Jordan's arms. She steadied him and kept him tight in her grasp. "What can we do after we get him home?"

"Let him rest to start with. I've ordered in-home physical and occupational therapy for him. That should help with his mobility and motor skills. Whatever you were doing before to slow the dementia, it's been working. He remembered who I was this morning. I'm going to go ahead and move him to a private room off the critical care wing. His blood work looks good, and all signs show that he's improving."

Sam shook Dr. Tennant's hand with enthusiasm. "Thank you, doctor."

"No thanks needed. It's a pleasure to deal with caring family. Many have great difficulty handling the changes in their loved ones. Max looks like he has wonderful support. Hopefully we can get him past this acute issue and back home."

Jordan shook the doctor's hand and helped Sam back to the chairs. "See, 'Dad' is going to be fine. Hopefully, he'll be in a room soon and we can check on him."

About an hour later, they were informed that Max had been moved and they were able to visit freely. Sam went out for coffee, and Jordan sat at the bedside with Max's hand in hers. He looked more fragile than the last time she'd seen him. His pallor closely resembled the grayish-white hospital sheets he lay under. She'd closed her eyes for a moment, resting her head back against the headache exploding behind her eyes—a symptom of a lack of sleep and a slightly broken heart. She hadn't taken much time to think about Noeul or how they'd left things. She'd need to deal with that at some point. Right now, she was where the need was the greatest.

A thin frail voice broke the silence. "What are you doing here?"

Jordan startled and sat up to meet Max's light-blue eyes. "Max!"

Max gave her a weak smile. "Easy now, I'm an old man. I startle easy."

Jordan pulled the clasped hand close to her lips and kissed it. "I've missed you."

"Missed you too, kid. What are you doing here?"

"You're here and that's why I am."

"And Noeul?"

"That's a story for another day. Right now, I want you to rest so Sam and I can take you home."

Max craned his neck a bit. "Where is my wonderful husband?"

"Finding me some coffee that doesn't taste like it's been run through a radiator. He is not impressed with the sludge they serve here. I already devoured the first cup he brought me."

Max laughed, and Jordan saw color return to his face. "My dear husband has always been a coffee snob."

"True...he's been worried about you."

Max squeezed her hand a little tighter. "I know, I'm doing all I can to stay around as long as I can. Today feels like it's going to be a good day. Tomorrow, I might be lucky if I remember my own name. You can't have the mindset that time is on your side, Jordan. It's a mere whisper in the grand scheme of things. Don't put anything off and leave nothing left unsaid."

Jordan thought about the truth of Max's statement. Her stomach flipped over all the things she and Noeul hadn't discussed. She knew what her own heart and mind were telling her. The questions all lay in what she didn't know about Noeul's feelings. What she hoped would come to pass while they were apart, was that the beautiful, green-eyed woman would have her own moment of clarity. For now, there was nothing Jordan could do until Noeul was willing to reconcile her past with the present.

Chapter Twenty-four

NOEUL PULLED HER SMALL wheeled carry-on behind her in the departure line at the Charlottesville Albemarle Airport. Ticket in hand, she would board a plane that would stop in Philadelphia, Pennsylvania before traveling on to Ithaca, New York. She'd driven more than two hours to Charlottesville the day before, and this was the best flight she'd been able to book, short of hiring a private plane. A car rental would be waiting for her, and all she could think was to get to Jordan. *Now to figure out what I'm going to say.*

The line progressed, and soon she was buckled in her seat with her leather-bound journal on her lap. Noeul listened closely to the attendant's emergency instructions, before she closed her eyes while the plane roared to life and taxied down the runway. The moment the aircraft left terra firma, the ascent pushed her into her seat. Her eyes were drawn out the window to the large white clouds that stood out starkly against the idyllic blue sky. *How small we humans are in the grand scheme of things.* Pen in hand, she opened her journal.

It's extraordinary to think about what Jordan did to find me. She took a sabbatical, deciphered coded messages, and traveled thousands of miles across the United States in her quest. Those extraordinary efforts make the five hundred and fifty or so miles I'm currently traveling seem insignificant. Sadly, the physical miles that separate us feel less of a barrier than my reluctance to take a chance on love again.

It's only been a little over twenty-four hours since I reached for her in the night. Nothing tastes right, nothing quenches my thirst. The reasons are simple. The hunger and thirst I feel aren't for food or water. I long to taste the salt on her skin and drink in the sight of that phoenix wrapping around her body. I'm desperate to feast on her lips and drink in her kiss, to fill my heart and soul with her. Those are the things my mind and body are starving for. They come with a price that, up until meeting Jordan, I've never been willing to pay. Now, I'd give every dime I have for one more minute in her arms.

Aggie's gone. I've spent years mourning what I lost instead of celebrating what I had. Miranda's right, the way I've been going through my life isn't what Aggie would have wanted. I know it's not what I would have expected of her.

I've wasted years of my life merely existing and not truly living. Now that I can look at it without my sackcloth and ashes, I realize I was just going through the motions, not waking up grateful for every day. I used Aggie's death as a reason to put everything on hold and isolate myself from even the slightest chance of pain. Slowly living to die, and not making the dash in between...count.

With the slight layover, she arrived in Ithaca three hours later. Without knowing where to find Jordan, all she could do was go to the hospital and hope to run into her there. Picking up her rental car, she loaded her luggage and decided to call back to the girls to let them know she'd arrived. As she listened to the ringing, her nerves started to get the better of her. She drew in a sigh of relief when she reached the calmer of her two friends. "Hey, Kelly, wanted to let you know I made it."

"I was wondering and praying you wouldn't get to Philly and turn around. Jordan's worth it, and more importantly, so are you."

Noeul played with her ponytail. "I won't lie and tell you I'm not scared to death. I hurt her. This trip might be in vain."

"You won't know until you let her know how you feel. Don't put words in her mouth, Noeul. Don't take anything for granted, and don't leave anything left unsaid. Put your cards out on the table, face up, and let the hand play out as it will. We love you, honey, and we'll be here for you one way or another."

"I love you, Kelly. You and Miranda are all that's kept me going all these years."

"We always will be. Now, put that car in gear and go get your girl."

"From your lips to God's ears."

One deep breath later, Noeul started the car and drove out onto roads and streets she hadn't been on in almost a decade. A tightness in her chest was a powerful reminder that she was driving to the hospital where she'd lost Aggie, and where she hoped she'd find Jordan.

The road took her by Stewart Park, where she and Aggie had often ridden the carousel. So many memories flooded back. Tears rose in her eyes, forcing her to pull over to get herself under control. The panic she was already feeling was only the beginning of what she'd soon experience walking through the hospital doors. She needed to talk herself down.

Just breathe, Noeul. None of that can hurt you now. What will hurt is if you lose Jordan. That's something you can try to change. Now get a move on. You can't change anything by sitting here in a parking lot.

She put the car back in drive and concentrated on the road and not the past. Minutes later, she was putting the car in park again, and staring at a place where she'd experienced an unbelievable amount of grief and pain. Noeul pushed those thoughts to the side, slid out of the car, and grabbed her purse. *Deep breath, deep breath.*

The smell of artificially cooled air assaulted her. Far removed from her mountain-fresh, unpolluted air, she steeled herself to put one foot in front of the other as she stepped across the tile floor and made her way to information. She wasn't sure if they would tell her where Max was because of privacy policies. She was pleasantly surprised to be given his room number and said a silent prayer to Aggie for any assistance she might have given in that endeavor. The elevator opened, and she met a face she hadn't seen in a long time.

"Sam?"

The blond-headed man looked confused at first before he went wide eyed with recognition. "Noeul Scott! Oh my God." Sam stepped out of the elevator and wrapped her in a gentle, warm embrace.

She sunk into his arms, as she drew strength from a man *she* should have been consoling. Instead, it was the other way around and she soaked it up. After a few moments, she held him at arm's length. "Sam, how is Max?"

Sam's bright albeit tired smile told the story and alleviated one of her greater fears.

"It seems he's come out the other side of this. The doctors say they'll send him home tomorrow if all goes as planned. I was running out for more coffee. I hate the garbage they serve here. I'm pretty sure that's all that's keeping me upright, that and the nap and shower I got in when Jordan stayed with him last night."

The sound of the one name she was desperate to hear perked Noeul up. "Uhm, Sam, is Jordan still here?" The way Sam's face pinched told her she wouldn't get the answer she'd hoped for.

"I sent her home about forty-five minutes ago. She came straight here when she got off the plane and wouldn't leave. She let me go home to rest and shower and stayed until Max told her to go home because she smelled like a horse."

Noeul tried to cover a grin with her hand. "Oh, that's probably because she had to ride Thor down the mountain to meet her transportation to the airport. We're a far cry from what most would consider the civilized world at Topside."

Sam threaded his arm through Noeul's and punched the elevator button. "She hadn't left since the moment she walked through those doors. Good Lord, I had to threaten her to get her to go home for a bit. Come on. Max will want to see you, and Jordan will be back in about an hour. I tried to get her to stay home and sleep." He shook his head. "Stubborn soul insists she's coming right back."

Noeul closed her eyes and breathed a sigh of relief. If she stayed where she was, Jordan would find her this time. "I'd like to see Max." She hesitated, not wanting to cause Sam more pain. "Do you think he'll remember me? Jordan's told me about his condition."

Sam held up one hand, palm up. "Only one way to tell. He remembers the past much better than simple things like what he had for lunch. I don't understand it all. It has to do with the difference between long-term and short-term memory. Jordan's been talking to him about you, so I won't be surprised if he does. If not, try to let it roll off your back. It's not intentional." Sam closed his eyes and sighed.

"Don't worry, if he doesn't, we'll make friends all over again," Noeul assured him.

"Thank you. It's hard at times. He is such an incredible man, and I'm losing parts of him day by day. I dread the day he doesn't remember me."

"I don't think that will happen until much later, Sam. Love is the strongest memory and our greatest bond."

Sam tipped his head at her as they stepped off the elevator. "I keep telling myself that. How about you? It can't be easy being back here, although I imagine your reason for coming overshadows that some, yeah?"

Noeul felt the heat creep up her neck. "I had a small panic attack on the way here from the airport. I kept thinking that who I was coming for was a stronger pull than the memory of what once was."

"And here you are. Don't worry, Jordan will be back soon. Until then, visit with Max. Hopefully it will do you both some good."

Noeul's smile felt genuine as they walked into the room. Max still looked very much as he had the last time she'd seen him all those years ago. He was so handsome, with his gray hair and clear blue eyes. She waited to let Sam make the introduction.

"Max, look who's popped in to see you. It's Noeul, Noeul Scott." Sam reached out his hand and brought Noeul closer to the bed.

Max's smile gave Noeul a second of hope that he indeed might recognize her.

"Oh, I don't know about that." Max furrowed his brow.

Noeul's heart sank at Sam's deflated countenance and at what she thought was Max's inability to remember her.

"I'd say she came here for an entirely different reason than to see an old codger like me." Max squinted and grinned. "I'd say it was more our *daughter*, Jordan—as you told the doctor, my dear husband—that she's popped in to see."

Sam's laughter mixed with the tears streaming down his face and eased the lump in Noeul's throat, as she watched him lean up to kiss Max. Sam reached out a hand and drew her up beside him.

Max reached out and took her hand in his. He kissed it and let it rest on the bed. "My dear, Noeul, you grow ever lovelier. I dare say the mountain air has restorative properties. Have you found the fountain of youth up there in that rare air?"

"Hi, Max. It's good to see you. I wish it was under better circumstances." Noeul leaned up and kissed his cheek.

"Take my word for it, getting old sucks, as does dementia. Be glad we made friends twenty years ago, though it doesn't feel that long ago. It's wonderful to see you and opportunistic that you've found me on a day when I know who the hell I am."

Sam smiled. "I'm going to go get that coffee before my caffeine meter runs out. Can I get one for you, my dear?"

Noeul quirked a grin as she turned to Max. "Yes, that'd be wonderful. I'll sit and catch up here with this smooth talker while you're gone."

Sam leaned in past Noeul and kissed Max once again. "Don't go getting yourself into trouble while I'm gone."

"And how could I do that when I'm tethered to this hospital bed by a spider web of wires and tubes? Run along and come back to me." Max raised a shaky hand to cup Sam's face.

"I'll never be far away, my love." With that, Sam exited and Max patted the side of the bed, indicating for Noeul to sit down.

"I'll sit in this chair beside you."

Max eyed her. "No, I want you to sit right here beside me, so I can hold your hand and look into those beautiful green eyes, so much like your father's. I miss my old friends. To see you here would scare me into thinking I was on death's door, if it weren't for knowing the true reason you left your sanctuary."

Noeul sat down on the elevated bed, struggling to get there with her short stature. Once she did, she took Max's frail hand in hers.

"Now, as much as I would love to walk down memory lane, I never know when I'm going to have lucid moments like now. My thoughts are clearer right now than in a very long time, and it's important I say a few things to you, while my much younger husband runs down to Café Kôfē to appease his refined coffee addiction. Noeul, I want you to listen to me until I'm done."

Noeul laughed and shook her head. "Okay, I'm listening."

"I hope you are, my friend, because I'm going to tell you a story about a young man, a very persistent young man. He was a successful chef and had every red-blooded gay man drooling at his feet, all except one extremely pigheaded mathematics professor. The chef created special dishes, dropped off pastries at the professor's office, and even managed to be in the right place at the right time on numerous occasions. The stubborn professor felt he was too old for the chef. You see, the handsome young chef, was twenty years younger than the professor. What could they possibly have in common, and what the hell could a charming young man with his pick of the litter want with a fifty-two-year-old professor, who reveled in numbers and formulas?"

Noeul started to shake her head. "I think I know where this story is going, Max, and I..."

"Has living alone all these years affected your ability to follow directions my dear, Noeul?" Max chastised.

Noeul bit her lip and pretended to lock it shut.

Max pushed back into his pillow. "That's better. The dashing young chef never gave up. He explained to the stubborn old man that age was relative and that it wasn't the quantity of years they could have together that mattered. What did matter was the quality. He explained that, as a chef, he could turn out mass-production meals that lacked flavor and distinction. Instead, he'd chosen to do a smaller menu full of dishes that were memorable. That chef has been my husband for the last twenty years, because he chose a life that might never set a longevity record by any means. What it certainly would not lack was substance or memorable experiences."

Max took a few minutes and rested while the silence hung between them. "Unfortunately, or fortunately depending on how you look at it, our life together has been shorter than we'd hoped for. I've had the perfect partner, and most of the memories we've made stay with me. Sam has repeatedly assured me I haven't forgotten a moment of our time together. I believe the reason is because the quality of the time we've had far outweighs the span. Twenty years is nothing to scoff at, I know. What I can say, without a doubt, is that I'd give him forty more if I could." Max stopped and closed his eyes.

Noeul grew worried. "Are you okay, Max?"

Max smiled at her again. "Yes, dear, I'm gathering my thoughts, or what's left of them. I only regret one thing...that I waited the year I did. Don't make my same mistake. Jordan loves you, that much I can assure you. She had her heart ripped out many years ago by someone who didn't deserve her. You had yours ripped out by Aggie's death. No one ever said life was fair. As I face my own mortality, I can tell you living is certainly better than the alternative. The only thing stopping you from having what I've been able to enjoy with my wonderful chef, is you. Don't look back on this five, ten, fifteen years from now and ask what if. Look back and be grateful for what has been."

Noeul felt a burning in her chest, igniting a fire that had been little more than warm ashes moments ago. Max's words were exactly what she needed to hear. She leaned up and wrapped an arm around him and hugged him gently. She sat back down in the chair at his bedside and closed her eyes. "Now if I can convince Jordan."

"Convince me of what?"

Noeul was afraid to open her eyes, afraid that the voice she'd heard was an illusion. Afraid that her lack of sleep in the last forty-eight hours had caused her to hallucinate. Could that voice belong to the one person she wanted to see more than any other? She clenched her eyes tightly closed and felt Max squeeze and release her hand. Another sensation passed through her body as a very warm hand cupped her cheek.

"Convince Jordan of what?"

The voice came again, the one Noeul hadn't been able to get out of her thoughts. She opened her eyes and leaned into the touch. Dark eyes danced and darted from her own green ones to her lips. "Convince you to give me another chance to say I'm not only falling in love with you, I am in love with you."

Warm sunshine crept across Jordan's face and pierced the storm clouds. When it broke out into that full Kodak-moment smile, Noeul let her heart beat again.

Jordan leaned close, so close only a whisper could pass between them. "Say it again?"

This time, it was Noeul's face that broke out in a wide smile. "I love you, Jordan Armstrong, for all you are and for the joy you've brought back into my life. For the first time in a very long time, I feel alive. And that is completely your fault. I love you so very much." Noeul punctuated her words with a brush of her lips against Jordan's, leading to a much deeper and more passionate kiss.

When a throat cleared, Noeul smiled and turned to Max. "What? You said don't look back on the what if. You said revel in what is. Excuse me for following your instructions, Professor."

"I think she's got you there, Max. How about we take this someplace a little more private?"

Noeul felt Jordan lean into her and whisper along her jawline. Words felt more clearly than heard made her body shiver and her center pulse.

"I love you too, and I want to feel you in my arms with nothing between us." Jordan kissed her again.

Noeul felt herself being pulled to her feet and wrapped up in strong arms. She pressed her face into the warm chest in front of her and luxuriated in the smells so uniquely Jordan, rich earth and sunshine. Not close enough, she wanted to crawl inside Jordan's skin to feel her everywhere. Before she could get lost in the sensation completely, she loosened her grip and turned to Max. She leaned over, kissed his cheek, and whispered, "Thank you, my friend, for making me see exactly what I would be missing out on."

Max looked up to her and to Jordan, as Sam came to his side. "Be good to each other. Love and cherish every moment."

"You two get out of here before you cause a scene ripping each other's clothes off. I seem to remember someone has an apartment above ours and nobody other than Bandit is home."

Noeul blushed, as Sam winked at her when he leaned over and hugged them both. She looked back to Jordan and slid her arm around her. "I think we have our marching orders."

***

Jordan kissed the top of her head and stepped over to hug Sam, before she came to Max's side. When she leaned down, she looked directly into his eyes, trying to convey all the love and gratitude she could. Close to his ear, she whispered, "Thank you for whatever you said."

Max looked back at her. "Remember, she came looking for you. I reminded her what's possible when you get out of your own way. Be happy, Jordan, love's a precious gift, and I don't know anyone more deserving. Now go, take that woman home and remind her why she came." He winked and embraced her before shoving her back and reaching for Sam's hand.

Jordan stood and took Noeul back into her arms. "I love you both. I'll check in on you later."

Max scowled at her. "Unless you hear from the chef, all is well. Now go."

"Yes, Dad." Jordan winked at him and kissed Noeul's head. "I think it's time we go get reacquainted."

Noeul looked up at her. "I'm all for that."

Hand in hand, they made their way out of the hospital and down to Noeul's rental. Jordan accepted the keys and held open the passenger door for the woman she had only imagined might be there with her. Before shutting the door, she leaned down and kissed Noeul soundly again, parting the soft lips and drawing out a small groan from the woman she loved.

"Jordan?" Noeul questioned.

Breathing hard, Jordan tried to answer. "What?"

"Get in this car and get me somewhere I can rip that shirt off you. Now."

Jordan stood up so quickly, she hit her head on the roof of the car. She nearly knocked herself down, running around the front of the vehicle to stumble into the driver seat. The keys fell onto the floor, as she fumbled to get them into the ignition. Her hands trembled with need as she searched for the keys.

Noeul's laugh filled the interior, and Jordan couldn't help joining in with her. When she looked at the woman beside her, the smile she saw was so wide, it reminded her of a child being allowed to stomp in a storm puddle. Pure joy was all she could see, and she wanted more of it. The key found its way into the ignition, and they were off to give in to the growing desire forty-eight hours apart had created.

Fifteen minutes later, they drove up to the house, and Jordan pulled Noeul from the car and up the stairs. Bandit danced around them at the threshold. Jordan sent him outside and pinned Noeul against the door, attacking her mouth with need and passion. Her tongue was met stroke for stroke, and she felt Noeul fumble with the buttons on her shirt. Impatience sent the small pieces of plastic bouncing off the hardwood floor, as Noeul ripped fabric away from sensitive breasts. Warm lips covered Jordan's nipple, nearly dropping her to her knees.

Jordan scooped Noeul up in her arms, carried her to the bedroom, and laid her on the soft comforter. "Trust me, I want you so much. I prefer it to be in my bed and not there in my kitchen. Well, at least not the first time." She covered Noeul's body with her own and drove her knee between the smaller woman's legs, eliciting a deep groan. She kissed down Noeul's slender neck until her lips met fabric. She pulled Noeul up and stripped the shirt over her head, throwing it to the floor, as she moved in to taste the skin now exposed.

Their heated kisses were interrupted only long enough to remove some piece of meddlesome clothing. Noeul's hands were pulling off the rest of the opened shirt that still hung on broad shoulders and started on the buttons of Jordan's jeans. "God, I missed you. I'm so sorry."

"Shh, don't talk."

Jordan kicked off the final leg of her jeans and pulled on the hem of Noeul's pants legs, stripping them off until a pile of denim lay on the floor. She could smell Noeul's arousal and buried her face at the apex of the thighs below her. Jordan wanted to taste her, feel her, drink her in. Noeul's hips were bucking under her touch, and she took advantage of the rise and fall to pull off the red lace bikinis that covered her final destination. When she'd removed the last piece of fabric, she sat up long enough to let her eyes consume the beautiful body that lay across her bed. She watched Noeul's chest rise and fall in deep gasps. Hands reached for her, pulling her up, until once again her body covered the woman she loved. *Yes, I do. I love her with everything I am.* Jordan shuddered with the arousal coursing through her body.

Noeul's tongue snaked up her neck and swirled around the curve of her ear. The sensation of Noeul sucking that earlobe into her mouth sent Jordan into overdrive, and she shifted her mouth until she met the warm, soft lips with intensity born of passion and desperate need. Tongues danced in and out, and hands searched for purchase.

Jordan felt blunt nails scrape over her shoulders and down her back, as their naked bodies slid along sweat-dampened skin. Jordan felt a searing heat around her breast, down her side, and across her back. The phoenix on her skin was being consumed by fire and reborn in the touch of the one woman for whom her desire could never be quenched.

Jordan could wait no longer and pushed herself down the bed until her shoulders nestled between the shapely legs that automatically draped themselves over her back. "I have missed you so much." She wrapped her arms around Noeul's hips and slid her tongue along the entire length of her center in one swift movement. She drank in the heated silk that met her tongue, lapping until she could no longer hold back. She drove her tongue deep inside, as cries of pleasure were pulled from her lover.

"Oh shit, Jordan. Don't you dare stop. Please don't stop! I'm so close!"

Spurred on by the request, Jordan shifted and brought a hand to Noeul's center. She drove two, and eventually three fingers, deep inside Noeul. She could barely hold on, as passion soared and Noeul bucked against her mouth and hand. Fevered groans fueled Jordan on, as she pumped her fingers deeper and pulled Noeul's clit into her mouth. Fingers wound into her hair and held her close, refusing to allow even a fraction of distance between them.

Come on baby, let go. Jordan felt the spasms start, as Noeul arched off the bed and heels dug into Jordan's back, and she curled her fingers up. A guttural cry pierced the room, and Noeul climaxed in Jordan's mouth. She continued to softly suck and lick, until shaky hands reached for her and draggedher up. Their mouths met again. Soft kisses and tender touches followed. The rest of the world was completely forgotten outside the bedroom walls.

Noeul whispered into her mouth as she held her close. "I love you, Jordan. I need you."

Jordan worked to bring her own breathing under control, as she rolled over and drew Noeul into her arms. The need to shelter her lover, to protect and care for her, was the most powerful rush Jordan had ever felt. She nestled Noeul into the crook of her neck. She held her close and felt aftershocks rock through the small body she held.

Jordan felt Noeul calm in her arms. Beads of sweat were rolling down her own temple from the exertion. The peace in the moment was not lost on her. For the first time in many years, Jordan felt complete and knew she was loved.

She felt Noeul trace her collarbone in small, soft, gentle touches and marveled at the simple pleasure of holding this woman.

"Jordan?"

"Hum?"

"I'm sorry for not saying it before."

Fingertips pressed on Jordan's lips, preventing a response. She kissed them, remaining silent to allow Noeul to exorcise her demons, uninterrupted. The room was cool. A soft breeze from the ceiling fan floated across her heated skin. Noeul's touch made her shiver slightly. The late afternoon started casting shadows on the walls, while she lay there soaking up her lover's touch, waiting to hear what was in Noeul's heart.

Jordan turned her head and kissed a fevered brow, still warm from the passion they'd shared. If Noeul never said another word, Jordan would be happy knowing that Noeul had admitted her feelings. *That's truly all I need right now. I'm in love and she loves me too.*

***

Noeul's pulse rate was finally calming down, and the pounding heartbeat in her ears was fading. The way Jordan had taken her was unlike anything she'd ever experienced. Her need for Jordan was growing again. She forced herself to push pause, because there were things she wanted to say. *Things I need to say.*

She placed her fingers on Jordan's lips, knowing that Jordan would likely protest her next words, regardless of their accuracy.

"I was an ass, a scared ass, but an ass nonetheless. I was terrified of letting you in, because I was afraid of caring too much, then losing you. I was also worried about this huge age gap between us."

Jordan struggled under her finger, so Noeul placed her whole hand across her mouth.

"Shh. Now I mean it. Let me finish." Noeul chuckled when Jordan stuck her tongue out and poked it between her fingers. "God, you are so bad." She felt Jordan shake her head at the comment.

"When I got to the hospital, Max reminded me that age is only a number, that he and Sam have the same age separation as you and I do. He reminded me that, in the years we could have, it would be up to us to make quality win over quantity. When you left to come back here to Ithaca, I felt more alone than I ever have, even after Aggie died. I'd grown used to being by myself. Without any warning, you waltzed in and turned my life upside down. And just as quickly, you were gone. In less than a month, you'd woven yourself into my life in a way I didn't think was possible. I looked around and saw memories we made everywhere. The final straw was finding your faded Cornell T-shirt by our bed. I realized that I missed not just you. I truly missed who I am with you."

Noeul leaned up and kissed Jordan's throat. "I snapped at Miranda so fiercely, she actually left and took Kyo with her. Right after that, Aggie spoke to me again and said something similar to what Max said after I got here. She reminded me that it's the dash in between that matters.

Noeul saw Jordan's eyebrows scrunch together in confusion. "Aggie's grannie had a saying. The gist of which, is that what's important is the dash in between. Do you understand now?"

Jordan shook her head.

Noeul traced Jordan's cheekbone with her fingertips. "I didn't think I could love again. I didn't even want to try, because I was afraid of the pain a loss like that could cause. Jordan, Aggie's death nearly destroyed me. The key in that statement is *nearly*. I didn't die. Aggie did. I've been going through life without really living, until you trekked across the country to hunt me down. The minute we met up, I started living again, making the dash in between count. You did that, my love. You showed me it was possible. Miranda and Kelly told me I was making decisions for you without giving you a chance to speak up for yourself."

Jordan enthusiastically shook her head and held up her hand.

Noeul rolled her eyes. "In a minute, still my turn." She tapped Jordan's lips and kissed them gently before covering them again with her hand. "My friends reminded me that until you came, I wasn't living, only existing. They also said you'd proven yourself already in your search for me. I know there are forces at work beyond our understanding. I think Aggie brought us together from wherever she is. Somehow, she's gone to extraordinary measures to make sure you could find me, when I couldn't even find myself. It's a gift that would be a sin to waste. I almost took it for granted, and I won't ever do that again, if you'll have me. I love you, Jordan Armstrong, and however we must make it work, I want to be with you. I'm afraid of what will happen at the end of your sabbatical, but I'm all in. I have to trust that we can work it out together. So, with all that being said without your interruption, I want you to know that I love you and that won't change."

Jordan's smile under her hand was contagious, and she finally released her lips only to capture them again with a kiss. She felt Jordan melt into her and reached to touch her.

Jordan spoke softly, as she settled Noeul on top of her. "Can I tell you some things now?"

Noeul shook her head affirmatively.

"When I started this journey, I was looking for one thing, a way to make something grow where nothing could. A way to feed the world. I traveled near and far, following things I couldn't always understand. I had to have faith there was a reason. I have no doubt there are powers beyond our understanding that want us together. As you said, someone wants us to spend the dash in between, fulfilling a new bucket list. A list with memories we make together. We will work it out *together*. I strongly believe we can solve the problem I started with. The bigger issue, on a personal level, was that I wasn't letting anyone in either. Until you, I'd put my eyes to a microscope and stopped looking at the world outside of that very small field."

Jordan kissed her softly, and Noeul felt her heart start to beat harder.

"So, Professor Scott, what do we do about all this?"

Noeul smiled. She shifted so she could run a finger down Jordan's chin, across her chest, and down her chiseled abs. When her hand brushed the soft curls at the base of Jordan's belly, she looked at her tenderly.

"I say, we do a little more research and add a few things to our own list. Are you up to the challenge, Professor Armstrong?" Noeul dipped her finger into Jordan's wet folds, drawing a gasp from her.

Noeul laughed, as Jordan tried unsuccessfully to talk while her clit was teased.

"I see a few checkmarks we can make right now. Sign me up for a lifetime commitment." Jordan kissed her and covered her hand, sliding it farther down into her own center, until Noeul's fingers found their way inside.

"I see a lifetime of research on that subject, Professor Armstrong."

Epilogue

ONE YEAR LATER

JORDAN STOOD AT DAVA'S side, as soft music played. They looked down the aisle and out over Jordan's Pond, where Sarah had popped the question. Down near the water's edge, Sarah stood at the archway looking anxious. Her eyes were glued to their approach, as she stood fidgeting in the slate-gray, Armani tuxedo with a monochromatic shirt.

Jordan smoothed her hands down her own tux jacket and bent to pull both her sister's hands in hers. "You ready?"

"I still can't believe it." A tear threatened to spill down Dava's cheek.

Jordan reached into her pocket and pulled out a white handkerchief that had been her father's. She dabbed under Dava's eye for her. "Hey now, you'll ruin that beautiful makeup you aren't wearing." She smiled at her sister.

Dava chuckled. "Never been a fan, you know?"

"You've never needed it. You're beautiful exactly as you are. Ovelay ouyay ittlelay istersay."

Dava, unusually stoic, answered in English. "Love you too, big sister."

Jordan moved behind her sister to push her down the aisle. "I'm so proud of you. How about we get you down to Sarah before she passes out?"

"Well, big sister, it's like when you were my buddy during our Challenger League days on the baseball diamond. I trust you to get me up to the plate. Let's roll, JJ. I've got a home run to hit with that beautiful woman in the rainbow tie."

"You ready to dance down that aisle?" Jordan joked.

Dava's mischievous grin said it all. "If we end up ass over tea kettle, I'm blaming you. Let's roll, Sherlock."

Jordan popped Dava up on two wheels, bent over, and kissed her cheek. "Batter up, Watson!"

The wedding march Dava and Sarah had chosen was as unorthodox as the couple themselves. Jordan turned on her heel to the recognizable riff of Lady Gaga's, "Born This Way", spinning them around on the hard surface they'd temporarily erected for the occasion. She pushed Dava a few feet, pulled her backward, then tipped her up again, while she spun them the opposite direction. They danced the entire way down the aisle to a clapping Sarah, whose beaming smile rivaled the sun.

Jordan stopped at the end of the aisle and leaned down to kiss Dava one more time. She squeezed Sarah's arm before moving to stand on her sister's left. Sarah knelt at Dava's side. Jordan looked back at her lover and winked. Sitting beside Noeul in the front row, her mother held the hand of Colonel Margo Bishop. Noeul shook her head, stifling a giggle with her hand while winking back.

The ceremony was full of laughter and several emotional moments. When the couple had exchanged vows and rings, their minister and friend pronounced them bound in holy matrimony. Jordan watched as they shared a sweet kiss, before Sarah danced Dava back up the aisle to the reception area.

Margo wheeled herself out into the aisle and pulled Dalia into her lap to roll her up the walkway. Jordan smiled at her mother, who wrapped her arms around Margo's neck and kissed the colonel's cheek. Jordan offered her arm to the love of her life, and she and Noeul danced to meet the rest of the family in front of the smiling and clapping guests.

Later in the evening, as the reception was winding down, Jordan held Noeul in her arms as they swayed to the music. Noeul was tucked into her chest as they worked their way across the parquet floor.

Jordan sighed. "I can't believe my baby sister is married."

Noeul looked up at her. "She was a beautiful bride."

"That she was. They both were. Did you see the smile on Mom's face when Margo pulled her into her lap?"

"I did. Don't be surprised if we're doing this again not too long from now."

Jordan spun them slowly. "Could be. I'd be happy to walk her down the aisle. I'm getting pretty good at it."

"You think so, huh?"

"What? You didn't like our style today?"

Noeul cupped her cheek. "I like your style every day, and I really like you in a tux." Noeul smoothed her hands down Jordan's lapels.

Jordan kissed her forehead and nuzzled her neck. "So, are we ready to go to Kenya for our crop trial?"

Noeul hummed appreciatively. "The bags and equipment are all packed."

"Including the Nutella?"

"Yes, my love, we barely take a walk around the block without a jumbo-size jar in a backpack."

Jordan ran her hands through untethered, long, black hair that cascaded down the back of Noeul's stunning, green dress that so closely matched her eyes. "Sam and Max have all our contact information?"

Noeul kissed her. "I made sure of it."

Jordan thought about what they were about to embark on. They'd been perfecting their grafts and found they were getting consistent results. They had collaborated with the Kenyan government. Moiben was known for wheat production, so she and Noeul felt it would be a good place to start with some trials. Locals would help them plant and cultivate the test crop. "I'm looking forward to the time there with you. Leo is watching over Topside, and Deena is watching the trials at Cornell."

Noeul unbuttoned Jordan's jacket and snaked her left arm inside. "You know, I had a dream once, where I saw a rider on a black horse that got off and walked through a field, brushing her hand along the grain heads and pulling at the plant bases. When we went over there a few months ago, I watched you do exactly what I'd seen in my dream. There are days I still can't believe how we came to be."

Jordan held her close and kissed her. "I'd do it all again to find you. That whole journey to you, my rooted dragon, taught me a very important lesson."

"What's that?" Noeul nuzzled her face against Jordan's chest.

"That a bucket list has to be more than things you dream of doing. If you never take the journey and put checkmarks by the items, there are no memories made. It's just a list."

"Very true, my love. Have I ever told you how grateful I am that Dava is so good at decoding puzzles?"

Jordan pointed to the stage. The bandleader nodded his head to the rest of the musicians. "A time or two, and amen to that. How about a little dance lesson, my love?"

Noeul furrowed her brow. "What did you have in mind?"

Jordan looked at the woman she was positive she would spend the rest of her life with, checking boxes off their own bucket list. "Oh, it's a little number Max taught me, one more memory for the dash in between."

Jordan pointed to the band who broke out into a perfect rendition of "Ain't No Mountain High Enough." Jordan swung Noeul out and pulled her close. "Nothing in this world will ever keep me from your side."

The End

About CJ Murphy

I grew up a voracious reader, feeding my imagination with books. I spent hours exploring the woods around my farm, pretending I was "Hawk-eye", surviving in the wilderness. I climbed into the hayloft of our barn, looking for "Charlotte" among the spider webs. Later, I looked in every wardrobe I could trying to find "Narnia and Aslan". As an adult, I can still remember reading my first novel with a lesbian character and how it made me feel to finally identify in an entirely new way.

My adventure into writing came at the suggestion of my wife. Several years ago, she asked me to write her a story. I began crafting her personalized gifts for holidays and special occasions, by writing stories for her. I'd weave in pieces and parts of our life. My brain started asking *"what if"* after she mentioned forgetting I'd written the story until something sounded familiar.

My wife and I are part owners of an active produce farm and a U Pick strawberry operation on my wife's family land all while I continue into my twenty fifth year as a full-time firefighter. On top of all that, we built our dream home in 2016, on property we've been clearing and preparing for fourteen years. Now we reside on 221 acres of woodland in the mountains of West Virginia, with three cats as I pine away for another promised Border Collie. We love to go watch our Mountaineers, Pittsburgh Pirates, and Steelers. We love leading our great niece and nephews on adventures to fuel their imagination and creativity as we watch them grow.

Connect with CJ:

Email: cptcjldypyro@gmail.com

Facebook: CJ Murphy (Murphy's Law)

Note to Readers:

Thank you for reading a book from Desert Palm Press. We have made every effort to edit this book. However, typos do slip in. If you find an error in the text, please email lee@desertpalmpress.com so the issue can be corrected.

We appreciate you as a reader and want to ensure you enjoy the reading process. We would like you to consider posting a review on your preferred media sites such as Amazon, Smashwords, Bella Books, Goodreads, Tumblr, Twitter, Facebook, and/or your blog or website.

For more information on upcoming releases, author interviews, contest, giveaways and more, please sign up for our newsletter and visit us as at Desert Palm Press: www.desertpalmpress.com and "Like" us on Facebook: Desert Palm Press.

Bright Blessings

37898047R00212

Made in the USA
Columbia, SC
02 December 2018